I know a bit about this castle because I was stuck
there for a month once, under circumstances
you really don't want to hear about.

At that time it had been spruced up a bit by the conqueror
before last and several of the larger rooms were watertight and
partially draughtproof; there were shutters on the windows
and floorboards on the floors, and someone had hacked a path
through the brambles and nettles in the courtyard, and if you
wanted to keep warm you could always break off some of the
dead branches from the elder trees growing out of the cracks
in the curtain wall, though elder doesn't give a lot of heat at the
best of times. I imagine I'd got the job of storming the place
because Praeclara knew I was familiar with it. Anyway, I knew
enough about it to be painfully aware that for its size it was
pretty well unstormable; as for a siege, forget it. Besiegers have
to eat, too, and getting supply carts up and down the sides of
the combe would be a hell of a job; you'd have to unload at the
top and carry everything down on your back, and in my experience there's a limit to how much healthy exercise the average
fighting man is prepared to put up with. In any case, Praeclara
had made it pretty clear that I was on a schedule, so starving
the buggers out wasn't an option.

For some reason, I decided not to share these insights with
Polycrates, Papinian and the rest of the lads. I had no intention
of storming the castle.

Praise for the Novels of K. J. Parker

"Full of invention and ingenuity.... Great fun."
—*SFX* on *Sixteen Ways to Defend a Walled City*

"Readers will appreciate the infusion of humor and fun-loving characters into this vivid and sometimes grim fantasy world."
—*Publishers Weekly* on *Sixteen Ways to Defend a Walled City*

"Parker has created a world full of wit, ingenuity, unlikely tactics and reluctant heroes and there is nothing else quite like it."
—*Fantasy Hive* on *How to Rule an Empire and Get Away with It*

"With a steady pacing, solid, lean writing and variety of twists, the novel keeps on surprising the reader."
—*Fantasy Book Critic* on *Sixteen Ways to Defend a Walled City*

"Parker's acerbic wit and knowledge of human nature are a delight to read as he explores the way conflict is guided, in equal measure, by the brilliance and unerring foolishness of humanity.... Thoroughly engaging."
—*RT Book Reviews* on *The Two of Swords: Volume One*

"A ripping good adventure yarn, laced with frequent barbed witticisms and ace sword fighting.... Parker's settings and characterizations never miss a beat, and the intricate political interplay of intrigue is suspenseful almost to the last page."
—*Publishers Weekly* on *Sharps*

As K. J. Parker

As Tom Holt

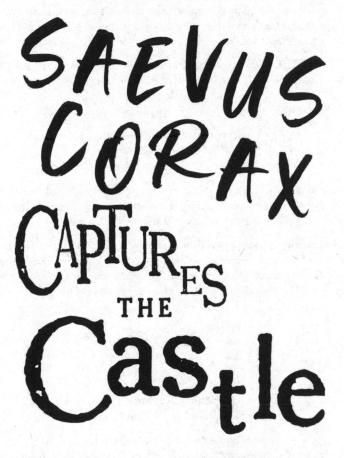

SAEVUS CORAX CAPTURES THE Castle

The Corax Trilogy: Book 2

K. J. PARKER

orbit

orbitbooks.net

Copyright © 2023 by One Reluctant Lemming Company Ltd.
Excerpt from *Saevus Corax Gets Away With Murder* copyright © 2023 by One Reluctant Lemming Company Ltd.
Excerpt from *Notorious Sorcerer* copyright © 2022 by Davinia Evans

Cover design by Lisa Marie Pompilio
Cover illustrations by Shutterstock
Cover copyright © 2023 by Hachette Book Group, Inc.

Orbit
Hachette Book Group
1290 Avenue of the Americas
New York, NY 10104
orbitbooks.net

First Edition: November 2023
Simultaneously published in Great Britain by Orbit

Orbit is an imprint of Hachette Book Group.
The Orbit name and logo are trademarks of Little, Brown Book Group Limited.

The publisher is not responsible for websites (or their content) that are not owned by the publisher.

The Hachette Speakers Bureau provides a wide range of authors for speaking events. To find out more, go to hachettespeakersbureau.com or email HachetteSpeakers@hbgusa.com.

Orbit books may be purchased in bulk for business, educational, or promotional use. For information, please contact your local bookseller or the Hachette Book Group Special Markets Department at special.markets@hbgusa.com.

Library of Congress Control Number: 2023937591

ISBNs: 9780316668910 (trade paperback), 9780316668958 (ebook)

Printed in the United States of America

LSC-C

Printing 1, 2023

For Zara, with thanks

1

The other day, for want of anything better to do, I tried to figure out how many people I've killed over the course of my life so far. I came up with a total of eighty-six. That surprised me.

A note on methodology. I'm talking here about people I've killed with my own hands, not the rather large number for whose deaths I could arguably be held morally responsible. Also excluded are those – twenty-seven, give or take – whose deaths I've ordered at the hands of others. If you count them in as well, we get a bottom line of one hundred and thirteen. Either way, that's a lot.

Bear in mind that I'm not and never have been a professional soldier. In my defence, I think I can honestly say I've never killed anyone out of malice, spite, idealism, revenge, for financial gain or just for the sheer hell of it. All those homicides were, as far as I'm concerned, justified: it was them or me. Either directly, because they were coming at me with a weapon, or indirectly, because they were trying to catch me or prevent me from escaping, or they knew something about me I daren't let anyone else find out; not my fault, because I didn't start it. I've never started anything in my entire life (well, hardly ever) and all I ask is to be left in peace.

A number like eighty-six begs a serious question. Has my life – to date – been worth eighty-six lives of my fellow human beings? To which I reluctantly but without hesitation answer: no, no way. Worth a single one of them? By any meaningful criteria: no.

Define meaningful criteria. For example, some philosophers claim that in a fight or any form of serious conflict the better man always wins, because winning is the definition of being better. If I'm just that split second quicker with my block, parry and riposte, I'm a better fighter, therefore a superior animal, therefore I deserve to win; by the same token, if I'm a tad slower than you are or your feint high left suckers me into walking straight into your low right jab, God or natural selection has spoken and I've got nothing to moan about as my lifeblood soaks away into the sand.

Actually, I'd happily accept that, if it wasn't for the inconvenient fact that the first man I ever killed – my brother, as it happens – was incontrovertibly the better man: not just morally, ethically, intellectually, so on and so forth, he was also a brilliant swordsman who'd have been remembered as probably the leading fencer of his generation if he hadn't died at age fifteen, on the point of my sword, during a practice bout I'd tried my best to avoid taking part in. Who was worth more, him or me? I'm not even going to bother answering that. I only mention it to prove that the best man doesn't always win, and therefore the proposition is flawed. A shame, but there it is. You can't argue with the facts, though I've spent my life trying.

Meaningful criteria: what, for crying out loud? Making the world a better place – no, I reject that. Making the world a better place isn't my job, I never signed up for it and it's not my responsibility. I would argue that the world is probably just fine as it is and people are about as good as they're capable of being. I've seen a lot of change and a lot of idealists. The change has invariably been disastrous and nineteen times out of twenty an idealist was to blame. Not making the world a worse place: well, on occasion I've tried, even put myself to a certain degree of inconvenience – as witness the ghastly mess on the island of Sirupat a few years back, which (four parts miracle, one part me) didn't end up as the biggest, most destructive war in human history. The objection to that is that, for all I know, I've done loads of things that have led to really bad stuff not happening and never even knew it, let alone intended the consequence. I may have failed to save a child swept away by a river, and that child would've grown up to be a second Odovacar or Felix the Conqueror, who'd have slaughtered millions in pursuit of some crazed messianic dream. By the same token the sixpence I tossed in a beggar's hat yesterday morning may have made the difference between starvation and life for the same kid. Or maybe it was you who tossed that coin. I wouldn't put it past you.

The hell with it. Eighty-six is definitely not something I'm proud of, but neither am I cripplingly ashamed. Definitely, the next time someone comes at me with a knife or a warder tries to stop me escaping from the condemned cell, the thought of the eighty-six martyrs isn't going to stop me or even slow me down. I am who I am, I do what I must, I didn't start it, it's not my fault. Now read on.

*

The worst thing about my line of work is when we're called in late. We need time – to get there, to plan out the job, decide how many carts and barrels and sacks and wicker baskets we're going to need, how we're going to do the clearing up and then shift the stuff to where we need it to be. Most of all, we need to get on site before the bodies start swelling up and the flies get into them.

It's probably very wrong of me, but I don't much care for flies. Crows I can take or leave alone – they have so much in common with me, after all – and dogs and foxes run away before you come close; even slugs don't get to me the way flies do. It's an irrational reaction. Flies don't do nearly as much repulsive physical damage as birds or mammals. They don't chew off extremities or peck out eyes. And what's a fly, compared to a human being? They're so small, they really shouldn't register, let alone matter. Logically, therefore, Brother Fly and Sister Bluebottle shouldn't bother me to the extent they do. Logically, it should be quite the reverse. Crows and foxes and rats come to gorge, stuff their beaks and muzzles with everything they can get for free; flies are *constructive*. They firmly believe in the future: a better future, for their larvae and their larvae's larvae. To them, taking account of scale, a dead body is a promised land, given to them by Providence as a place where they settle down, lay eggs, raise families, improve themselves, develop an orderly egalitarian society under the rule of law, quite possibly evolve in due course into a race of perfect beings, like the gods only rather less self-centred.

Even so, I dislike them. Their buzzing gets to me, and the way they move in swarms, one shape made up of thousands of restless, fast-moving components. Maybe it's because they aren't scared of me, the way crows and rats and foxes are.

Maybe it's because they have no real cause to be scared of me, because I'm too slow and predictable to be a threat. I like being a threat. It means I get left in peace.

In my line of work, we aren't nearly as constructive or positive as the flies. We get called in when there's been a battle, to clear up the godawful mess. In return for gathering up and burning or burying the bodies, the dead horses and the smashed-up hardware, we get to keep the armour, weapons, clothes, shoes and personal effects, which we patch up and sell. For this privilege we pay good money, cash in advance; and, since there are always two sides to a quarrel, we have to pay double, to the ultimate winner and the ultimate loser, because beforehand there's no way of knowing which will be which. Factor in the overheads – I employ five hundred men; the bigger outfits, such as the Asvogels or the Resurrection Crew, field squads four times that – and make provision for the occasional disaster, like a whole train of fully laden carts getting washed away in a flooded river or ambushed by bandits, and you'll be forced to agree with me that we earn our profits, such as they are. Vultures and parasites we may be, but we put in a lot of hard, dirty work for our disgusting and inhuman gains. Morally, that makes no difference whatsoever, but a lot of people can be fooled into thinking it does, and I sincerely hope you're one of them.

Imagine my joy, therefore, when Count Sinderic, instead of fighting a pitched battle with the Avenging Knife on a flat, level plain half a mile from a major seaport, decided to send his cavalry to intercept the enemy as they crossed the Tabletop, a plateau eight hundred feet above sea level, only accessible through a narrow pass through the foothills of the Spearhead Mountains.

I was tempted to wash my hands of the whole thing and go home, but I couldn't. I'd borrowed money at silly interest to buy the rights to this war, which I normally wouldn't have touched with a ten-foot pole, but it was the only war in town, so to speak, and we hadn't worked for a while. An unfortunate consequence of my noble and heroic acts on Sirupat (see above) had been an abnormally long spell of peace, and such action as there had been recently had been snapped up by the Asvogels, who paid stupid money for the rights with a view to starving out the smaller operators like myself and thereby achieving a monopoly. Thanks to them, I'd had to bid well over the odds for this idiotic scrap between Sinderic and his latest crop of rebels. My margins were already as thin as a butterfly's wing, and now I had to go zooming off into the mountains or risk defaulting on my loans, which would spell death for my business and a deplorable number of broken bones for me personally.

We got there in the end. Sinderic had sent his cavalry because he needed to cover a lot of ground quickly; we therefore had to do the same, but we had carts loaded with empty barrels and hampers, which tended to bounce off and scatter all over the ground every time a wheel ran over a rut or a stone. There comes a point, travelling in that manner, that the faster you try and go the less progress you make. We settled down into a grim, earnest trudge. We tried travelling by night as well as by day, but that was hopeless because we wore out the horses; quite a few of them went lame, and that slowed us down even more. "The hell with it," I told Gombryas when he nagged me about how slowly we were going. "We'll just have to take our time and get there *properly*."

It's all about perspective. I was muddy and bruised after helping fix a cracked axle; he'd been sitting on the box of a wagon all day, with nothing to do except experience the passage of time. "At this rate," he said, "by the time we get there, everything'll be maggots. You hate maggots. You've told me that enough times, God knows."

"Absolutely true," I told him. "But if we rush, we'll break more axles and take longer getting there, and then there'll be even more fucking maggots. Nice and steady does it. That's being sensible."

Gombryas is my friend. Define friend. I see him every day. I talk to him without having to think carefully about what I say. If I broke my leg, he'd do what it took to see me all right, provided he didn't have a very good reason not to; and vice versa. I know a lot about him, and he knows a certain amount about me. Some things he does amuse me, and his more disgusting habits don't offend me, because his value to me outweighs the revulsion. He works for me (at a flat rate plus a share of the profits) and he's very good at his job, which is an important one. If I tell him to do something, it generally gets done, so on balance he makes my life easier. If he died tomorrow, I'd be sorry and upset. If he died tomorrow and someone equally good at his job stepped immediately into his shoes, I'd still be sorry and upset. We choose to overlook each other's faults. He's familiar, like inherited furniture. Just occasionally, he says something that hadn't already occurred to me, and there are some things he thinks about so I don't have to. He knows me very well (which isn't the same thing as knowing a lot about me). We trust each other, up to a clearly defined point. He's my friend.

"Fuck you," said my friend. "Why don't you and me and Polycrates go on ahead on the riding horses, and then we can make a start before everything's gone completely shit, and the wagons can catch us up?"

I hadn't thought of that; and I'm supposed to be smart, and he's supposed to be thick as a brick. I spent a frantic moment trying to think of a reason why not, but failed. "That's not a bad idea," I said. "See to it, would you?"

Immediately he started whining. I was supposed to be in charge; why did he have to do every single bloody thing? I explained that it was because he was so smart, and thought of things I was too dim to envisage. He didn't know what envisage meant. He called me some names and stopped the cart, so he could get down and run around organising things. He likes doing that, though he always moans about it.

There are lots of little valleys and combes all around the edge of the Tabletop, and you could have a quite substantial battle in one of them and nobody would ever know, because you'd be completely hidden from sight. But we had no trouble finding the right place, thanks to the crows, and the stink.

And the starlings. Starlings aren't big carrion eaters, but they like flies, grubs and maggots. A huge flock of them whirred up off the ground, so loud we could hear them as soon as we broke the skyline. They lifted before the crows did. Starlings getting up are a cloud, whereas crows are like snow falling in a blizzard, only in the other direction. It always makes me feel guilty when I disturb so many thousands of my fellow creatures. They're getting along just fine, minding their own business in these hard times in the carrion trade, and then I come along and spoil everything. Foxes and badgers and other mammals always act like criminals caught in the act. They lift their heads, give you a horrified stare and run for it, like they know they're doing something wrong. But crows yell abuse at you, and threaten you with lawsuits for restraint of trade.

"Told you," Gombryas said. "God, what a stink."

But after a while you stop noticing it. For a while I lived next to a tannery, and people passing by in the street would stop dead, cover their faces and retch; as far as I was concerned, it was just ordinary breathing air. You can get used to all sorts of things. "It's not so bad," I said. Gombryas threw up. Maybe it was that bad after all.

The first thing you do when you find a battlefield, after making absolutely sure there's no active soldiers on site and, if you're Gombryas, wiping the last dribble of sick off your chin, is make a thorough skirmish of the field. It's amazing how often you think you've done it all and finished, and then you come across a dell or a dip or a little fold of dead ground, and guess where the heaviest action was, the heroic counter-attack, the desperate last stand of the Imperial guard. By that point you're already behind schedule, in grave danger of being caught out by the spring floods or missing the ships you've booked all that expensive cargo space on; furthermore, you've calculated precisely how much food and water you need to supply five hundred men for the return journey, not to mention oats and hay for the horses . . . So Gombryas and Olybrius and Carrhasio and I trudged through the swollen, purple bodies, figuring out what had happened. If you know what happened, you know where to look. Simple as that.

On this occasion, to begin with, it didn't make sense. Then I realised why.

"Stone me," I said. "The Knife won."

"Don't talk stupid," Carrhasio said. He was a soldier most of his life, so he reckons he knows about strategy and tactics. "They never stood a chance."

Not long after that we found a sunken river. The bulk of

Count Sinderic's army, running for their lives, had slithered down one side, then found the opposite bank was too steep and slippery to climb. The Knife, meanwhile, had crossed the river further up, which meant they could station their archers on top of both banks and shoot up Sinderic's men, floundering in the deep, fast-running river below. There was no cover, the current made it hard to stand up, let alone shoot back with any accuracy or effect; escape upstream was out of the question, so a fair number of the poor bastards tried to go downstream, and were caught at a sharp bend, where the water suddenly got deep; the Knife's archers on the bank enfiladed them as they tried to swim back against the current, and the few who weren't shot drowned.

"Piss and fuck," Polycrates observed, gazing down at the tangle of sodden bodies. "That's no bloody good."

I could see his line of reasoning. A significant percentage of our profit comes from clothing – shirts, trousers, tunics, coats, boots, hats. Nearly a week of being buffeted about in fast-running water does even the sturdiest fabrics no good at all. There was no point stripping the bodies: all their clothes and footwear were irreparably spoiled. Basically, all we'd be able to salvage from this site would be metalwork; and iron, especially chain mail, isn't exactly improved by being soaking wet. It goes without saying, the principal form of defensive armour issued to Sinderic's men was a knee-length long-sleeved mail shirt. By the time we got them back to somewhere we could work on them, they'd be solid blocks of rust.

"Some people," Eudo observed solemnly, "have no consideration for others."

Absolutely. We wouldn't be able to burn the bodies in their sodden clothes, which meant either stripping them and dumping the clothes, an exercise which I felt might prove distasteful, or else digging a very big deep hole (in thin, stony soil) and burying them. Leaving them in the water to let nature take its course was out of the question, since the river feeds the aqueduct that supplies fresh water to Audoria, a substantial market town and our next destination if we wanted to get to the coast in time to catch our ships.

Mercifully, half a mile downstream from the main killing point was a dense reed bed. It had acted as a filter, keeping the bodies from being carried any further. I gave Eudo a hundred men and left him to it. Gombryas and a hundred more went back up the hill to deal with the rest of the battle, where at least the salvage would be dry, the bodies would burn and we might even pick up some stuff somebody might eventually want to buy. The rest of the crew stayed with me, and we tackled the worst of it. There's a considerable degree of inherent technical interest in what we do, and you'd probably find a detailed account of how we solved our various problems both informative and useful, but I'm afraid you're out of luck. I can't face reliving all that again just to satisfy your morbid curiosity. We got the job done, that's all I'm saying.

By the time we'd finished we were all miserable, except for Gombryas. He collects body parts from famous people (he rents a converted smithy in Boc Bohec, where he's got them all on display, desiccated and nailed up on boards or carefully pickled in bottles), and to his great joy he found Count Sinderic, dry and reasonably well preserved apart from a hole in his skull, which ruined it as a collectible. After a certain amount of careful thought, he decided to keep an eye and six fingers for himself, and the other eye and fingers, nose, toes, ears, dick and scalp to use as swapsies with other collectors.

The residue, after much soul-searching, he chucked on the bonfire along with those of the common people who were dry enough to burn. On balance, he told me later, there was more to be gained from scarcity value than selling or trading additional pieces, not to mention the aggravation involved in getting any of the larger bits home.

"Gombryas," I asked him, as he meticulously smeared the inside of the scalp with saltpetre, "will you keep a bit of me when I'm gone?"

He looked at me. He doesn't like it when I get morbid.

Essentially we work on a departmental basis. I'm the boss, and also head of disposal, which means I'm in charge of getting rid of the bodies. Each department head has his own squad and looks after a specific stage in the process. Gombryas and his boys collect up all the weapons and armour. Armour used to be Polycrates's side of things, but he and I don't always see eye to eye . . . We had a major row on the job before last and I told him to take what was owing to him and go to hell. He realised I was serious and backed down, albeit with a lot of hissing and snarling and tail-puffing-up; I accepted his apology (if that's what it was) but sideways-promoted him to head of footwear. That looks like a demotion, because he now has thirty fewer men in his gang, but footwear is actually rather more profitable than weapons and armour, so his percentage of the gross tends to be slightly higher than it used to be. I gave Gombryas armour and twenty more men because Gombryas doesn't like Polycrates much either. Gombryas was happy because he now had two slices off the top rather than one, which meant he could afford to buy more bits of interesting and sought-after people. Footwear used to be Rutilian, but he caught something nasty from a mouldy boot a while back and died. Olybrius ran his department for a while, along with his own clothing operation, but the two portfolios are too much for one man, which Olybrius freely confessed, so I took on Eudo as a sort of floating trainee head of helping out the others until we could all decide what he'd be best at. Papinian is chief medical officer, and he and his twenty-odd ghouls patch up any wounded survivors overlooked by the soldiers, so we can sell them back to their owners. We do this at cost plus fifteen per cent, more as a public relations exercise than anything else – the industry has a bad reputation with pretty much everybody, mostly thanks to the Asvogels and the College of Vultures, who simply don't give a shit; I have this naive belief that snatching a few mothers' sons from the jaws of death and restoring them to their loved ones at sensible prices might go some way to reversing that, but my breath remains resolutely unheld. Papinian has the most amazing knack of healing people and raising the very nearly dead, but he doesn't like me, so I find it hard to warm to him. Athanaric is head of supply, Dodilas is i/c transport, Inguimer does shipping and handling, a massive undertaking which he makes look far too easy, and Carrhasio is head of small items of value – cash money, rings, brooches, prophylactic amulets and gold teeth. That isn't really a cabinet-level portfolio, but Carrhasio's been with the firm since before I took it over, and I felt obliged to give him something to do now he's not up to heaving corpses about any more. If I told him he wasn't wanted at staff meetings he'd barge in anyway, so what the hell. As it happens he runs his department at a healthy profit, and his habit of cutting off the nose of anyone caught pilfering portables from the deadstock is probably quite good for corporate morale.

We ended up having to dig a pit, so I appointed Eudo acting

head of digging, a promotion he accepted with a wry smile and a few uncouth words, and we all joined in except for Papinian's medics, who are above that sort of thing. Just to add to the general feeling of joy and contentment it started to rain heavily, which it wasn't supposed to do for another two months. The pit filled up with water when it was about half as deep as it was supposed to be, so we revised our design parameters and went scrabbling round for rocks and big stones for a cairn instead. Properly speaking, cairns are extra, and very few customers are willing to pay, but we decided that the avenging Knife's extraordinary achievement in securing victory over a superior enemy called for some sort of monumental recognition. We even stuck a wooden pillar in the top, leaving it blank so the Knife could add their own inscription later on, if they decided they could be bothered.

By this point, needless to say, we were so far behind schedule that wasn't worth worrying about it any more. The ships we'd booked space on would be sailing the next day, and we were nearly a week from the coast; no chance whatsoever of getting my money back, and no way of knowing when there'd be more ships going where we wanted them to go. Palaeopolis isn't your regular trading port, where ships come and go all the time. It only exists to service the indigo trade, which is where all the money in those parts comes from. I don't know the first thing about indigo, except that it's a sort of plant with ferny leaves and little bean pods; I don't know if you make the dye from the leaves or the roots or the pods, nor do I care particularly. I know that it's one of the things they use for making blue cloth, the alternative being whortleberries, and it only works on fabric; if you want blue paint, you have to save up or steal a vast fortune and buy a tiny scrap of lapis lazuli, which is why the

Holy Mother always has a blue gown in the high-class paintings whose donor's name appears in small gold letters in the bottom right-hand corner of the frame. Indigo, by contrast, is relatively inexpensive – the Holy Mother most likely did wear a blue gown, because she was cheap trash and brought up in Poor Town, an irony that probably has deep spiritual significance if you're into that sort of thing. Anyway, indigo moves around in bulk at certain times of year, but once it's gone on its way ships don't call at Palaeopolis until it's time for the next stage in the cycle. What that meant for us was waiting till the indigo freighters came home empty from Scona or Perimadeia, at which point we might be able to hire half a dozen to ship us and our loot fifty miles up the coast to Boc Bohec, which trades all the year round; more expense, calling for more money, which I hadn't got, so I'd probably have to sell an advance share of the loot to the Asvogels, care of their agent in Boc Bohec, for delivery on Scona, which would mean a detour – long story short: if I handled all of a complex string of interrelated deals exceptionally well, I'd probably come out of it with enough to pay off my loans before my legs got broken, but I'd then have to take out more loans to pay my employees their shares off the top, and yet more loans to finance the next job, which I'd need to undertake to pay off the debts I'd already incurred. I believe the technical term for this activity, as applied to my particular line of business, is war profiteering. Fair enough, except where the profit part of that comes in, I'm not entirely sure.

We loaded up what we'd managed to get and set off back the way we'd come, only to find that the heavy rain had flooded the higher ground, and what had been dry gullies when we came up the mountain were now foaming torrents, which we had no hope of getting across. Luckily, Papinian (of all people) knew the country; he'd been there before, many years ago, and pointed out that if we went back up the mountain, crossed the plateau at the top and went down the other side, there was a relatively straight road leading down to the Ochys valley. This road had been built by military engineers about four hundred years ago and ran along the top of embankments designed to keep it clear of floodwater streams, so we ought to be able to get the carts down it without too much trouble. Of course, that would bring us out on the wrong side of the mountains, which in turn would mean a gruelling overland slog all the way to Weal Bohec, where we could hire barges to float us downstream to Boc. On the other hand, it would save us the cost of the indigo freighters at Palaeopolis, not to mention the time wasted waiting for the fleet to return from Scona. If all went well, it'd all be as broad as it was long, apart from the agony of the overland hike, and we'd be in Boc at around the same time we would've got there if we'd followed the original plan.

"That's a bloody stupid idea," Polycrates said, which surprised me. Usually, he and Papinian agree about everything. Mind you, usually the subject for discussion is me and my shortcomings. "If we're going all that way overland, where the hell are we supposed to pick up the extra supplies we'll need? Fat lot of use getting the stuff to Boc if we all starve to death along the way."

Papinian gave him his most patrician look (he's Echmen, so all westerners are naturally inferior) and pointed out that all he'd done was suggest a possibility. It wasn't up to him, he added, to thrash out the minutiae; that's what our fearless leader was for, and if he couldn't figure out a way to do this perfectly simple thing—

"We've enough to get us over the mountain and down into the valley," I said firmly, not having a clue whether or not it was true. "There's villages in the valley; we can buy what we need as we go along. The alternative is ditching the stuff and the carts and walking back to Palaeopolis empty-handed. We can do that if you like, but I'd rather give the doc's idea a go. What do you think?"

Polycrates pointed out that even if there were villages along the way, which he wasn't prepared to admit, there was no guarantee that they had surplus food or would be willing to sell it to us – perfectly true, and entirely unhelpful, like most of the things Polycrates says. "Fine," I said. "In that case we dump the carts right here and get ready to try swimming the flooded rivers. It's entirely up to you. You can all swim, can't you?"

I knew for a fact that Papinian and Dodilas can't, and I had a shrewd suspicion about Athanaric and Carrhasio. "Shut your face, Polycrates," Gombryas put in at this point. "Unless you can come up with a better idea, I vote we go with what Doc says. It'll be a piece of piss."

I've known Gombryas for quite some time now and I've never quite been able to work out what a piece of piss is: something vaguely positive, I think, but that's as far as I'm prepared to commit myself. "Fuck swimming," Carrhasio said. "And if we dump the stuff, that's it: the end of the company. And you," he added, turning his head to glare at Polycrates, "can go fuck yourself."

There are times – few and far between, but worth waiting for – when democracy actually works. "Let's vote," I said. "In favour. All right. Against?"

Against, Polycrates's solitary paw, upraised to an unheeding heaven. Papinian abstained, like he always does. Voting, in his view, is for slaves. "That's fine, then," I said. "We do what the doc said."

"It wasn't my idea," Papinian said. "I just happened to mention there was a road."

(Just to go back to what we were talking about earlier: friends, my definition thereof. Friends? These people were my friends, more or less the only ones I'd got. At least, they met the definition I gave you just now – even Polycrates, whose drinking water I could cheerfully spike with foxglove juice if I thought he wouldn't notice the funny taste; my friends, my crew, the people I know and work with. The people I'm responsible for. When you get to know me, you'll understand that I'm responsible for an awful lot of people, and things, most of which I didn't intend but which somehow happened anyway.)

If my life had gone the way it should have, instead of melting into shit not long after my seventeenth birthday, I'd have spent three years at the military academy at Hago Sagittarum learning how to be an officer. There they'd have taught me, among other things, leadership – how to inspire and deserve the confidence and loyalty of your men, how to make wise decisions, how to anticipate events and plan accordingly, how to take responsibility (that word again) for the lives of those under your command and balance it against the imperative of achieving the greater objective, as ordained by the chain of command.

I missed out on all that useful stuff, owing to a mistake with a sharp rapier. The irony of it is, I've spent the greater part of my adult life as a leader of men, and all the things I should have learned at Hago I've had to make up as I go along. That's just silly. If I believed in Destiny, I'd be so angry I might even write a letter of complaint to somebody. Why set before me a life of duty and obligation, but deprive me of the training necessary for me to do my duty properly?

Shucks. Instead, I get on with it as best I can. I keep score by asking myself, each year end when I do the accounts: how many of us got killed this year, and are we still solvent? If the answers to that are less than five and yes, I figure I'm doing all right. When a day comes when I don't get those answers, I've promised myself I'll pack it all in and find some other way of earning a living. Of course, I tend to break my promises.

Climbing back up the mountain was no fun, and crossing the Tabletop wasn't much better. It rained and carried on raining, so we spent more time pushing the carts out of bogs and flooded ruts than riding on them. The rain washed most of the mud off, but when you're soaked to the skin and you've got no dry clothes to change into, your perspective on life changes: all the downside of being a fish and none of the advantages. We broke open the barrels where we'd packed such clothing as we'd managed to salvage from the battlefield and shared it out, but that didn't help much; and then it was all sodden, too, so wet we daren't repack it or it'd all be ruined by mould by the time we got to Boc; we piled it up in the carts, draped over the luggage, and squelched on our sad way down the disused military road.

Which at least existed. I'd had my doubts, which was wrong of me, but Papinian doesn't make mistakes. The road was exactly where he'd said it would be.

It was a good road, too. Someone had been to a lot of trouble. Their engineers had sort of averaged out the landscape, cutting off the high ground and using it to fill in the dips, the way the social reformers in Aelia wanted to do with people fifty or so years ago, before the First Social War. On top of their nicely level surface they'd laid a thick layer of rubble topped with meticulously puddled clay and finished off with limestone slabs three inches thick and perfectly square – limestone absorbs moisture, which meant the road didn't get slick and slippery in the wet. It was such a splendid achievement that I asked Papinian where the road started and where it went to. He didn't know. Apparently nobody did. The military had built it, presumably to achieve some objective, but by the time the road was finished history had moved on and the objective no longer mattered. It was, he said, a perfect example of the means justifying the ends. He says things like that occasionally, and all you can do is smile and pretend you understand them.

Anyway, it did us proud, and then it came to an abrupt halt in the middle of a swamp, something Papinian had neglected to mention. There was no way in hell we could get the carts across it, so we turned round and tramped twelve miles back up the beautiful road to where we remembered the going offroad was still reasonably hard, and tried to figure out where to go from there.

"Those," Polycrates said, pointing to the cloud-blurred horizon, "must be the Cantrips, which means that if we head basically south-east, sooner or later we'll hit the river, and—"

"The whats?" I asked.

"Cantrips. The Cantrip hills. Those big sticking-up things on the skyline."

My eyesight is better than his. "Those," I told him, "are clouds."

"No, they're not, they're mountains. Once we hit the river, we just follow it down to where the treeline ends and we'll be in the valley, where there's farms and people we can ask."

"Clouds," I repeated. "Besides, if you're right and those are the Cantrips, right now we should be standing up to our necks in Lake Houba. Are you standing in a lake, Polycrates? I don't think I am."

"I've got a map," Eudo put in, "if that's any help."

A map. Joy kept me from smashing his face in. "Where did you—?"

"I found it on one of the bodies. I don't know if it's any good or not."

Valid point. The events I'd reconstructed on the battlefield had led me to the conclusion that Sinderic's men had gone badly astray in their geography, which was how they'd ended up in the death-trap riverbed. A dud map might account for that. Even so. "Give it here," Polycrates said. I intercepted it before his fingers could close on it, so he came behind me and peered over my shoulder, breathing heavily in my ear.

Polycrates had been right, in a sense. He hadn't seen them, because they were wreathed in cloud, but behind those clouds were the Cantrip hills. The lake was the other side of the Tabletop. The beautiful road we'd just come down was clearly marked. It ended at a large town, with walls and a cathedral, more or less where we'd run into the swamp. An old map, I reckoned, or a new copy of an old map. "You arsehole," I said to Eudo, not unkindly, "why didn't you—?"

"Sorry," he said. "I thought you knew where we were, so I didn't mention it."

With an actual map to go by, we had no trouble figuring out our next step. If we left the road and held a bit north, we could cross a nice dry moor and come down into the gently rolling, intensively farmed valley whose market town was the terminus of a road that led straight to Weal Bohec, and all our troubles would be over. Nearly all of them, anyway.

I outlined my proposals to the heads of department, who looked bored. "Let's do that, then," Gombryas said, as though it was the most obvious thing in the world. Mildly stunned by their unanimous support, I agreed. Dodilas wandered off to organise the carts – we'd been in column and now we needed to be in line, apparently – while I took another look at the map, just to make sure everything was right and I wasn't holding the stupid thing upside down.

"Who do you suppose they are?" Olybrius asked, pointing at something I couldn't see.

"No idea," I replied. "Shepherds, probably, or someone out hunting. Life goes on, and all that. How many of them are there?"

"Oh, not many. A few horsemen and a cart."

"Fuck them," I said tolerantly.

2

Sleep and I don't get on, like an old married couple who squabble all the time. When I want Sleep, it refuses to come near me. When I particularly need to keep awake, one lapse in concentration and I'm away with the fairies. There's not much I can do to punish Sleep for its annoying behaviour except swear and think hard thoughts. Doc Papinian has a recipe for some kind of syrup that puts you out like a snuffed candle, but he won't let me have any. He says it's bad for you and only for emergencies. I point out to him that my life is one long, continuous emergency, and then he calls me a prima donna.

Another thing. Most of the time, the slightest noise will wake me up and then I can't get back to sleep again and lie there in the dark, worrying about every damn thing. The rest of the time, once I'm off I can snore my way through anything: earthquakes, trebuchet bombardments, the end of the world, doesn't matter. Up to the point where Eudo produced his map I'd been getting by on maybe an hour when I went to bed and forty minutes just before dawn, the rest of the night being given over to peering into the pitch dark and fretting myself to death. Once we left the road and began the long, slow rumble across the moor, all that changed. Logs and lead ingots weren't in it; I closed my eyes and was dead to the world until rosy-fingered dawn, and some kind friend nudging me in the ribs with his boot to get me moving again.

"Wake up." I knew that voice. "Wake *up*, for fuck's sake." Then the toe again, rather harder than absolutely necessary.

Something in the voice chased away the fog and the chewed stubs of dream like a dog putting up partridges. "I'm awake," I said, and opened my eyes to prove it, and saw Polycrates standing over me, dripping blood from a huge gash on the side of his head. A fat drop shook loose and plopped on my cheekbone. "What?" I said.

Minor scalp wounds bleed alarmingly. "You've got to come *now*," he said. "We're under attack."

These things happen. We don't exactly conduct our business under a heavy cloak of secrecy, and we're not hard to find or follow. People assume that our carts are loaded down with jewel-encrusted parade armour, fine vintage wine from the command staff's baggage train and millions of staurata in payroll coin. They also assume, equally accurately, that we're bad and mean and not worth picking a fight with, but from time to time someone's cocky or greedy or desperate enough to give us a tumble, and then there's trouble. Because we have ready access to weapons and armour, our would-be predators tend to attack from ambushes or in the middle of the night. "What time is it?" I asked.

"Fuck what time it is. You've got to come *now*."

I scrambled to my feet, glanced around for some sort of weapon, saw none and decided I couldn't be bothered. It also occurred to me that Polycrates was being inconsistent. Most of the time he reckons I'm completely useless, but as soon as there's a problem it's *you've got to come now*, implying that only I'm capable of dealing with it. I looked up through the open tent flap at the sky, which was dark. Night, then. It wouldn't have killed Polycrates to tell me that, but what the hell.

We'd been attacked all right, but they didn't seem to have taken anything. They'd made no effort to rifle the carts, though it turned out they'd run off all the horses. Three sentries had been beaten up – I think it's bad form to hit a man while he's sleeping – and one of Papinian's medics who'd been out taking a pee had been stabbed from behind: nasty, like all puncture wounds, but Papinian reckoned he'd make it. Apart from that—

"Don't ask me," said Eudo, who alone of my senior staff had had the wit to light a lantern. "All I heard was a scuffle and some angry voices. I thought some of the men were fighting over something, so I grabbed a light and came to take a look. I can't see where anything's been stolen."

"They must've got scared and run for it," Polycrates said.

"Scared of what?" I said. "The men they hit on the head, or the one they stabbed?"

"My lamp, maybe," Eudo suggested. "Like I said, I haven't got a clue. You'd have thought they'd have taken *something*."

It was all too much for me to take in. "Get the others," I said. "Meet me at my tent. Then we'll get some torches and have a proper look round."

I went back to my tent, pulled some clothes and boots on, swallowed a mouthful of truly disgusting brandy we'd found in some poor devil's saddlebag and found, somewhat belatedly, the Mezentine Type XIV which masquerades as my personal sidearm, though mostly I use it for splitting kindling and prising open crates. I was a pretty reasonable fencer when I was younger, but after I killed my brother with a rapier I sort of lost the taste for swords, and these days I tend more towards a bow and arrow, or a knife. I was looking for my hat, which wasn't where I distinctly remembered leaving it, when the tent flap opened and Polycrates came in. "They've gone," he said.

Another inconsistency. If I'm as stupid as Polycrates maintains I am, surely you'd expect him to explain things to me, rather than assuming I know everything? "Who's gone?"

"All of them. Gombryas, Carrhasio, Dodilas, Olybrius, Athanaric. We looked everywhere. They just vanished."

Which made absolutely no sense. "All of them?"

"Me and the doc," he said, "and Eudo, and you. Apart from us, they've all gone."

"The money," I said.

"Fuck."

Actually he couldn't have been expected to know, because I'd been at some pains to keep it from him, but our cash reserve, war chest and working capital, which lives in a steel box bolted to the chassis of the big six-wheeler cart, wasn't really worth looting at that point in the proceedings. I hadn't told anyone that we were practically broke because they didn't need to know and it would only have worried them. Accordingly—

But the box was still there, unforced and pristine. "You'd better look and make sure," Polycrates said.

I didn't want to do that, since if I opened it he'd see how little money there was inside, and then we'd have tantrums. "No need," I said. "There's only the one key." I pulled it out on its string from under my shirt. "If they'd wanted to take the money and run, they'd have had to bust it open. And anyway, they wouldn't do that. Come on, you know them as well as I do."

Even Polycrates could see the sense in that. "Then where the fuck are they?"

Excellent question, and if only I could get Polycrates to stop talking, maybe I could think about it and find the answer. "I don't know," I said. "It doesn't look like they've—" Couldn't think of the right word. "Run away," I said feebly. "And if they did, why beat up the sentries? They'd just have snuck out. And why run off the horses? And why haven't they taken anything with them?"

Which, I reckoned, was a significant point. They'd departed without clothes, shoes, hats, weapons, money; most telling of all, Gombryas's accumulation of bits of dead heroes was still in his tent. No way in hell would he go far without that.

Polycrates had his stupid look on. "They had to leave in a hurry."

Now there he was touching on a subject on which I'm an expert, something Polycrates is well aware of, worse luck. I had to leave home in a hurry when I was seventeen, and I remember it vividly to this day. I jumped out of a window with a bloodied rapier in my hand, and not long afterwards my father set the dogs on me. "I don't think so," I said. "They obviously haven't killed anyone or stolen anything. And maybe one of them, or possibly even two might've done something stupid and bolted. But all of them?"

I had a point. There'd be evidence, raw and bleeding, and all we had was concussed sentries and a wounded medic – events arising from the act of departure, not the cause of it. In which case—

"Bastards," Polycrates said suddenly. "They've sold us out."

The drawer is overflowing with knives sharper than Polycrates, but, honestly, that hadn't occurred to me until he said it. But it made sense. "Oh, hell," I said. "Right, you know what to do."

Overstating the case somewhat. We have a drill, which we sometimes actually practise. We form the carts into a square with the horses inside (only we had no horses); we issue weapons and armour; we go to our assigned defensive positions and wait to be attacked. We waited till dawn, and then we waited till midday. Then we started to feel a bit silly hunkering down behind the carts with our fingers on the bowstring, so I sent a couple of scouts to see what they could see. Nothing, they reported back, apart from the horses, well, most of them, peacefully grazing about a quarter of a mile away.

My back was hurting from crouching under a tailboard all morning. I stood up, wincing, and told the scouts to go and get the horses. "Everybody out," I announced, and people started to emerge, like lovers from cupboards in an Adelphi farce.

The drill had been a bit of a mess, largely because most of the department leaders hadn't been there to organise it. Polycrates came and found me; I'd been free of him all morning. "I don't get it," he said.

"There's only one explanation left," I said. "They didn't run. Someone stole them."

He gave me that look. "That's crazy," he said.

"Yes," I said, "I know. But they didn't kill anyone or steal anything, and we haven't been attacked, so they didn't betray us to an enemy. Also, there's the angry voices Eudo heard."

"What about them?"

"I'm guessing they were saying something like: you're

coming with us, like hell I am, shut your face and come with us or we'll do you." I shrugged. "I know, it makes no sense. But we've disproved everything else. And Saloninus says, once you've eliminated the impossible—"

Polycrates wasn't in the mood for Saloninus. "Why would anybody kidnap that bunch of losers? They're not worth anything. We haven't got any money."

I knew that. "There's the stuff," I said. "Armour and weapons. And maybe they don't know we haven't got any money. People assume."

"Then they're going to be disappointed."

He was making my head hurt. Suppose I was right. The kidnappers would be disappointed, and then my heads of department (my friends) would be dead. "There's got to be a trail we can follow," I said.

"Over moorland? Get real."

Yes. In a desert, maybe, or deep mud; but tracking is a skill, and to the best of my knowledge we had no practitioners on the team. "Maybe we could've sent out scouts and got a sight of them," Polycrates went on, "if you hadn't had us all hiding behind barrels all morning. As it is, they'll be long gone."

I nodded. "If someone's snatched them," I said, "we'll hear about it. Meanwhile, we'd better get moving." Tell Dodilas to get the horses spanned in, I didn't say, because Dodilas wasn't there. So I went and saw to it myself.

We got ready, then stopped and did nothing. We had no idea which direction to go in. It also occurred to me that if I was right and someone had abducted my heads of department in the hope of getting money for them, sooner or later the abductors would want to get in touch and start talking figures. If we launched off across the moor (leaving no tracks, see above) they might not be able to find us, and then they'd give it up as a bad job, slit my friends' throats and go home. The list of ways in which I could make the situation even worse was a short one, but that possibility was near the top of it.

Fortuitously we didn't have long to wait. A man on a horse materialised on the skyline. He didn't seem to be in any sort of a hurry. We watched him amble towards us – it's hard to be precise about distances on the moor, because everything looks the same and everything's so small; no trees or big bushes, just heather and clumps of gorse. Polycrates wanted to go out and meet him, but I was afraid that a bunch of us charging straight at him would scare him off. Polycrates said that was stupid, and I think he was probably right.

He stopped about fifteen yards from the lead cart, which I happened to be sitting on. "Which of you," he called out, "is Saevus Corax?"

That's the problem with having so many different names. Polycrates nudged me. "Here," I called out.

"We've got your friends." I couldn't quite place his accent, which was unusual. It's something I'm good at. "You want them back?"

"Depends," I said.

"You what?"

He couldn't hear me. "Depends," I bellowed. "How much do you want for them?"

"You've got to come with me," said the man on the horse.

Verbal communication sucks. Was that the price, or just a condition? I could think of a lot of people – double figures – who'd be prepared to go to this degree of trouble to get hold of my body, living or dead. It goes without saying, none of them were people I was in any hurry to meet. "The hell with that," I said. "Tell me how much money you want."

"You need to come with me," the horseman said. "Now."

Greater love, according to Scripture, hath no man than this, that he lay down his life for his friends. That's a wonderful sentiment, and of course it cuts both ways. Gombryas, Carrhasio, Dodilas, Olybrius and Athanaric were my friends. Doubtless they'd be only too happy to lay down their lives for me; it would be downright churlish to refuse to accept such a sacrifice of grace. "Well?" Polycrates hissed.

"Well what?"

"They want you. Get moving."

Nuts, I thought. Then I called out, "I haven't got a horse."

"That's all right," the rider called back. "You can walk."

I despise walking. There are people who enjoy it; there are people who enjoy pretty much everything. I take the view that since mankind is master of things with hooves and things with wheels, any situation that involves me having to walk more than a hundred yards must represent a breakdown in efficient organisation. That or active malice.

Like I said just now, distance is different on the moor. You walk for a long time, then you look round and you don't seem to have come any distance at all. Then you walk some more and take another look, and suddenly everything's different, all the landmarks have dipped down below the horizon and you have absolutely no idea where you are. You look up at the sun, but even that seems to have been swallowed up in banks of low grey cloud. My sense of direction is slightly better than most people's, but it doesn't work worth a damn on the moor.

The only good thing is, you see things coming a long way off. I saw a cart. At first I thought it must be something else, because it was the wrong shape. Then it got closer and we got closer and, yes, it was a cart: two wheels, one small horse and the weird thing on top that made it look unrecognisable turned out to be a parasol.

I kid you not. It was round and flat and navy blue; not an umbrella, because they tend to be arched, like an upside-down bowl. Parasols are flat. I know, because I've seen them out east, on the Sashan border, where important officials insist on them for special occasions. Surely not, I thought, followed immediately by, hell and damnation.

I could think of someone who'd think a parasol appropriate and necessary for a trip across the moor. Someone I tried not to think about if I could possibly help it.

But there you go. "Hello," I said.

She looked down at me. "So it's Florian now, is it? Why am I not surprised?"

Florian's the name I was given when I was born. It sort of fell out of my pocket when I jumped out of that window. During the godawful mess on Sirupat I found it again, or, rather, it found me. I have absolutely no use for it, needless to say. But she'd always known me as Saevus.

"Please don't call me that," I said. "And what have you done with my friends?"

"They're safe," she said. "Is it true you've got five hundred men working for you now?"

"What's that got to do with anything?"

"That ought to be enough."

She'd always had that annoying habit. When I talk to her,

she asks me a question, completely ignores what I say and continues on the assumption that the answer given was the one she'd wanted to hear. It's much ruder than spitting in my face or calling me an arsehole. "Enough for what?"

"For the job I want you to do."

She's somewhere between sixty-five and eighty, quite small and thin, with a great cloud of silk-fine white hair always done up in a sort of heap on top of her head and tied with a ribbon, which makes her look like an onion. She has pale blue eyes and a mouth you could cut diamonds with, and I gave up trying to understand her many years ago. From time to time she happens to me, like earthquakes, economic collapse or the plague, and so far I've survived all the outbreaks, but a man only gets so much luck in one lifetime. "No," I said.

"As soon as you've done the job," she said, "you get your friends back. If you fail, I'll have them killed. It's quite a tight schedule, but you should be able to manage."

She has a high, clear, pure cut-glass voice, rather like my mother's, only my mother was a duchess. She, by contrast, was a hedger-and-ditcher's daughter, and mostly communicated in grunts until she ran away from home at age thirteen and ended up, unbelievably, on the stage. She married a retired lieutenant-colonel of mercenaries when she was thirty and he was seventy-two. She had one daughter. "I said no," I told her. "Forget it. Kill the lot of them for all I care. You can kill me, too, if you want, but whatever it is, I'm not doing it. Are you listening to me?"

She had a new driver since the last time I saw her; a huge fat Blemyan with a shiny bald head. "Get in the cart," she said. "I'll tell you all about it as we go."

*

She is, of course, my mother-in-law.

Her name, incidentally, is Praeclara. You've probably heard of her. A mother-in-law presumes a wife. I no longer have the wife, but apparently I've still got Praeclara, or she's got me. We never liked each other much. She disapproves of me. I feel about her the way most people feel about death.

"There's a castle," she told me, as the cart bumped and rumbled across the moor. It was, of course, totally unsuitable for the terrain, having been built to take well-bred young ladies for drives in a park, or somewhere they could sketch or collect flowers for pressing. "I need you to capture it for me. It's defended, but that shouldn't be a problem."

She says things like that. "Make your goons do it," I said. "You've got plenty of them."

"My people aren't expendable," she said. "You'll have odds of three to one in your favour. The classic ratio for an assault is five to one, so you'll have to try a bit harder."

Strange as it may sound, I've never quite managed to figure out what she and her organisation are about. Sometimes they seem to be religious fanatics; other times they're political. They're not just ordinary bandits, because for one thing they never make a profit, and she has to make up the shortfall out of the vast wealth her late husband earned by burning down cities for money. She talks about the Cause, though not all that often. I've given up trying to work out what it is. As far as I'm concerned, it's not the Cause that worries me, it's the effect.

"I know absolutely nothing about storming castles," I pointed out. "You need a proper soldier for that, and sappers and engineers and God knows what. It's a science; people write books about it. I'd be completely useless."

"My people will give you food and water for fourteen

days," she said. "That ought to be enough, provided you don't dawdle. The defenders are amateurs. They shouldn't give you any trouble."

I'd neglected to mention that I'd read the relevant books, not that it mattered. She'd know I'd read them. She knows everything. "You need specialised equipment," I told her. "Expensive stuff: springals and worms and escaliers and assault towers and rams and fascines—"

"Fascines aren't expensive," she said. "They're only bundles of brushwood. Besides, you won't need any of that rubbish. It's just a little castle. Really, it's more sort of a fortified manor house. I don't know why you will insist on making difficulties all the time."

"I'm not a—"

"Soldier, yes, I know, you said. My late husband, now, he was a soldier, so I happen to know a thing or two about military affairs, and this is something you're perfectly capable of doing. It's little more than casual breaking and entering. I'm sure that's entirely within your capabilities."

I'd been doing sums in my head. "You said three to one. That means there's a garrison of a hundred and seventy. Chermaneric held Paragetae against the entire Vesani army with a hundred and seventy men."

"Your best bet," she said, "would be to sneak up quietly in the middle of the night and climb the wall. Once you're inside I don't imagine they'll give you any trouble."

"My men won't do it. They're not soldiers either. We don't work like that. I can't just order them to charge to their deaths. We're a business, not an army."

"Whatever you do," she said, after a short pause, "don't set fire to the place or anything like that. I want as little damage done as possible. That's very important. As far as possible, it's to be taken intact. And if you could keep the casualties down, that would be good as well. The situation is a bit awkward politically, and the last thing I need is a lot of fuss."

"Out of the question," Papinian said, as though I'd just proposed we walk to the moon. "We're not soldiers."

"She's got our people," I repeated. "If we don't do it, she'll kill them. I know her. She's perfectly capable of it."

"And if we try and do this ridiculous thing, a lot more of our people will be killed," Papinian pointed out, absolutely fairly. "Undoubtedly more than five of them, so you'd be sending dozens of our people to their deaths in the hope of rescuing five men who happen to be your personal friends. I happen to find that disgusting."

"And we'll fail," Polycrates said. "What did you say the odds were, three to one? That's not nearly enough. Five to one minimum if you want to have any chance at all. Less than that, they'll wipe the floor with us, specially if they're real soldiers."

"I know," I said. "But it's not like we've got any—"

"Furthermore," Papinian said, "you clearly haven't given any thought to the possible repercussions. Is this woman legally authorised to go storming castles? Because if she isn't, we could be letting ourselves in for all sorts of horrible problems. You can't just start a private war in the middle of a civilised country. We aren't bandits. She is, but we aren't."

Years ago, before I left home, I had a tutor who made me read books. One of them was called *Types of Political Theory*, or something like that. Basically it was a rehash of Saloninus's *Republic*, but cleverly rewritten so as to be extremely boring. It went through all the various ways of governing a country – monarchy, oligarchy, democracy – and proved (not a difficult job) that all of them are useless and counterproductive, before coming to the conclusion that the only way that stood any chance of working was to have a king or dictator with unfettered authority but under the constant supervision of a panel of economic and constitutional experts with the power to order the palace guard to cut his throat at a moment's notice. I didn't deliberately set out to structure my own organisation along these lines, but that's more or less how it's worked out in practice. Basically, I can command my men to do whatever I want, provided they don't mind. "Listen," I said: "Gombryas and Olybrius and Carrhasio are your friends, too. Are you saying we should let them be killed and not do a damn thing about it?"

"It's not up to me," Papinian said. "I don't give the orders around here. I think you'd find that if I did, things would be rather different, but let that pass. This is your decision."

"Like hell it is," Polycrates said helpfully. "If he wants to go charging about starting a war, that's up to him. I'm not going to get myself killed for anyone."

"Fine," I said. "Go away."

He glared at me. "It's always you, isn't it? You're always the one who gets us in the shit."

"Yes," I said. "Yes, I think you can say that. But it's all right, because you can just walk away and leave me to it. You, too," I added, before Papinian had a chance to contribute. "Well?"

Polycrates gave me a look of pure loathing. "When this is over," he said, "and we've rescued Gombryas and the others, there's going to be some changes made around here. We can't go on like this, it's stupid."

"Agreed," I said. "Now go and span in the horses."

He scowled and went away. Papinian didn't move. "What?" I said.

"He's quite right," Papinian said. "It is always you, isn't it?"

"Yes, worse luck. What about it?"

Papinian was a real doctor once, and a very good one, in Echmen, where medicine is a science rather than a licence to kill people for money. He started as an army surgeon and quickly worked his way up to chief medical officer for an entire regiment. Then one day he made a bad mistake, which is unfortunate but not a crime, and tried to cover it up, which is stupid but not a crime, and poisoned one of his colleagues who was a witness, which is a crime . . . Because he'd saved thousands of lives his sentence was commuted to thirty years in the galleys, around the time of the Echmen–Tarsali war. His ship survived three battles with the Tarsaliot navy, but (as previously noted) you only get so much luck; the fourth time it was sunk, and the oarsmen were, of course, chained to their benches. Papinian survived by cutting a chunk off his heel, just enough to slip his foot through the manacle. These days he wears a special shoe, his own design, which lets him stand up and walk about almost as well as a normal person, though I gather it hurts like hell all the time. Maybe that accounts for his miserable disposition, though I think he was probably born that way. He's the only man I know who can regularly beat me at chess without cheating, and whenever we have occasion to travel by boat, he's as sick as a dog.

"Nothing," he said. "It's just a fact, that's all."

Praeclara was as good as her word. She turned up just before sunrise with eight large carts loaded with barrels: flour, oats, salt cod, bacon, apples, all the cheapest and lowest quality. She also gave me a map with a big red circle painted on it.

"There," she said, stabbing the red circle with her stubby finger. "You can read a map, presumably."

"On one of my good days," I said. "How are we supposed to get across the river?"

"What river? Oh, that." She gave me one of her looks. "Be resourceful," she said. "I gather you're good at that. Once you've taken the castle, send word to me here." She prodded a square inch of map apparently devoid of any feature whatsoever. "That's all you have to do, and then you can have your friends back."

In case you were wondering, I'm not a complete idiot. I'd had scouts out trying to find where she and her gang were hiding out, but no joy. I wasn't surprised. After many years in pursuit of her weird agenda, Praeclara was an expert at not being found. My guess is, she'd got some hidden combe or cave or similar infuriating advantage, and the moor's ideal for that sort of thing. Back when I knew her better, she tended to have a staff of about thirty with her at any given time, with the rest of her forces dispersed in cells, whose location only she knew. Trying to sneak up and rescue my pals by force was, therefore, not a viable option, as I'd tried to explain to Polycrates, who chose not to listen.

"One more thing," she said. "If I don't hear from you by the third after Ascension, I shall kill Gombryas. Five days after that, I'll kill Dodilas. Is that understood?"

"Yes."

"Splendid. I shall look forward to hearing from you. You may be a complete waste of a human being, Saevus, but I'll say this for you. You can be trained to perform simple tasks."

Which happened to be the nicest thing she'd ever said to me. I tried not to let it go to my head.

*

"Obviously," I told Polycrates and Papinian, as we started out on our long trudge north, "we can't do this stupid, horrible, dangerous thing. You agree with me?"

They nodded.

"Fine," I said. "So what we need to find is a way of not doing it. Any suggestions?"

They didn't have any. No surprise there.

My dialogue, incidentally, wasn't exactly original. It's cribbed from a famous exchange between Cyprian the Great and his brilliant, appalling son-in-law Prisca. Cyprian was just coming to the end of his fourth term as First Citizen of Mezentia, at which point he'd be obliged to account for all the public money that had passed through his hands over the last ten years. One evening, Prisca came across him in the rose garden, crying his eyes out. It's no good, he sobbed. I can't think of a way of rendering my accounts.

Fine, said Prisca. In that case, we'd better come up with a way of not rendering your accounts. Whereupon they sat down and devised the Third Social War, which caused unthinkable devastation and loss of life and ultimately led to the fall of Mezentia; but in all the confusion, Cyprian was never called in front of the Treasury Committee, and the shortfall never came to light and very soon ceased to matter because of the eye-watering deficit caused by the war ... Cyprian died in office three years later. Prisca succeeded him, changed sides, burned Mezentia to the ground and was crowned emperor. Moral: always fight the war you can win, not the one you can't; if you can't win this war, start another one. If I have a core belief, a creed, a moral kernel, it's that story.

"We need a plan," Polycrates said, after a long silence. The rear offside wheel of the cart was making a creaking noise, once every revolution, presumably where the axle fouled a raised spot in the hub. I'd been using it to calculate our speed, and he made me lose count.

"Of course we need a plan," I said. "Have you got one?"

He gave me a sour look. "You're supposed to be the incredibly resourceful and inventive leader," he said. "Though if you ask me it's all shit."

"A lot of it, yes," I said. "But with a core of genius. Sort of a reverse pearl. Layers and layers of rubbish built up around a tiny speck of—"

"Shut up, will you?" Polycrates said. "You make my head hurt."

By this point I'd lost interest in my mathematical speculations, so I gave them up and tried to think of a plan instead. No, no plan. Pity about that. "Our orders," I told him, "are to take the castle intact."

"Really? That'll be so easy."

"No," I said. Polycrates shouldn't be encouraged to use irony. I'm not entirely sure he knows how it works. "But that's not the point. I think that tells us something about the nature of the operation."

"Sure it does. It tells us it can't be fucking done."

I tried thinking about the something it told me, made a certain amount of progress, folded down the corner of my reflections for further study and went back to counting wheel creaks. In case you're interested, using Saloninus's third law of distance we find that a wheel whose spokes are eighteen inches long travels a whisker under three and a quarter yards each time it squeaks. The answer to my original question was, therefore, too bloody slow.

*

Some people consider the moor to be beautiful. I can sort of see where they're coming from. But I defy anybody to find it interesting. There's an awful lot of it and it's remarkably, depressingly uniform. Even the differences – combes, goyles, lone thorn trees, stone outcrops – are just the same few features repeated over and over again, because one combe, goyle, thorn tree or outcrop is very much like another, and once you've seen one, trust me, you've seen them all. In consequence it's lethally easy to get lost on the moor, particularly when the mist comes down – really it's low cloud, not that that helps at all – and you can't see the sun or, for that matter, your hand in front of your face. We were in luck. The mist didn't come down, the sun was shining and it was the dry season. In the wet season, there are soft places on the moor where a cart can be swallowed up in the time it takes a bored monk to mumble the general benediction, but we didn't run into any of those. To be truthful, I found that mildly vexing. As I think I may have mentioned, you only get so much luck, and I was vaguely but painfully aware that in crossing the moor safely I was using my ration up rather fast.

About two hundred years ago, there was a man who made a great deal of money in the bone trade in Calisy. He decided he wanted to be a great feudal lord, but he wasn't quite rich enough for that. He cast around for some land to buy, and about that time the lease on the moor came up for renewal and the great feudal lord who held it decided he couldn't be bothered any more, so the bone magnate nipped in and secured it, paying silly money for the privilege. What he got for his money was a vast area; on paper he was suddenly the fifth biggest landed proprietor in the Duchy. The sheer extent of the property was the only reason his predecessor had taken it on, because of the bragging rights, but the bone man had a one-track commercial brain. If he owned something, it had to be useful for something. The moor, as anyone who's lived there can tell you, is good for absolutely nothing.

The bone man wouldn't accept that. So he bought ploughs and harrows and horses and people, and thus began the Improvement, which went on for the rest of his life and most of his son's, and achieved very little. They ploughed up 250,000 acres of heather and gorse, built banks and planted beech hedges, dug drains and rines, quarried about a million tons of lime to try and sweeten the useless soil, recruited an army of tenants and issued them with grass seed, livestock and buildings . . . These days you come down off the high moor and there it still is, what's left of the Improvement. A lot of it flooded and is now impenetrable bog, but the rest of it is short, thin-soiled, wind-burned grass, cropped by the saddest sheep you ever saw. One of the dictators, I think it was Victorinus II, made a grand gesture of liberating the serfs about fifty years ago, so the poor bastards who live there now own the land they're chained to, and I'm sure it's a great comfort to them. It's blazing hot in summer, except when it rains, and absolutely perishing cold in winter. It has a certain rugged charm, but I wouldn't want to live there.

I know the Improvement quite well because a lot of battles get fought there. It's a great place for battles. The open country is ideal for cavalry, and the bogs are marvellous for luring your opponent's cavalry into; you can see for miles, so there's no excuse for unwelcome surprises, except that the combes and folded valleys allow scope for clever tactical exercises – you can make, or lose, a reputation quite easily on the Improvement, and a lot of ambitious generals like to fight there. Collateral damage to infrastructure and the national wealth is practically nil, and it's on the borders of three small nations (the Duchy, Permia and the Olethrian Protectorate) which serve as buffer states for the big boys. Like I said, I wouldn't want to live there, but it sometimes feels like I do.

In fact it's been fought over so often that it's easy to lose track of who's won, especially since the victor immediately goes away again, understandably enough. Actually, that's the best thing about the Improvement. When there isn't a war actively going on, it doesn't really belong to anybody. Therefore there's no effective government, and you can feel moderately sure of being left alone. Bandits and tax collectors don't bother with it because there's nothing there worth stealing. At one point a bunch of rich men's sons who'd just come a very poor second in a civil war in the Protectorate drifted out that way, built themselves a castle and tried to earn a living robbing the locals, but they found they couldn't make a go of it and drifted off somewhere else. They're long gone, but the castle's still there, apart from the cartloads of stones liberated by neighbouring farmers to build hay barns.

The met'Einae (that's the rebels I just told you about) chose a good spot for their castle. It's built on a tall, steep outcrop around which a river obligingly forks, in the bottom of a sheer-sided combe overgrown with holm oaks; if you didn't know where it was, you'd have a job to find it, because the trees obscure it, even if you're looking down from the beacons on top of the high moor. I guess you could climb the outcrop if you had ropes and time and leisure to cut steps into the granite. Lesser mortals go up and down on the one passable track, which zigzags half a mile to climb two hundred yards. Near the foot of the track there's a place where you can ford the northern fork of the river with horses and carts. The southern fork runs

in a deep goyle, and you'd need a battalion of Imperial engineers to build a bridge over it. The entrance to the track is a
crack between two colossal boulders, as good a defensive position as the Great Gate at Lonasep; farm carts can go through
one at a time, or three horsemen abreast, and the met'Einae
had a sort of portcullis arrangement on a counterweight that
dropped sideways. The castle itself is nothing special, because
it didn't need to be. There's a low curtain wall of the local
sandstone, and inside that a square slab-sided four-storey
keep with an arched gateway. The keep is built round an open
courtyard, about the size of one of the smaller quadrangles
at the university in Choris. You could knock the whole thing
flat in an hour with a dozen type three trebuchets, except you
couldn't, because there's nowhere flat enough to put them with
an unobstructed field of fire. Sapping is out, because the whole
thing's built on solid rock. The one clever thing the met'Einae
did was to build a large lead-lined cistern on the third floor of
the keep gatehouse tower. It rains a lot on the moor in winter,
so water simply isn't a problem.

I know a bit about this castle because I was stuck there for
a month once, under circumstances you really don't want to
hear about. At that time it had been spruced up a bit by the
conqueror before last and several of the larger rooms were
watertight and partially draughtproof; there were shutters on
the windows and floorboards on the floors, and someone had
hacked a path through the brambles and nettles in the courtyard, and if you wanted to keep warm you could always break
off some of the dead branches from the elder trees growing
out of the cracks in the curtain wall, though elder doesn't give
a lot of heat at the best of times. I imagine I'd got the job of
storming the place because Praeclara knew I was familiar with

it. Anyway, I knew enough about it to be painfully aware that for its size it was pretty well unstormable; as for a siege, forget it. Besiegers have to eat, too, and getting supply carts up and down the sides of the combe would be a hell of a job; you'd have to unload at the top and carry everything down on your back, and in my experience there's a limit to how much healthy exercise the average fighting man is prepared to put up with. In any case, Praeclara had made it pretty clear that I was on a schedule, so starving the buggers out wasn't an option.

For some reason, I decided not to share these insights with Polycrates, Papinian and the rest of the lads. I had no intention of storming the castle. What I needed to do, obviously, was find out who was in charge of the defence, do a deal with him and then double-cross him. That, I felt, was entirely within my capabilities. It's the sort of thing I'm best at, after all.

It rained for three days, and then stopped as we reached the head of the combe, which is the only angle you can approach from if you've got vehicles. The track was a proper metalled road once, thanks to the bone man; these days it's mostly ruts, down which rainwater happily races if there happens to be any about. The carts kept bottoming out on the ridges between the ruts and we decided they were more trouble than they were worth; most of the stuff on them was the junk we'd picked up on the battlefield, and we wouldn't be needing that. So we left the carts and walked the rest of the way, which was no fun at all.

"So what's the plan?" Eudo asked.

"It's complicated," I told him.

"Ah." He seemed entirely satisfied. The more complicated the better, presumably: the more complications, the more genius must've gone into making it. I can handle Polycrates's and Papinian's scepticism and naked contempt all day long, because they feel about my abilities roughly the same way I do, but Eudo's blind faith disturbs me. I imagine God feels the same way a lot of the time. In any event, I felt an itchy sort of need to amplify, just so as to fill up the yawning maw of Eudo's faith. "Just thinking aloud," I said.

"Yes?"

"Well," I said. "Once you're past those two rocks and up the path to the top, the castle itself shouldn't be too much of a problem. There's a blind spot just under the gatehouse—"

"Is there?"

"Sure," I said. "Hadn't you noticed?"

Of course he hadn't, because you can't see it from where we were. I knew it was there because I'd lived in the horrible castle for a month. "Sorry," Eudo said. "I'm not very observant."

"It's like everything," I told him. "You need to train your eye to notice things. Anyway, yes, there's a blind spot. If you get there, you're sheltered by the angles. They can't shoot arrows at you, and they can't drop things on your head. So all you'd need to do would be to stack up dry logs against the gate and start a fire, and once the gate's burned through, in you go. You'd want to lock shields, of course, going in through the gateway, but force of numbers would be your friend, which it isn't always. And once you're inside it's just going room to room, assuming they don't just cave in straight away and surrender. Depends on how motivated they are. But it shouldn't be a problem."

"Ah." He was smiling, the poor fool.

"Which leaves the small matter," I said, "of how you get past the two rocks and up the path. That could be awkward."

He grinned at me. "But you've got a plan."

"Yes," I lied, and then an arrow whistled past my ear and hit him. I stared at it for a small fraction of a second: Eudo, not the smartest man I've ever met but basically all right, with an arrowhead sunk about three-fifths of an inch into his collarbone. That must hurt, I thought, and then I hit the deck.

Lying flat on my face I wasn't in a position to gather and collate useful data, but I already knew a great deal. I knew the direction the arrow had come from, and the depth it had penetrated told me that the enemy were either using light bows or shooting at extreme range. That aside, anybody's guess. Those horrible trees – a holm-oak wood is a beautiful thing, but not when you're inside it getting shot at – crowded round the path on both sides, and of course it was only to be expected that the bad guys would have archers out, to give us a hard time even if they couldn't do any real damage. I lifted myself on my hands and craned my neck to make sure the rest of my people were down and safe, then went back to nuzzling leaf mould. The flatter you are, the safer it is. A metaphor for life, and all that.

Sometimes in my line of work – quite often, in fact – I come across stuff that looks like it's worth good money, but which proves impossible to shift. One such item was a presentation copy of Marcian's *Art of War*, no doubt given to a young officer as a graduation present by a rich uncle. It was codex-bound in elaborately tooled and gilded Olbian kid, it had twenty-six full-page illustrations and lots of quarter and half-page pictures and diagrams, illuminated capitals, ivy and acanthus trails in the margins, the whole nine yards, and could I find anyone who wanted to buy it? Could I hell. The best offer I got was twelve gulden, which was a joke, so I kept it for myself. Furthermore, I actually read it, which is how I know that the main purpose of suppression archery is to mask an open manoeuvre – translated from the military, that means when someone shoots at you at long range from cover, it's not just to be annoying. They want you to lie down and hide; and while you're doing that, they can sneak up on you without you seeing them and surround you with a view to slaughtering you like sheep, or something of the sort. It comes quite early in the book, chapter three or four, so it's pretty elementary stuff. So is how you're meant to respond. All you do, Marcian informs us, is stand up, form a shield wall and charge the archers, who are by definition light infantry and yellow as a buttercup, and can be relied on to run away at the first hint of an orderly, disciplined deployment. That's it. It's so standard and orthodox, and the outcome is so inevitable, it's hard to see why people bother. After all, we've all read the same book. Wouldn't it be much simpler and more convenient if the captain of the archers called out, "Chapter four, paragraphs six to nine", and the lieutenant commanding the heavy infantry shouted back, "Chapter six, paragraphs twelve to fifteen inclusive", and then both of them could get on with something useful instead of wasting each other's time.

My lads aren't soldiers. Asking them to stand up and charge a bunch of vicious bastards they couldn't even see was not a viable option, and a refusal often offends. Nuts, I thought, we're dead.

Then I remembered that Eudo had just been shot in the collarbone. I scriggled over to where he was lying, on his back, with his wrist in his mouth to stop him from screaming. I call that thoughtful. "Hold still," I said, and yanked at the arrow. It stayed put, so I had to wiggle it about before it came loose. I can't begin to imagine how much that must've hurt.

He looked at me with damp cow eyes. "Is it poisoned?" he whispered.

Is what poisoned? Oh, the arrow. Eudo likes reading war stories. "Don't be stupid," I said, hoping it wasn't. "You're bloody lucky it hit the bone, or you'd have been in trouble. Can you move?"

It wasn't a question he'd been expecting to be asked, but I needed him. Or at least, I needed someone, and he was all I had. "I think so."

"Good lad. Now, it's quite simple. You and I are going to make our way nice and quiet over there—" I nodded toward the castle "—and then we're going to make a lot of noise and shout orders to a lot of imaginary soldiers. Think you can manage that?"

"Yes."

In his shoes I'd have told me to go to hell, so it's probably a good thing we're not all made alike. "Splendid," I said. "Now then, nice and easy does it."

That particular manoeuvre isn't in Marcian, because it's downright silly, but it's how Armanarich won the battle of Seppa. I know that because I was there, watching from a safe distance, and Armanarich told me about it later. There wasn't much else I could do, he told me, so I did that, and it worked. I quite liked Armanarich; he was a decent sort, for a soldier. Gombryas has his shoulder blade, though he didn't pay a lot for it.

So we did that, and it worked. The genius lay in my choice of direction; I'd guessed more or less where they were and made it seem like I was bringing up reinforcements from directly behind them. Nobody, however brave, likes taking it in the rear. There was a sort of multi-directional rustling, and the woods were full of people we couldn't see, running.

"It's the deal their captain made with them," I told Eudo, as he leaned against a tree, out of breath and white with pain. "We're just going to soften them up a bit and give them a scare, he'll have said. First sign of trouble, I'll have you out of there." I smiled at him. "We were the first sign of trouble. Nothing to it, really."

He beamed at me: true worship, which made me feel sick. "That was brilliant," he said. I wanted to tell him to fuck off and die, but that would've been ungrateful.

Papinian emerged from a clump of holly. He had holly leaves in his hair, and his face and hands were scratched. "You lunatic," he said to me. "We were nearly killed."

"No, you weren't," I said. "Eudo and I made a noise and they ran away. They're chickenshit. Like you," I added. "We know that now. Useful information."

I was watching over his shoulder as more of the lads emerged from cover. There are few things as inherently funny as watching cowards come out from where they've been hiding. I speak as one who's given a great deal of amusement to other people, over the years. "Any casualties?" I asked Papinian, whose department it was to know.

He was staring at Eudo's shoulder. "I don't know, do I?"

"Then find out." Which was him told. "Let's get out of here," I said. "We've got what we came for."

We trailed back up the combe, looking nervously about in case the trees started spitting arrows at us again. It wasn't likely, but it was possible. "What did we find out?" Eudo asked.

"That the other side aren't soldiers either," I said, "but whoever's commanding them is. How's the shoulder?"

"Hurting rather a lot. Can the doc do anything, do you think?"

"He'll probably bathe it with something that stings like hell and stuff bits of moss in the hole. Don't worry. He's really good. He'll see you right."

If it doesn't get infected, I didn't say, in which case you'll probably die. I try and be positive in these situations, which calls for a great deal of lying. He went off to be patched up. I went looking for Polycrates, and found him sitting with his back to the wheel of a cart. There was dried blood on his face.

"Bashed my head on a stone when I hit the deck," he explained, with a sheepish grin. "How many dead?"

"None," I told him. "Four actual arrow hits, nothing serious."

"First time I've been shot at like that," Polycrates said. "I pissed myself."

"And why not?" I sat down beside him. "It's not something that should happen to anyone, in an ideal world. But I've got the advantage of having read Segimerus."

"Who the hell is—?"

I'd brought a bottle. I gouged out the pitch it was stopped with and handed it over. "A general," I told him, "about a hundred and fifty years ago. It occurred to him to wonder what men actually do in battles, so he asked them, and then when he retired he wrote a book. I used to have a copy, but I lost it. Interesting stuff."

"Really?"

"Oh yes. He used to go round the campfires after every engagement, talking to people. The result of his research is Segimerus's law of participation, which states that in a missile exchange – that's arrows and javelins and slingshots – only one man in five actually makes any sort of effort to aim at the enemy. The rest just loose off in the vague direction. Partly it's because they're too scared to bother, but mostly, he reckoned, it's the innate instinct in all of us not to hurt people. It really surprised me when I read it the first time, but if he says it, I guess it must be true."

"Sounds like bullshit to me."

"Oh, I don't know. A colonel told me once about a time when he and fifty slingers were supposed to be guarding a river crossing. They were all bored out of their heads, and there were these bits of greenery floating down the river – you know, bits of branch with leaves on, like you get when a river's in spate. Some of the slingers started taking bets on whether they could hit the floating branches, and it wasn't long before they found the range, and soon they were picking them off like nobody's business. And then dead men started floating to the surface, because it wasn't branches and bits of wood, it was men in camouflage wading across the river. So the colonel yelled at the men to get the bastards, and suddenly they couldn't hit them at all; they started slinging wide or too short, and the next thing they knew, the bad guys were across the river and coming at them, so they turned and ran. You see, when they thought they were just targets, they could hit them, but when they turned out to be people, they missed."

Polycrates frowned. "It didn't feel like that," he said. "It felt like they were aiming all right."

I shrugged. "Figures," I said. "An arrow is still an arrow, even if it hits you by accident. But if you get down flat, you'll probably only get hit if you're unlucky, or God hates you. I was scared rigid, as it happens."

He looked at me.

"But," I went on, "I was lucky. I couldn't afford to be scared, because fixing it was up to me. That kept my head clear, so I couldn't drown in panic. If I hadn't been in charge, I'd probably have pissed myself and shat myself as well."

He opened his mouth to say something, thought better of it, and shut it again. Definite progress. Usually Polycrates isn't the sort of man who ever thinks better of anything. "Don't worry about it," I said. "Anyway, it was a useful exercise."

"Was it?"

"Oh yes," I said. "Now we know everything we need to know, and on that basis I now know exactly what to do. We'll be fine, you'll see."

Which was perfectly true.

I'd learned two vitally important facts. One: my men weren't soldiers. Two: neither were the enemy. That made it all very simple and straightforward. Now there's a difference, a vast difference spanning life and death, between simple and easy. Simple is not complicated. Easy means it can be done without genius or mortal peril. Lifting a five-ton rock is simple, but unless you're a giant it's not easy. But to a giant, a piece of cake.

I'd also learned, or formed an informed opinion, that my counterpart was probably a soldier, or at the very least had read Marcian. That made him dangerous, just as potentially I was dangerous. There are several passages in Marcian, such as chapter nine and bits of chapter twelve, dealing with how to achieve military objectives using terrified and rebellious troops. I'd read them, and so presumably had he. Something we had in common: if we ever got together, maybe we could talk about our common love of Marcian over a slice of seed cake and a carafe of the house red. Meanwhile, I had facts to face. I had to win this pathetic little war, and I had to do so by means other than military force. He, on the other hand, could get what he wanted simply by doing what it says in the book. You don't need proper soldiers to cower behind walls and a locked gate; you have what's known as the advantage of position – like that idiot a thousand years ago who held the city of, I forget the name of the city, against half a million men with a few hundred terrified gardeners.

3

"You're kidding," I said.

Polycrates looked at me. "Straight up," he said. "You can look for yourself if you don't believe me."

For crying out loud. One commodity you get plenty of in my line of work is fabrics, textiles – shirts, trousers, coats, blankets, tents, cart canopies, you name it, we peel it off the dead, darn the holes and sell it on. Even the pitiful haul we'd acquired from Sinderic's last stand had yielded two full carts. "And you're telling me," I snarled at him, "there's not a single bit of white cloth in the whole consignment?"

He gave me his hurt look. "Not much call for white in the army," he said.

Which is essentially true. White gets grubby; also it costs money to bleach wool and linen, so why bother? Endless variations on the theme of dingy light brown, but that's not the same thing at all.

"All I need is enough for a stupid flag," I told him. "Come on. You can't have looked properly."

It turned out we did have just enough milk-white cloth for a flag of truce. It was my best shirt, the one I jealously preserve for meetings with important people and my once-in-a-decade days off. We tied the arms to a stick. It would have to do.

"You must be out of your mind," Papinian said, as I hefted my flag. "As soon as you break cover, they'll shoot you."

"Shoot at me," I corrected. "I have absolute faith in their marksmanship."

Eudo had begged to be allowed to come with me. I pointed out that his presence would achieve nothing, he couldn't protect me, he'd only get himself killed as well as me, and I didn't need an idiot along to screw things up. Polycrates had found me a mail shirt to wear under my coat; it would've come down to my knees and slowed me up horribly if I had to run for it, so I told him where to stick it. Besides, I already had my very expensive genuine Echmen-made brigandine, though I didn't tell him that.

My brigandine is made up of over a thousand small steel plates rivetted to canvas and backed with gorgeous red velvet. The individual plates are made of thin spring steel, hardened and tempered, and the weight is so perfectly distributed that you barely notice you're wearing it. True, it didn't save the life of its previous owner, but only because he got his head smashed in by a catapult shot. I hadn't mentioned it to anybody because they'd have wanted to know where I got it, and why I'd kept something so eye-wateringly valuable for myself instead of adding it to the overall take, to shares of which they were entitled. It's just that sort of petty dishonesty that wrecks the confidence in each other that you need in a business like ours. It'd be terrible for morale if I told them what I'd done, so I didn't.

But it was nice to know it was there as I walked up the path through the holm oaks. Trees make a difference. If you're watching someone through a curtain of trees, you only get part of the picture. Important details, such as a white flag, can get obscured by an inconvenient branch. I'm being pretty brave doing this, I said to myself, as I flinched at an imagined movement off to one side. Idiot, I thought. But it had to be done, so I did it.

They let me get to within sight of the two rocks. Then they came out from the trees, pointing bows at me. I could tell they were clowns because they had their bows at full draw. First thing they tell you in archery training: don't hold your bow at full draw for a moment longer than you have to. It strains the wood and ruins the bow; also, your fingers might slip and you might shoot something you don't want to. Such as me.

"That's far enough," said a tall, skinny man with a long beard. He was terrified. "Don't try anything or we'll kill you."

The temptation to try something was almost irresistible, mostly because they'd crowded round me in a ring; if I ducked and they all shot, they'd wipe each other out. That would be satisfying but counterproductive. "I'd like to speak to your commanding officer," I said. "Please," I added. My mother would've been proud of me.

The skinny man looked at someone behind me I couldn't see, then nodded. "Nice and easy does it," he said. "This way." I decided I loved him. He was a clown, and they'd put him in charge of the sentries.

"Do you mind if I leave this here?" I asked, giving the flag a little wiggle. "Only it's my best shirt, and I don't want anything to happen to it."

"Shut up," the skinny man said. His throat was dry with

terror. It was almost certainly a trap, and any second now he was going to be hacked to pieces by monsters. I felt sorry for him. In his shoes I'd have been terrified, too. Actually, come to think of it, I was scared out of my wits. But I was used to it, and he clearly wasn't.

"Sure," I said. "I'll be as quiet as a little mouse."

He'd have belted me for that, only he was scared of initiating violence. I was, after all, known to be dangerous; I might duck, weave, come up behind him and snap his neck with a single chop of my cupped hand. Instead he treated me to a glare of pure hatred. "This way," he said, neither moving nor pointing. I waited patiently for further and better particulars, and we might all still be there if I hadn't started to walk, slowly and with my hands behind my back, in the general direction of the two rocks.

Things had changed since I'd been there last. Someone had built a brick arch between the two rocks, narrowing the gap slightly but contributing nothing to the defensibility of the position. I saw pintles for hinges let into the brickwork but no gate; held up in committee somewhere, at a guess. The gap was guarded by armed men, who took a step back when they saw me.

If ever I'm emperor, my first official act will be to have all the mountains and hills levelled and all the buildings reduced to a single storey. I hate walking up things. I get out of breath, and the backs of my legs hurt. Down with up. I arrived at the top of the hill with the knees of my trousers glued to my skin with sweat, and a stitch in my chest. To be fair, my escort weren't much better; I'd made a point of setting a stiff pace, which they struggled to match. It's the little details that make all the difference, and first impressions are so important.

A short, fat man was standing in front of the castle gate, which was open. He looked at me as if I was a unicorn, then at the skinny man. "What the fuck have you done?" he asked.

"Prisoner." The skinny man was out of breath. "Caught him in the forest."

"Actually," I said, "I'm here to negotiate, under a flag of truce."

"What flag?"

"I left it at the bottom of the hill." I turned to the skinny man. "Tell him there was a flag," I said. The skinny man glowered at me and nodded. "Take me to your leader," I said to the fat man. "Please," I added.

The fat man had forearms like a blacksmith, and I got the impression of a sergeant with twenty years' service, demobbed and gone to seed. Fine. He could be useful, too. Like I said, first impressions. He summed me up with a glance that read me as an officer – not a compliment, as far as he was concerned – then nodded. "With me," he said. I followed him through the gate. The skinny man and his patrol stayed behind, relieved that they were still alive.

There were a few people milling about in the centre yard, loading sacks onto wheelbarrows, carrying jars. There was also a man in a pourpoint (that's a padded jacket you wear under your armour) sitting on a barrel next to a mounting block with three steps. I thought I recognised him from somewhere. Surely not—

He saw me and stood up. "Where the hell did he come from?" he said.

"Caught him in the woods," the sergeant replied.

"Actually, no," I said. "I'm here to open negotiations, under a flag of—"

"Shut up," said the man I thought I recognised. "Have you any idea who this is?"

The sergeant looked at me.

"He's Florian," said the man I thought I recognised. "That lunatic who did all that shit in Sirupat and nearly got us all killed. He's worth an absolute fucking fortune."

"And you're Crabia," I said. "Thought I knew you from somewhere. How's her ladyship?"

He gave me a look you could've smeared on arrowheads. "Ask her yourself," he said. "I'll let her know you're here."

Many years ago, when I was sixteen and even more arrogant and stupid than I am today, I dressed up in an old coat I found in the stables and went drinking in the village. Everything was going fine and I was having a great time, making new and interesting friends and buying drinks for people; and then I must have said something, because one of my new friends suddenly spun round and hit me in the solar plexus. I treasure the memory of that punch, though it was no fun at all at the time, because it taught me more about human nature than all sixteen books of Theodotus's *Humanities* – its relevance at this juncture was that stunned, winded, witless feeling, not being able to breathe because your lungs have been drained of air and your mind has been emptied of all traces of thought. I distinctly remember standing there, staring at the man whose name I'd just recalled to mind. That's where I knew him from: he'd been one of her assistant goons, and during a long cart ride we took together we hadn't hit it off at all. Maybe the penny should've dropped, at terrifying speed, like a meteor. But there are some contingencies you can't possibly prepare yourself for, not if you want to stay sane and sleep at night. I remember thinking, well, at least it's not my sister, and then someone grabbed me by the shoulder and shoved me through a door . . . And there she was.

"Oh, for God's sake," she said. "You."

Which was, oddly enough, exactly what I was thinking at the time.

We go way back, Stauracia and I. Sister Stauracia she calls herself, though the religious order of which she's founder and sole autocrat is a gossamer-thin front for an operation very similar to mine. They call themselves the Sisters of Mercy or something like that, and the idea is that they go round battlefields tending the wounded and giving spiritual comfort to the dying. Like hell they do; and what annoys me is that she doesn't pay for her scavenging rights, like me and the Asvogel boys and everyone else in the trade. Instead she puts on her snow-white wimple and goes and simpers at generals and princes (she's very nice looking, which helps) and they give her the run of the carrion for free, often when they've already taken my money for the actual rights. If I boot her off she goes whining to the victorious general, who shouts at me for interfering with angels of mercy and confiscates everything I've painfully and expensively collected, and as often as not hands it over to her as a charitable donation. She saved my life on Sirupat, but only after she'd tried to kill me a couple of times. If I have to be scrupulously honest, I confess I like her a lot. I have no idea why, but liking someone isn't the same thing as approving of what they do, not by a long shot, and you can like a real genuine hundred per cent proof pain in the arse, which she is, and so am I, for that matter. The fact that she's one of my favourite people in the world says a lot about the world, if you ask me.

*

"You first," I said politely.

"What the fuck," said Sister Stauracia, "are you doing here?"

"Besieging you, apparently. What are *you* doing here?"

She gave me a look that should have shrivelled me like a hundred years in the desert. I'm used to that look; it means I've got past her defence, which doesn't happen all that often. I'd put her in an awkward position. In order to answer my question and continue the conversation, which she was clearly anxious to do, she'd have to send away the half-dozen or so of her people who were standing around earwigging like mad; doing that, however, would give the impression that she was about to conspire with me behind their backs.

"Take him away and lock him in the charcoal store," she said. "And watch him. He's as tricky as a snake."

Precisely what I'd have done in her shoes. Just as well I'd brought a book to read.

I'd managed a chapter and a half of *The Garden of Entrancing Images* – it was a tiny, pocket-size edition and it's just not the same without the pictures – when the door opened and she came in. "You shouldn't read in this light," she said. "You'll strain your eyes."

"Hello, Stauracia," I said. "Sit down, relax."

She was too smart to sit down in a white dress in a charcoal store. "You're kidding, right? Tell me you're just kidding."

"I'm just kidding. No, actually I'm serious. How about you?"

"Never mind about me."

"I mind about you terribly. Are you really in charge of these pinheads?"

She gave me her best hurt scowl. "It's all your fault."

"Of course it is. How, exactly?"

She looked round for something to sit on or lean against. It was a charcoal store. She stayed standing. "That stupid mess on Sirupat you got me into."

"What about it?"

A roll of the eyes; one of her signature gestures. "I ended up having to command an army."

"You did it ever so well."

"Too bloody well. These—" Pause to find suitable word; quest abandoned as impossible. "These lunatics needed someone to defend this place and they heard about Sirupat. They couldn't hire a real soldier for various reasons, so they picked on me. Like I said, your fault."

"Picked on."

Slight nod. "You could say I'm not here through choice."

"Me neither," I said. "Are you getting paid?"

"That's neither here nor there." Then she looked at me: a curious look, one which I couldn't immediately classify, and I collect her looks the way Gombryas collects dead people's bits. "Saevus, they've got my son."

When I was a kid, one of the gardeners had a tortoise. It was a phlegmatic beast, given to walking slowly and in deadly earnest in a straight line until it bumped into something. If you picked it up and turned it through a hundred and eighty degrees and put it down again, it would pause for a second then carry on walking, the same slow, determined pace, towards a completely different destination. I guess it must've been confused for a moment, but it took it in its stride. I envy that tortoise. When you pick me up and turn me through a hundred and eighty degrees, as she'd just done, I don't recover half as smoothly.

"Your what?"

"Son," she said impatiently. "Male child. You're one, if that helps at all."

"You've got a—"

"Had," she snapped. "They broke in and stole him, and I won't ever see him again unless I do exactly what they tell me to. Saevus, he's only three. I can't let anything happen to him, I just can't."

"You've got a kid," I said. "My God."

Her eyes are the colour of well-seasoned walnut heartwood; or, if you prefer, of diarrhoea. "Yes," she said. "I found him under a gooseberry bush, and it's none of your stupid business. But if I don't do this job for these people, they're going to kill him. Got that?"

"I think so."

"Splendid. So, what you've got to do is, you've got to lose."

I kept perfectly still. "I'd love to," I said. "Only it's not that simple."

"Yes, it is."

"No, it isn't. They've got my friends. My lot," I explained. "The lunatics I'm working for."

A tiny movement around the eyebrows indicated a sudden spurt of anger. "Tough," she said.

"Stauracia—"

"No, shut your face. Look, I've met your friends. They're not worth spit. This is my son we're talking about."

"They're my friends."

"Oh, for God's sake, how can you be so selfish? Look, it's easy. All you have to do is mount an attack in force. I beat it off with heavy losses. You lose half your men, and then it's plainly impossible for you to take this castle with the resources remaining to you. You explain that to your bosses, they see it's unreasonable to expect you to proceed, they let your pals go and that's it, problem solved. And my son doesn't get killed."

"You aren't listening," I said. "They're my friends."

"So fucking what? You can always get new ones. No, I take that back, you'd have problems in that direction, I grant you that. But they're just—" vague but impressive hand gesture "—people. They're a bunch of strangers you happen to spend a lot of time with. He's my *son*. Part of me."

When Stauracia decided to make robbing the dead her career, the stage missed out on a great actress. She can say practically anything like she really means it, and sometimes even I can't tell the difference. If she's stopped at *he's my son*, she'd have been fine. It was the *part of me* that was overdoing it. A great actress; not quite so good at writing the script. "You haven't got a son," I said. "Have you?"

She kicked me in the face. The upshot was that she got charcoal marks on the hem of her gown. I count that as a partial victory. "Arsehole," she said.

She'd caught me on the cheekbone. It didn't feel like anything was broken. Probably just a big, cheerful bruise for a week or so. "Tell me about it."

"Why the hell should I? It's none of your business."

"Tell me about it," I said, "and then, when I know all the facts, maybe I can figure a way out of this mess. Like I did on Sirupat."

Stauracia feels about trusting people the way a cat feels about swimming: she can do it if she absolutely has to, but she knows she's completely out of her element and it makes her mental fur feel all wrong. And, like me, she tends to regard telling the truth as an admission of failure. There's no angle to be gained from telling the truth, no mechanical advantage: it's like driving in a nail with a chunk of flint instead of a hammer. The truth is a gobbet of raw meat, not a casserole with herbs and red wine. I was asking her to do something that went entirely against the grain, and what was in it for her?

"I was young," she said. "It was just before they arrested my dad and I had to go into service. There was this boy, our neighbour's son. Like I told you, none of your fucking business."

"Agreed," I said. "Go on."

"His father had a stall in the market, wicker baskets. He said they'd look after the kid, provided I moved away and had nothing more to do with any of them, because of the shame of my father being in jail. That suited me fine. Anyway, the boy I – the kid's father, he took over when his dad had a stroke, the year after I left. He did all right, nothing special. We hadn't talked in years. I don't think he'd ever forgiven me, because of my dad's spot of trouble, and I never gave him a moment's thought. He was just there, in the background, like home if you were born in Poor Town. And then these bastards came, the ones I'm working for. They wanted the kid, so I'd have to do what they wanted, but there was a scuffle and they smashed his head in, and then they took the kid." She took a deep breath, then let it out again slowly. "One day I'll deal with them, you can be absolutely sure about that. But first I've got to get my son, and I can't do that until they decide I've finished the job. I don't know where he is or anything. For all I know they've already killed him, but that doesn't matter. One thing at a time, it's the only way. Otherwise—"

She didn't need to enlarge on otherwise. "Who are these people?" I said.

She shrugged. "Not a clue," she said. "I know who they aren't. They're not government, they're not guilds, they're not part of any of the big trade syndicates, they're not the Knights or the Poor Sisters or anyone we've heard of. They've got some money and some people, not a lot of either. I think they probably believe in something, politics or religion or shit like that. Apart from that, not a clue. And I care less. I just want to give them what they want. And then I'm going to kill them."

Fair enough, I thought, if she was telling the truth. "So what do they actually want?" I asked. "Yes, they want you to defend the castle. But in aid of what?"

"Don't know, couldn't give a damn." I could feel her patience run out. That could be awkward. "Look," she said, "I'm really sorry, but I haven't got the time or the energy for you to weave your special brand of magic. Really I ought to cut your stupid throat, but I feel bad enough about the kid's father as it is without you loading guilt on me as well. So you're going to have to stay here and be a hostage. It's not all that hard. You just sit still and quiet. You can manage that, can't you?"

"Now hang on a minute," I said. "I came here in good faith—"

"That's so sweet. Still and quiet, and I promise I won't kill you if I don't have to. For old times' sake."

Call me a naive, trusting halfwit, but I hadn't anticipated that. Which is another way of saying I hadn't expected to find Stauracia here. I'd assumed – never assume, that's rule two. Rule one is, don't get involved. I'm not good with rules.

"My boys aren't going to be happy about that," I said.

She smiled at me. "Is that who you've got down there? Your happy band of tame jackdaws? Oh, that makes everything a lot easier. Once they've heard I've got you chained up, they'll piss off and find something else to do, and then all our problems will be over. You never did have the knack of instilling

discipline among your employees. I thought you had *soldiers*.
Well, that's a weight off my mind. You've really cheered me
up, you know that?"

The Garden of Entrancing Images is widely regarded as a classic of its genre. The plot is garbage and the characterisation
isn't up to much, but the descriptions – and it's got a strong,
independent-minded female lead who wears black leather
when she's wearing anything at all, not to mention an uplifting
message and a happy ending, so you can see why it's popular.
But to get the full effect, you really need the pictures.

I sat there reading it until the light through the tiny grating
in the ceiling died away and I couldn't make out the cramped
little letters. Then I laid it down on the floor, open more or
less halfway, and ripped off the spine. Wedged into the now-
exposed stub end, where the folded leaves are stitched together,
was a little something I like to have by me for emergencies. It's a
whisker under six inches long, about half an inch wide, flexible
spring steel and usefully sharp, with a point on it like a needle.
I wrapped the strip of leather binding round the bottom two
inches so as not to cut myself, and then I was ready to face the
unfolding course of events.

Which turned out to consist of some poor slob bringing me
my dinner: rye bread, a generous knob of cheese and a thumb's
length of smoked sausage, on a wooden tray. I was lying on the
floor when he came in, doing my best to look like someone sunk
in morbid depression. He looked down at me, I whimpered a
bit, and just when he'd decided I wasn't a threat I grabbed his
ankles with one arm and cut the tendons behind his knees with
my little thingamajig.

I recommend that approach, by the way, if ever you find

yourself in an awkward spot. There's not a great deal a hamstrung man can do to make a nuisance of himself. He goes down like a felled tree, and the shock empties his mind completely, and the pain isn't so bad that he starts yelling the place down; you should have plenty of time to boot the side of his head and send him to sleep, and all done neatly, efficiently and without any tiresome fuss. If you haven't had the foresight to equip yourself with a handy equaliser, anything reasonably sharp will do – bit of broken glass, potsherd, lengthwise-cracked flint, whatever – and the nice thing is, you haven't had to kill anybody. Crippled for life, maybe, but still very much alive, and I think it's important to care for your fellow man, even though he's just some goon, if at all convenient.

I hadn't explored that part of the castle in any detail when I stayed there before, but I know a bit about buildings and how they work. A charcoal store in a castle is going to be near three things: the kitchen, the main boiler for the hypocausts and the gatehouse, for ease of deliveries. Usually there's a hatch or grating in the roof, or a chute, but I'd looked carefully and hadn't found one, so presumably the stuff was lugged there in sacks, a stupid arrangement if you ask me. Still, it suggested to me that I couldn't be all that far from the gatehouse. They'd put a bag over my head when they brought me down there, so all I had to go on was counting the number of footsteps. That number included crossing the main courtyard from the main hall, which was where I'd had my chat with Stauracia, and the hall was opposite the main gate. I'd done my best to reconstruct the geography of the place from what I could remember, but the hard data at my disposal was scant and vague, and I decided not to rely on it.

Out through the door, remembering to close it behind me.

I figured I had a couple of minutes clear before the goon's colleagues noticed that he hadn't come back yet. Nobody had any reason to be in the corridor I found myself in, which was just as well. I stood still and listened – it wastes time, but it's worth it for the information. In this case, silence. Valuable data. There's always people coming and going round the kitchen, but the boiler only gets stoked five times a day. I slipped my little metal friend between the pages of *The Garden of Entrancing Images* bookmark-fashion, and walked slow and flat-footed up the corridor, which led me into, guess what, the furnace room.

Now of course I knew where I was. Whoever built the castle was, I'm guessing, not from around there. He came from a warmer climate, and felt the cold. Therefore he designed the central keep around a system of hypocausts, which are square brick-lined shafts designed to circulate hot air throughout a building. Naturally, he put the furnace that produces all the heat as close to the centre of the structure as he could manage, and underground because hot air rises. That agreed quite well with the twelve steps down I'd counted on my bag-obscured way in. Being a cunning bastard, the castle builder would have had the kitchen backing onto the furnace, so that all you had to do was swing open a cast-iron door, and the furnace doubled as a range and a roasting oven.

It was nice to know where I was, but I couldn't help wishing it was somewhere else. There would be two flights of stairs connecting the kitchen, furnace and cellars to the ground floor. One of them, the kitchen stairs, would lead up into the hall, where people gathered to eat. The other one, if I was very lucky, would come up into the yard next to the gatehouse; or it could come up in the gatehouse itself, in which case I'd push open a door and find myself nose to nose with a couple of armed sentries. That wouldn't necessarily be the end of the world if I managed to preserve the element of surprise, but I've learned by experience that surprise tends to work both ways. All you can do is press on, expecting everything to go wrong in a manner you didn't anticipate, and hope for the best.

Sure enough, the back stairs came up in the gatehouse. And, sure enough, directly in front of the door I pushed open was a goon in a pourpoint, eating an apple. He looked round as I made my entrance, and I smashed his face in and he fell over, which was fine. But, of course, there was another goon directly behind me, where I couldn't see, and by the time his mate hit the floor, the second goon had recovered from the shock and figured out I was up to no good. Luckily for me, he drew his sword, which made a grating noise as the blade cleared the chape of the scabbard and told me he was there; I had just enough time to take a long step forward, pick up a spear which some fool had left leaning against the wall – rule one: don't leave unsecured weapons lying around in an area where you can reasonably expect bad things to happen – spin round and jab with it in a threatening manner, designed to cause fear and alarm.

Actually, I did better than that, if better's the right word in this context; I stuck the poor sod neatly in the base of the throat, that handy gap between the collarbones that God put there to help hard-working killers. His eyes rolled as he went straight from living to dead – no matter how many times I see it, it always freaks me out – and he fell backwards onto a chair and was no longer any concern of mine.

And there I was, with a spear in my hand, thinking, is that it? Apparently it was. I listened, but all I could hear was someone whistling, a barrel being rolled across a cobbled floor, two men having a cheerful conversation some distance away, somebody knocking in a nail.

I envy those people who can take things in their stride. I've worked with men, and two women, who'd have been out of that gatehouse like a rat up a drain, completely unfazed by what they'd just done, their minds perfectly and exclusively centred on the next stage of the operation. Not me. I had to stop and let my brain catch up.

Well, what was I supposed to do, sit there like a good little boy until she decided on the best way to make use of me? The hell with that. I don't react well to being locked up, or under authority in any shape or form. I don't like violence, it makes my skin crawl, but I didn't start it, by ignoring a flag of truce. I have my faults, God knows, but on my day I can be usefully sharp, so people who play with me can expect to get cut.

Did that make me feel any better? Of course not. But it gave me a chance to get a grip, and now it was time to go. I could see sunlight coming in through the gatehouse door, which meant the gate itself was open. The next stage might involve a certain amount of running, but what the hell. All in all—

There was a table, and on the table was a bag. I'd seen bags like that before. It was a particular grade of coarse grey linen, neatly stitched and sealed with a lead seal. I couldn't make out the impression on the seal, because it was in shadow, but I didn't need to. Those bags are sewn by prisoners in a jail on the outskirts of Kudei Gaion, to a rigidly set pattern. Everything about them is uniform, down to the number of exposed stitches in the fold through which the drawstring runs; from time to time a guard comes and counts the stitches, and if there's one more or one less he finds out who sewed that bag and bashes him across the face with the rim of his shield. I've still got the scar.

Strictly speaking, that bag didn't belong to me. But, I figured, I'd already killed one man and viciously assaulted two more. Compared to that, theft of a bag whose intrinsic value was a couple of coppers didn't really signify. Besides, those bags are made to contain documents, and I fancied something to read, and I was sick to death of *The Garden of Entrancing Images*. I slipped the bag inside my shirt, peered round the doorway to make sure I had a clear run, and ran.

There were a couple of archers outside the gate, purportedly guarding it. They got off a couple of shots at me as I ran, and arrows have got to go somewhere, even if loosed by incompetents. One of them hit me right between the shoulder blades, hard enough to knock me off my feet. That's it, then, I thought; then I remembered my beautiful and expensive brigandine, decided I was still alive, scrambled to my feet and carried on running. Along the way I passed my shirt on a stick, still leaning against a tree where I'd left it, but I couldn't be bothered to stop. There are times when shirts matter, and this wasn't one of them.

"Where the hell did you get to?" Polycrates said. "We were just about to pack up and go home."

Home in that context would be Auxentia City, the last place God made, where we bought a couple of sheds not long after the Sirupat debacle. I wasn't in favour of the purchase, mostly because owning real property in Auxentia City, even a couple of semi-derelict sheds, might be construed as some kind of endorsement of the place; it's the slave-dealing hub of the Friendly Sea, it has bad associations for me and I have an idea

that technically I was condemned to death *in absentia* there
for killing a guard a few years back. What the hell do we need
a shed for, is how I phrased my objection, and they all looked
at me. After all those years living in tents and carts, the poor
bastards wanted somewhere, some infinitesimal slice of geography they could call their own, and, yes, it was Auxentia, but
the price was right, so I was overruled.

It's different for me. My family collected geography. A man
can't really call himself a gentleman, my grandfather used to
say, unless he's got at least one of everything: his own house,
his own estate, his own deer park, his own quarry, his own
lake, his own river, his own mountain, his own town, his own
forest, his own coal mine, his own seaport. If he can't sit on the
highest point of his domain and see nothing in any direction
that doesn't belong to him, he tends to feel cramped, belittled,
put upon; he can't breathe, or he shouldn't be able to. When I
left home I left that mindset behind, along with some clothes,
a few books and a stuffed felt lion called Smiley; from time to
time I miss Smiley and one or two of the books, but not the
land, the buildings, the live and dead stock. Home is just a
nail that secures you to the cross; home through one palm, love
through the other, conscience driven economically through
both insteps.

The subset love in this context includes friendship. They
were just about to pack up and go home, to Auxentia fucking
City. I told myself he hadn't really meant it. The hell with the
truth; who needs it?

"You'll never guess," I told him, "who I've just been
talking to."

The point being, I told myself, that they hadn't packed up
and gone. "Who?"

"Sister Stauracia."

Sometimes I like saying things that have the effect of a stone through a stained-glass window. This was one such time; I felt he'd deserved it. His mouth fell open, and he had that look on his face.

"Large as life," I reassured him, "and just as pretty. She's defending the castle. Don't ask," I added, before he had a chance to speak, "because I don't know. I mean, she told me some story, but I know she's lying."

"Fuck," said Polycrates. I don't have a lot of time for him generally, but occasionally he has the knack of putting things rather well.

"Yes," I said.

So I called a heads-of-department meeting (four barrels under a beech tree). "Suggestions," I said.

They looked at each other. Then they looked at me.

"Quite," I said. "For what it's worth, her people are negligible. As far as I could tell, it's about twenty of her regular crew and thirty-odd deadheads she must've picked up at a hiring fair. Probably," I added, "in the late afternoon or early evening. But the castle is a bastard, even if we can get up close to it, and offhand I can't think of a way of doing that. And let's face it, we're not soldiers. I don't know about you boys, but as far as I'm concerned our percentage of acceptable losses is nil. Of course, that includes Gombryas and Olybrius and the rest of them. Frankly, I don't know what to do. Any thoughts?"

"Starve them out," Polycrates suggested.

I gave him my patient look. "They've got more food than us," I said. "I give it a week, and then someone's going to have to go to their front door and ask if we can borrow a bowl of flour and half a dozen eggs. Also, please bear in mind that we're on a schedule."

"A night attack," Eudo said. "We wait till it's dark, then we sneak up on them, silently eliminate the guards – yes, all right. But you did ask."

"You've talked to her," Papinian said. "What did she say?"

"Plenty," I said. "Very little of it true. Her orders are to hold the fort, and I think she's got a pretty good incentive, though I don't know what it is."

He nodded. "She's only a girl," he said. "And you've read all those books you're always quoting from."

He was just trying to be annoying. "That girl commanded an army of regulars on Sirupat," I pointed out. "And she'd have won, if I hadn't been there."

If I hadn't been there, she wouldn't have been commanding anything because there wouldn't have been a war. Everything is my fault.

"We need to do a deal," Papinian said. "Like that wisecrack you're always quoting. The one with the donkey."

Indeed. Attributed to Cyprian the Great: no fortress can be considered impregnable if it can be approached by a man leading a donkey loaded with money. "I don't think she's for sale," I said. "No, that's not true. She's out of our price bracket."

Papinian looked down his nose at me. "Leverage," he said. "Something she wants."

Occasionally Papinian says something clever. "Such as?"

"I don't know, do I? You know her better than we do. Think of something."

Working on that, I didn't tell him. "In other words," I said, "we have no ideas. In which case, I propose we prepare for a straightforward frontal assault, textbook style. It's not what I'd have chosen, but I don't think we have an alternative."

"Are you out of your mind?" Polycrates asked, reasonably enough. "You said it yourself, that place is as tight as a drum. And we aren't soldiers."

I sighed. "That's why I asked for suggestions," I said. "Pity there weren't any."

4

If you're going to do a really stupid thing, my brother used to say before I killed him, do it as well as you possibly can. Wise words, and, I think, original. If we were going to attack the castle, we had to think hard, plan carefully and prepare for as many contingencies as possible. Fortunately, I'd read all the right books.

That sounds like a really stupid thing to say. You can't fight a battle with a textbook open in one hand, you're yelling at me. Actually, you can. I've known (and buried) enough generals to have a certain degree of insight into the art of war and how it's usually conducted; books play a large part in modern strategic planning. It's all in there somewhere, if only you can be bothered to look. Theories of war, practical guides to tackling specific military tasks; above all, records of past campaigns – the brilliant stratagems and, above all, the stupid mistakes made by generations of leaders of terrified men; hundreds and thousands of carefully recorded examples of what can go wrong, how people can get themselves killed, how victory can be turned into defeat by the tiniest, razor-thin little thing. It's all been done before; there's nothing original; the wheel has been reinvented a million times in a million killing fields. What do they do in military academies? They read books. A good book, a morbid imagination and a certain degree of familiarity with human nature, that's all you need. I have all three. I could do this.

"What we need," I said, early the next morning, "is artillery."

(I'd had a chance to look in the bag I stole from the castle. It contained a rolled-up military-issue belt with a broken buckle, a small whetstone, a letter from an unidentified correspondent speculating about the whereabouts of a missing pretender to the Sashan throne and two links of dried Aelian sausage. Because not everything is significant, and sometimes my instincts are just plain wrong.)

"You what?" Polycrates said helpfully.

"Artillery," I said. "Never send a man where you can send an arrow. Or a lump of rock, or, better still, a jar of burning lamp oil. How many jars of lamp oil did you say we've got in stock?"

"I didn't," Polycrates said.

"Thirty-two," said Eudo. "Nine of ours and twenty-three from the battlefield."

"Oh well," I said. "That'll have to do. Now, then, this is how you build a catapult."

One thing at a time, like she'd said. The first thing was to get control of the two rocks, the narrow and horribly defensible gateway to the hill on which the castle stood. We couldn't rush it with men, not without heavy casualties. If we pelted it with rocks, all we'd achieve would be to fill up the gap and make it completely solid. That left fire. Many great and famous generals have, so to speak, played with fire; most of them have got their fingers well and truly burned. Even so. A dozen jars of lamp oil dropped squarely on the two rocks would clear out the defenders, leaving it open for a sudden rush, and then it's our gateway, not theirs. Once we had possession of it, there would at least be some point to developing a strategy for attacking the castle itself. Without it, no point even trying.

"Also," I said, "barrels. Empty ones, that we can fill with water."

Already it was horribly complicated and technical. First, plaster the two rocks with burning oil, to roast or drive out the defenders. Then, since nobody likes charging into an inferno, drench the burning rocks with barrels of water, to put out the fire by the time we get there. That calls for timing, and accurate artillery. Also, a barrel of water weighs four times as much as a jar of oil. If we had plenty of jars and plenty of barrels we could practise, find the ranges, adjust the tension in the torsion ropes to compensate for the difference in weight and aerodynamics between the two different sorts of projectile. Or, if we were soldiers, professional bombardiers, we'd probably have a handy chart with all the differentials written down for us. But what we had in practice was some trees, some axes, some coils of rope and my vague recollections of some pictures I'd once looked at in a book I no longer owned.

This, as an idiot once told his friends, is how you build a catapult.

First, catch your tree. Having done that, chop it down, trim off the branches, rough-hew it into a beam of approximately square section. Do it again, and again until you've got a stack of nine beams. Now you have lumber. That's the easy bit.

Seven of the beams want to be eight feet long, the other two around twenty-five feet. Make a rectangle with the long beams and two short ones; the shorts go inside the longs, if you see what I'm getting at. Then, three-quarters of the way down the long sections, set two uprights at right angles to the base and fit a crosspiece at the top between them; a rectangle with two posts sticking up out of it, the two sticking-up posts joined at the top by a third. With me so far? Now brace the two stickers-up with beams placed diagonally (the key is in the word *brace*) and that's it, you're nearly done.

Back to the long, twenty-five-foot beams. In the middle of each beam, seen from the side, bore a six-inch hole on the long side of the uprights. That's the hole your ropes will go through. These ropes, twisted round the spoon (we'll get to the spoon in a minute) provide the torsion which will power the projectile. Now then, the spoon: choose a tall, straight tree about ten inches diameter at the base, fourteen feet long, with a bit of taper to it. That's the bit that actually moves when the catapult goes off. The ropes (passing through the holes in the base) are twisted round one end of the spoon, which rides halfway between the legs of the frame . . . You haven't the faintest idea what I'm talking about, have you? That's me, I'm afraid. I can visualise, but I'm not so good at explaining. If I could draw you a picture, you'd get it in the blink of an eye. Instead, you're just going to have to trust me, regardless of what you already know about my attitude to the truth. So many things eventually come back to blind trust, and I guess this is one of them.

Maybe you don't trust me, maybe you do; my men trusted me, at least as far as building a catapult was concerned. I told them what to do, they did it, and, after a long day, the death of a dozen innocent trees and a lot of chopping and swearing, there it was.

You twist the rope as tight as it'll go, and then nine turns more on each side; left side clockwise, right side anticlockwise. Then a lot of you pull on a rope, to haul the spoon down until it touches the rear crossbeam of the frame; at which point some brave, nimble soul nips in and fastens it with a hook, to which is tied a bit of string. I hadn't figured out how to get the spoon down the last eighteen inches and the book had neglected to cover that, so we had to improvise with pulleys and an iron hoop driven into the ground; it was getting late and we were tired and I still wasn't sure that the mortice and tenon joints in the frame would be man enough to withstand the shock when the spoon went slamming against the crosspiece. A lot of things could happen at that point. The crosspiece could fail. The spoon could snap off like a carrot. The rock we were using as a test projectile could fall off the spoon, or limp sadly through the air and land five feet away. The rope could break. The whole thing could shake itself apart. All I could confidently predict was that something would go wrong, because nothing ever works perfectly the first time; and if something went wrong, the thin filament of trust that bound my friends to me would snap, the whole catapult idea would be dismissed as impractical, and we'd end up charging the two rocks and getting shot down in windrows, like newly mown hay, and it'd all be my fault—

A man called Steleco, who usually pulls earrings out of dead men's ears but who'd volunteered to be deputy chief engineer, darted forward, secured the hook and did a standing jump backwards to get out of the way in case the hook failed. It didn't. We all let go of the breath we'd been holding, and stared at what we'd accomplished that day. What we were looking at was a catapult, life-size, spanned, locked and suddenly plausible. If you didn't know better, you could believe it was real.

"Don't just stand there like a prune," I told someone. "Get the stone on."

Two men lifted a stone. I'd chosen it because it looked like it weighed roughly the same as a barrel full of water; that's how scientific I am when I'm tired and my back hurts from hauling lumber. They nestled it into the hollowed-out bowl of the spoon – did I mention that? Well, I have now. "Stand back," I said, superfluously. I nodded to Eudo, who had the end of a bit of string between his fingers. "All right," I said. "Here goes nothing."

Eudo pulled the string. The string jerked the hook out of the spoon. The spoon shot forward and slammed into the crosspiece, which amazingly didn't break. The stone left the spoon and sailed through the air, very fast and quite high, and then it dropped and hit the ground. We felt it land through the soles of our feet.

"Fuck me," Polycrates said. I chose not to construe it as an invitation.

A moment of stunned stillness and quiet. I let it play out, then we all went forward and checked the machine over for cracks, fractured or sprung joints, frayed ropes, right angles knocked out of true. The machine had bounced sideways about eighteen inches, but that was all.

People were looking at me. I smiled. "Piece of cake," I said.

I've dwelled on this episode for two reasons. It worked, which I really hadn't been expecting, and it changed things. That morning, before the first tree fell, we were a bunch of amateurs completely out of our league. By nightfall, we had a weapon and a plan. The plan might, just possibly, work – in the morning I'd have said it probably wouldn't, but I'd have said that about the catapult, too, and that had worked just fine ... The plan involved shooting fire at a bunch of strangers who'd never done me any harm, then capturing a strategic position that significantly changed the balance of power. If we did that, we stood a chance of taking the castle by storm. We could win this—

Begging the question, do we want to? Do *I* want to?

I like Stauracia and I suspect that at times she likes me, but that's never led either of us to pull our punches; there are always more important issues at stake, and we have this unhappy habit of getting in each other's way. But now I had a working catapult, a real and rather powerful asset, a significant advantage. Now, just suppose—

I tried reassuring myself with the probability of failure. Everything would be bound to go tits-up, so the question won't arise, so don't worry about it. I can usually get away with thinking like that because nearly everything I try and do goes horribly wrong. But the catapult hadn't, and that bothered me. Maybe my luck had changed. Scary thought. It all came from reading books, of course. You read too much, my mother used to say, you'll ruin your eyesight.

Target practice.

If we'd been proper soldiers we'd have had ammunition to spare. We could've blazed away with burning jars and water-filled barrels until we knew exactly where to point the catapult and how many turns of the rope we needed to gain one minute of elevation. Instead we had rocks.

We made a balance – sapling with the ends cut off dangling from a rope with a basket hung on each end – and weighed rocks against oil jars and water barrels, which broke the sapling, start again, try and get it right this time. We couldn't find rocks big enough, so we filled bags with stones, allowing us a greater degree of precision. But a bag doesn't fly like a jar.

Still, the hell with it. We found we could throw a jar's weight of stones two hundred and thirty yards, which is further than effective bowshot – I had a lively discussion with Polycrates about the definition of effective in this context. That was fine, but we couldn't throw a barrel of water's weight more than ninety yards, which was hopeless ... Wheels, someone suggested (I have a horrible feeling it was me): why don't we put the catapult on wheels? We shoot the jars and make the area round the two rocks a living hell, then we drag the catapult a hundred and forty yards closer, lob in the water and everything's fine ... So we made some solid wooden wheels and a couple of axles, which we attached to the underside of the frame with bent-over nails, which pulled out as soon as we ran over a large stone.

If at first you don't succeed, fail, fail, fail again. We tried really hard, but we simply couldn't get it to work. The hell with that, someone suggested, there's plenty of us, let's just carry the stupid thing. That actually worked better than the wheels, and once we'd taken them off again the catapult didn't bounce up and down and topple over after every shot, which was nice.

But at two hundred and thirty yards, our accuracy with a jar's weight of stones was not impressive. Sometimes we overshot, sometimes we undershot, sometimes we hit a perfect length but pitched ten yards either side. If we closed the range to a hundred and fifty yards, we found we could hit the target one shot in ten—

("How many jars did you say we've got?"

"Thirty-two. No, make that thirty, we broke two.")

Which meant three hits, if we were lucky, and I wasn't going to go charging up to the two rocks in nothing but a helmet, shield and brigandine with anything less than six solid hits, ten for choice, twelve would be even better. So we closed to a hundred yards, and got sixty per cent accuracy; and a hundred yards is only ten yards more than ninety, which was extreme range for water barrels and medium range for arrows—

"Pavises," I said.

"You what?"

Pavises, I explained, are large shields, mounted on wheeled frames. You trundle them in front of you as you advance, and you don't get shot. All the best armies use them, I said. The best ones are made of oxhide, because it's dense enough to have good stopping power, and slack enough to absorb energy, thereby hindering penetration ... But we didn't have any oxhides. We had canvas tents, courtesy of the late General Sinderic; three ply of tent fabric isn't as good as a quality oxhide, but we lobbed a few shots into a prototype at a hundred yards and reckoned it would do.

"If I was your lady friend," Papinian said, "as soon as I saw you wheeling these contraptions down the slope, I'd send out a sortie and smash them up."

I smiled at him. "Wouldn't that be nice?" I said. "She's only got fifty men, and they're almost as chickenshit as us."

He had the grace to concede the point and confined himself to pointing out that wheeling anything as top-heavy as a pavise over the sort of ground we'd have to cover would be a disaster waiting to happen ... Fine, I said, we'll carry them, too. But that would mean the men doing the carrying would be stuck out at the ends of the pavise, therefore not sheltered by it; or else, if we carried them from behind, they wouldn't be able to see where they were going, and they'd fall over. Also, Papinian said, had it occurred to me that an arrow doesn't fly in a straight line? Instead it describes a graceful curve, which makes it perfectly feasible to lob a shot over an obstacle and hit the people standing behind it? I had a good, scientific answer to that, involving parabolic curves and dead zones, which I could have proved conclusively with the help of a few simple sketches. What I didn't have was time and patience to argue, in front of five hundred terrified eavesdroppers, so I told him that I'd already got everything covered, and that unless he shut his face I'd smash it in—

"Sorry to bother you," Eudo interrupted, "but there's men over there watching us."

So I should damn well hope, I didn't say. You're starting to get to know me by now, so you've probably figured out that shooting jars of burning oil from a catapult hidden behind a screen of pavises was definitely my Plan B. Plan A was to let Stauracia know that I was serious about doing my job, and I had the knowhow and the capacity to get it done. Accordingly, I'd made it as easy as possible for her scouts to watch us, short of building them a grandstand with an awning in case it rained. The scouts would go back and tell her we now had a significant artillery capability, which would concentrate her mind on the possibilities of double-crossing her bosses and doing a deal with the devil she knew, namely me. The more time she had to think, within reason, the better. On the other hand, time was on her side, not mine. But that was all right. If the very worst came to the very worst, at least I had a Plan B—

So what would I do, if by some miracle I managed to cram

my enormous feet into her dainty little shoes? Answer: I'd wait till dark, choose the ten least chickenshit of my men, sneak out and set fire to the catapult. I'd do it very reluctantly and only after a great deal of thought and bad language, but I'd see that I had no choice. And although I don't like getting my hands dirty, I'd realise the depressing fact that, since none of my deadhead crew could be trusted to do the simplest thing, I'd have to lead the sortie myself . . .

That was my Plan A. In fact, it was my Plan A+.

I had a lot of private tutors when I was growing up. I had one for theology, ethics and calligraphy, one for arithmetic, logic and calculus, one for fencing, one for law, history, rhetoric and public speaking, one for music and fine arts (three, actually, one after another; for some reason, they didn't stay for very long in our house) and one for horsemanship and archery. I was the sole focus of their attention; my brothers had their own tutors, because they were smarter than me.

I can't say they taught me a great deal, because my attention was always wandering, and (certainly compared to my brothers) I wasn't very bright. I can do long division in my head, but music and fine arts flowed over me like water over an oilskin, achieving no penetration whatsoever. You can probably gather from what I've told you about my life the extent to which I took to heart what I was taught about law and ethics. I'm no great shakes as a fencer, people tell me I sit on a horse like a sack of turnips and my handwriting is so bad that only two people in the world can read it, one of whom I am not.

I wasn't much good at archery either, but I did learn one useful and important lesson from the poor devil who had the job of teaching me. He was a fat man, formerly a sergeant-major in the Guards, after that a champion archer in the Summer League; I disappointed him a lot, but I think he liked me in spite of everything. I remember clearly as anything the day (early morning, straight after family chapel) when he presented me with my first proper bow. I didn't really want it, but your first bow is supposed to be a big deal, so I was trying to convey enthusiasm. He took a long, rectangular wooden box out of a sack and put it down on a bench. I went to open it. He put a huge chubby hand on my chest and said, not so fast.

"That," he said, "is a lethal weapon. I want you to remember that."

"All right," I said.

"No, it's not all right. You could do someone a mischief with that thing. You could kill someone."

I could kill someone with a stone or a chair leg, I didn't point out; and as things have turned out, I've killed more people with stones, chair legs, crockery (broken and unbroken), garden and hedgerow plants, lengths of rope and the toe of my boot than with all the finely crafted and deadly weapons that have passed through my damp, sweaty hands in the course of a career crammed with the wretched things.

"I understand," I told him. He looked at me. "Mind you do," he said. "And always remember, good shooting is no accident."

Whereupon he flipped open the lid and there it was, a handsome object, gleaming under seven coats of varnish, and to me for ever thereafter always vaguely menacing and untrustworthy, as if it was just waiting for me to take my eye off it so it could dart sideways and bite me. It was only twenty pounds draw weight and the arrows tended to bounce out of the straw mat at more than thirty yards, but the message had well and truly sunk in. This is not a toy. Above all, never ever point it at anybody.

Gombryas never had a day's teaching in his life, not even in prison, where they're supposed to train you in a useful trade. He just picked up a bow one day (it didn't actually belong to him) and played with it until he could skewer a squirrel running at fifteen paces. Carrhasio learned to shoot in the army, where the targets are dressed up in captured armour and have faces painted on them, an extra point if you get it through the eye socket. I'm a better shot than both of them, not that that's saying much, if we're shooting at a hat on a stick or tree stumps. But pointing an arrow at someone and letting the string pull itself off my fingers is something I simply can't do to this day. I've shot people, and hurt and killed them, but only because I was trying to miss and failed.

So, as night fell and I finished assigning my sentries to their carefully chosen positions, I went to the back of one of the carts, pulled open a sack and chose myself a bow. Sinderic had spent a lot of money on quality kit, and the bows he issued to his archers were well made, ash backed with rawhide, hemp strings, sixty-eight inches between the nocks, drawing around ninety pounds with better than average cast for their weight. There wasn't much to choose between them so I picked the one with the least string follow, and two dozen standard arrows with conventional bodkin heads, what we call in the trade the flying nail. When doctors qualify they're supposed to take an oath which includes the words *First, do no harm.* I'm not a doctor, but when it comes to fighting in a battle I try and follow the same precept.

Actually, bearing in mind the doctors I've come across – Papinian is the exception – I suspect the famous medical oath has strayed a bit in translation from the original Aelian, and what it should read is, *at* first, do no harm. "She's not going to attack," he told me firmly, as I wandered round the camp making sure everybody was in position. "She's got too much sense."

"We'll see," I said. "Now get in your tent and stay there."

"I must have been mad to join up with you," Papinian said. "I could've made a good living in private practice."

Everything was as good as I could make it, and I'd covered all the details, apart from one: where I was supposed to go while we waited for Stauracia to make her move. I considered climbing a tree, but in the end I opted for ducking under one of the carts. Arrows often go high but rarely low.

She's not coming, I thought for the sixteenth time, and then I heard a noise. There's no sound like it in the world: terrified men trying to be quiet.

Some practical information for you. If you need to go somewhere and don't want to attract attention, the best thing you can do is walk normally but carefully, thinking about what you're doing. Don't do that silly half-crouching thing, which screws up your balance; don't walk on tiptoe for the same reason. Breathe normally. And for God's sake don't flit from tree to tree, because what catches the eye more than anything else is rapid, jerky movement. Nice and easy does it. Relax.

I counted nine of them, crouching, tiptoeing, flitting from tree to tree and snorting through their noses like a herd of buffalo. Stauracia wasn't one of them, but she knows how to do that sort of stuff, experience no doubt acquired by moving about in other people's houses when they're asleep. My guess was that she'd have led the way then hung back, so that if things went wrong she'd be best placed to make an unobtrusive exit while her ape-like warriors were being slaughtered. Fine. The cart I was under was some way back on a straight line to the catapult. Slowly and carefully I squirmed out and stood up, and someone put a hand over my mouth and pricked my neck with something very sharp.

At which point the yelling started. I'd told my boys to make plenty of noise, with a view to driving the intruders into the ambush I'd prepared for them. I heard shouts, horrified yelling and the trampling of heavy boots, then another loud shout as my men jumped out of cover to block the way and encircle the fugitives. All exactly to plan apart from one small detail, which had just drawn blood an inch below my ear.

"Tell them," Stauracia hissed in my ear, "to let them go. Now."

Ambiguously phrased, but clear enough in context. I made a mumbling noise, and she took her hand away from my face. "Go *on*," she said. "Tell them."

I never learned much from my tutors, but experience has given me a first-class education. My specialist subject is what to do when you've been captured, and someone's holding a weapon close to your skin. You may object that I'm self-taught and quote the old proverb, the self-taught man has a fool for a teacher. Fair enough, but I'm still alive and (for the moment at least) at liberty, so clearly I haven't done too badly.

What you do is, you lift your right foot off the ground, assuming you're right-handed, and bend your knee, while simultaneously moving your left hand upwards across your body. Then you grab for the wrist of the hand with the knife in it, and a split second later you kick back with your right heel at where you hope his, or her, kneecap is. You secure the wrist and you feel his (or her) weight slump against your back; that's when you pull sharply downwards with your left hand, twist your whole body sideways and heave, with a view to throwing your assailant over your right shoulder. If all goes well, you should end up with him (or her) lying in a sprawling heap at your feet, nicely placed for an enthusiastic kick to the side of the head, and no harm done.

I've had a lot of luck with that manoeuvre over the years, but not this time. The grab, the kick and the throw went splendidly, but as I pulled down with my left hand I contrived to stab myself in the chest, just above the right nipple, with the knife clenched in her hand. Nuts, I thought as she sailed over my shoulder, that's done it. I was so shocked by the pain and the stupidity of it all that I nearly forgot to kick her in the face as she tried to grab my ankles.

"You stupid bitch," I yelled at her. "Now look what you've made me do."

I should've known better than to expect sympathy from someone so pitilessly self-centred, let alone an apology. She was too busy moaning and writhing and clutching her jaw, which I concede I'd just dislocated. I took two long steps backwards and started tearing at my shirt. It was too dark to see how much damage I'd done, but the shirt was sodden with blood. "Get the doctor," I howled. "I'm hurt. Quickly. I'm bleeding to death here."

"Talk about a cry-baby," Papinian said, as he stuffed the wound with moss and spiderweb. "And next time don't bother me unless it's something serious, such as a hangnail."

I was too weak from pain and shock to argue, but I hung around to watch him fix her jaw. It's one of those things: no matter how many times I see it done, it always amazes me. Papinian is very good at it, though he approaches the operation with his usual degree of sensitivity and compassion. He bears down on you, filling your personal space, and grabs your head in both hands. Then he sticks his thumbs in your mouth and stretches it painfully wide, and then he does this extraordinary thing, pressing down on your teeth with his thumbs and lifting your jaw with his fingers, and just when you think he's going to rip your face in half, there's a click and you're all better.

"There'll be some swelling," he said, to me not her, "and it'll hurt for a while, but that's normal." He was wrapping a bandage under her jaw and over the top of her head, then round behind her neck. He was looking at me; he didn't need to see what his hands were doing. "She'll need her food cutting up into little baby chunks, and if she yawns she'll need to put her hand under her chin, like that, see? You know the drill."

It's a habit of his. He tells me, but loud enough so the patient can hear every word. I think it's because everything – all the sick and wounded and dying people who pass through his hands – is my fault.

"Right," Papinian said, washing his hands in the bowl of water that one of his people was holding in just the right place, so he didn't need to look down to know it was there. "You're fine, just lay off sharp, sudden movements or you'll open it up again and it'll need stitches. I hate sewing you up, you're such a coward. Next."

Next was one of Stauracia's goons who'd tried to make a run for it and sprinted straight into a spear; the man holding it had tried to get it out of the way, but there hadn't been time. "More cobwebs," I heard Papinian growl. "Come on, it's a forest; it's crawling with bloody spiders." He enjoys his work, mostly, I think, his capacity for making people rush madly about doing things. A bit like a dog chasing a squirrel up a tree, what he likes most is the movement.

Stauracia stood up, and suddenly I felt nervous. There were people about, my men drifting aimlessly around, like they do, but I could see a straight line between Stauracia and the eaves of the wood with nobody much in it; if she made a run for it along that line, the only man in position to tackle her would be me, and she'd just heard the doctor tell me not to make sudden movements – she and I think alike in tense situations. She caught my eye, just as I turned my head to look at her. Two minds with but a single thought, as Saloninus says somewhere, two hearts that beat as one.

There's a game they play in Echmen. You have a perfectly flat table and a dozen coloured ivory balls, and you poke the balls with the end of a stick to make them whizz across the table. The trick is to hit one ball so it collides with one or more of the others, and if you're good at it you can hit ball A so that it hits ball B in such a way as to bash into ball C and send it skittering across the table into a hole at the corner. I've never had a go at it, but I've watched it being played, and it's all about angles and time and force and speed, and as a metaphor for my life it's profoundly and depressingly apt. I'd probably be hopeless at it, just the way I'm hopeless at my life. But I can size up angles, estimate speed over time; I call it doing the geometry. I yelled a couple of names, and two men started to come towards me, cutting off that perfect straight line that she and I had both noticed. That earned me Stauracia's pet scowl. It emphasises her cheekbones and is therefore no bad thing.

The men I'd called over ambled up to me. "Get some rope," I said, "and tie her up real good. I'm holding you two personally responsible for her not getting away. Got that?"

The two men – I never forget a face but I'm not great at names – got busy, and I supervised the actual ropework in considerable detail. Tying up Stauracia is a bit like tying up water, so overkill is the best policy. "And loop it twice round the back and tie it off with a double sheet bend," I told them. "There you go, that's the ticket."

I inspected their work, then let them go. "Arsehole," she commented.

"Yes," I said. "Now, we need to talk."

"Not supposed to talk. Weren't you listening to the doctor?"

"Yes," I said, "but this is an emergency. People are going to get killed if we don't sort this mess out."

"I had it sorted," she pointed out. "And then you murdered a man and maimed another man for life and spoiled everything. You're a vicious bastard, Saevus, did anyone ever tell you that?"

I shook my head. "I'm a victim of circumstances," I said. "And I was there under a flag of truce, and you—"

"That really bugs you, doesn't it?"

"We need to start again," I said. "Hello, Stauracia."

"Saevus."

Suddenly I felt tired. "This is silly," I said. "You should've anticipated the catapult."

"I've only got fifty men and they're all useless." She shrugged, not an easy thing to do under all that rope. "The catapult was just to get me to come and burn it."

I nodded. "It doesn't actually work," I said. "We'd need to get within ninety yards, which means pavises, and my bunch of clowns aren't up to that sort of thing. I could probably have stormed your stupid castle, but it would've meant people getting killed and I don't hold with that sort of thing."

She frowned. "You killed Birenna," she said. "That's the name of the man you murdered. When you escaped, remember?" She did her sad smile, unfortunately hampered by the bandages. "It must be difficult for you to keep track. After all, you kill so many people."

No point in saying anything. She'd scored her point. It was a valid one, but coming from her, meaningless. Score one, therefore, and on with the game. "Now then," I said. "What are we going to do?"

"He mostly worked in the stores," she said. "He could add up a column of figures just by looking at them. And he was practically supernatural when it came to finding keys. I'm always losing them. Birenna, I'd say, have you seen the keys to the cash box, and he'd just sort of sniff the air like a dog and tell me where I'd left them. I shall miss that."

"Have you finished?" She glared at me. I took that for a yes. "We've got a problem," I said. "A shared problem."

"I don't think so. You could solve it by untying these ropes."

"A shared problem," I repeated. "Our problem is, we're both under the control of unreasonable people."

"I am, certainly."

"We both are. That bloody woman's got my friends, and your lot have got some kind of hostage—"

"My son, you arsehole."

"Some kind of hostage," I said. "So there you are, we're both in the same boat. We can't fix the problem by fighting each other without a lot of people being put in harm's way. Therefore, let's fix it by not fighting."

She took a deep breath and let it go slowly, a classic way to keep your temper in the face of extreme provocation. "How nice it would be if that was possible," she said. "As it is—"

"Why do your lot want this castle?"

"I don't know, do I? Why do your lot want this castle?"

I shrugged. "It's a castle," I said. "A small one, in rather poor repair. What are castles for?"

I know her humouring-idiots look. "Well," she said, "traditionally they're used to control potentially hostile territory and guard lines of communication."

I looked at her. She looked at me.

"All right," she said. "You can use them as bases of operations, from which to conduct mobile campaigns."

"There's a whole lot of that going on, I can see. What else?"

"Shut up just for a moment and let me think. They're a classic post-subjugation tool in newly conquered territory. They're the foundation of classical defence-in-depth theory. I don't know," she said, "what do you use them for?"

I had no idea, until she asked me. "Keeping things in," I said.

She opened her mouth to say something caustic, then closed it again. "You mean people," she said. "The prisoner of Castle Whatsisname, the man in the iron mask."

"People can be things," I said. "But things don't have to be people. Look, there's two ways of keeping something safe. You hide it where no one's going to look, or you put it in a safe place. Option one is the best, naturally, but only—" I was thinking about half a step ahead of what my tongue was saying. "Only if you can trust the other people in your gang. Like, if you bury it and only five of you know where it is, sometimes that's four too many."

"Maybe."

"Entirely possible," I said. "For instance, if you and I suddenly came into a million staurata. If we buried it under a stone somewhere, neither of us would be able to sleep at night for worrying about the other one sneaking out with a shovel. So we'd have to put it in a safe place."

Her eyebrows squeezed together. It makes her look about fourteen when she does that. "Maybe," she repeated.

"Now then," I said. "You say you don't know anything about your lot, but I bet you do. Like for example there's more than one of them."

She nodded. "I got the impression there's a sort of committee running things," she said.

"Thought so. Now, imagine you and me on the committee of a shadowy organisation with a secret agenda, and we've got hold of something valuable. We'd stick it in a safe place, so neither of us would be tempted."

"Maybe. I don't know. You call that a safe place?"

"Yes, if you're the one guarding it, and you don't know what you're guarding."

She likes compliments, especially from me. "It's possible, I suppose. What sort of thing?"

"I have absolutely no idea," I said. "But one step at a time. Let's just go back and look at what we've got so far."

"Do we have to?"

"Slow and steady wins the race," I said. "We agree that this castle is valuable to your lot, but not for the usual reasons. It's not controlling strategically important territory, because they're not a government and there isn't a war. Same goes for lines of supply. It could be a base of operations, except that it isn't, because otherwise it'd be crawling with your employers doing whatever the hell it is that they do. Instead, they tell you, there it is, we want it defended. At all costs."

She looked like someone trying to stop the sun from rising

by sheer force of will. "Fine," she said. "For the sake of argument let's assume you're right. What sort of thing?"

I sighed. "Good question," I said. "But at least we've got a few clues to help us."

"We have?"

"Yes. We've got a castle with stuff in it. All we do is go through all the stuff until we find something that might be valuable to someone."

She gave me her snake look. "Oh, right," she said. "And you and your merry band of pirates are going to be really kind and help us look. Which means opening the gates and letting them have the run of the place."

"Yes," I said. "Something like that. It's called trust," I explained. "It comes about when two people know each other well and have a common objective, and realise that they can only get what they both want through co-operation and good faith."

"You honestly think that. How sweet." The snake look turned into the tiger look. "In your dreams," she said. "I know you."

"Then you know that unless you play nicely I'll storm your silly castle and kill a lot of your people, which ought to be fairly straightforward if you're not there to lead them, and then I'll be able to search the place at my leisure. In fact, why don't I just do that? I don't need you at all."

She looked at me. "Quite," she said. "Why don't you?"

The thought had crossed my mind, but in the same way as a messenger crosses a battlefield: quickly, with people shooting at him. I don't think it made it to the other side. "I have absolutely no idea," I said. "Do we have a deal?"

*

Of course I hadn't told her about the time I'd spent in the castle, on my own, quietly exploring. Everyone doesn't need to know everything, and most definitely not straight away.

I'd expected the news that Stauracia and I were now on the same side would be met with a degree of hostility by my friends, and I wasn't disappointed. "That bitch," Polycrates said. "I wouldn't trust her further than I could fart her out of my arse."

"Nor me," I said. "We'll have to be careful, that's all."

"The hell with that," he replied. "She'll stitch us up and screw us over. She's sharp."

"So is a chisel," I said. "Wouldn't be much use if it wasn't. Sharp tools are good, provided you mind what you're doing with them."

The contempt in his eyes ... "She's smart," he said. "Smarter than you."

"Quite possibly."

"She screwed you over on Sirupat. She could've sold you to your sister if she'd wanted to."

Tact isn't one of Polycrates's strengths. "But she didn't want to," I said. "Think about it. She could've had more money than you can possibly imagine, but instead she let me go."

I ought to mention that my sister and I don't get on. She's married to an Elector who loves her dearly and likes to buy her things. What she'd like most in the world would be my head, pickled in a jar of honey, and the Elector was prepared to go as high as half a million staurata to indulge her. Stauracia had the chance to sell me to him, dead or alive, but she turned it down. I'm still not entirely sure why; neither, I suspect, is she. "So what?" Polycrates said. "That woman is trouble. Even you couldn't be that stupid."

"Really?" I said. "Watch me."

I suspect Stauracia had one or more similar conversations with her people. She'd summoned half a dozen of them from the castle; they didn't want to come, not surprisingly since it was clear that the conventions regarding safe conduct didn't seem to apply any more, and I heard raised voices coming from the tent where she talked to them: hers mostly, occasionally interrupted by dismayed baying. I was happy to leave her to deal with her own problems while I bashed my head against mine.

"I don't see what all the fuss is about," Eudo said. We were sitting on a log, watching the sun set and listening to Stauracia winning over hearts and minds about a hundred yards away. "You fixed it so we get the castle without a single arrow being shot. That's great, if you ask me."

Eudo hadn't been with us on Sirupat. "I thought so," I said. "Still, what do I know?"

"Papinian says you're an idiot to trust her."

"I would be if I did."

"He says you're – well, keen on her. You know."

"I suppose I am, in a way." I yawned. "She makes life interesting, I'll give her that. But she has the knack of wanting the same thing as me, and not giving a stuff about how she gets it. It shows we have a lot of shared tastes, but that's not necessarily a good thing in a relationship. Particularly when the shared taste is money." I felt like I'd been sitting still for too long, but I'd done everything I could think of that needed doing. "Papinian is right about her, and so's Polycrates. She's as slippery as an eel and as poisonous as a viper, just like me. But the only alternative is violence, and you know how I feel about that."

"I'm sure you know what you're doing," Eudo said. "I just wish the others wouldn't bitch about every damn thing. It's not constructive."

Eudo takes some figuring out, and I have a suspicion I haven't devoted as much time and energy to the issue as it deserves. He turned up one day when we were selling our stuff in the big twice-yearly fair at Mesoquai; he was going from stall to stall, passing the time of day with people, and we all assumed he must be a buyer. Then, quite out of the blue, he asked me for a job. He could do most things, he said. I told him to get lost; he smiled, thanked me and drifted away, not looking particularly concerned. Later that evening I had a drink with Chusro Asvogel, our biggest competitor, and he happened to mention that he'd just hired a new man, who seemed like a good thing. Really? I said. Sure, said Chusro. For a start he's ex-military, he was a captain in the Mezentine foreign legion, and you don't get further than lieutenant in that outfit unless you're pretty hot stuff. Go on, I said, feeling a slight quiver in the hairs on the back of my neck. Good family, Chusro continued, there's money there somewhere, you can tell by the voice. Experience in shipping and banking, too. Quite an asset.

So why would this paragon of all the virtues want a job in the battlefield salvage industry, I didn't ask; I finished my drink and went back to my tent, feeling like someone had just thrown a red-hot ten-staurata piece at my head and I'd ducked. Not that it mattered any more, because Chusro Asvogel had got him now and once Chusro's got something he doesn't tend to relinquish it without intrusive surgery . . .

The next time I saw him was three months later. We were unloading at the dock at Busta Sagittarum, after a long and tiresome crossing from north-east Blemya. I don't know if you've been to Busta lately, since they rebuilt the long break-water and moved all the deep-water berths over to the north side; they've ruined the place if you ask me, which is why we've taken to plodding the extra twenty miles overland and loading and unloading at Port Fabilla. I can't remember what stage we were at, but we were interrupted by Daresh Asvogel and about thirty men in armour.

"All right," Daresh said. "Where is he?"

His men looked like they were in a mood, and I could smell trouble. I gave Daresh my big smile. "Who are you after?" I said.

"You know perfectly well."

Oh boy. "Actually, I don't. Be more specific."

"That bastard," Daresh said. "That arsehole my idiot brother hired, the one you recommended to him. I know he's on your ship. I'm going to kill him."

There are eight Asvogel brothers plus a brother-in-law and two cousins; they don't like each other much. "He's not on our ship," I said. "Feel free to have a look."

That got me a scowl. I called my boys out onto the quay and let Daresh and his goons get on with it. Sometime later he came back up the gangplank and gave me the world's most grudging apology.

"Don't mention it," I said. "What's all this about me recommending someone to Chusro? I did no such thing."

"He said you'd sent him." Daresh scowled, then shrugged. "I believe you," he said. "Chusro's an idiot; obviously he didn't check. Look, if you see the arsehole, let me know. Better still, break his arms and legs and then let me know. Drink in it for you if you catch him."

"I'll bear that in mind," I said. "What's he done?"

"Taken things that don't belong to him."

"Ah," I said. "Well, rest assured, if he comes my way I'll let you know. I don't hold with people taking my name in vain."

I waited half an hour, then I went on board the ship. There's a bulkhead between the forward and aft cargo holds that isn't strictly speaking necessary. I thought I was the only one who knew about it, but apparently I was wrong.

I reached in and pulled him out by his ear. "The Asvogels are looking for you," I said.

He was dirty and scared-looking, and he had dried blood caked in his hair. "I didn't do it," he said.

"Yes, you did. You told Chusro I'd sent you. That's the only crime I'm interested in."

He made a sort of whimpering noise, then tried to trip me up. Being cramped in a space almost but not quite big enough for a human being to breathe in isn't good for your reflexes. I avoided him easily and decked him. "Get up," I said.

"You're going to give me to—"

"Worse than that," I said. "You're going back in there, and you aren't coming out again until we're safely back at sea."

Which is how Eudo joined the firm. Not by my choice; but if I'd turned him loose Daresh would've found him and killed him, and for some reason I felt that that would be a bad thing. Besides, the Asvogels had clearly made up their mind that I'd planted Eudo on them to spy on them and rob them blind, so the damage was already done. Meanwhile I'd acquired an assistant sufficiently well qualified to walk into a job with the main opposition, so presumably he was worth having, and I like employing people who owe their lives to my generosity of spirit. I still don't trust them, but it's a good foundation for a working relationship.

Since then, Eudo had turned out fine. He was smart, resourceful and got on well with everybody. You could give him a job and he'd go away and do it, and you didn't need to be peering over his shoulder all the time. There were things about him that made my skin crawl, but if I refused to employ people who have that effect on me I'd be overworked and very lonely. I did ask him once, why the salvage business? He replied that it had all the good things about being in the army and not so many of the bad things. Coming from him, that made a weird sort of sense, so I decided to let it go.

Shortly before midnight Stauracia's friends and colleagues came storming out of the tent and demanded to be taken back to the castle. I lent them a few lanterns, then went to see how things stood.

"Ungrateful shits, the lot of them," she said.

"But you insisted."

"Yes. Bastards. They'd have left me here to rot."

"So we're on. Like we agreed."

"Like you said, and I reluctantly accepted because I had no choice." She looked tired, which is unusual. "Yes, we're on. First thing in the morning we all go up to the castle together."

No wonder she looked tired. Presumably she and her people had tried to think of some way of either rescuing her or ambushing us, and hadn't been able to come up with anything sensible. That, of course, remained to be seen, but I reckoned that if she'd been able to think of anything, I'd have been able to read it in her face. As it was, she looked depressed. A good sign, from my perspective.

(And now, not because it's directly relevant to the narrative but because I feel like it, a short homily about normal people. Most people are normal; I'm not. The circumstances of my birth, the life I've led, the things I've done and had done to me, have turned me into something similar to a human being but different. A few years back the Vesani sold off about two dozen of their old warships – bloody stupid thing to do as it turned out, because shortly after that they got into that scrap with the Aelians over Terulam, and for want of about two dozen ships they lost a valuable province, but there you go – and the Uttach brothers bought them and turned them into oyster boats, for just long enough so that the Vesani forgot about them, where-upon they resold them to their cousins in the piracy industry, to whom they were a godsend. Now, I feel like I'm an oyster boat, misguidedly sold off and converted into a warship. You look at the basic hulk and you think, they've both got enough in common, a hull, three masts, a row of oars on either side, one's got a pointy bit up the front end and the other hasn't but that's not a problem; a ship is a ship is a ship.

And a man is a man is a man, and so on; only it's not true. Warships aren't normal ships. You can use them for oyster fishing, but everything about them is slightly wrong, just as it's exactly right for ramming, boarding and fast, tight manoeu-vres in deep water. Now, take me. I was built for a purpose; I was built to be the King of Sirupat (long story; maybe I'll tell you about it someday), failing which I was designed, con-structed and fitted out regardless of expense to be the duke of somewhere or other when my father eventually died, governing substantial estates, owning places and things and people, care-fully and lovingly looking after my possessions, which is only simple business sense, after all – a combination of bad luck and stupidity saw me repurposed as an industrial contractor. You can use me for catching oysters, but everything about me is slightly wrong. I can, for example, like people. When it comes to feeling affection I have a hull, three masts, two banks of oars. But a lifetime of bad luck and stupidity get in the way, and it's never quite right.

Not that it matters very much in day-to-day practical terms. But what happens when someone like me finds he likes someone like her? An aunt of mine had a dog, a little yappy thing that got under your feet and bit your ankles. Don't make such a fuss, she used to say, it means she likes you. Biting as a way of expressing affection (and scratching and growling; to this day I think my aunt probably misinterpreted what the wretched animal was trying to communicate, but never mind about that) – I don't know the answer, so I tend not to think about it. When one converted oyster boat bears down on another, oarsmen working up to ramming speed and the marines crouched nervously in the bows, they recognise each other as kindred souls, soulmates, with more in common with each other than with all the rest of the world, but they have their orders, and the punishment for mutiny doesn't bear thinking about, so I don't. That's Stauracia and me. If we ever ran into each other when we weren't compelled to tear each other to pieces, I suspect we'd get on famously. And by the same token I bet you I could fly like a dove, if only I had wings and a prodigiously muscular chest.)

Early next morning she was still there, probably because I'd had her chained to the axle of our biggest cart. A short pause while one of my blacksmiths cut the rivets he'd so carefully peened a few hours earlier, and off we went to the castle.

Let's go back to Saloninus's definition of love, which I quoted earlier: two minds with but a single thought, two hearts that beat as one. Foremost in Stauracia's mind the previous evening, when she was shouting at her colleagues, would have been an ambush, somewhere between my camp and the castle. The logical place would be the two rocks, which was why I'd sent seventy of my boys on ahead to secure it before we got there; she'd foreseen that, of course, so that's not where the ambush would be. Nor would it take place before we reached the two rocks, because then she and the ambush party would be cut off from home. Accordingly, not ideally (no choice in the matter; story of our lives), she planned to jump me somewhere between the two rocks and the castle gate, in territory she fondly believed I'd only seen once and was therefore unfamiliar with.

We reached the two rocks, where my men were waiting for us, green with fear. I'd put Eudo in charge of them, and when we got there he was sitting on top of one of the rocks, eating pickled walnuts out of a small jar.

"Get down from there," I told him, "take thirty men and go up the road about a hundred and fifty yards. On your left you'll find a sort of fallen-down shack hidden in a load of ferns and brambles. Tell the dozen or so blokes inside it to lay down their weapons and come out. Try and be polite."

Stauracia gave me a look that should have stripped all the enamel off my teeth. I smiled at her. "I know," I said. "You can't trust anyone these days, not when there's money involved."

She called me a much-maligned part of the human anatomy, which gave me a sort of warm glow somewhere inside. If she believed that one of her boys had sold out to me, it would make my life much simpler from then on. "Who?" she said, and I smiled at her.

Eudo had got the ambush party rounded up like sheep to be

dipped. I told him there was no need for that, now that we were all on the same side. "Run along and secure the castle, would you?" I said to him. "These gentlemen can stay here with us."

That's the sort of thing Eudo is good at; probably it comes from having been in the army, which I would have been if my life hadn't taken that one wrong turn so many years ago. I'd have served about five years, joining as a captain and ending up as a major, by which time I'd have learned to perform simple tasks, such as securing positions and bossing people about. When I try and do that sort of thing, people answer back and make suggestions. Eudo just tells them what to do in a loud voice and they do it, even if it's obviously a stupid way of going about it. I think it's because he makes it plain from the start that he's not going to listen, no matter how right they are. I wish I could do that, but I can't. "All sorted?" I asked him.

"The position is secure," he replied, soldierspeak for Yes. "I've confined the garrison in the main hall."

"Good boy. Now add this lot to them" – I pointed to the ambush party – "and tie them up good and proper. Her, too," I added. "And watch her like a hawk. She bites."

Stauracia started to say something in a loud, clear voice, but I'd brought a suitable bag with me and Eudo popped it over her head. She carried on talking, but the words were too muffled to be understood.

"Job done," I said.

Polycrates and Papinian looked at me. "You what?"

"I said, job done. We captured the castle. Told you I could do it without anyone getting hurt."

There was one of those silences you come to relish. "I thought you'd done a deal with your girlfriend," Polycrates said.

"So did she. But what the hell." I gave them a big smile. "Right," I told them, "I want someone to take a letter to my mother-in-law. The sooner it goes, the sooner we get Gombryas and the lads back." I turned the full force of my good nature on Polycrates. "See to it, there's a pal."

"But I thought—"

"Yes," I said. "You were wrong. Move."

And off he went, looking worried. I went and found Eudo. He was guarding the prisoners in a marked manner.

"Leave that," I said. "We need to search this place from top to bottom."

"Sure," he said, not quite leaping to attention but definitely quivering. "What am I looking for?"

"I have absolutely no idea."

Which wasn't entirely true. All I knew for the moment was that it was something that hadn't been there when I spent my enforced holiday in the castle. Probably. But I wouldn't know that for sure until I found it. Anyway, the orders seemed to make sense to Eudo. "Anything out of the ordinary," he said.

"Yes and no."

"Fine," he said. "I'll let you know what we find."

Something out of the ordinary. Define ordinary. An uncut diamond looks a lot like a pebble. A piece of paper is just a piece of paper, useful for writing on or lighting a fire with, unless it happens to have a confession written on it, or Saloninus's lost seventh eclogue, or directions how to find a million staurata in buried gold bullion. And a ship is a ship is a ship; we've already been through all that.

For a short – would that it had been longer – period in my life, I made a sort of a living writing plays for the theatre in

Roul Bohec; happy days, and if I could go back I would, but I can't. The experience taught me a bit about structure. A play has either three or five acts, which is another way of saying that stuff happens (on the stage) in compartments – rooms, if you like, on which a door closes when you reach a certain point. The rooms in my life, for example, include a privileged, miserable childhood, a short but peaceful time in Roul earning an honest penny, and a sort of cellar or warehouse where I am now, robbing dead bodies and burying them. Act One of the current episode (scene: a castle) seemed to be drawing to a satisfactory conclusion. Our hero, having double-crossed the heroine, finds the hidden whatever-it-is and is therefore in a position to tackle the challenges that face him in Act Two. In order for that to happen, however, I needed to figure out what I was looking for, which is not the same thing as finding it. I'd already done that; it was in the castle. Like the old story about the three men who saved up and took a trip to Choris to see the Blue Pavilion. They got there and climbed up Hill Street, where there's that amazing view over the whole city. One of them pointed: that's the Blue Pavilion there, he said. Another one pointed at something else: no, that's the Blue Pavilion, he said. No, you're wrong, said the third one, also pointing; that's got to be the Blue Pavilion over there, look, next door to the big round building. It was a hot day and they were tired. They looked at each other. Anyway, we've seen the Blue Pavilion, one of them said. Let's go home. I knew how they felt. It was here somewhere, if only I could recognise it.

At one point I thought I'd found it, but I was wrong.

At the top of the tower, facing out over the gatehouse and the surrounding countryside, was a room that had clearly been designed as the seneschal's lodgings. Actually, I think seneschal is going it a bit. It's the proper term to describe the commanding officer of a castle garrison, but that sort of assumes a proper castle, its white limestone walls blazing defiantly on a sunlit summit. If there's a proper term to describe a poor sod lumbered with running a middle-of-nowhere blockhouse, I hereby authorise you to scrub out the word seneschal and write it in.

It was the best room in the house; I've been in bigger, better ventilated prison cells. Whatever the weather, it would always be too cold in winter and too hot in summer, and the doorway was so low that even I nutted myself on the lintel twice – once going in, once going out again, when I should've known better; I remembered to duck, but didn't duck low enough. The damp had got into the door so it didn't shut properly. There was one big window. That made sense. The whatever-you-just-wrote-in would need a commanding view of the besieging enemy, and the tower was too high to reach with arrows, so it didn't need to be a slit. It also meant the wind and the rain could come and visit you whenever they happened to be passing; likewise the sun, when what you wanted most in the world was a bit of cool shade. There was a stone shelf for a bed, just like in a prison; a hole in the wall that opened into the garderobe shaft, for emptying your chamber pot; and a set of bookshelves.

Which hadn't been there before. It shocked me that I'd been inside the room for well over a minute before I noticed them. Bookshelves, for crying out loud; and on them, a load of old books.

Consider the book. It can be worth a great deal of money. The Blue Star monastery in Perimadeia produced the finest books the world has ever seen. The quality of the vellum has never been equalled – they had some technique for treating the skins after they'd been skived and ground that nobody's ever been able to reproduce; the pages have a semi-translucent quality that means that in daylight they shine, as though there were tiny candles trapped inside them. The Blue Star specialised in small books, nothing bigger than a roof tile; but the calligraphy is so amazingly clear that you can read the tiny letters easy as anything, even by candlelight, and the letter shapes are things of exquisite beauty in themselves – they're highly prized by collectors in Echmen, where they write in little pictures, not letters, because they're so delightful to look at, and the hell with what they happen to mean. The illuminations are extraordinary. Every page is a blaze of gold leaf and incredibly expensive ground-up lapis lazuli; a blue sky, with the Invincible Sun blazing up at you from the page instead of down on you from heaven. The pictures of men and women and animals are outstanding, but what really gets into your bloodstream are the abstract borders. At first glance they look like a tangle of primary-coloured briars; but take a moment and trace them one by one, and you'll see that the primary-coloured strands weave in and out of each other in a pattern that slowly begins to make sense the more you look at them. The idea was that you used them as an aid to meditation. A bit like life, they said: the more you gaze at the tangle, the more clearly the patterns emerge. Other people say that they represent mathematical principles, expressed in intervals and the ogives of curves rather than mere numbers, in the way that music conveys information that can't be expressed in words. A Blue Star missal or book of hours will cost you the price of a well-established vineyard or a five-masted freighter; the rarer pieces – Amalrich's *Reflections*, for instance, or a three-volume

Collected Saloninus – don't come up very often, and when they do, they fetch sums that would pay for a whole war. Books can be valuable things, believe me.

There were no Blue Stars on the shelves in the seneschal's lodgings. Nor were there any Silver Horns, Seventh Milestones or examples of the work of the Master of the Studium. They were just books: practical books, mostly, in dog-eared vellum bindings; books about mining and brass-founding, agriculture, architecture, refining lamp oil from pitch, glue-making for beginners, the properties of different sorts of wood, how to distil plant extracts for medicinal use and dyeing cloth, shipbuilding, roadmaking, the principles of double-entry bookkeeping and how to make pencils on an industrial scale. Looked at from one perspective it was the greatest storehouse of treasure I'd ever set eyes on in my life, because it told you useful stuff you needed to know about useful things; I estimated the resale value of the whole collection at twelve staurata, half what my father used to pay for a falcon. Standard works on a variety of subjects; you could find copies of them in every prefecture and priory anywhere west of the Friendly Sea. Worth their bulk in toilet paper, and that was about it.

I stood gawping at them for a long time. A tiny silver bell rang somewhere in the back of my mind, but when I tried to drag out whatever was ringing it into the light, it slipped away like a rat in a dark shed and I gave up trying. Then I remembered the golden rule. When all else fails, ask someone.

5

She wasn't pleased to see me. "You arsehole," she said, as soon as I lifted the bag off her head. "You complete and utter shit."

"Yes," I said. "But it wasn't that I wanted to talk about. You know all those books in the seneschal's room."

"Fuck you," she said. "What books?"

My head was starting to hurt, probably because the little seized-up cogs were trying to turn. "You know," I said. "The books in the room at the top of the tower. Technical manuals, mostly."

"I have no idea what you're talking about. Saevus, you're a turd. I trusted you."

"The books," I reminded her gently. "You're saying you didn't bring them with you. They were there when you came."

"I don't know anything about any fucking books. Now get these ropes off me. You know being tied up gives me panic attacks."

"Sorry," I said, "but you're too good at getting away. It's a compliment, really. I happen to think the ability to escape is one of the most beautiful qualities a person can have, and you've got it in spades. You sure you don't know anything about the books?"

A serpentine look lit up in her eyes. "If you showed me what you're talking about," she said, "it might jog my memory."

"I doubt it. So you didn't bring them with you."

"No. Saevus, *please* untie these ropes. They're so tight I can't feel my legs."

I considered for a moment. "I'll ask your carters," I said. "They'll remember if there was a big box full of books. I don't suppose you'd forget carrying that lot up eight flights of stairs in a hurry."

"Saevus, I mean it. I'm really suffering. I saved your life once. If you don't let me go I'll never forgive you."

I spread the hem of the bag out with my fingers. "If you do remember anything," I told her, "do let me know." Then I popped the bag back over her head, and she started yowling like a cat.

Not that that told me anything, apart from the fact that she has a thing about confined spaces, which I already knew. If Stauracia didn't want to tell me about the books, she'd be prepared to put up with a lot of personal discomfort before she gave way. I know her well enough to be aware that I don't always know when she's lying: useful knowledge, but essentially negative. Still, negative data is still data. "Are you all right in there?" I asked.

I couldn't make out the words, but the tone of voice told me what I needed to know. I wasn't going to get anything useful out of her, and she didn't like having the bag over her head. I took it off. She tried to spit at me but her mouth was too dry.

"All right," I said. "Let's assume for argument's sake that you don't know anything about the books. In that case, I'd be grateful for your opinion. Let's go for a walk. I expect you'd like to stretch your legs after a night on the floor."

As we strolled round the courtyard I listened patiently to her mostly accurate summary of my character, then pointed out that she'd have done exactly the same thing if she'd been in my shoes. She had the grace to admit that, yes, she would. In fact, she looked forward with eager anticipation to proving me right, the very next time she had an opportunity.

"That's fine," I said, "we understand each other. Now then, about these books."

"I don't know anything about any stupid books," she said. "And I haven't even been in that room."

"Haven't you? You're sure about that."

"Of course I'm sure."

"You've been up the tower."

"Of course I have, to the platform on the top. But I didn't go in any room. No need to."

"Funny," I said. "You're curious by nature, you'd have wanted to see if there was anything in there worth having."

"Fine." She glowered at me. "I tried the door but it was stiff and I couldn't get it open. So I thought, I'll come back with a couple of men and a big hammer. And then I forgot all about it."

Possible but unlikely. The door opened just fine when I tried it; in fact, it wouldn't shut properly, because of the damp. Of course, if it was seized and someone had kicked it in, that would account for its deplorable lack of function. "Who the hell," I said, "would store a load of perfectly ordinary, not especially valuable books at the top of a tower in an abandoned castle?"

The question made her pause and think. "I don't know," she said. "Someone who'd stolen them and needed to stash them for a while."

"Yes, but they're only worth about ten staurata."

"Ten staurata's a lot of money to some people. We aren't all the sons of dukes, remember."

"Yes, but – all right, what do you think they're doing there?"

She stopped walking and frowned. "You can hide something in a book," she said. "You can cut out a page and paste in a new one. Or you can write something in a margin. Vital information."

What I'd been thinking. Two minds, et cetera. "Yes, in one book," I said. "There's forty-two of them."

"Camouflage. One book on its own—"

"Might just have been left there by accident, so you'd take no notice. Forty-two are hard to miss."

She sighed. "All right," she said. "Someone stole them or got hold of them, knowing that one of them had something valuable in it. But he didn't know which one, or what the valuable thing was. So he pinched the lot and stashed them, intending to come back later and figure it out."

"That's what I figured," I said. "So let's go and look, shall we?"

We looked. We went through all the books, me first then her, in case I missed something. But all the pages followed on from each other, the writing in each book was all in the same hand, and there were no notes in any of the margins. Just a load of useful technical books. Useless.

"A code," she suggested. "You can do a code by using the first word on each page, and then you substitute the letters—"

"Yes, I know. But you could get a copy of any of those books anywhere in the West. If it was a particular copy, the relevant words would be underlined or have a pinhole next to them. There's nothing like that."

"Fuck," she said, with feeling. "In that case, I don't get it. It makes no sense. So it can't be the stupid books."

"Then account for them being there."

She shrugged. "I don't know, do I? Look, they're all useful books. Lots of useful stuff about how to do things. Somebody wanted a library of useful books, because they were getting ready to do stuff."

"So?"

"So maybe the people I'm working for want to do stuff. To be honest, I haven't got the faintest what they want, but for all I know maybe they're planning to found the Perfect Society. Nutcases usually do, and I'm pretty sure they're all nutcases. If you were founding a utopian colony, you'd need to know about preserving fruit and making barrels and all that kind of thing. And they're probably all city people who don't know spit about anything useful, so they'd need to read about it in books."

I thought about that. It made sense. "Really," I said. "Someone's planning to set up the ideal republic, so naturally they desperately need a book about how to make stained-glass windows."

She glared at me. "Probably a job lot," she said. "In an auction catalogue: useful books, various. Look, these people aren't the sharpest arrows in the quiver. And there's really useful stuff in there, too: crop rotation, basics of animal husbandry, how to build a house. I bet you anything you like that's the explanation."

And making stained glass isn't a bad idea, either. A new

colony needs exports, and people pay good money for stained glass, and the raw materials are basically sand. "It's got to be the books," I said, "for the simple reason that I've been all over this stupid castle and there isn't anything else."

"Or you haven't found it yet. Because it's really well hidden, or you don't know what you're looking for."

I sighed. "You're not helping," I said.

"Why the hell should I?"

"Because—" I hadn't meant to shout. "Because if we can identify and find what it is, we can play your lot off against my lot, and get what we want: my pals safe and sound, this kid you're concerned about—"

"My son."

"This kid," I repeated, "whoever he is. We can both win, and everybody goes home happy. But if I can't find it and use it to do a deal, I'll have no alternative but to hand this castle over to my lot, in order to get Gombryas and Carrhasio back, and you'll have failed in your mission, and I have to take your word for it that there'll be repercussions that you won't like."

"Fuck you, Saevus. My *son*."

I still couldn't make my mind up about that. I'd tried reconstructing what I knew about her, looking out for a gap of say four months when she'd been out of sight and unaccounted for. The trouble was, there were several gaps of suitable duration; I'd assumed she'd been on the run, hiding out or in prison, but maybe she'd been off somewhere giving birth to an actual human child. Or maybe not. "I wish I could believe you," I said. "I really do. The trouble is, faith is like sleep and—"

"Love." She stifled a yawn. "Yes, you've told me that before. It's one of your party pieces. You repeat yourself a lot, did you know that? Like an old man telling war stories. Look," she said, lowering and softening her voice – it was supposed to inspire confidence but in me it had the opposite effect, unfortunately. "Just for once in your life, believe me. I know, I've lied to you a lot and there's no reason you should ever believe a word I say, but this time it's for real, and it's important. He's all I've got. If anything happened to him, I'd die. Really."

She's lying, I sixty per cent decided. But that didn't really matter. I wanted to fix the problem without her getting hurt, with her getting what she wanted. But unless I could figure out what the castle's hidden treasure was, I couldn't do that. "How often do you report back to your lot?" I asked.

"You what?"

"The people controlling you," I said. "The ones you claim kidnapped your suppositious child. Do you send them regular reports? How regular? Once a month? Once a week? Daily?"

"When I feel like it," she said. "What's that got to do with anything?"

"I'm guessing," I said, "that they hear from you regularly. If they don't get a report, they know something's wrong and they arrive with reinforcements. So how long is it since you last reported in, and when can I expect the reinforcements to get here? Don't answer that," I added, "I find it hurtful when people tell me lies."

She answered the question, though. She did it with a little twitch of her mouth. It's a habit of hers. I don't think she knows she does it, though maybe that's what she wants me to think; that would be very useful, of course. "Oh, come on," she said.

"I'll assume they're on their way," I said. "But that's all right, because my lot are on their way, too. And I've got five hundred men to hold this castle with, until my lot and your lot get here and we can have a nice three-way siege, just like in bloody Sirupat. But we don't have to do that," I said, as impressively as I could manage on the spur of the moment. "Not if you know what the special thing is and where it's hidden. If only you knew that, we could fix this and go home."

I looked at her. It was like looking into a mirror.

"I'm glad I'm not you," she said, after a moment. "I'd hate to have a mind like yours."

About Praeclara. My mother-in-law.

She's not someone I like thinking about, let alone talking about or describing. I'm not a hateful sort of person. I meet a lot of hard cases and nasty pieces of work in the course of my daily grind, but they don't bother me as a rule; I don't like them, but I don't hate them. Usually I can sympathise with them, since they tend to have done the same sort of horrible and unforgivable things as I have; I don't approve, please note, but I can sympathise. I don't happen to believe in Evil with a capital E. I think there are nice people and nasty people, people who think nice thoughts and people who think nasty ones; and generally speaking, the bad stuff in this world is much more likely to emanate from the nice people with nice thoughts. Such as: well, liberty, equality and fraternity, for a start. Those concepts have started more wars and killed more human beings than dear old greed and selfishness could possibly ever aspire to. Show me a genuinely serious war, not just a border dispute or a scrap about trade but a million-killing, city-burning, depopulating, starvation-inducing nightmare, and I bet you ten staurata I can show you the idealist who started it. True, there are people who do appalling things not for idealistic reasons; mostly people with mental problems. There are people who stab strangers in the street for no obvious motive, or set fire to buildings because they like the glow. They cause unspeakable grief to a few individuals. That's not evil, that's illness. Compared to the visionary who longs to free the oppressed or lead the chosen people to the promised land, the damage they do is so limited as to be, in the great scheme of things, inconsequential, and you might as well hate the sky because of the occasional flash of lightning.

So: I don't hate many people. My mother-in-law Praeclara is one of about five people I genuinely loathe. And Praeclara isn't evil. She's just intensely self-centred, incredibly focused and, goes without saying, an idealist. She believes in the Cause. I've known her a long time and I've never quite managed to figure out what the Cause is, but she knows and she lives, breathes and has her being exclusively for it. I imagine the Cause is probably something fundamentally decent. It usually is.

I first met Praeclara shortly after I met her daughter. This isn't easy for me to write, by the way, so please excuse me if what follows lacks my usual hard-glazed charm and meretricious flippancy. Let me start this again, now I've had a moment to catch my breath.

The first time I met Apoina, my wife, was at an Ascension Day service at the Flawless Diamond temple in Leal Defoir. I don't know if you ever went there before they tore out all the old seating and replaced it with all those ghastly modernist benches; before that, you had the high altar in the centre of the nave, where it is now, and all the seats surrounded it in a series of concentric rings. I can see why they changed it, because at any given time a quarter of the congregation had a splendid view of the back of the celebrant's head and not much else. I think it was supposed to symbolise the centrality of the Light Made Manifest in all aspects of human life or something like that, but it was all pretty silly and no wonder they scrapped it, though needless to say they replaced it with something worse. Anyway, I was kneeling in the front row during the Sanctus – what was I doing in a temple? You've jumped to the conclusion that I was casing the joint with a view to stealing the gold ornaments off the rood screen, but in actual fact I was only there to listen to the music; the choir was due to sing a Procopius anthem – "Rejoice, Ye Lands", if memory serves – and I happen to like that sort of thing. Anyway, I was kneeling for the Sanctus, looking down at my hands like you do, and at the edge of my peripheral vision I caught sight of something that looked remarkably like a knife. I glanced sideways, and, yes, it was a knife; double-edged, tapered, about five inches. It was being gripped in the left hand of a thin-faced young woman who was muttering something very rapidly under her breath, and I sort of intuitively knew that the moment she'd finished reciting this whatever-it-was, she was going to jump up out of her seat and stick the knife in the back of the Lord Archdeacon.

That sort of thing happens, from time to time; see above, under Evil, non-existence of. You get some poor fool who honestly believes that the Invincible Sun ordered him to do it, so what choice did he have? Personally I don't think the Invincible Sun did anything of the sort, mostly because He doesn't exist, but that's just my opinion; it's stuff that happens, and the more you agonise over it, the more collateral damage is likely to occur.

Fortunately, thanks to my long association with sharp

objects, I know how to take a knife away from someone without making a fuss or getting cut. The trick is to clamp the flat of the blade between your thumb and fingertips, squeezing it as hard as you can, then give it a sharp turn through ninety degrees to break the owner's grip. Use your left hand; the object of the exercise is to get the knife as far away from its owner as possible, so if you use your left there's the whole of the width of your body between you and him; also, if the operation goes wrong and you end up getting cut to the bone, you don't lose the use of your more valuable right hand. Don't rush; nice and easy wins the race, as my old archery tutor used to say, and you can apply more controlled force if you keep it smooth rather than being tempted to jerk.

So I took the knife away from her. It was a piece of cake, since she hadn't been expecting it. She turned to stare at me; I put my right forefinger to my lips, ssh, then lowered my head once more in conventional prayer. As the Sanctus wound up I slid the knife down the inside of my left boot, where the hem of my coat would conceal the handle.

The precentor sang the last phrase of the Sanctus, cue for the congregation to stand up for the Miserere, and I glanced at my left hand, which was dripping blood. It was only a minor slice, diagonal rather than square on, so no danger to the tendons. I wriggled my sleeve down my arm and clenched my fingers on the cuff to check the bleeding.

I'd expected her to get up and walk out, but she stayed where she was, eyes fixed straight ahead. For a moment I thought she had another weapon, but the tension had gone out of her neck and shoulders; the poor kid was stunned and confused, no idea what she was supposed to do next. By this point, according to the schedule, she ought to be dead or being dragged across the floor on her way to a prison cell, but everything had changed and she was cut off from her chain of command, like a half-platoon of soldiers at the extreme edge of a battle who've just seen the rest of their army wiped out.

I assume they sang the Procopius but if they did I wasn't paying attention. My hand started to throb and I was afraid to look at it, in case I saw something I didn't like. It was essential not to draw attention to her or myself, so I made a point of saying the prayers and responses loudly and clearly, looking straight ahead, taking no notice of my neighbours on either side – on my left there was a middle-aged woman in a yellow silk gown, and the last thing I needed was for any of my blood to get on it, so I had to keep my left hand in my lap. All told, it was a pretty weird three-quarters of an hour.

The service ended, the choir and clergy processed out through the west door and everybody did that sitting-around-until-it's-polite-to-leave thing that you only ever see in places of worship. I looked to my right to see if the woman was still there. She was. She had this sort of dead look in her eyes, which I interpreted as: I've made a mess of it; my life is over. Silly girl, I thought, but I knew I was being unfair. Maybe she had some entirely valid cause of action against the Archdeacon, he killed her father or raped her sister, and I'd interfered and screwed everything up. Interfere at your peril, my uncle Cyprian used to say. Good advice, which I'm usually smart enough to follow.

People all round us were standing up to go, but she just sat there. God only knows why, but I tapped her on the shoulder and tipped my head in the direction of the east door; come on, the gesture, said, we need to talk. So we went out into the cloister, and we talked.

Correction: after a sticky beginning, she talked and I

listened. It all came rushing out, like fish sauce out of a bottle when the mouth of the bottle's caked up, so you give it a good shake . . . Her name, she said, was Apereisi Apoina, and her mother had made her do it. For the Cause, she said, in a leaden sort of a voice. It was time to send Bad People a message, one they couldn't ignore. She didn't say what the message was (obviously something short and pithy enough to be written on the back of a dead Archdeacon) but she knew it was important, because out of all the Brotherhood her mother had chosen her own daughter to deliver it, and now it had all gone wrong and she'd failed—

"What do you want?" I asked. "An apology?"

She looked at me. "No," she said. "I don't know what to do. I should be dead by now."

I took a deep breath. "Let's pretend," I said. "Let's make believe it all went swimmingly and you're dead."

She laughed, then burst into tears. "I'm not, though. Am I?"

"You're left-handed, aren't you?" I asked.

"Yes. How did you—?"

"You were holding the knife in your left hand," I said. "If you'd been right-handed, I wouldn't have seen it in time, if I had seen it I couldn't have taken it away from you without a hell of a fuss, and there'd have been blood everywhere. And I'm sorry if it sounds feeble, but I regard blood as an admission of failure. I see so much of it in my line of work, and it's sort of my golden rule: whenever you see blood soaking into the dust, somewhere close at hand you're bound to find an idiot in charge of something."

"Your line of work." She stopped short and frowned. "You're a soldier."

"No."

"Yes you are." She looked straight at me, and if she'd had hackles they'd have risen. "You weren't just there by accident."

"I was, actually. I heard they were going to sing a Procopius anthem, and I had a bit of spare time, so I dropped in for the service. If you remember, I was there first."

"No, you weren't."

"Yes, I was. You arrived late, just before the introit. You sat next to me because there was only one empty seat in the front row."

Actually that proved nothing, but I said it as though it was conclusive evidence. I could see her fighting it, then reluctantly giving way. "So if you're not a soldier, what are you?"

"Me? I'm a businessman. I deal in second-hand goods. Actually, more like a glorified rag and bone man."

"You see a lot of blood in the rag and bone business?"

I decided I'd better change the subject as quickly as possible. "You say your mother told you to do this."

"Yes, that's right."

"But—" No, I thought, forget it. None of your business. It's like flies in buckets of water. You see them thrashing desperately, trying to get out before all their strength is used up, but they can't, and when they're utterly exhausted they drown. So you have a choice. You can scoop them up in your cupped hand and put them somewhere safe, or you can leave them to it. I don't think even Saloninus could calculate precisely how many millions of flies drown in buckets of water on any given day, and you know what? You can't save them all. In Echmen they have these fairy tales where the fly turns out to be the daughter of the Dragon King of the West, who in due course rescues her saviour from certain death and ends up marrying him, but Echmen is a long way away and we don't have dragons in these parts. The hell with it. The world is crowded to bursting with dying, helpless innocents. There's nothing you can do about it. Really there isn't. And you can catch something nasty from dipping your hand in stagnant water.

I thought about all that, and then I looked at her. "I lied," I said. "I'm a soldier. You're under arrest."

Which left me with the question of what to do with her. I couldn't let her go back to her mother, who'd simply issue her with another knife and tell her to try again. I couldn't hand her over to any form of authority; either they wouldn't believe me or they'd hang her. I couldn't find a job for her in my business, which is what I generally do with the waifs and strays I lumber myself with – Stauracia lives and thrives on battlefields, but she was clearly no Stauracia. I felt like a man who wanders into a saleroom to get out of the rain and comes out again having bought a stuffed elephant.

"You'll end up marrying her," said my friend Amphilyta, to whom I'd unwisely told my troubles. "I can see that happening, clear as day."

"Bullshit," I said.

Amphilyta runs the Crystal Garden. I'd asked her if she needed a bookkeeper. "You haven't got a choice," she said. "You've backed yourself into a corner and now you're screwed."

"Absolutely not."

"Absolutely. You've taken responsibility for her: that's where you made your big mistake."

"Which makes her a nuisance," I said, "not a prospective bride. Look, I've got her locked up in a room out back of the distillery in Coopers Yard, for which I'm paying sixteen stuivers a day. The sooner I can get shot of her, the happier I'll be."

"Your own silly fault," she said, as if I hadn't spoken. "And anyone can see you're besotted."

"No."

"Yes. How long have we known each other? I can read you like a book."

Amphilyta is illiterate, which is why I'd thought she might need some clerical assistance. "No, you can't," I said.

"The way you talk about her," she said. "Besotted."

"Drop dead."

Which got me a smile; more like a leer. "I suppose I could use someone to look after the accounts," she said. "Of course I can do them in my head far better than any silly girl can written down, but since you asked so nicely—"

I'd made a mistake, but it was too late. Amphilyta had made her mind up, and that was that. When I'm in Leal I spend most of my time in the Crystal Garden; it's where everyone knows where to find me, and I know I'll be safe there. Amphilyta knows people who can arrange that sort of thing. I helped her out of a scrape once, a long time ago. I had a nasty feeling this would, in her view, be her way of repaying her debt.

The main thing, I told her, was to make sure Apoina's ghastly mother didn't find out she was there; also, while we were on the subject, what was known about her, and why would she want her daughter to kill an Archdeacon? Amphilyta knows everything that goes on in Leal. The mother's name, she told me, was Praeclara, and her outfit was the Golden Spider—

"Oh, for fuck's sake," I said.

"Precisely," Amphilyta said. "And in all the years I've known you, that's the first time I've ever heard you swear."

If you want to start a conversation in any bar in Leal and be confident that it'll end in shattered furniture and broken teeth, walk up to someone and say, "So what do you think the Golden Spider is really trying to achieve?" There are plenty of theories. They're out to overthrow the government. They're the government's top secret black ops squad, blending deniability with utter ruthlessness as they wipe out the regime's more troublesome opponents. They plan to drive a stake through the heart of the military-industrial complex that really runs things. They're a bunch of religious fanatics. They're a bunch of atheist maniacs hell-bent on toppling established religion. They're a pseudo-political front for organised crime. They're out-of-control vigilantes fighting organised crime because the government can't or won't. They're misguided idealists trying to stop the next war. They're misguided idealists trying to start the next war. All of the above.

Opinions, therefore, vary. The facts are pretty universally agreed. A hundred and seven murders, ninety-eight major robberies, over a thousand arson attacks, woundings, beatings and destruction of property too numerous to particularise; those are the facts they cheerfully admit to.

Not evil people; certainly not. I have no doubt whatsoever that they consider themselves to be saints and (if at all possible) martyrs; they're not evil, they're *fighting* evil, and with such utter devotion that they'd happily give their lives to further the long, twilight struggle. But dangerous people – yes, very much so, and I make it a rule to keep as far away from dangerous people as I can get, myself excepted, naturally. I wasn't overjoyed, therefore, to find out that I'd effectively kidnapped the daughter of one of them. It struck me as possibly the most stupid thing I'd done since I left home. Amphilyta clearly agreed with me.

"I'm not having her here," she said. "Sorry, but no deal. And come to think of it, you can piss off as well, and don't ever come back. I like you, Saevus, and you did me a good turn once, but you're not worth that much trouble. And if they come here and ask where to find you, I'll tell them. Like a shot."

I admire honesty. "Give me twenty-four hours, all right?"

She gave me a sad look. "Not if they come here looking for you. Sorry."

Well, the world is a big place. The previous day I'd put in a bid on a silly little war in Teuda, right up in the armpit of the Friendly Sea. I'd bid low because I didn't really want the job. I went back to the factor who was taking the bids and raised my offer somewhat.

He looked at me. "Seriously?"

"Seriously."

"Fine," he said, his eyes very wide. "You got it."

That was late afternoon. The soonest we'd be ready to leave would be early the next morning. I told Gombryas and Polycrates to get the stuff loaded. Then, as soon as it was dark, I went round to Coopers Yard. They were there waiting for me.

That was the first time I met Praeclara. An interesting woman: clearly very smart, focused, motivated, not one to suffer fools gladly. "He's not a soldier," she told her daughter. "He's a scrap merchant. He makes his living robbing dead bodies."

In case you'd formed a mental picture of a dark cell with straw on the floor, chains and rats, I'd spent rather a lot of money – forty stuivers – on making the room as comfortable as possible. I'd provided a decent bed and a table and a chair, a nine-stuiver brass lamp and sheepskin rug. The door was bolted on the outside, but I'd seen to it that there was always a scuttleful of charcoal for the fire, a jug of water and a basin, edible food sent in from the Clarity of Purpose round the corner and a box of books for her to read. "I'm assuming," Praeclara went on, "that he'd got some silly idea about demanding a ransom."

To make matters just a little bit worse, I hadn't told Gombryas and the boys anything about it, so they had no idea where I was and weren't going to come bursting in through the door to rescue me. In fact, as far as I could tell, I'd come to the end of a long and pointless road; a stupid place to die, for a stupid reason, but nobody lives for ever. It was probably going to hurt, but what the hell.

"No," I said. "No ransom. Matter of fact, I felt sorry for her."

I've probably already told you the story of the friend of mine who stopped by the roadside for a piss and found himself nose to nose with a lion, so I won't repeat it; but, trust me, I know how he felt. Absolutely terrified, of course, but he also mentioned a sort of brittle, petrified calm, in which he could hear a bird singing in a nearby thorn bush and his own heart beating, as clear as anything. "You felt sorry for her. How come?"

"Because," I said, "her lunatic of a mother had sent her off to be killed. I ask you. What kind of a monster would do a thing like that?"

She looked at me. I interested her. I imagine the lion had a similar expression. "And what business is that of yours?" she asked.

"None," I said. "And I got my hand all cut up and I'm out of pocket a gulden thirty. Serves me right for giving a damn."

Consider the lion. It's so big and strong that it's afraid of nothing. It's so successful at hunting that it can afford to be lazy, belay that, leisured in its approach. It's not starving hungry all the time like most predators; it can afford to play

with its food, or even – the supreme indulgence – occasionally
let it go. She looked at me for a long time, then put her hand in
her sleeve and took out a small lace purse. "Two gulden," she
said, holding out the coins. "Keep the change."

I knew the situation, as though it was a scene in a play I'd
watched a dozen times already. I reach out to take the coins,
someone standing behind me bashes my head, I fall on the
ground and they all crowd round me and stomp me to death.
They were waiting for their cue. I let them wait.

She stood there holding out her hand with the coins in it
for maybe five seconds, then shrugged and put them back in
her purse. The lion was intrigued with me. "I found out about
you," she said. "You're a real piece of work."

"Thank you," I said. "Coming from you that means a lot."

"Funny man." Again, an obvious cue for the beating to
start. She could have started it with the slightest nod, but she
chose not to. Interesting. The dynamics of mass stompings are
very delicate and precise, like the mechanism of a Mezentine
clock. Set the mechanism in motion and the outcome is inevitable, but there are points where, if you keep your nerve and
don't do what's in the script, you can save your life. I was still
undamaged, and I was gleaning tiny amounts of data, like a
bee getting pollen on its legs. "I gather you're off to Teuda."

"That's right."

"I've never been there, but I gather it's a real dump."

"It's not so bad," I said.

She nodded. "Fine," she said. "Have a safe trip. And if you
ever show your face in Leal again, I'll cut it off. Got that?"

"Yes."

"Good boy."

So that was it. She wasn't going to have me kicked to death

in front of her daughter. Later, maybe, but not where her little girl could see. Meanwhile, the Queen of Beasts was extending disdainful clemency to the gazelle trapped under her paw. "Just one thing," I said.

And why I said it, I have no idea, to this day. Brave, as far as I'm concerned, is just a speechwriter's synonym for stupid. I knew there was nothing useful I could achieve, and it was none of my business anyhow. At that moment it suddenly dawned on me, like the sharp unexpected pain that tells you that you've just torn a ligament, that Amphilyta was probably right and I was besotted. Pity about that, I decided, since it was going to get my skull crunched under someone's boot.

"What?"

"You're the biggest heap of shit I've ever come across in my entire life. Would you like me to justify that remark?"

So I had her undivided attention. Lucky me. "I think you'd better," she said. "If you can."

"No problem," I said. "You send your own daughter to be a martyr to the Cause and get killed. That's all right," I added quickly, before she could interrupt, "I can understand that. I think it's disgusting and ridiculous, but I can see why someone might think it was the right thing to do."

"Thank you," she said sweetly. "I do admire an open mind."

"It's not your lunatic fanaticism I'm taking issue with," I said. "It's you being so utterly selfish and self-centred that you don't mind killing your own child for the Cause, but you don't want her to watch you having a man beaten to death, because then she might see you for what you are and you won't be her Great Goddess any more. I know that's trivial compared to all the killing and burning you get up to, but I happen to think it's particularly low, that's all."

It was one of those moments that could have gone either way. She could have decided that the damage had been done, so there wasn't anything to lose by having me killed on the spot; there was also her dignity and authority to think about, since I'd insulted her in front of a dozen of her goons. Or she could prove me wrong by letting me live and being magnanimously amused about the whole thing. In her shoes I'd probably have had me killed. "Finished?" she said.

My heart stopped, because for a moment I thought she'd said, "Finish it". My bowels had started to open; I managed to get control of them back just in time. "Yes," I said. "I think that more or less covers it."

Nobody said anything or moved. It was up to me. I turned round and headed for the door. If it was going to happen, it would be now; I'd lost the eye contact, my back was turned. I got as far as the door. "Just one thing," she said.

I stopped but didn't turn round.

"My daughter wasn't in any danger," she said. "I had seventeen men in the congregation, carefully positioned to screen her and make sure she got away. But you had to interfere."

I put the palm of my hand against the door and gave it a gentle push. It opened. I walked through and kept going. Ten yards brought me into Coppergate; I turned left. Seven doors down on the right is the Clarity of Purpose. I plunged through the door and went straight up to the bar, where my friend Despoina (actually my friend Amphilyta's friend Despoina) started to say, "You've got a nerve, showing your face in—"

"I need to hide," I said. "Now."

"Oh, for crying out loud."

There's a trapdoor to the cellar. It's a nice cellar, cool and airy and not too many spiders. Sometime later, Despoina lifted the trap. "You can come out now," she said.

"They've gone?"

She nodded. "Five of them," she said. "I don't know them so not from round here, but definitely trouble. And you owe me forty stuivers for the dinners."

I gave her a gulden. "Won't be needing them any more," I said.

She looked at me. "Walked out on you, did she? Can't say I blame her. If ever I decide to live in guilty splendour, it won't be in a grubby little kennel out back of Coopers Yard."

I went back to the Crystal Garden but didn't go inside. Instead I hung about in the street. Eventually Olybrius came and found me. "What the hell is going on?" he asked.

"Let me guess," I said. "Strange men have been looking for me."

"We didn't like the look of them, so we caught one and Carrhasio talked to him." He smiled. "Told him he'd cut his toes off one by one with the poultry shears. You remember, there was a pair in with all that kitchen stuff from Duke Ousia's baggage train."

"And?"

"Nothing," Olybrius said, clearly impressed. "Carrhasio was all for snipping some toes but we wouldn't let him. He's still in there if you want to have a try."

"Let him go," I said. "I know who sent him."

So much for all that, then; all in all, I was glad we were leaving and heading for Teuda, a dismal place but not nearly as complicated as Leal. I was furious with myself for getting besotted (that was the word I made myself use) and acting like a stupid teenager over some thin-faced girl who'd barely said ten words to me. A month on the road followed by heaving about heat-swollen corpses would set me straight again and serve me right. We all act a little crazy from time to time—

I'd finally managed to get to sleep after a lot of staring up into darkness when that idiot Gombryas woke me up. "She says she needs to talk to you," he said, grinning horribly. "She says it won't wait."

It was that sort of grin. I didn't need to ask who she was.

"I got away," she said. "I climbed out of a window onto the roof, then I lost my footing and slid the rest of the way. Is it bad?"

She'd lost a lot of skin off her palms and knees. I sent Gombryas, who'd been standing there smirking his head off, to fetch Doc Papinian. "You'll live," I said. "What the hell are you doing here?"

"I'm coming with you," she said. "To Teuda."

"Like hell you are."

I'd spoken quite loudly but she can't have heard me. "I'm not going back," she said. "I've finished with her and the whole lot of them. I hate her."

I sighed. "All daughters hate all mothers," I said, "just as all mothers hate all daughters. But only part of the time. Go home. Stop putting me in mortal peril. I don't like it."

"You've met her," she said. "Well?"

Besotted. Buy me one drink more than I can handle, and I'll explain to you, convincingly and in great detail, why love is the most harmful force in the universe. Actually it is, but I don't suppose I'll ever be able to convince you, so I'll save my breath. "Yes, all right," I said. "But you can't come with us. Where we're going it's not – nice."

She shrugged. "I was brought up in the Spider camp," she

said. "When I was ten my mother made me kill a hostage, in front of everybody, to prove I could."

"And did you?"

She nodded. "They held him still, so it wasn't difficult. When my mother tells you to do things, you do them." She breathed out slowly through her nose. "But not any more."

She'd been parted from her mother for four days. She must hate her very much.

Of course I needed a lot more data before I could make an informed decision. How many men did she have, and where? Was she strong enough to be able to come after us to Teuda? If not, did she know people who could? It wasn't a simple decision. There were so many factors to be taken into account, and a great many lives depended on it.

"Fine," I said. "You can come with us."

I had a lot to put up with on that trip, from Gombryas and Carrhasio and my so-called friends. As it turned out, the war wasn't the total dead loss I'd expected it to be. The winning side pulled off an amazing ambush in a mountain pass, wiping out an opposing force that outnumbered them four to one with remarkably little damage to property. We actually made a profit; and to celebrate, Apoina and I got married in the chapel of the Mercantile Exchange in Sphoe Theon. I don't know if you know it, poky little place, but with the remains of some rather fine Fourth Empire mosaics. As a wedding present I made her head of department responsible for saddles, bridles and horseshoes. The other heads of department acknowledged that she'd probably do a fine job. Never thought I'd say this, Gombryas said, but she's not bad at it, for a girl. Coming from him, that's the sort of accolade you want on your tombstone.

From Teuda we went straight on to another job, a useful

little border war in northern Baesia. I spent a day piling up dead bodies ready for burning, then went to look for her. "Well?" I asked.

We'd piled up all the dead horses. There are two schools of thought about the most efficient way. One way is to cut off the legs at the knee; it's a lot of work, but rather less time and effort than hauling all those half-ton corpses about, just to salvage a few horseshoes. I, on the other hand, take the view that time is money. Hacking off legs takes time, therefore costs me money. Much better to collect and stack the dead horses in such a way that you can get at the hooves without too much scrambling and heaving; only we'd never been able to figure out how to do it. It took Apoina half an hour. She stood there looking at the scattered mess, where a cavalry charge had been turned back by mass archers. It's the sort of sight that gives most people the horrors. It keeps coming back at them in their dreams, and sometimes they're never the same again. She stood and looked at it, like I just said, and I was just starting to think I'd done the wrong thing and I was about to have a basket case on my hands for the rest of my life when she turned to me and pointed out that if you stacked the horses alternately – one level with the legs sticking out one way, the next level with them sticking out the other way – the pile would be much more stable and you could do the hooves quickly and efficiently without being scared to death the whole lot was going to collapse and come crashing down on you like an avalanche.

"I'm happy," she said.

I looked at her. She was filthy with mud and other stuff you find on battlefields. "You spend your life prising the shoes off dead horses and you're happy," I said. "You're weird."

"Colybas made me a special prybar," she said. "He reckons

I need a longer handle, to make up for being a girl." A little flick with the lower hand, and off the shoe came. She picked it up and tossed it in a bucket with the others. "For the first time in my life I can be me," she said. "Of course I'm happy." She walked on her knees to the next hoof and dug the sharp lower edge of the bar into the thin line between horn and iron. "We've been over this," she said.

"I can't take yes for an answer. Thank you. It's a good line, but it doesn't really cover everything."

"It's all you're getting, so you'll just have to make do." Another shoe came loose and joined the pile in the bottom of the bucket. "What's the deal with these things, anyway? Do we straighten them out and reuse them, or do they go in the melt?"

Neither, as it happens. We sell them to the fancy shops in places like Choris, where they hammer them out into thin strips, twist them like cornstalks, heat them white hot and forge-weld them into the finest patterned steel, out of which they fashion miracles of the swordsmith's art, which rich men buy and never use. I mention it at this point because of the obvious analogy: love, friendship, besottedness, all that stuff. Why horseshoes I have no idea, but apparently nothing else is half as good.

"Ask Colybas and he'll tell you all about it," I said. "It's really boring. You say you can be you. Define you."

"I said, we've been over this." She scowled, then decided to humour me. "I can't," she said. "I can't define me, just like that. It'll take me years to figure it out. But at least I can make a start, which I couldn't when I was—" The scowl came back. "Like an eclipse," she said. "The moon covers up the sun. Actually, that's a lousy comparison."

I nodded. It was. She thought for a moment, the said, "All

right, more like an occupied country. There are foreign soldiers on every street corner and you aren't allowed to speak your own language: you've got to speak theirs. They even want you to think in it. But when you drive them out, you can start again. That's why I'm happy. Liberation."

I nodded. "Seen a few of those in my time," I said. "And over the next five years either there's a civil war or someone comes along and makes himself First Citizen, and next thing you know, taxes are higher than they were under the occupation. Liberation only lasts a week or so, and then you're back with government. I suspect it's more or less the same with happiness; it just marks the transition between different phases of misery. But I've never been happy, so I wouldn't know."

"Poor baby." She grinned at me. "Why are you trying to make me miserable?" she said.

"Out of a sense of duty," I replied. "It's what husbands do."

The grin vanished. "You mean mothers," she said. "No, screw her, I don't want to think about her any more."

"Probably best if you don't," I said.

"Quite. As far as I'm concerned, the world is divided into two sections. There's a great big one called my mother, and a much smaller one called everything else. I'd never have got away from her if you hadn't—"

"Probably not," I said. "But you're here now, so that's all right." The sun came out from behind a cloud. I felt it on the back of my head and winced. Bright sunlight isn't good for dead bodies, and we still had a lot of work to do. *You are my sunshine* isn't a compliment in my line of work. "You sure you're all right?" I asked her. "Doing this."

"Yes," she said, without hesitation. "It's so much better than anything I've ever done before. All these people are already dead, and we didn't kill them."

It didn't last, needless to say. After we'd finished in Baesia we shipped the stuff we'd collected back to Beloisa for the big twice-yearly fair, and guess who was waiting for us when we got there.

I was manning the stall, on the second day of the fair. We'd already shifted most of the stuff – the real action at a fair happens on the first day, in the hour before the main gate opens – and we were at the stage I like best, when everybody mooches round talking to the friends and enemies they haven't seen since last Beloisa Fair. I'd just been chatting with Curosh Asvogel (Is it true? Did you really get *married?*) and then Laelian Andrapodiza from the College of Vultures; Laelian and I go way back, and he'd just agreed to buy my fifty dozen unissued seven-foot spear shafts, warranted genuine cornelwood, some water damage. I was leaning back in my chair with my hands folded behind my head feeling moderately content, and then Praeclara showed up.

"Relax," was the first word she said. "I'm not going to hurt you."

Beloisa Fair is as close as I ever get to feeling safe. When I say close, I mean you can see safe from there, if you stand on a chair. "You're a long way from Leal," I pointed out.

She nodded. She was dressed for the occasion. Sartorial restraint isn't what Beloisa Fair is about. She'd gone for the Warrior Princess look that was so in that year. I don't know if you remember it: red leather, gilded chain mail, exaggerated gold pectorals and lots of flesh. You wore it if you were a middle-aged businesswoman with a lot of money to spend. "Buying?" I asked her.

"This is a good place to buy armour and weapons," she said. "We use a lot of that sort of stuff."

"Feel free to browse," I said. "And all at sensible prices."

"Actually, I'm selling." She looked at me as if I was a castle someone had built in the middle of her lawn; she didn't like it, but being realistic, there wasn't a lot she could do about it. "I suppose I ought to thank you," she said.

"Really? Why?"

"For rescuing my daughter."

"You said she was never in danger."

"From me."

"Ah." I thought for a moment, then kicked a chair in her direction. She sat down.

"It was the right thing," she said. Her sword – purely decorative, not a practical item – was digging into her armpit. She took it off and laid it on the ground. "It was good for her to leave. I'd lost my sense of perspective, I guess. I'd stopped thinking of her as my child. She was just another soldier, and not a particularly good one. And that pissed me off, because I expected her to be the best."

It was my turn; my cue to give her a mouthful, about being a monster and so forth. I've found that if you listen when it's your turn to talk, people tell you useful things. But Praeclara is as smart as me, or smarter. "Well?" she said.

I shrugged. She was dressed like that because she wanted to look ridiculous; I was supposed to underestimate her. The lion turns out to be just another mutton-dressed-as-lamb follower of fashion. "Tell you what," I said. "You can have five per cent off. Special discount for family and in-laws."

"We don't buy equipment," she said. "We take it from our dead enemies. But it was sweet of you to offer. How is she?"

"Happy," I said. "Or so she says. Personally I think she's overstating the case. Make that happier."

She nodded. "I imagine she probably is. I thought I'd miss her terribly, but instead I just miss her."

"Only yourself to blame for that," I said.

"What the hell." She stood up. I managed to override my impulses and not flinch. "You can keep her. I don't want her any more."

"That's very generous of you," I said. "Sit down, I haven't finished yet."

She looked at me, and sat down again. "Well?"

"It's what I'd do," I said. "If I were you, and I wanted her back. Let her go. Like loading a pig in a cart."

The more you drag it, the more it resists; so you drag it away from the cart, which means it backs away from you right up the ramp, and then all you have to do is slam the tailgate, next stop the slaughterhouse. She gave me a faint smile. I like it when I don't have to explain.

"I made the mistake of assuming she was me," she said at last. "Then I realised she wasn't. I love her, but she's no earthly use to me. You can have her. For now."

"Until?"

"Until she realises that all she wanted was to get away from me. You were just the getaway horse. She'll cut you loose as soon as she figures that out."

"Probably," I said. "I'm not getting my hopes up. But you never know."

She gave me a curious look, as though she'd just noticed a sixth finger on my left hand. "You really love her, don't you?"

"The word I choose is besotted," I said. "Not mine, a friend's. But it covers it quite well."

Another nod. We understood each other. "In that case I'm sorry for you," she said. "If I were you, I'd make my hay while the sun shines. But who knows, I might be wrong." She stood up again, and retrieved her stupid toy sword from the floor. "Just keep well away from Leal," she said. "Anything less than twenty miles from Leal Cross and you're a dead man. All right?"

"Fair enough," I said. "Do you want to see her? I can ask. I don't know what she'll say."

"I do, so don't bother. And I mean it. The next time I see you, you're dead."

Anyway, that's more than enough about Praeclara. She stayed away, and Apoina and I were happy for a while, until she lost the baby. Afterwards she was too sick to come with us to General Sichyon's big war in eastern Blemya. I offered to stay with her but she said no, you go, I'll be fine; a bit of time on my own will do me good. So I went to Blemya and we did good business; there was a big cavalry skirmish with plenty of dead horses, and I missed her a lot. Then, on the way home, I got a letter from my friend Gaularia. Apoina had been staying with her while I was away. Apparently she'd caught the fever and died.

Gaularia and I go way back. It was quick, she said in her letter. Did I want her stuff sent on to me at Beloisa, or should she sell it and set the proceeds off against what I owed her for rent?

That was all some time ago. I'm still here. I think that's about all I can say on that score.

And now Praeclara was on her way, with her guerrillas or disciples or whatever the hell they were, and I was expected to do what she wanted me to do, or else. I'd often wondered if she blamed me for Apoina's death. I wouldn't be at all surprised if she did. If she hadn't gone off with you, she'd never have caught the fever and died; sometimes it was Praeclara saying that inside my head, sometimes it was me; it's got so I can't tell which of us is which, and I don't suppose there's any real difference. Neither of us did much of a job of looking after her.

Water under the bridge, I told myself. What signified was that the lion was back, the only difference being that this time I was tied to a tree. Happy days.

6

"It's got to be the books," I said. "I'm working on the assumption that it's the books."

Stauracia had been giving me a hard time about being chained to the cart, reasonably enough, so I'd relented. Instead of a long chain wrapped three times round the cart axle, she now wore a short chain attached to a staple driven into a sixty-pound log, which she was free to carry about with her, cradled in her arms like a baby. This arrangement gave her back her mobility, or as much of it as was good for her, together with a degree of basic human dignity. "I'm not talking to you," she said. "You're an arsehole."

"It's *got* to be the books," I said. "I've been all over this castle, and there's nothing else."

"And you've been all over the books and they're dogshit," she pointed out. "Admit it: you're beaten. You had a good idea but it turned out to be wrong. On this occasion, your much-vaunted insight into other people's cunning schemes simply hasn't worked. You gambled everything on your theory, and it turned out to be drivel. You're just not as smart as you think you are, that's all."

Two minds with but a single thought. "I'm going to have one more look," I said. "You can come, too, if you like. Bring the log."

Up all those flights of stairs. "This is pointless," she said, as I pulled down a book at random and opened it. "We've looked, both of us. There's no scribbled marginalia, no pinpricks next to keywords for a code, nothing slid between the pages or stuck down the spines. You're barking up the wrong fucking tree, and that's all there is to it. You know what you are? Stupid."

She was sitting in the windowsill, the log balanced awkwardly in her lap. I think I must be attracted to difficult women. "I think I know where these books came from," I said.

She looked at me. "Really?"

"Yes," I said. "I think these are some or all of a load of books stolen from the Silver Apple monastery on the island of Ogyge, not long before the Sirupat thing blew up."

"Interesting. What makes you think that?"

"I was there," I said. "At least, we were the first ones on the scene after the robbery, or at least I think we were."

"I remember."

"Of course you do. The thing is, I noticed some books were missing from the library and I had a pal make a list of everything that should've been there but wasn't."

"And you've got this list with you."

"No," I said. "And my pal's dead. But a couple of the titles ring a bell; Marcian on viticulture and Thenderic's *Principles of Metallurgy*."

She nodded. "Why did they ring a bell?"

"Because there were copies of them in my dad's library at home."

And now she smiled. "Proving that they're commonplace, the sort of thing you can find anywhere. Admit it, Saevus, you're wrong. All right, these may be the books that were lifted from the Silver Apple, but so bloody what? They're still not worth having, and meanwhile a bunch of lunatics has got my son, and they're going to kill him unless you give me back this castle." She stopped talking, and a sort of pale glow lit up in her eyes. "Tell you what," she said. "You're right, of course."

"Am I?"

I don't think she's aware of the pale glow; well, why should she be? "Absolutely you're right. It must be the books; it can't be anything else. Like Saloninus says, once you've eliminated the impossible, whatever remains—"

"Yes, thank you."

"In which case," she went on, "you take the books and give me back the castle."

I looked at her. Two minds and all that; having distracted my attention with an interesting proposition, she was figuring out the geometry of throwing the log at me, knocking me out and using me as a hostage. It all depended on the length of the chain and how far away I was. I knew how long the chain was; oddly enough, it was thirty inches shorter than the distance separating us at that precise moment. But if she were to hop down from the windowsill and take a long step forward – I took a long step back.

"That way," she went on, "I get what I want, and you've got what your precious Praeclara wants, and everybody's happy. Well? How about it?"

I shook my head. "If I'm wrong, I'm screwed. If you're

wrong, you're screwed. Oh, and have you allowed for the weight of the log?"

She scowled at me. "I've got a better idea," she said. "We join forces. Your people and my people against my lot and Praeclara. We shut the gates, barricade the two rocks and let them sort things out among themselves. A nice three-cornered siege, just like Sirupat. You're good at that sort of thing, remember."

She was making my head hurt, undoubtedly on purpose. "I'm trying very hard to see things from your point of view," I told her. "Look, I've got the castle. I've achieved all my objectives. I've won. It's your stupid neck I'm trying to save. So will you please stop giving me a hard time, because it makes it difficult for me to think straight."

"Poor baby." She glared at me. "All right, take this stupid thing off me and maybe I'll consider it."

"No, because the moment I do you'll be off and away, and then I'll have you to contend with as well as everything else." I sighed. "It's not fair," I said. "I'm trying to do what's best for both of us, and you're only interested in yourself."

She shrugged. "It's not ideal, I grant you," she said. "Look, if it's any consolation, I really wish it had been the stupid books. But obviously it isn't, and meanwhile we're in the shit and I can't see a way out that includes both of us. And neither," she added, "can you. So do the decent thing for once in your life and let me go. Please. It's my son."

It had to be the books. But it couldn't be. "The hell with you," I said. "They're my friends."

"I know. It's a cruel world sometimes."

We went back down the stairs, her first, naturally. I yelled for Polycrates and Eudo. "Get the stuff ready," I said. "We're leaving."

"You what? Are you out of your—?"

"Yes," I said. "Eudo, I want you to take a couple of men and a trunk or a big box or something. Go up to the top of the tower, you know, the room I showed you. Pack up all the books and load them on the big six-wheeler cart. Pack them up carefully with plenty of straw, and look sharp about it. It's time we weren't here. Polycrates, I want a word with you. Over here."

He scowled at me. "What? And what the hell do you think you're playing at?"

I grabbed his arm and moved him out of the way. "You remember Ogyge," I said. "The Silver Apple. When we got there and the place had been ransacked?"

"Sure. What about it?"

"We got there and all the monks had gone," I said. "And whoever did it left all the gold and silver plate and the money, and all they took was a few books. Remember?"

"Of course I remember, I'm not stupid. What about it?"

"What if someone stole the books before the monastery got turned over? Did you ever consider that?"

He looked at me as if I was simple. "No," he said. "Why should I?"

I sighed. "No reason," I said. "All I'm asking is, do you remember anything that would be inconsistent with the books having been stolen before the place was raided and all the monks were herded away? It's important."

Blank stare. "No," he said. "But I wasn't paying attention, so that doesn't mean spit."

"Thank you," I said. "Now go and load the carts."

He gave me a long look, because there were no words to express what he was thinking about me at that precise moment, then stumped off to do as he'd been told. I looked round and she was where I'd left her, the log in her arms like a rich woman's lapdog. "What?" she said.

"It's the books," I told her. "It's got to be. Which means, when your lot gets here, you're going to be in so much trouble. But I can't help that. Don't say I didn't warn you."

A terrified look crossed her face. "You really think it's the books?"

"Only one way to find out," I said. "And if I'm wrong and it was the castle after all, I guess I'll have to come back and capture it." Artless shrug. "I've done it once. I can do it again. It might not be quite so ludicrously easy the second time, but that's a risk I'm prepared to take."

I think I know her. That's a weapon she can and does use against me. "If it's the books," she said, "are you going to give them to her?"

I smiled at her. "Depends," I said. "See you around."

We withdrew to our original position. I had a few preparations to make; they didn't take long. Which was just as well, because I'd only just finished them when Praeclara arrived.

She loves dramatic entrances. You can see it as a brilliantly intuitive tactician thinking outside of the box, or you can call it showing off. I find the way to deal with it is not to be surprised. Expect the unexpected, and then when it arrives it's just another day at the office. Very well, then. I'd anticipated a dramatic *coup de théâtre*; no idea what it would be, just absolutely sure there'd be one, so plan accordingly. In practice, that meant keeping it simple and, as far as possible, watertight.

I was sitting on a folding stool reading a book when there was this godawful yelling noise, coming from every side. We were surrounded. I yawned and marked my place in the book with a dock leaf. Out of the corner of my eye – over the years I've trained my peripheral vision – I saw a crowd of armed men springing out from behind trees or jumping up out of the long grass. They wore hoods and masks, and they were making as much noise as they possibly could. I figured, without actually looking, that there were roughly as many of them as there were of us; possibly slightly fewer, definitely not significantly more. Hence the amateur dramatics, to draw attention away from the fact that we weren't outnumbered—

Praeclara strode out of the ring towards me. No mask or hood for her. I kept my eyes on the book closed on my knee. "That's far enough," I said.

She stopped. The reason she stopped was a big stack of wood, all nice dry stuff, on top of which the books from the castle were neatly stacked. The wood was soaked with lamp oil. To hell with the expense; I'd used two jars of the expensive perfumed stuff, formerly the property of a political officer who'd neglected to leave before the battle started, now deceased. The stuff reeked to high heaven of violets or something such. You could smell it half a mile away. Evidently she had.

Slowly and carefully I put the book down on the ground and picked up a lantern. I opened the little window, gave the wick a gentle puff, closed the window again, rested the lantern on my knee. One little flick of the wrist would send the lantern sailing through the air. It would hit the pile of firewood and the glass would break. A good, steady archer might be able to shoot me before I had a chance to throw it, but then again he might miss, or not kill me instantly; it wasn't a shot I'd fancy taking, if I knew how much was riding on it.

I heard her sigh. "It isn't going to work," she said.

"Yes, it is."

"I've got you surrounded. There's only about an hour's worth of oil in your stupid lantern. I can wait."

The lantern had a little wire handle. I put my finger through it. "Surrounded."

"Yes. See for yourself if you don't believe me."

"I refer you to book six of the *Principia Mathematica* by Prosper of Schantz," I said. "To refresh your memory, it's the bit about concentric circles."

Very short pause, then the penny dropped, hitting her like a meteorite. Praeclara is smart, but she lacks the rigorous clarity of mind that would make her great, or terrible, if only she had it. Her greatest shortcoming in that respect is a lack of attention to detail.

"You're bluffing," she said.

I can do quite a few clever and useful things: whistling isn't one of them. So I'd forearmed myself with a little silver bell, hidden in my left sleeve. I took it out and rang it. "See for yourself," I said.

She didn't bother. If she had, she'd have seen three hundred of my men coming out from behind trees or standing up in the long grass, directly behind her lot. Attention to detail would have revealed that there were only two hundred of my boys in the camp, doing their best to look like five hundred. She's smart; where she goes wrong is in assuming that everybody else is stupid.

I stood up. "Let's talk," I said.

She breathed out through her nose. "Why is it," she said, "that you can never do as you're damn well told?"

"Conflict of interests," I said. "Here's the deal. You give me back my people, I don't burn the books. This offer is time-limited."

"You wouldn't dare."

I shook my head. "Actually, I would," I said. "There'll be a fight and some of my boys will get hurt, but all of yours will be killed. I'd like to avoid that, which is why we're talking. The word you're looking for," I added, "is yes."

Her eyes were fixed on the lantern, which is where I wanted them. I had, of course, exaggerated slightly. The strategic position I'd engineered was very much in my favour, but it was far from conclusive. If there was a fight, it could just conceivably go her way. But she wouldn't figure that out, because her attention was focused on a naked flame perilously close to a heap of flammable material. "Fuck you," she said.

"Fuck me meaning yes?"

"No." She hesitated, and I felt a sharp pang of unease. There are people in this world who don't go into a fraught confrontation with a knife hidden in the calf of their boot. Praeclara isn't one of them.

"Spit it out."

"I haven't been entirely honest with you," she said. "There's one thing I may not have mentioned."

I stood up. The main danger was that if I threw the lantern too vigorously, the wick would blow out. A gentle lob was what was needed. I mimed the backswing for a gentle lob.

"She's not dead."

It was the little wire handle that saved me. If my finger hadn't been looped through it, I'd have dropped the lantern. I stared at her. Stupidly, I'd forgotten how to talk.

"She's alive," Praeclara said. "And I know where she is."

You think you're so clever, she didn't say, so I said it for her, under my breath. I couldn't have said it out loud because my tongue had gone to sleep. Luckily she was in a chatty mood, so I wouldn't have got a word in edgeways even if I'd wanted to.

"She's not dead," she said. She took a step forward. I remembered the lantern in my right hand. She stopped where she was. "I'm afraid I lied to you."

You know what it's like – possibly you don't, in which case I envy you – when someone hits you in exactly the right spot, and all the air is forced out of your lungs, and the blood stops flowing in your head, and you're vaguely aware that you're alive, but that's about it. A sort of dumb reflex was telling me to throw the lantern if she got closer than a long double stride, but apart from that I was the proverbial blank sheet of paper.

"Your friend Gaularia," she went on, "was my friend first. She owed me a favour."

Who the hell was Gaularia? It took me a while, like a librarian who's lost the catalogue, looking for a book by going along the shelves painstakingly taking down each book in turn and squinting at the flyleaf. Gaularia: my friend in some place or other who'd promised to look after Apoina while I was away on business. She'd written me a letter telling me Apoina was dead. Got you: that Gaularia.

"You think you're so clever," Praeclara went on, "but actually you're as stupid as a little kid. You thought you could take my daughter away from me. Like I'd let you."

A little voice in the back of my head was yelling *she wants the books*. It made me realise I was still in the game. I took a long step forward, closer to the pile of firewood. It was all I could do, and it wasn't very much. She appeared to take no notice.

"So there you have it," she said. "Give me the books and I'll tell you where she is."

Pins and needles, right? First your hand or your foot or

whatever goes numb. Then, as it slowly comes back to life, it starts hurting like hell. The slightest pressure on it is agony. At that moment I was all foot. "I don't believe you," I lied.

"Why the change of heart?" She shrugged. "Let's just say she's been a big disappointment to me. For which, incidentally, I blame you. You ruined her. I thought if I could get her away from you, I could straighten her out, but apparently not. So, yes, you can have her back and the hell with it. But I want the books."

Just out of interest. "Why?"

"None of your business. I want the books."

There were various issues for me to consider at that moment, if I was to make the right decision. One of them was Polycrates. He whines all the damn time, usually with good reason. He, after all, tags along with us in the hope and expectation of making money, not out of love or loyalty to me. He'd gone along with this whole capturing-the-castle business because Gombryas and Olybrius were his friends, too. Was he likely to stand for a radical change of plan, possibly involving fighting and danger, to help me with my own purely personal problems? Him and four hundred and ninety-odd like him. Maybe, but more likely not. Quite apart from the practicalities, I was duty bound to consider his interests and point of view, and I flatter myself that if only I'd had time and the mental resources to think the thing through, I'd have done just that. But I didn't. I recognised a valid claim on me, but I had to ignore it, simply because my brain had just come back from being numb and was now packed full of very sharp spikes. "All right," I said, "let's do this sensibly. Baby steps. First, you give me back my friends. Then I put this lantern out. Then we talk."

She laughed at me. "Saevus," she said, "you're so pathetic it's almost endearing. You've lost. Give it up. Give me the books."

My head hurt so much I nearly threw the lantern then and there, just to be rid of the whole thing. She must have seen a tiny movement in my arm, the precursor to the gentle lob. "Fine," she said. "You can have your friends back. Then you give me the books. Then we talk."

Baby steps, I told myself. I transferred the lantern from my right hand to my left. This meant I could take the little silver bell from my left sleeve and ring it.

A gamble on my part, since I hadn't actually briefed my men on what to do if the bell rang a second time. But she didn't know that. I rang the bell; she assumed it was the signal for my boys to close in, disarm her goons and tie them up. She gave me a scowl that would've curdled milk. "All right," she called out, in a loud voice, slightly unsteady, "let them go."

A gap appeared in the front rank of her people, and through it some men came stumbling. I recognised Gombryas, Dodilas and Athanaric; I couldn't see the others' faces. I yelled for Polycrates, and he came pushing through the cordon with a dozen or so of my lads. They secured the hostages and marched them away, and Polycrates gave me a nod: all secure. I looked past him and saw Eudo, who also gave me a nod. I had no idea what it was supposed to signify.

"Eudo," I called out. "Get over here."

He came bounding towards me like a happy dog. "All done," he said.

"What are you talking about?"

He gave me a slightly puzzled look. "You gave the signal," he said. "So I moved in and neutralised the bad guys. That was right, wasn't it?"

I like Eudo, but I can't always anticipate what he's capable of doing. "Neutralised?"

"We came up behind them and took away their weapons." He saw me staring at him. "What? We can give them back if you want."

"No," I said quickly, "that's fine. That's marvellous. Well done. Now don't do *anything* until I tell you to."

He nodded and went back to where he'd come from. Then I looked at her. I don't think I've ever seen so much anger on a human face. "Sorry," I said, "I've changed my mind. New deal. I keep the books, you tell me where she is, your men don't get slaughtered like sheep."

A hundred fun ways of playing with fire. Still, she'd asked for it. Also, as a very bad man once said, when you have them by the balls, their hearts and minds will follow. "No deal," she said.

"Fine." Suddenly I felt very tired, and sick of her company. "In that case we'll hamstring all your men, take the books and go somewhere. I expect you'll be able to find us when you're feeling more reasonable."

If only there was a prize for making enemies. I'd win it every year. It'd look nice on my mantelpiece, if I had one, which I don't, and in a life otherwise devoid of lasting achievements it'd be something I could be proud of.

"Sorry to rush you," I said. "But fairly soon your mortal enemies will be showing up to relieve the siege. I don't suppose you'll want to be around to meet them, with no weapons and all your men trussed up like chickens. Tell me where she is and once I've verified it I'll let you have the books. Now I can't say fairer than that, can I?"

Come on, my little voice was telling me, this is Praeclara, you know she's got a third knife tucked down inside her third boot. But as usual I was out of options. "I don't trust you," she said.

"Why should you? We hate each other and I just stitched you up. But you want the books and you can't have them unless you do as you're told." I could feel my dislike of her soaking into my judgement, like broken eggs in a basket of shopping. She'd be counting on that, of course. "The hell with it," I said. "Why don't I just burn these books and slaughter all your men and get on with my life? Getting rid of you would make me feel so much better about myself."

We both know why, she didn't have to say. "Fine," she said. "The place you're looking for is a village called Deisidaemon. There's only one street. Go up the hill to the top and on your left there are two towers. You want the smaller one. Say Mimo sent you." She stopped. I waited. "That's all you're getting," she said.

"The hell with that. Where is this village?"

She smiled at me. "Two miles from another village called Cynosoura. They're both on the map."

"Which map?"

She shrugged. "The relevant map," she said. "Come on, Saevus, you're supposed to be smart."

I opened the door of the lantern and blew on the wick, making it glow. No effect on her. I could burn the books and kill her and her men; nothing to stop me except the thought of getting to Deisidaemon, wherever the hell it turned out to be, and finding nothing there. I looked at her. I know her quite well. What should have been giving me pause for thought was getting to Deisidaemon and finding something I wouldn't like one bit. The third knife, tucked into the third boot, is always going to be the sharpest, because it's the one you're most likely to end up using.

I licked the tips of my thumb and middle finger and pinched out the flame in the lantern. "Who's Mimo?" I asked.

"No idea."

"Enjoy your books," I said. "Oh, one thing I neglected to mention. My scouts tell me they saw a large body of men coming through the mountain pass the day before yesterday. About fifteen hundred, they reckon, possibly more. I'm guessing they've come to relieve the castle. They should be here by tonight, maybe early tomorrow morning." My turn to smile. "You can try and bash your way into the castle, but I wouldn't recommend it. There used to be a weak link in the defences, but I expect that's been dealt with by now. If I were you, I'd make myself scarce."

She looked at me as though I'd just stamped on her toe. "Don't believe you."

"Good," I said. "In that case, stick around. I'll enjoy watching what they do to you."

I was, of course, lying. On the balance of probabilities she knew I was lying, but there was something like a twelve per cent chance I wasn't. I can quite see why she hates me.

"Maps," I said. "Where do they have maps?"

"Fuck maps," said Polycrates. "We need to get this stuff to Beloisa and sell it. You nearly got us all killed with your stupid games. We're not going through all that again."

I didn't say anything. Neither did any of the other heads of department, gathered under a large beech tree in a forest through which passed the Southern Military Road. It was one of those trees that had been there before the forest grew up; you can tell them because their branches spread wide, like a tree in a hedge, rather than reaching up towards the light. We'd chosen it because it gave superior shelter from the rain, which was bucketing down. Polycrates looked round at the other heads. "Well?" he said. "You tell him. If he wants to go charging off on some stupid adventure, let him. We're not going."

I felt sorry for him. Here he was, trying to talk some common sense into a bunch of idiots, and they were refusing to listen, out of misguided loyalty to the man who'd just saved their lives. The fact that he was now about to get them all killed ought to outweigh their gratitude, but because they were stupid, it didn't. I think my friends the heads of department could see the force of his argument, which was why they said nothing, but he wasn't going to change anybody's mind. It must be so annoying to be right and have nobody listen to you.

"There's the military cartulary in Sosis," Eudo said, closing the book he'd been reading and slipping it into his sleeve. It looked like the same book I'd seen him with quite often over the last few days, and every time he saw me looking at it, he shoved it away out of sight. That sort of book, presumably: badly written and lots and lots of pictures. "They've got maps of pretty well everywhere."

"The what where?" asked Dodilas.

"The military cartulary," Eudo said. He's the sort of man who believes repetition constitutes explanation. "It's the biggest cartulary this side of Choris."

"Place where they store bits of paper," I said. "And you're probably right and we could be there in a week, but we'd be wasting our time. They don't let just anyone in there."

"That's all right," Eudo said, beaming. "I could go. I've got clearance."

Stunned silence, as though he'd announced he was the crown prince of Sashan in disguise. "No," I said, "you haven't."

"Yes, I have. I'm a captain in the Guards. Well, I was, but I've still got this." He fished inside his collar and brought out something on a bit of string. "And my name's still on the roll. Bound to be."

He lifted the bit of string over his head and passed me the whatever-it-was. It proved to be a lead seal, folded over the string and stamped flat. The design was a double-headed eagle, a bit the worse for wear from rubbing against Eudo's chest for God knows how long. On the back were two columns of tiny numbers. A security pass, issued to junior adjutants assigned to the general staff. I've got an oil jar full of them in a shed somewhere.

"Sorry," I said, handing it back, "but that's useless. You can buy them anywhere."

"I know that," Eudo said. "But like I said, my name's on the roll. That and a letter from General Alcidas ought to do fine."

Gombryas laughed. He's got one of Alcidas's ribs; he used to have two, but he swapped one for the nose of Marshal Droizen, preserved in honey. I waited. Eudo looked at me. "It's no bother," he said. "I was his secretary when I was a second lieutenant. I can do his handwriting, no problem."

I looked at Gombryas, who grinned. "He's dead," he said.

"Doesn't matter. The letter would still work."

Sudden thoughtful silence, which lasted until Olybrius said, "He's right, you know."

"Of course I'm right," Eudo said. "And, actually, it's perfect, because eight years ago, when I was on Alcidas's staff, if you wanted a letter from him it'd have been written by me. Pretending to be him, if you see what I mean. And all those letters were perfectly valid, or we'd have had complaints. And if they were valid then, they'd still be valid now: that's how the system operates. So anything I write now will be as good as the real thing, because to all intents and purposes—"

I raised my hand to shut him up. "Well," I said. "It's worth a try. Better than climbing in through a window."

"We could sell the stuff in Sosis," Athanaric pointed out. "There's always factors from the big combines hanging around, because of the army base." Polycrates pulled a scornful face, with good reason; if you sell that way, you tend to get no more than two-thirds of what stuff fetches at a fair. "It'd probably work out about the same as lugging it all the way to Beloisa, when you take off the shipping and the harbour dues."

Not strictly true, but nobody seemed inclined to take the point. I got an eerie feeling of people bending over backwards to be helpful, which I really hadn't expected. "Good point," I said. "And while we're there, we can see what's coming up to bid on. No reason why we shouldn't do some paying work while we're—"

I stopped, but not in time. Polycrates gave me a look that would've poisoned a river. "You're all idiots, the lot of you," he said, and stormed off.

Negativity. I seem to run into more than my fair share of it, maybe because I'm always asking people to do stupid, dangerous things they didn't sign up for. I tell myself that this isn't through my choice. Life delights in loading me down with stupid, dangerous things I didn't sign up for, and I'm simply passing them on. The way I see it, misery is like caviar or plovers' eggs. It isn't something you greedily keep to yourself. It's something you share with those you love.

I made various excuses for hanging round a mile or so from the castle; we had a long journey coming up, so it'd be a good idea to overhaul the carts – which was true, incidentally; every now and again life tricks me into telling the truth and doing the sensible thing. So we jacked the carts up on piles of stones, pulled off all the wheels, took the tyres off, cut them, shrank them and put them back on again; we repacked the hubs and fettled the axles and cut new planks to replace the split or perished boards, all the sensible things you're supposed to do but never get around to doing. We were patching the canopies, for crying out loud – when did you last patch a canopy *before* it started letting in water? – when one of the scouts came bustling up and told me there was a column of horsemen coming up the valley. A couple of hundred, he reckoned, armed but not military. I played it cool. Fine, I said. That'll be the relief column for the castle. We won't bother them and they won't bother us.

Another thing about Eudo: he's an idiot, but also a natural leader of men. It's like the old soldier's joke: his men would follow him anywhere, if only out of curiosity. In his department he'd got a hardcore of a couple of dozen men who were clearly into playing soldiers; he barked military-type orders at them and they snapped to it, almost but not quite saluting. This gave a certain degree of harmless amusement to everybody else, and I let him carry on, just in case it might be useful. It was now useful. "Eudo," I said. "Get your private army fell in. Job I want you to do for me."

Eudo likes to do things properly. He'd been through the stock and picked out twenty matching sets of everything and dressed his pet soldiers up in them. They were practically in uniform. "What's the plan?" he asked me. Note: not, what are we doing or what the hell do you think you're playing at? No. Just, what's the plan?

"We lie up in that small copse on the left of the road," I said. "Sooner or later, there'll be either a covered chaise with outriders or a small group of horsemen. We intercept them and rescue someone, trying not to kill anybody or get killed in the process."

He nodded. "Got you," he said.

Mind you, Eudo is an idiot but he's not stupid. He'd probably figured out what I was planning to do about the same time I did. I made sure everybody else had plenty of work to be getting on with, and then we slipped away and went quietly down the hill to the fortuitously placed copse.

"We need to saw through that tree there," Eudo was saying, "leaving just enough of a hinge so that when the riders show up, we can give it a little nudge and it'll fall over and block the road. Then you attack frontally with eight men while I engage them in rear echelon with the remaining twelve. How does that sound?"

I hadn't really been listening. "Aces," I said. "See to it."

It was the small group of horsemen rather than the covered chaise. I can't be right all the time. It was a big tree, and when it suddenly came screaming down and hit the deck with a loud thump, it scared the horses witless and they shied. While the riders were trying to get them back under control, we all jumped out and started pulling them out of their saddles. The horses rearing and bucking all over the place made that distinctly awkward, but in the end they did the job for us, throwing eight of the ten riders, who we promptly set on. Eudo killed the ninth in broadly defined self-defence. The tenth, keeping her seat superbly well in spite of all the fuss and having her hands chained to the saddle, was Stauracia.

"It was the least I could do," I told her, after she'd called me an arsehole and a lunatic. "If I hadn't taken the books, your employers wouldn't be pissed off with you. True, you wouldn't believe me when I told you it had to be the books . . . "

"I could have been killed," she said. "Jumping out like

that, shooting arrows everywhere. I could've been thrown off my horse. I could've been shot—" She took a deep breath and forgave me. "They should have told me it was the stupid books," she said. "How the hell was I supposed to know if they didn't tell me?"

"They didn't trust you not to walk off with them," I said. "Quite rightly so. Anyway, no harm done and you're safe now."

She shot me a furious look. "No, I'm bloody well not. I've been captured by the fucking enemy."

"What? Oh, you mean me." I made a sort of vague gesture. "In a sense, yes. But that's all water under the bridge as far as I'm concerned. Look at it this way," I said, talking over her protests. "You made a bad judgement call, you lost, they were sending you back to HQ to be found guilty and executed. Luckily for you, you had a friend who was prepared to put himself out to save your life."

She looked at me. "What do you want?" she said.

"I was coming to that."

Time to go. Our beautifully maintained carts made good progress on the road, with me looking over my shoulder every two minutes in case we were being chased by a couple of hundred angry cavalrymen. That was bad luck; I'd been anticipating foot soldiers because what sort of an idiot sends cavalry to relieve and reinforce a garrison? If they'd come after us we'd have had a bit of a scrap and people would've got hurt. Luckily, Stauracia's head on a pike wasn't sufficiently important to them to be worth the effort.

"We've got a plan, naturally," I told her, as we rode together on the lead cart, "but it involves my man Eudo and he's an idiot. Also, I don't altogether trust him."

"You don't? Fancy that. He's the tall one with the weak chin, isn't he?"

"He reckons he can just stroll into the cartulary using his old military ID," I said. "I think that's highly unlikely. But that's fine. If he succeeds, I'll know for a fact he's up to something. If he fails, I'll be rid of him, problem solved. Meanwhile, I need a proper plan. One that'll work."

She gave me a sour look. "Involving me."

I nodded. "Simple little job," I said, "won't take you very long. And then you'll be free as a bird and you can go about your business."

"I don't like it," she said. "If it all goes wrong, I'm going to be left with my leg in a bear trap. Couldn't you just burgle the place or something? Much easier."

"No."

I could understand her attitude. As far as she was concerned, things weren't going well for her. She'd screwed up her mission so she wasn't going to get paid. Her crew, who she'd always looked out for and trusted (up to a point), had deserted her and gone over to the bad guys on the paper-thin pretext that she'd made a series of disastrous mistakes and nearly got them all killed (my heart really did bleed for her on that score) and, besides, they hadn't been paid for six months ... She was alone in the world with nowhere to go and no goons to do her bidding, and I was asking her to do something stupid and dangerous, simply because I'd got her out of the ghastly mess I'd got her into in the first place. Fair enough. I didn't expect gratitude. In fact, the only thing I could offer her was summed up in the two words *or else*. Even so.

"I need your help," I said. "Please?"

"Go fuck yourself," she said. "Look, have you been listening to a single word I've said? Those maniacs have got my son."

I sighed. "While we're on the subject," I said. "Your son. How old is he?"

"Four. Why?"

"Thought so." I paused, relaxed my shoulders, took a deep breath and let it go slowly. "You forget, I know quite a bit about you. Four years and nine months ago you were six months into a life sentence for dealing in counterfeit currency in Oudei City. You managed to wangle a pardon, and here you are now without a stain on your character, but the fact remains. Four years and nine months ago you were in an all-female prison on a rock in the middle of the sea. Barring immaculate conception, I don't see how it's possible."

She closed her eyes. I think she was trying to turn on the tears, but she was too angry for that to work. "Fine," she said. "It's not my son, it's my nephew. But he's all the family I've got left."

I shook my head. "You have one surviving sister," I said. "Three children, all girls. One of them's married to a corn chandler in Zeugma, one of them works in a cathouse in Busta Sagittarum and the third—"

"All *right*." She gave me a scowl that nearly broke my heart. "They were going to pay me a great deal of money. And you were involved, and I know you're a soft touch. It's what you'd have done."

"Absolutely not. You know my family history. You'd never have believed me."

"Saevus, I really need that money." She paused, as her mental librarians consulted the catalogue of lies: twelve massive volumes bound in tooled leather and chained to the desk. "It was my chance to get out," she said. "Retire. Stop doing this ridiculous stuff. Maybe even live to be forty."

I nodded. "But they neglected to tell you it was the books, because if you'd known, of course you'd have stolen them. Some people."

Just after the Sirupat business, I'd robbed her of half a million staurata. That was the bounty she could have got for me if she'd turned me in, but she didn't. Morally, therefore, I owe her that half-million, plus interest. It's a debt I take seriously. If only she'd said that in the first place, we'd have understood each other. "I never seem to win," she said. "I don't know why. I create the most amazing opportunities, and then you come along and they go all to pieces, like picking up a sheet of thin, wet paper. You just keep on doing it to me."

"I'm sorry," I said.

"Oh, you don't do it on purpose," she said. "You don't set out to screw up my life, it just happens. It's sad, though. All I ask out of life is the one really big score, that's all. Just one really good hit, and then I'll settle down and be good and not be a nuisance to anybody. That's not too much to ask, is it?"

"Certainly not," I said.

We rode on in silence for a while. Then she said, "So, what's all this about?"

I told her. It took a bit of time. When I'd finished, she turned a stone-cold face to me and said, "You want her back."

"Yes."

"What in God's name makes you think she'll want you, after all this time?"

I told her what Praeclara had told me, shortly before we parted. While I was away on business, Praeclara had gone to visit her daughter at our mutual friend Gaularia's house. She'd told Apoina that I wasn't coming back. I'd found someone else. She had proof. She had witnesses.

"Did she?" Stauracia asked.

"No. It was all lies."

"Really? Of course, you would say that."

"She told Apoina the other woman's name. It was you."

She went bright red. "All lies, then."

"Exactly. But her witnesses must've been convincing. She told my wife that now I'd found you, the next thing I'd need to do was kill her. Apparently you insisted on that."

She didn't say anything. Language is useful but often inadequate.

"So Praeclara arranged a new life and a new identity for her in Deisidaemon—"

"Where?"

"Good question. And now she's living there, with my daughter, firmly convinced that I want her dead so you and I can be together. According to Praeclara. Who may well be lying, but I've got to *know*. If that makes any kind of sense."

She looked as though I'd just slapped her across the face. "It sounds like a trap to me," she said.

"Of course it's a bloody trap." I hadn't meant to shout, or swear. "Yes," I said, "I think you're probably right. Praeclara wouldn't tell me something like that just to get a load of books, even if they're worth a million staurata. But there's a ring through my nose and she's got a rope tied to it. I don't see what else I can do."

"Forget about it," Stauracia said. "Forget the whole stupid thing. Get on with your life. Help me get hold of those stupid books and make the big score. Fifty-fifty, on my word of honour. I mean it."

Something in the way she said it made me catch my breath. "That would be the sensible thing to do," I said. "Unfortunately, I'm an idiot. Can't be helped, it's just the way

I am." I hesitated. For some reason I didn't like what I was about to say. "I'm not asking you to come to Deisidaemon," I said; "Just help me to find out where it is."

"Thanks a lot." She closed her eyes, then opened them again. "Funny how things work out. I was in Sosis only recently. I got offered a job."

"Really?"

She nodded. "Abbess of the Iron Rose priory. They own forty thousand acres of prime arable land, two copper mines and the biggest rosewater distillery outside of Mezentia. My job would've included keeping the books. But I turned it down."

"Ah. Because of the big score."

"Precisely."

I nodded. "Still," I said, "it was nice to have been asked."

That got me a foul look and stony silence as far as Baul Cross. No bad thing.

"I don't get it," Eudo said, reasonably enough. "You want to go with my idea, but you're sending her in as well."

"That's the plan," I said. "Two bites of the cherry."

He looked confused, but I didn't mind that. "You're the boss," he said. "I've written the letter." He pulled a thin brass tube out of his sleeve. It was an old tube, polished mirror-bright by constantly rubbing against cloth in someone's knapsack, and the embossed decoration was mostly worn away. "I used old parchment," he went on. "I bought a bundle of old letters in the market and scraped one down and went over it with sand. They reuse parchment in the military until it's so thin, the ink soaks into it like a sponge."

He insisted on showing me his handiwork. "Shouldn't there be a seal?" I pointed out.

"Properly speaking, yes. So I tore the end, look, where the seal ought to be. It happens all the time and nobody cares."

Shocking. Your tax money at work. "Very nice," I said. "Right, you know what you're looking for."

A brisk nod saves words. "Deisidaemon, location of. Now there should be a general gazetteer in the catalogue room, which'll tell me which map to look at in which archive. Of course, there could be more than one place called Deisidaemon, in which case I cross-verify by looking for an adjoining village called—" He paused and glanced down at the palm of his hand. "Cynosoura. If I can, I'll draw a sketch, though you're not supposed to without prior written authorisation. It'll depend on whether there's an archivist on duty in that particular room at that particular moment. Probably not, but you can't be sure. If there is, I'll memorise it thoroughly."

"You do that," I said. "All right, carry on."

He'd dressed the part to perfection. It helped that we'd picked up several hundred as-issued pourpoints, only one unlucky owner, at the last battlefield. He went through them and chose the one with exactly the right degree of use and staining for the character he'd invented for himself; ditto officer's cloak, cavalry breeches and ammunition boots bulled to a blinding sheen. In an army base he'd be so normal as to be practically invisible. "Your hair's too long," I told him.

"You what?"

"Think about it. You've been on active service for months, what's the first thing you do when you get back to civilisation?"

He nodded gravely. "You're absolutely right," he said. "I'll find a barber's shop on my way to the base."

Stauracia had also prepared thoroughly. She'd spent ninety gulden of my money on a snow-white floor-length gown with ruffed sleeves, which together with the wreath of white roses in her hair made her look like one of the angels in an Assumption. No rings, earrings or jewellery of any kind, no rouge or eye shadow. Luckily, she can get away with it. "You'll be fine," I said. "Knock 'em dead."

So Sister Stauracia asked the cartulary commandant for a few minutes of his valuable time. He was delighted to oblige the army's favourite angel of mercy, and she was in. Four hours later she came out again with a little metal tube: silver, not brass. "Piece of cake," she said.

"Told you."

"Only," she went on, "the commandant was a bit puzzled why I wanted to know about a place a hundred and seventy miles the wrong side of the Hetsuan border."

One of those moments. "You what?"

She pulled a bit of paper out of the tube. "See for yourself," she said.

I got shot once: did I ever tell you? My own silly fault. I was on a job; we'd just arrived at the battlefield; I went ahead to check it out. It was cold, so I grabbed the first coat that came to hand. It proved to be an Aelian officer's greatcoat, and the battle had been a major victory for the Aelians against the Aram Chantat. A wounded Aram trapped under his dead horse took me for one of the bad guys and shot me. The arrow hit a rib, which according to Doc Papinian is why I'm still alive; an inch to the left, et cetera. I can clearly remember the shock, which is like absolutely nothing else. No, belay that. There is one thing that's very much like getting shot. Namely, hearing that your next destination is in Hetsuan.

Nobody knows anything about the Hetsuan Confederacy

because nobody's been there; or, more accurately, nobody's been there and come back. About fifteen hundred years ago, the Hetsuan arrived in an endless caravan of ox carts. They came from somewhere north-east, they were starving and desperate, every man's hand was against them and all they wanted was somewhere to go. The generally accepted view is that they picked up the habit of cannibalism on the Great Trek, out of necessity, and once they'd found their new home they carried on with it, either because it had acquired a strong degree of cultural symbolism or because they liked the taste. Everyone who's studied the very little we know about the Hetsuan agrees that they're not savages; perish the thought. They're the heirs of a rich and mature civilisation, forced by circumstances to abandon their homeland and heritage and do the best they could in an implacably hostile world. More sinned against than sinning, is the scholarly consensus, by a ratio of roughly 51:49.

The Hetsuan live a long way away and since their arrival they've shown no interest whatsoever in expanding their territory, which is why you and I can sleep at night. One thing we do know about them is their language: they're basically Sashan-speaking, like our dignified neighbours to the south-east of the Friendly Sea.

There are slight variations in dialect. One of them is to do with strangers. In Hetsuan, foreigner belongs to the subset of linguistic terms that differentiate living things from food. For example, we talk about sheep, pigs, cows, deer and chickens when they're alive, but mutton, pork, beef, venison and poultry when they're for dinner. In Sashan, stranger and foreigner are the same word but pronounced with a different tone. Stranger in the Hetsuan dialect means someone you haven't met before.

Foreigner means something best served with lentils on a bed of wild rice.

I'd hired warehouse space for the stock. Actual warehouses are at a premium in Sosis and they want you to pay silly money, so I opted for a derelict tannery instead. There were two long sheds next to what used to be the tanks, which stank to high heaven, and we piled the stuff in there and hoped it wouldn't rain. There was a third shed with only a vague memory of a roof. We pitched our tents in it. Sosis is an expensive town.

Eudo came back – ah well – in a state of high excitement. "You'll never guess where Deisidaemon is," he said.

I proved him wrong. He looked at me.

"Well, anyway," he said, nobly masking his annoyance, "while I was there I pulled the latest dossier on the Hetsuan and made a few notes. Actually, we know rather more about them than we let on."

I really wish I could like Eudo more than I do. "Brilliant," I said. Then (an afterthought is better than no thought at all), "You got on all right, then. No problems with the pass or anything?"

"What? No, piece of cake. I told you they'd go for it. I know how their minds work." He paused and looked at me again. "You're not seriously thinking about going there, are you?"

"Depends," I said. "What did you find out?"

We know more about the Hetsuan than we did, Eudo said, because about fifty years ago the Serica, an offshoot of the Aram no Vei, got sucked into a border dispute with them; realising that they'd made a serious mistake, the Serica appealed for help to their allies the Sashan. The Sashan refused, but not before they'd got as much information as they could out of the

Serica, who subsequently lost the war and were exterminated; these days there's about two dozen of them living in a valley somewhere deep in Sashan territory, and that's it. Anyway, some clerk copied out the report and sold it to someone, who sold it to someone else, and after a considerable sum of money had changed hands a copy ended up in the archives at Sosis, where it's been kept very quiet, for reasons that should become obvious.

The main things to bear in mind about the Hetsuan, according to the report, are that they're a deeply spiritual people, and there are a lot of them. An exact figure is hard to arrive at. The Serica encountered them nearly two generations ago and their mathematics was of the one-two-three-lots variety; the report gave a figure of ten thousand times ten thousand, which happens to scan a perfect dactylic hexameter in Aram and is used in their epic poetry to convey any number greater than forty. Anyway, the Hetsuan are a numerous people, and their territory is extensive.

Their deep spirituality takes the form of being in tune with nature (they use the same word to mean God). They believe in reincarnation, a process that applies to all animals (defined as creatures capable of moving themselves from one place to another); consequently, with one notable exception, they follow a strictly vegetarian diet. The cycle of reincarnation, they believe, is broken when a human being (not a lower animal) eats and digests flesh; essentially, what happens is that the soul of the eaten gets turned into shit – the Hetsuan are passionate about cleanliness and hygiene   and is lost for ever. If you eat a sheep or a fish, you may well be destroying the soul of your mother.

But the Hetsuan have a vindictive streak. The Sashan

officials who transcribed the report speculated in comments in the margin that this probably derived from their experiences during what the Hetsuan call the Great Trek, their traumatic emigration from wherever the hell they came from to where they live now. During the Trek they got no help from any of the people whose territory they passed through; they were attacked, shot at, moved on with extreme prejudice; crops were burned and wells deliberately stopped up in attempts to starve and parch them to extinction; they had to fight literally every step of the way. This made them into exceptionally efficient fighters, a tradition they have since maintained, and left them with a jaundiced view of everyone who isn't Hetsuan. A fundamental credo in their society is that the good man loves his friends and hates his enemies. Accordingly, no Hetsuan ever goes hungry or lacks shelter; they are the most benevolent and egalitarian nation on record, according to the Sashan scribes. By the same token, their rage against their enemies knows no bounds. And, since the worst thing you can do to an enemy is to kill his soul, they eat them.

Only their enemies. Cows, pigs, sheep and chickens are not the enemy. Murderers, rapists, traitors, blasphemers, heretics and foreigners are. Just as you gain a reward in Heaven for nursing a leper and giving a tithe of your income to the widow and the orphan, you earn absolution for all your sins by turning an enemy's soul into shit through the wondrous alchemy of the digestive tract.

A system that offers complete remission of sins in return for a simple act is, of course, open to abuse, so there are rigidly enforced checks and balances. Their legal system, for example, is scrupulously fair, to make sure that innocent people aren't convicted of capital crimes simply in order to provide a supply of soul food. Likewise, a declaration of war can only be made by both kings (they have a dual monarchy) and has to be endorsed by all three chambers of the popular assembly with a majority of not less than seventy-five per cent. Even then, it can still be vetoed at any stage by the college of priests, and requires a positive omen from both of the Great Oracles, situated at opposite ends of the country. It takes at least a year to start a war, during which time most diplomatic emergencies tend to have worked themselves out. Furthermore, a king who proposes a war which is not approved by the people and the church is guilty *ipso facto* of treason, leading to death and the casserole dish. The Sashan archives record only fourteen instances in fifteen hundred years when the Hetsuan have gone to war, the elimination of the Serica being the most recent. They won all their wars, and their opponents no longer exist.

The Hetsuan have the highest standard of living of any nation this side of Echmen and the highest proportion of adult literacy. Life expectancy is eight years longer than in the Sashan Empire, therefore fifteen more than in the West. Their closed-border policy means they've never experienced the plague or most of the epidemic diseases that sweep through the rest of the world from time to time, killing millions. Next to nothing is known about their literature, art, religion or philosophy, except that all of these elements are very highly prized in Hetsuan society, and the handful of Hetsuan artefacts that have drifted across the borders over the last fifteen centuries are uniformly exquisite in design and excellent in function. The Echmen emperor drinks his noonday tea from a Hetsuan porcelain bowl; entirely plain and unadorned, its perfect form makes it the most beautiful object in the Empire, and the emperor himself washes and dries it after use because nobody else is worthy to touch it.

Being a foreigner is a capital offence, strict liability, anywhere in Hetsuan territory. Because of the highly integrated and benevolent nature of the society, foreigners are very easy to identify. Everyone in a Hetsuan community knows everyone else, and there are no beggars, vagrants or refugees. Merchants and government officials travel freely throughout the country, but the settled nature of society and the fact that trades and professions are hereditary means that they are rarely strangers in the places they go to; a newly appointed official will make his first visit accompanied by his predecessor, and a merchant will introduce his sons and daughters to his regular customers as soon as they're old enough to accompany him on his rounds. There's no Hetsuan equivalent of the bands of wandering lepers and lunatics we're used to west of the Friendly Sea; it's a solemn duty in Hetsuan to look after the physically and mentally ill. There are no gangs of seasonal labourers roaming the countryside, and slavery is both illegal and impractical in a country where there are no outsiders to enslave. Consequently, any foreigner rash enough to attempt to infiltrate the Confederacy is quickly detected, restrained and eaten. The number of defectors who have voluntarily left Hetsuan can be counted on the fingers of one hand; leaving the country is by definition treasonable, and, besides, nobody wants to.

"Which means," Eudo concluded, "that you're screwed. Well, doesn't it?"

Hard to argue with that. "Not necessarily," I said. "There's bound to be a way, if we apply our minds."

"Besides," Stauracia pointed out, "surely it means Praeclara was lying. Your stupid ex can't be living in Hetsuan because if she'd gone there she'd have been eaten as soon as she crossed the border. This is just Praeclara trying to get you killed."

I shook my head. "I don't think so," I said. "I think that's where she is. And if she got there, so can I."

"Hang on," Stauracia said. "If nothing's known about this godawful place, how come Deisidaemon is on the map?"

"Ah," Eudo said, and that quiet plonking tone came back into his voice. "It's a very old map. Or at least it isn't, but it's copied from one. Deisidaemon was the name of the village fifteen hundred years ago, before the Hetsuan arrived. As there's been no new information since then, the current maps are just the old ones traced over dozens and dozens of times. I don't suppose Deisidaemon is called that now, assuming it still exists."

"That's mad," Stauracia burst out. "There isn't even a village. You're talking about trying to get to a place that was probably burned down fifteen hundred years ago. Come on, Saevus, use your tiny brain. It's a trap. She wants you to get eaten: that's all there is to it."

"Yes, I imagine so," I said. "But not straight away. I'm fairly sure she wants me to do something first."

"Do what?"

Big shrug. "I expect I'll find out when I get there."

7

There's a Sashan consulate in Sosis, as you'd expect in a town whose function is mostly military. Its purpose is to provide a secure base where Sashan spies can deliver their reports and seek sanctuary if they're detected. By the same token, the Western nations have consulates in all the equivalent Sashan army towns. Every now and again someone makes a fuss, all the diplomats are expelled and sent home and new ones come out to take their place. Nobody minds; it's a stressful posting, so it's a comfort to know you won't be stuck there indefinitely.

I didn't know anyone in the consulate, but Peros Asvogel had a couple of contacts there, as he'd gloatingly pointed out to me when he beat me out of a potentially lucrative deal. I didn't say anything at the time, mostly because as he was telling me all about it I was stealing his personal seal. It had slipped out of his purse when he paid for the round of drinks he'd bought to celebrate cheating me, and my hand somehow came to rest on top of it. The loss wouldn't have inconvenienced him greatly – he had four identical seals made, one for him, three for his secretaries – and I could foresee circumstances where such a thing could come in handy. Clever me.

I wrote myself a letter of introduction, sealed it and sent it to the deputy chief political officer, who Peros had mentioned by name. Back came an appointment and a sealed pass, leading me to speculate what Peros had done to merit such high favour. I washed my face, brushed my hair, polished my shoes and went to see the deputy consul.

I remember learning Sashan as a kid and thinking to myself that it was stupid cramming my head with a language I'd never use when I could be outside in the sunshine collecting beetles in a jar. It's a difficult language, and anything you say in it comes out like someone shouting. "My pleasure," the deputy consul replied in flawless Aelian. "Anything to help a friend of Peros Asvogel. What can I do for you?"

"I need to go to Hetsuan."

He smiled. "Seriously, though. How can I help you?"

"I need to go to Hetsuan," I said. "To be precise, a little village that used to be called Deisidaemon about a thousand years ago, though what it's called now I have no idea—"

"I know where you mean," he said quietly.

My mouth was still open, with a view to finishing some sentence or other. It took me a moment to pull myself together, then I said, "You do?"

He nodded. "But it's impossible," he said. "Sorry, but there it is."

I was still too shocked to be able to think, and I needed my brain to be working at full capacity. "So you know what it's called now?"

He was a man of about thirty, good-natured and

good-looking. It clearly gave him no pleasure to be so negative. "Obviously," he said. "And obviously I can't tell you. But
really, that's beside the point. You'd never get there. I'd never
get there, not if I had ambassadorial credentials sealed by the
emperor. You know the score, you must do if you're a friend of
Peros. Nobody gets in and nobody leaves. It's one of the few
immutable laws of the universe."

"My wife got there," I said. "Safely."

"Your *wife*." He gave me a blank look. "Really?"

"Really. And if she could, so can I."

His face said I-don't-want-to-know more clearly than language ever could. "In that case, bloody good luck to you. I don't
think I can help you, though. I'm sorry."

It was at that point that I realised that I had no leverage
whatsoever. "I understand. That's fine," I said. "Peros told me
I'd be wasting my time, and now I've wasted yours. Of course,"
I added, "that's not the only thing he told me."

The good-natured young man gave me an evil look. "Is
that right?"

I nodded. "Peros used to owe me a substantial amount of
money," I said. "I told him he could forget about it, in exchange
for a bit of help with the Sashan authorities." I stood up. "I'm
not quite sure who the appropriate person to go to would be,"
I said. "I'm guessing that if I wrote to the embassy in Choris,
telling them what Peros told me, they'd see to it that the information percolated through to the right desk."

Silence. It occurred to me that I'd just cost Peros Asvogel
a useful contact and possibly a personal friend. Ah well.
Omelettes and eggs. "Sit down," said the good-natured
young man.

"Thank you."

Sashan officials keep a bowl on their desks, containing strips of clay soaking in water. When they want to write something they take a strip, dab it dry with a fluffy white cloth, and prick the message onto it with a sharpened reed. The idea is that you then take your strip of clay down into the basement, where there's a furnace roaring away day and night, and the man there puts your clay in to bake and you call back for it in the morning. I wasn't planning on coming back, so when he handed me a bit of clay with some little wedges poked into it, I glanced at it, memorised the name, scrunched it into a ball and dropped it back in the bowl. "You're sure about that?" I said.

His face, admirably suited to nonverbal communication, told me not to push my luck. "Thank you," I said, and left.

To make sure I didn't forget the name between leaving his office and getting back to the tannery, I scratched it on my forearm with a brooch pin. By the time I got back my shirt sleeve was soaked in blood, but you can't be too careful.

"How did you know Peros Asvogel was blackmailing him?" Eudo asked.

"I didn't. I guessed." I dabbed the blood away with a towel. "Anyway, now I know where I'm headed for, which is nice."

Eudo peered down at my arm. "Nidons."

"Midons," I said. "That's an M."

"Oh. Are you sure?"

"Midons." I'd been repeating the words over and over, ever since the good-natured man's door closed behind me. "Don't confuse me. Anyhow, it's none of your business."

He frowned at me. "Didn't it strike you as odd," he said, "that he knew the name, straight off, just like that?"

"Now you mention it." I'd pressed harder with the pin than

I'd intended. A permanent scar might be inconvenient, at some point in a future I almost certainly wasn't going to have. "Please go away," I said. "I've got a lot to think about."

I didn't get the chance. "So you're back," she said. "Dear God. What happened to you?"

"Cut myself on a pin."

"What did you find out?"

"The new name of the village," I said. "Also, the Sashan are deeply involved with the Hetsuan at some level, so much so that even a junior intelligence officer knows about it. Oh, and the Asvogel boys are going to be very angry with me quite soon."

She shrugged. "Not that it matters," she said. "After all, you aren't going to Hetsuan."

"Yes, I am."

She rolled her eyes. "Lunatic," she said. "You need to put vinegar on that before it gets infected."

Eudo had been quite right. It did strike me as odd. The thing about Sosis is, everybody working as a diplomat there is obviously a spy, at some level. Peros's friend had, however, been there some time, because it was at least eighteen months since the Asvogels had had a major contract in those parts. Accordingly, Peros's friend hadn't just arrived from another posting where whatever it was about the Hetsuan was common knowledge; it was therefore likely that he'd heard about it while he was posted to Sosis – which meant a general all-branches memo at the very least, something that the whole of the Sashan intelligence service needed to know about, at every level. Something, therefore, big.

I paused to speculate about what Peros could have had on the good-natured young man that was so dreadful that he was

prepared to pass on something that big to a stranger . . . Not
my problem, and I had plenty of problems of my own to deal
with. But if the Sashan were involved in Hetsuan there had to
be an avenue of communication of some sort. Your *wife*, the
good-natured man had said. Now you could just conceivably
parse that as meaning *you mean she's your wife* . . . suggesting
that Sashan intelligence knew about the existence of a woman
who was involved in Hetsuan – in which case, maybe I'd
given the good-natured young man rather more than I'd taken
away. Maybe at that precise moment he was busy with a strip
of clay and his little bit of reed, stabbing a message he'd take
personally to the bakehouse: *She's married to a man called
Saevus Corax. What do we know about him?* To which the
answer would be—

The thought that you might suddenly be of interest to
Sashan intelligence isn't a comfortable one, but comfort is
overrated if you ask me. I don't mind sitting cramped up on top
of a stack of barrels if it means getting a ride to where I want
to go. It occurred to me that if I stayed put and didn't mind
getting jostled about a bit, the Sashan might be along quite
soon to offer me a lift.

I came back from a meeting with Auxiliary Services Area
Command, who turned out to be a young man with a turkey
neck and his old, fat, cunning clerk. They sold me the rights
to a tiny little war, only they didn't call it that; they called it a
limited scope police intervention, somewhere up in the mountains on the south-western shore of the Friendly Sea. I paid silly
money for it, because it was the only action happening right
now that wasn't already bought and paid for. A map came with
it, absolutely free.

"Gombryas and Polycrates," I said, "you'll be in charge. It should be just in and out, get the stuff, cart it down to the nearest port, which is here—" I prodded the free map "—and then it's two days sail to Beloisa. I hope I'll be there to meet you but, if I'm not, you can handle selling the stuff, I'm sure. It's a nice little job; you two can do it in your sleep."

They stared at me. "You're going," Gombryas said.

"Yes."

"You're out of your tiny mind," Polycrates said.

"Yes. Look, the result's a foregone conclusion so I haven't bothered trying to contact the other side, but if by some miraculous chance they should win, don't bother trying to do a deal with them, just come straight home and we'll just have to swallow the loss." I paused. "I think that's everything," I said. "You two know the score. Don't try and be clever and everything should go just fine."

Long, awkward silence. Dodilas hadn't touched his beer, and Olybrius's mouth was hanging open like a gallows in the wind. "I'm coming with you," Carrhasio said.

Carrhasio, let it be noted, likes to fight. He must be sixty-seven if he's a day and his back is a mess, which is why he heads the team that pulls rings off dead fingers and earrings from dead ears; no heavy lifting. But he still yearns for the thrill of cutting into living flesh, the way a thirsty man yearns for water. "No, you're not," I said. "You're too old; you'd be a liability. Besides, I need you with the team, in case there's any trouble. Thank you, though," I added. "It was a sweet thought."

Polycrates pointed at Eudo. "What about him?"

"He's coming with me," I said. "But only as far as the border. Look, since you're doing this one without me, I won't be taking my share, obviously. Split it up among yourselves, the usual proportions. Be good, be safe, and I'll see you in Beloisa."

I like it when people are too stunned to argue. It means they don't argue.

Next. "I'm not going," she said. "No way in hell."

"Yes, you are," I said. "But only as far as the border. I need someone I can rely on."

She stared at me, then burst out laughing. "You what?"

"Straight up," I said. "I need you to stop Eudo cutting my throat in my sleep. I think that may be a very real possibility. Either that or selling me to someone who doesn't like me."

"Then why take him, for crying out loud?"

"He's involved," I said. "I have no idea how or why, but he is, I know it. And the way he just slid into the army base confirms it. I don't know any details, but I'm pretty sure he doesn't have my best interests at heart."

"And I do, I suppose."

I smiled at her. "Your gang's been captured," I said. "You have no money and no way of getting home unless I lend you some. Your late employers want you crucified, and you're not exactly hard to notice. I'd say that means you need to stick close to your friends for a while. Sorry, make that friend. You only have one."

"And whose fault—" She decided not to bother saying it. "This is really stupid," she said. "Why don't I tag along with Gombryas and the boys? I know the work. I can make myself useful."

I shook my head. "Absolutely not," I said. "When I want to retire I'll sell the business, not give it away. Besides, you owe me."

She breathed out through her nose. "Arsehole," she said, which in her dialect means something like, Oh, all right then.

We were all headed in the same direction for the first forty miles or so; then the three of us would be taking the Northern Trunk, while Gombryas and the lads would stay on the Great East as far as Eutechne. Two days out of Sosis, we camped for the night in the ruins of an old priory. I waited till they were all asleep, then woke up Eudo first, then Carrhasio, then Eudo's squad of wannabe soldiers. "It'll be tonight," I explained to them. "This is just the right sort of place, and they won't want to go much further."

I was right. Shortly after midnight the moon went in behind the clouds, and not long after that we heard the unmistakable sound of very frightened men trying not to make a noise. I sent Carrhasio and six men round to the left, and Eudo with the rest of them off to the right. I stayed where I was, just in case there was any fighting.

But there wasn't, much to Carrhasio's disappointment. He did get to cut two fingers off someone's hand, but the enemy surrendered immediately after that. People can be so inconsiderate.

We woke up the rest of the boys, issued spears and posted sentries, just in case there were any more bad people out there. Then we lit a big fire, so I could see what I was doing, and I settled down for another cosy chat with my mother-in-law.

"I saw you coming," I explained. "You followed us from Sosis. You're really hopeless, you know that?"

Her fifteen men-at-arms were terrified, as well they might be with Carrhasio glowering at them. But she was just plain furious.

"You bastard," she said. "Where is it?"

I wasn't sure I followed.

"You cheated me," she said. "I want it. I want it *now*."

"You're not making any sense," I said. "What do you want?"

Sticks and stones may break my bones, and have on several occasions, but looks can never hurt me. This didn't stop her trying. "You know what I—"

"No, I *don't*." There now, she'd made me raise my voice, something I don't care to do. It makes me sound squeaky and shrill, instead of my usual soft, gravelly purr. "Honestly. I haven't got the faintest idea what you're talking about."

Another furious glare, then total bewilderment. "You don't, do you?"

Sigh. "No."

"The book," she said. "I want the book."

"I gave you all the books."

"No, you *didn't*." She closed her eyes. A world with me in it was intolerable, but she had to do her best, for the sake of the Cause. "The book I need wasn't there."

"Are you sure?" I said, but only to annoy her. "All right, what's it called? What does it look like?"

"About yay big." She shaped the size of a brick, then pinched an inch. "Dark brown, a bit tatty, there used to be a thin line of gold tooling round the edges but it wore off long since. *Concerning Textiles* by Deudel Agrippa."

"Never heard of it," I said. "And most of the books in the stash looked like that."

She sighed, breathing out a considerable volume of air. Suddenly she looked old, a thing she'd never done before. "Shit," she said. "You're telling the truth, aren't you?"

I nodded. "We went through the books several times," I

said. "We were trying to find out what was so special about them. I don't remember one called that." I turned to Stauracia, who'd been sitting there motionless, apart from her ears flapping. "Do you?"

She shook her head. "There was a *Practical Guide to Carpet Making*," she said. "But it was by someone else."

That got her an evil look, and she went back to sitting still. "That's it, then," Praeclara said. "I've been had for an idiot. It was never even fucking *there*."

I was feverishly trying to think. *Concerning Textiles*, for crying out loud. I strained my mental ear for the very faintest tinkle of a bell, but nothing came. "Sorry," I said. "It looks like you've been wasting your time."

She gave me an agonised look. "It does, rather. Those arseholes played me, and I fell for it."

I saw an opportunity to glean data. "Out of interest, which arseholes?"

She nodded at Stauracia. "Ask her."

"I did. She says she doesn't know them from a hole in the ground."

"Quite true," Stauracia put in. "They said I didn't need to know who they were or what they were about, just so long as I did the job."

"And now they're pissed at her and want to hang her," I said, "so it might be helpful to know something about them, just so she can keep out of their way. Isn't that right?"

"Yes," Stauracia said. "I don't even know what they call themselves."

Praeclara sighed. "I can tell you that," she said. "They're the Rose Revived, and they want to sweep away all existing hierarchies, abolish established religion and redistribute the land among the serfs and tenant farmers. Only they don't," she added savagely. "Really they're just a bunch of renegades and criminals, using the Cause as a blind for extortion and theft. They're thugs and heretics, and one of these days I'm going to wipe them off the face of the earth. Meanwhile they're a major nuisance, and if she's working for them I wouldn't trust her as far as I could fart her out of my arse."

Well, neither would I, I didn't say. "I see," I said. "Business rivals. I can sympathise." That got me a scowl, which I ignored. "And you think there never was a book, and they let you think there was just to mess you around."

"It's looking like it," she said wearily. "Stupid. Because unless she or one of her idiots took it, it should've been there. Only it was definitely there when the Rose robbed the abbey—"

"Ogyge."

"Yes, how do you know—?" She shrugged. "It was in their catalogue three years ago, I know because I saw it."

"The book?"

She shook her head. "A catalogue entry," she said. "But you know what monks are like. Meticulous, especially when it comes to books. It should've been there. But it isn't there now. We looked. So it must've been in the batch the Rose stole, and all of them were sent here, to this castle. Which means," she added, turning to glare at Stauracia, "*she* must've taken it. Have you searched her?"

No, I hadn't. "Yes, of course," I said.

"Do it again, right now."

To be strictly honest, the thought was crossing my mind. "Believe me," I said, "she hasn't got it, I looked. Which means your friends the – what did you call them?"

"The Rose."

"They must've taken it out of the batch and put it some-where safe, and sent you off wasting time and money looking for it where it wasn't. Smart," I added pleasantly. "These Rose people sound like they have a sense of humour."

"It figures," Stauracia put in. "That's why they hired me instead of using their own people. Me and my men, expenda-ble. You slaughter us, this stupid book isn't there, you end up looking like a bunch of idiots and the Rose doesn't even have to pay us, because we're dead."

Nobody spoke for a moment. Probably just as well, since if I'd said anything it would have been how clever I thought the Rose was for thinking of something like that. "Complete waste of time," Praeclara said eventually. Then she looked at me and glared some more. "Well, not quite. Not for you, anyhow."

That set the back of my neck tingling. The thing was, I believed her, about the book. "Ah, yes," I said. "I was meaning to talk to you about that. Hetsuan? Really?"

It's always nice to cheer people up when they're sad. "You found out, then."

"Yes."

She grinned at me. "Just a little present from me," she said. "I thought you'd like it. She's alive and well, and you'll never ever see her again. Something for you to think about for the rest of your life."

"I don't believe you."

Her face went hard. "Suit yourself."

"It can't be true," I said, "because no stranger can sur-vive more than five minutes in Hetsuan territory. Therefore you're lying."

"Am I, though?" The grin spread out into a smile. It took fifteen years off her. "In my right sleeve," she said.

"What about your right sleeve?"

"A letter. I didn't want you to think I was going for a knife."

She held out her arm. I poked about in the folds of the sleeve and found something small, hard and square; parchment, folded many times. "Go ahead," she said, and I read it. Then I looked at her.

"Her handwriting," she said.

"Yes."

"You saw the date."

"Yes. Who's Eudocia?"

The smile turned radiant. "Your daughter," she said. "You'll note that she's over the touch of fever she had in the spring and now she's fine. Nice name, Eudocia. After my mother."

Killing people is wrong, but I do think there ought to be an exception where Praeclara's concerned. "Fine," I said. "But there's nothing in the letter that means it came from inside Hetsuan."

"Look at the front."

I hadn't done that. "That scribble there," she said. "The bit you can't read. That's Sashan, only altered so it can be written on paper instead of clay. Written in letters, not symbols representing syllables. They use the Antecyrene alphabet, not that you're interested."

But I knew that, because I can read Antecyrene. Sure enough, it was Sashan written in Antecyrene letters: *Raimvaut to Juifrez, give this to our friend at the seventh milestone. Garsio sends greetings. Good health.* Or words to that effect.

Raimvaut, Juifrez and Garsio are traditional Aram names. The Hetsuan are Aram offshoots. I looked round for Eudo, who was sitting there with his usual vacant expression. "Is that true, what she said?" I asked him. "About using Antecyrene letters?"

"Yes," he said. "It was in the dossier. Sorry, didn't I mention it?"

"Before you say anything," Praeclara said, "yes, I can forge my daughter's writing. And I know Sashan and Antecyrene, and I can rub dust and soot into a bit of parchment to make it look worn. The question is, can I do it that well?"

I looked at the letter. She used to write to me – Apoina, I mean – when I was away on business. I lost her letters a while ago, but if I close my eyes I can picture them right now, every unintended flick of a frayed nib, writing fast to keep up with her thoughts. I took a deep breath. Apparently I'd been neglecting to breathe for some time. "Which begs the question," I said. "Two questions, actually. How, and why?"

"Ah." Praeclara was enjoying herself. "Why is easy. To get her away from you. Somewhere you'd never be able to reach her, ever again."

I looked at her and believed her. Some woman, my mother-in-law.

"All right," I said. "What about how?"

She settled herself more comfortably. "It wasn't easy, believe you me. But I know people. You can always get what you want if you know exactly which levers to pull. It was the Serica."

Who the hell are the Serica, I was about to say, but then I remembered the name. Some tribe who fought a war with the Hetsuan and got wiped out.

"The Hetsuan," she went on, "don't do things by halves. When they decide someone's got to go, they do a proper job. I found out that fourteen Serica families had escaped and gone

west, across the sea to Scona and then on down south. I finally
ran them down in Parcyr. That's in north-western Blemya, in
case you're interested. I scooped them up, and I traded them
to the Hetsuan in return for a favour."

Fourteen families. Well. "The Hetsuan went for that?"

"They're not nearly as unreasonable as they're painted, once
you get to know them. And they really wanted those Serica.
Apparently there's a few more survivors in Sashan somewhere,
but they're really hard to get at. They'd need to kill something
like a million people before they could reach them, and of
course by then the Sashan would've shifted them to somewhere
else. But they could have my Serica for practically nothing.
What's not to like?"

I happened to catch sight of the faces of my boys, listening
to what she'd just said. I agreed with them, of course. But I
had no choice.

"So you can go to Hetsuan?"

She laughed. "Not likely," she said. "If I did, I'd end up in a
sauté dish. They allow one letter out and one letter in a month,
through approved intermediaries. The letter gets put under a
certain stone on a certain spot right on the boundary line. And,
no, I don't know where. That's it."

"But she can leave? If she wants to."

She shrugged. "Don't know," she said. "That wasn't covered
in the agreement. But she wouldn't want to leave. You see,
she thinks Hetsuan's the only place on earth that she and her
daughter are safe." She beamed at me. "Safe from you," she
explained. "That's why she went there."

I vividly remember the time I got hit with a slingstone,
somewhere up in the Mesoge, of all the stupid places to get
hurt. It caught me on the collarbone and broke it neat as

anything, and the pain – that's why pain is so useful. Take fencing. Your enemy knows enough to keep his vital bits covered by his guard, the places where three inches of steel will put you out like a light. He covers these targets with other bits, things that won't kill him if they get penetrated or cut – hands, elbows, hips, or letting your chin dip in front of your throat when you're fighting someone shorter than you are. But a savvy fencer knows that these places can hurt if you tickle them up just right, and pain distracts the attention, blots out rational thought the way a baby crying smothers its mother's mind. While he's hurting, distracted by pain for just a split second, you can nip in and stab him, game over, which is why the cut or thrust designed simply to hurt as much as possible is a good business shot. Pain is like a jet of smoke in a beehive; all that organisation and grim purpose turned to heaving confusion, while the smart, cynical thief reaches past them and steals the honey. I know that pain is just a feeling; Saloninus says it's nature's way of telling you something's wrong and making you do something about it, just like the baby's squalling. Once you know what it's for and what it's doing, you can train your mind to ignore it and focus on the real priorities, which may be subtly different; killing the other man in a swordfight, or answering the door instead of imme-diately tending to the baby. I'm sure he's right and I've been trying to train myself – I've had enough opportunities over the years, God knows – but I haven't quite got the hang of it yet. Give me time. I'll get there in the end.

"Got you," I said. "So why tell me now?"

"To make you suffer," she said pleasantly. "Or to encourage you to go there and get eaten. Look, I needed something to buy the book with, when I thought you actually had it. I knew it'd get your attention, plus the added advantage of killing you or making you hurt like hell." Smile. "Worked, didn't it?"

"Why tell the truth?"

"You'd know if I was lying."

I took a moment to contemplate her, like someone who happens to be walking along the quay when fishermen bring in something truly weird, as they sometimes do; something white and flat and huge, all jaws, with its eyes in the wrong place or no eyes at all. She's a real piece of work, my mother-in-law, and I don't suppose there's many like her. Most of the time she lives really deep down, about as far down as it goes; when she comes up, though, she has the edge over the rest of us, because down where she's evolved they have to be able to withstand an unbearable weight of water, pressing hard on them all the time. Up in the shallows, therefore, she's incredibly strong and tough, and a thoroughgoing pain in the arse.

"Fine," I said. "Well, sorry about the book. What's so special about it, by the way?"

Maybe I'd been whispering and she didn't hear me. "So," she said. "Are you going to Hetsuan?"

"Do I look stupid? No, of course not." I nodded to Olybrius, who was standing directly behind her. He popped the bag over her head neat as anything and tied round her neck with a bit of hessian string, though not nearly as tight as I'd have liked. "Put her somewhere she'll be found," I said. "Eventually," I added.

Olybrius looked at me. I'd forgotten to mention something. "Alive," I said. "We're not like her."

He shrugged, and he and Dodilas scooped her up and bustled her off, not as gently as they could have done. When they'd gone maybe ten yards I heard a sneeze. I'd specifically asked for a barley sack. Barley sheds this incredibly hard, sharp dust; it gets in your eyes and particularly up your nose, and until you finally grind it away with your knuckles it's torture.

Off went my friends to their nice, safe little war. We parted from them at the fifth blockhouse on the North-Eastern Link, a bleak little road I always seem to find myself ending up on wherever I go. The blockhouses are military, but there's stabling and shelter for civilians if they're prepared to pay silly money. The buildings are perfectly square, made out of identical blocks cast in moulds on site using a mixture of the local red sand and some kind of powdered grey pumice which is the only big business in those parts; grind it up real fine and mix it with water, and next day it's hard as sandstone. They hack it out of the mountainsides and ship it off on carts, and send it all over the world because there's nothing like it anywhere else. That's what the North-Eastern Link was built for, and there's a constant flow of carts, empty and fully loaded. Nobody lives there except the miners. The air is permanently full of dust.

At Blockhouse Five the road forks. My friends carried on up the Link. Eudo, Stauracia and I took the other fork, rattling along in a two-horse trap I'd paid too much for in Etoima Elis. From there we plodded on north-east up a thousand-year-old semi-derelict road with no name until we reached Sunelonti. The main thing to remember about Sunelonti is not to go there. If you should happen to find yourself there, leave.

At Sunelonti you have three choices. Go back the way you came; go south; go north-east. We went north-east, following what's basically a drovers' track (luckily it didn't rain or we'd be there still) as far as the only ford across the Artaba for a hundred miles in either direction. The ford hasn't got a name because it doesn't need one. After the ford you can follow the riverbank north-west or south-east, or you can lunge off across the moor, aiming straight for the peak of Tor Chirra, which is plainly visible for miles around except on the three hundred days every year when the moor is shrouded in fog.

Two days on the moor brought us to the Etmo, which is navigable right the way up as far as Chirra; what you do then is sit down on the bank looking pathetic until one of the big slate barges pulls in to rest its horses. You offer the bargemen a stupid amount of money for the privilege of five days squatting on top of the bales of slate. We had to abandon the cart, but they allowed us to lend them our horses to help pull the barge. Anyhow, it was better than walking, and the Etmo eventually condescends to reach the sea; the Friendly Sea, up in the north-eastern corner of which lies Coine Andron, the big grain port. We hitched a ride to Coine on a slate freighter, and then we were practically there.

Coine is a big, sharp millstone of a town, always working, moving, hoppers feeding a constant stream of people in under the stones to be crushed and processed. It's a centre for the indentured labour industry; contractors trawl through Poor Town in their local cities and march their catch to the nearest seaport for onward shipping to Coine. It's not the slave trade, heaven forbid; if you want to buy people body and soul you need to go south to Auxentia City. At Coine you buy a rigidly defined slice of their lives, three, five or ten years, after which they're free to go and good luck to them. The labour is needed to work the vast grain prairies between Coine and the Neras Mountains. Once you leave Coine you're nominally in Sashan territory, but clever speculators like the Poor Sisters and the Knights of Equity leased something like two million acres from the emperor about a hundred and twenty years ago,

back when it was all wilderness and scrub, and spent a fortune on irrigation and soil reclamation, and now each year it
churns out some unbelievable quantity of the cheapest wheat
anywhere. In forty years or so the lease will come to an end
and the land will revert to the Sashan, and all the countless
people in cities in the West who depend on the cheap wheat
will have to find some other way of getting by, but that's not
my problem.

Crossing the Breadbasket is easy as pie, because there's a
network of good, well-maintained roads for the grain carts. I
bought a two-horse fly in Coine, the sort of thing favoured by
estate supervisors for getting about on their rounds, and we
trotted cheerfully through the prairie heading north-east. It
was that time when the wheat is just starting to change colour
and the grain is still quite milky and soft; that's when the
rooks and crows like it best, and there are tens of millions of
rooks and crows in the Breadbasket. You get sudden storms
of wind and rain at that time of year, which flatten patches in
the wheat. Down come the rooks to feed, and in a few hours
they've trampled and stripped a couple of hundred acres, till
there's nothing left but broken stalks; then along comes some
fool in a horse and cart to disturb them and they all get up at
once, screaming and yelling their heads off and swarming in
furious upward spirals, like smoke in a slight breeze. The sight
made me a bit homesick, if you must know.

Rooks, crows, most kinds of corvid make me depressed, so
it was relief to get off the flat and up into the foothills of the
Neras. It's not bad going if you're riding rather than walking;
mostly it's pine forest, which is pleasantly shady after the
baking heat of the Breadbasket. You trundle along for four
or five days until you reach the mouth of the Butter Pass. It's

called that because most of the traffic is skinny looking men carrying huge bales of butter, wrapped in oilcloth, on their heads. They meet with the buyers at Drapezi, where a lot of money changes hands; Neras butter is reckoned to be the best in the world, because of the quality of the pastures. Most of the money ends up in the Sashan state treasury, because the lease-hold ends at the foothills and the Neras is definitely Sashan territory. All the farms where the butter comes from belong to the Great King, whose guests we now were.

People are scared of the Sashan; I don't know why. I find them decent, cheerful and friendly, provided you don't accidentally say the wrong thing, which is unfortunately quite easy to do and then they stomp you. As soon as you set foot on Sashan soil, you can bet your life that some official somewhere knows about it. The Sashan live by lists. Every aspect of everybody's life is written down somewhere on one of those roof-slate-size clay tablets that all look exactly the same unless you can read them. They know the size of your house and the dimensions of all the rooms and the names of all your cows, pigs and chickens, not to mention how many piglets were in the last litter and how many eggs each chicken lays. Not surprisingly, therefore, we were met at Drapezi Gate by a bored-looking man with a shaven head (means he's a clerk) who asked us who we were and what we were doing and where we were going. I told him I was looking for my wife, who I hadn't seen in ages, and my two friends were two friends who were helping me look for her. The clerk wrote it all down without comment, thanked me and walked away. So long as it was all duly logged, he clearly had no opinion one way or the other.

*

The Hetsuan border doesn't look all that scary. You stand on the bank of a small river, which you've just crossed by way of an unobtrusive stone bridge. In front of you, you see the ground gradually rising towards a distant, obscure skyline. It's mostly merino grass and small thorn trees bent sideways by the wind. Two-thirds of the way up, it stops being the Sashan Empire and turns into hell. The actual line is marked by a deep ditch with a low, thick bank on the Hetsuan side, but because of how the land lies you can't see it until you're practically on top of it. The ditch is to stop Sashan sheep from straying into the Kingdom of Death and I dare say it does a thoroughly good job, not that I saw any sheep when I was there. Still, it was the wrong time of year.

"Doesn't seem to be anybody about," Eudo said cheerfully. "We could just stroll across and nobody would know."

He wasn't helping. As I may have mentioned, I find it hard to think when people are chattering away at me. Well, I was thinking, here we are; thus far and no further. The idea was, by the time I reached the border I'd have thought of something. After all, I'm very clever, and the way my cleverness works is, terrible dangers roll in like thunder clouds and suddenly I have an inspiration. But my mind had gone completely blank, even when Eudo obligingly shut up. Thus far, apparently, but no further. Nuts.

"Eudo," Stauracia was saying, "where are you from? Originally, I mean."

"Well," he said, "I was born in Beal Defoir, but that was just where my father happened to be posted at the time. He moved around a lot."

"Where was he from?"

"Good question, actually. You see, we've been either

military or diplomatic corps for generations, so we're not actually from anywhere, if you see what I mean. My great-great-grandfather on my father's side was the younger son of a sort of country squire in Auving, and when he was seventeen he joined the Fifth Dragoons—"

"How about your mother?"

"Army brat, same as my dad. Her grandfather on her father's side—"

I glanced round. She was looking at him. "What?" I asked.

"I was just thinking," she said. "It's such an utterly nondescript sort of a face, don't you think? I mean, he could be practically anything."

To be honest, I hadn't given much thought to how Eudo looked, same as you don't agonise over the colour of water. He was easy to recognise, but mostly because of his uniquely gormless expression. "True," I said. "What about it?"

"His hair's the wrong colour," she said. "But we could fix that."

I turned round and gave Eudo my full attention. "Come off it," I said. "The Hetsuan are basically Aram. He'd never pass for Aram; he's too tall and stocky. Besides, they all know each other."

"Not Aram," she said. "Serica."

Oh, I thought, I see. "What do the Serica look like?" I asked.

"I can tell you that," Eudo said. "Basically they're a fusion of Aram and Otremar. The Otremar are Sashan-speaking but originally they're part Dejauzi and part Cauda, from the central Sashan highlands. About eight hundred years ago—"

"So they're all sorts of things," Stauracia said. "Like you."

Eudo thought for a moment. "The Serica tend to be slightly below medium height, very pale white skin and red hair like the Aram but stockier and chunkier, high cheekbones and grey or green eyes. But you get some Serica who're quite tall and dark-skinned with black curly hair and brown eyes—"

"Like you," Stauracia said.

"I suppose so, yes. That's a thought," Eudo said.

I stared at him. "No, it's not," I said. "They'd eat you."

But Eudo's eyes were gleaming. "It would get us across the border," he said. "You could tell them I was a Serica, and you'd sell me to them in return for safe passage to Deisidaemon, sorry, Midons, that's what it's called now, isn't it? And then I'd escape and make my way back here, and you two could carry on to Midons."

"Not me," Stauracia pointed out. "No way in hell."

"That's stupid," I said firmly. "For a start, they aren't going to go for a deal like that, and even if they did, it means he'd get killed and eaten, which is probably too high a price to pay. Also, nobody's going to believe he's a Serica. At first glance, maybe, but three minutes later they'll figure out they've been had and then they'll be seriously annoyed."

"Who says I couldn't pass for a Serica? Bet you I could."

The sound of his voice was driving me mad, like a fly buzzing in a small room. "You can't speak the language, for one thing."

"That's all right," Stauracia said. "We could cut his tongue out."

"And even if you could, there's all sorts of things they could ask that you wouldn't know. The Hetsuan aren't idiots. They'd want to test the merchandise before they buy." I felt like my head was going to burst. "Look, why are we even talking about it? And what about you, you halfwit? You're practically volunteering."

"I am volunteering," Eudo said. "I think it's a great idea. Well, it's the only one we've got, anyhow."

"It makes sense," Stauracia said. "Think it through. We hear about the deal Praeclara made, so we know they're amenable to making deals to get hold of Serica. We happen to know where one is, so we grab him. We can only get one, but no matter, because now there's very few of them left, so naturally the price goes up, simple supply and demand. And it's all academic about whether he'd be able to convince them long term, because as soon as the deal's struck and you're safely on your way up country, he'll give them the slip, so it really doesn't matter. Does it? And don't look at me like that. I'm only trying to be helpful."

"I can get away from a few border guards, if that's what you're worried about," Eudo said.

So much enthusiasm all of a sudden. The usual drill is, I think of a good idea, people yell at me and make difficulties, I bribe or blackmail them into doing as they're told, much against their better judgement. Any departure from the norm makes me sweat. Unfortunately, my way of doing things is posited on me having a good idea, and my mind was a blank. "Go away," I said, "both of you. I need to think."

I thought for a long time but nothing came. I even walked up as far as the ditch and stood there, looking down into it; my shadow could cross the border just fine but I couldn't. I don't know how long I was standing there, but at some point I looked up, and on the brow of the hill above me I saw a horseman. He was standing up in his stirrups, looking at me.

So what? I looked back at him. The people in the village closest to the border told me that the Hetsuan keep sheep, only for the wool, so this horseman was probably just a shepherd making his rounds. Even if I called to him and he rode down to talk to me, which was incredibly unlikely, he wouldn't be authorised to do deals on behalf of his government, and I couldn't imagine that he'd be interested in going away and fetching someone who was. All he was doing was reminding me that if I crossed the border I'd be seen before I got very far, and that would be that. As for Stauracia's idiotic plan—

"Hey, you," I called out in Sashan. "Over here."

He didn't move. I yelled again, this time waving my arms. Then I gave up. The horseman stood looking at me for a long time, then sat down in the saddle and slowly walked his horse straight at me.

He was young, maybe eighteen or nineteen, short and slight, the way most Aram look to us, with skin so pale it was practically white and pale blond hair reaching down to his shoulders. He wore a loose coat of bleached linen, sandals and a broad, floppy hat. He came so close I could see the colour of his eyes. They were blue, something I've heard about but never actually seen before.

"What?" he said.

"I think a couple of your sheep got across the ditch," I said.

He shrugged. "Keep them."

"You don't want them back?"

"Not from you." Then he laughed. "You're lying," he said. "We haven't lost any sheep. I'd know."

"I'm lying," I said. "I just wanted to talk to a Hetsuan, that's all."

That seemed to make sense to him. "Sure," he said. "You're not from round here."

"No," I said.

"You talk funny."

212 K. J. Parker

"Sashan isn't my first language." I took a deep breath. "Are you all right talking to me like this?"

He shrugged. "Talking is fine," he said. "Just so long as you stay your side of the line."

"What if I didn't?"

"I'd kill you." He shifted the hem of his coat a little, revealing a quiver full of arrows hanging from his saddle. "But talking is fine."

I nodded. "I need to get to a place called Midons."

"Where's that?"

"Over there." I pointed. "A long way. Maybe a week's ride."

He thought about that. "Then you're out of luck," he said. "You can't go there."

"I've got to," I said. "No choice."

He shook his head slowly. Nobody actually knows wherein the secret of the Hetsuan's military success lies, because nobody has seen them fight and lived to describe it. They could be superb heavy infantry or exceptional hit-and-run skirmishers or invincible lancers or world-beating horse archers. The glance at the quiver made me think horse archers, but that was probably only because I was talking to a man with a bow on a horse. But nobody knows, because nobody's lived to tell the tale.

"You could help me," I said.

He looked at me. Blue eyes, for crying out loud. That's not natural. "Why would I want to do a thing like that?"

"I don't know. Money."

"What's money?"

Oh boy. "Gold," I said. "Silver. You could buy yourself all the stuff you could possibly want."

"I've got everything I want, thanks."

Yes, I thought, you probably have. See what a difference a

ditch makes. Nobody my side of it would ever say that, unless he was lying. "What's your name, son?"

"I'm not your son. Giraut," he added, looking down at his hands. "Giraut de Borneil. What's yours?"

"Saevus Corax."

He frowned. "Is that right? So why do you want to go to this place you want to go to?"

"My wife is there," I said. "And my kid. Who I've never even seen."

"And?"

"That's it," I said.

"Sounds like you need a new wife," he said.

Even so. We were still having a conversation. "You married, Giraut?"

"Sure."

"Do you love her?"

"Don't know yet. We've only been married a year."

"All right. Do you know anybody who loves his wife?"

He thought for a moment. "There's a man called Arnaut de Marsan, lives away down the valley from us. His wife died last fall and he went crazy sad about it. He just sits on the stoop all day crying. What of it?"

"Him and me both," I said. "Except my wife's still alive. About a week's ride over there." I paused for a moment. "What would Arnaut do, if he was standing where I am?"

He looked at me. "Trouble is," he said, "you're a foreigner. No foreigners on our side of the ditch. That's how it is."

"Suppose I said, the hell with you, I'm coming across. What would you do? Knowing my name and what's eating me up inside, what would you actually do?"

"Kill you."

I dropped to my knees. "Listen, I'm begging you. You don't have to do anything. Just look the other way for two minutes."

"Sorry."

So was I, because it meant I had to throw the stone, which I'd knelt down to pick up, straight into his face as hard as I possibly could. I felt bad about it even while I was doing it, because it was murder, but there you go. I don't make the rules.

He was dead sure enough. I've seen enough men hit right between the eyes with slingshots to know the exact spot. The horse shied when he slid off its back and ran a few yards, then dropped its head and began to graze. That was just as well. If it'd bolted off over the hill, poor Giraut would've died for nothing. I jumped down into the ditch, hauled myself up the other side and walked over, keeping well to one side of the horse so as not to spook it, picked up the reins and looped them over my forearm. Nice and easy does it, with horses the same as with people.

I had to kill him because otherwise he'd have woken up, gone home and told everybody there was a dangerous foreigner on the loose. But I could make it so that events had transpired in a very different way. Poor Giraut; his horse shied at something – a grouse getting up out of the heather, a bit of white rag fluttering on a gorse bush – and threw him, and his head hit this stone here, the one with blood on it, and he rolled into the ditch and that was that. And then some evil foreigner, whose tracks you can see parting the merino grass leading up to the ditch, came along and robbed him of his clothes. And his horse – good point.

I put the coat on over my own clothes, jammed the hat on my head, took off my boots and put on the sandals, which were way too small. But I wasn't planning on walking anywhere, so that was no bother. The horse stood perfectly still while I got on his back; nice horse, I was probably a bit too heavy for it but never mind. I brought it round in a half-circle and jumped it over the ditch. There now, the evil foreigner had even stolen poor Giraut's horse. Someone ought to do something about those bastards, once and for all.

I trotted a couple of hundred yards along the ditch, an obvious track through the tall grass, and jumped back onto the Hetsuan side. Absolutely ridiculous, of course. Stupid, suicidal (and murderous, too, of course; let's not forget the burden of guilt), I was committed to a course that could only end on a spit or a bed of charcoal, probably with a sprig of rosemary or maybe basil. But not as stupid as all that. Bear in mind that nothing on land moves faster than a galloping horse, including news. Provided I didn't hang about and the horse didn't die on me—

I gave the horse a vicious and undeserved kick, and off we went. As we flew along, I had to take one hand off the reins, which I was reluctant to do (I can ride, but it's not my best thing) in order to pat my pockets frantically to make sure I had the map, Eudo's surreptitious tracing on a scrap of translucent vellum. I'd forgotten all about it, and it was fifty-fifty whether I'd left it behind or still had it in my pocket because I'd forgotten to take it out and put it somewhere safe. Luckily I'd been careless, and there it still was.

It didn't matter, I told myself as the horse's back tried to bounce my spine up through my skull, if they chased me, the whole stupid Hetsuan nation. Let them, so long as I got to Midons first. After that, I'd have to think of something. Cross that ditch when we come to it.

*

Also, in case you think I'd acted rashly, not the first time I'd been in that position – racing desperately through hostile territory, knowing that if anyone saw me for more than a few seconds they'd try and kill me. Only the previous time I'd been on foot: that was when I killed my brother, jumped through a window and ran for it, with my father's expensive pedigree hounds on my scent.

Well, I thought, I've done it before, I can do it again. I was younger and fitter then – it was seventeen years ago and I was seventeen years old – but I was older and smarter now, and I had a horse, and I knew where I was headed, whereas the last time I was just running away, rather than towards anywhere in particular. The argument that a man, even a fool, has only so much dumb luck in this life and I'd probably used up all mine long ago, weighed heavily on me for a while, until I decided I didn't care. Being alive is just a habit, like drinking too much. The drunk keeps drinking because deep down he knows that the world is too horrible to endure without an anaesthetic; I stay alive because I'm scared of death. But losing this chance, Apoina, would be worse. Either I make it to Midons or I don't; both were preferable to the third alternative. The hell with it.

As I rode, I must confess I was troubled by the fact of poor Giraut de Borneil. I've done things which are technically murder rather more often than I care to think about, but up till then the men I'd killed had been guards, warders, jailers; all in some shape or form aspects of law enforcement. I'm all right with that. I take the view that anyone who chooses to make his living hunting down his fellow man and handing him over to the gallows or the prison yard is basically a predator; he chooses to be one, rather than a farmer or a carpenter or a mill-hand, and that's his decision. Fine. I have nothing against the wolf, the sparrowhawk or the crocodile, and I have nothing against policemen. I wouldn't ruffle a hair on their heads if I had any choice in the matter. But the predator lifestyle comes with the risk that the terrified prey might fight back, and I have a problem with the idea that the prey forfeits its right to live, and fight for life if needs be, simply because it's transgressed some man-made rule. Having been prey so often myself, maybe my judgement is impaired on this issue. I'm only telling you how I think, not how you should. That's none of my business.

I've taken this philosophy too far on a number of occasions. I've killed people because otherwise they'd have given me away. I once killed a friend because he recognised me for who I truly was – I was in the wrong on that occasion, but I had no choice. But Giraut de Borneil wasn't a predator. On that occasion, I was. I killed him because I wanted his clothes and his horse, especially his horse, and if he'd lived to tell the tale, it would've reduced my head start: no other, better reason than that. Now that's murder, wicked and unacceptable – the fact that he'd promised to kill me if I crossed the ditch is neither here nor there, since crossing the ditch was my choice, too. Except I didn't have a choice, because I needed to get to Midons, the way a salmon needs to swim upstream or die trying.

I try to comfort myself in this regard by thinking about soldiers. They kill people, and make children into orphans and wives into widows, because their leaders tell them to, and as often as not the justification is a trade dispute or a squabble about borders or some idealist's dream of a better future – no justification at all. But soldiers kill, and as often as not they rape and burn and trash while they're at it. And the people they don't kill tend to starve or die of cold or exposure, but that's all right because it's war, which is an extension of public policy.

I can make that argument sound really convincing if I set my mind to it; if governments can commit murder for the sake of expediency, why can't I? The government is the people, I'm one of the people, so why the hell not?

All garbage, of course. All it proves is that on my own I can occasionally be as wicked and evil as a government. And that's a rotten thing to say about anybody, even if it's true.

8

I could describe that ride in meticulous detail, because I remember it so vividly, but you'd be bored silly after the first hour or so. Mostly I remember the pain: a saddle, too small for me, hammering away at a spot that rapidly became very sore indeed. Well, every good story needs comic relief, though it didn't seem all that hilarious at the time.

And I remember the landscape, which changed agonisingly slowly but surely as I moved through it. And there's a thing. I knew I was going dangerously fast – one slip and either I'd fall and break my neck or my leg, or the horse would stumble and break its neck or leg, and then I'd be caught and eaten. That horse, incidentally, was the single most admirable living creature I've ever encountered in my entire life. It kept going at a ridiculous pace, even though it was bone-tired and hurting. I remember asking myself, why is the stupid animal doing this? It's not even my horse; in fact, I'd just murdered its owner, so loyalty can't explain it. All I can think of is the proposition – I think it's in Saloninus somewhere – that once in your life you

encounter perfection, in some form or other, usually unexpected. It was the perfect horse, and I was dead lucky to find it.

Anyway, the landscape. I was going dangerously fast, but
the landscape changed agonisingly slowly, just enough to
reassure me when I was about to lose heart that I was actually
getting somewhere. The moor seemed to go on for ever, but in
fact it only lasted about four hours. Then it began to fade into
short grass dotted with clumps of nettles and thistles and the
occasional copse of birch or ash trees. When the horse and I
were gasping for something to drink, we came across a stream,
actually a drainage rine; the water was brown and tasted of
leather. The map told me there might be a town up ahead and
I looked around for a way to bypass it without losing time and
speed, but as it turned out there was no town. Instead we came
down into a lot of little hills and valleys, green and parcelled
out into small fields, which I didn't like one bit. While I still
had enough height to get a panoramic view, I stopped and
figured out a way through that would avoid any patch of dead
ground where a house or a farm might be lurking. I hadn't seen
a building of any sort so far, or another human being, which
wasn't to say that other human beings hadn't seen me. But I
was high up enough to be able to look back the way I'd come
and scan for any fast-moving dots, and there weren't any. They
hadn't found poor Giraut yet, I decided, and nobody had come
close enough to me to realise I was a stranger. In which case –
it would be dark in an hour or so – I decided to squander my
hard-won advantage in disgusting sloth and idleness and rest
the horse for a few hours.

But not on top of a hill, naturally. Once I'd committed the
view to memory as best I could, we made for a thick patch
of trees, bigger than a copse, hard to account for in such a

managed landscape where nobody hunts. We got there and I realised my mistake; it was a working coppice and crawling with foresters. I don't think anybody saw me, or at least not close enough to realise there was something wrong; we changed tack and headed off due north, mostly because it was downhill and we could go fast. I overdid it getting away from the coppice and the people, and the horse was starting to make disconcerting noises; I saw a scrap of ash copse at the head of a goyle, and that was going to have to do.

Getting off the horse warned me of how hard it was going to be getting back on it again, but a lively foreboding of death is a great way to overcome those niggling aches and pains. The horse drank about half the water in the goyle, pissed like a fountain and set about stuffing its face with ground elder. I swallowed a few mouthfuls of water, then realised I hadn't eaten since the previous night and had no food. Shucks, I thought. Better not to eat than be eaten. I tried to think about something else, with indifferent success, and then I fell asleep.

I woke up some time after midnight, and, praise be, there was a big fat moon, the fugitive's friend. There is of course a risk in riding hell for leather in the middle of the night, because if anybody does see you they'll know you're up to no good; but by the time they'd seen me and reflected on what they'd seen and decided that on balance they really ought to do something about it, I'd be a long way away and still going strong. The horse gave me a sad look, and then I hauled the assemblage of aches and pains I was stuck with for a body into the saddle and off we went. Dawn greeted me by very nearly letting me wander into a village street; it sort of came at me from nowhere, like a lion at a Blemyan waterhole, and for a moment I panicked and contemplated riding straight through, because hauling round and going back would be more conspicuous. But I had the sense to do neither. I slowed to a trot, which hurt even more than the gallop, and we turned round slowly and calmly and went back the way we'd come. I saw a woman put down a basket to stare at me, which I took for a timely warning rather than the beginning of the end, and as soon as we were back in open country I was off like a greyhound on a slightly adjusted bearing.

Not long after that we got clear of the farmland and into rather more amenable territory, downs rather than moor, but we gained a lot of height, which pleased me because I could see for miles. Mostly what I saw was flocks of goats, and where there's goats there's goatherds, probably sitting under trees or in cool, shady nooks where I couldn't see them but they could see me. That thought gave me the shivers, so I piled on the speed rather more than was sensible, until the horse started making those noises again, and it wasn't even noon yet. But noon in those parts is hot, and sensible goatherds get under cover and close their eyes for a few minutes. I decided I had no choice but to do the same. I found a beautiful little pocket of cover where a stream fell down between two chalk outcrops, the assemblage shaded over with tall, droopy willows. The horse had a nice drink and a scoff of willow leaves; I tried a mouthful and spat them out. Then I saw one of those giant puffball fungi, and I remembered someone telling me that if you ate them they didn't actively kill you, so I ripped it up and stuffed it into my face. It tasted somewhere between stale bread and the hard rind off buffalo cheese, and chewing it took the very last of my strength, but at least I was kidding myself that I'd had something to eat, which was fine.

After I came off the downs, life started to get more difficult.

Below the downs was a big, wide river valley, flat as a mirror and perfect for growing grain. It was far too big to go around, there were villages every few miles – I could see the smoke rising, like tufts of floating wool – and this time of year there'd be people out all over the place, weeding, cutting back headlands, scaring the rooks off the laid patches. It was flat, so I couldn't see anything coming (but it was flat, so I couldn't be seen from a distance) and unless I wanted to make myself conspicuous and very unpopular by riding through the standing crop, I was going to have to trot demurely along established roads and tracks, with everybody stopping to stare at me as I went past.

Time for a big gamble. I glanced at the sky and it was nearly cloudless – no guarantee of a moonlit night, but on the balance of probabilities, worth the risk. While I still had a bit of height I went back to just below the skyline on the other side of the ridge and took a long, slow look. I couldn't see the sort of movement I've learned to associate with fast-moving horsemen. Fuck it, I thought (I rarely swear inside my head, but on this occasion I did), let's chance it. So the horse and I wasted five hours of perfectly good daylight in a clump of gorse and didn't come out till the sun had well and truly set.

The gamble was that I could get across the corn belt to the big forest I'd seen practically on the riverbank in one night of hell-for-leather dashing. I figured that under those circumstances the roads would be a help rather than a deathtrap; I could get up speed without being scared to death of the horse putting its foot in a rabbit hole. Anybody awake would wonder who the hell was riding by so fast at that time of night, but I devoutly hoped they wouldn't think it was worth getting out of bed to go and investigate. Besides, who's up and about in the middle of the night? Answer: lampers, long-netters, pool fishers and various other sorts of hunter, not a problem in a nation of pious vegetarians. I came to the conclusion that I was taking a stupid risk and putting myself into serious danger, but that I had no choice. Story of my life.

It was eight hours of exhausting pain, terror and boredom, but we made it, through the fields and into the forest, where I felt justified in feeling reasonably safe. As the sun rose, I dropped down at the foot of a massive holm oak, took my boots off and wondered if anywhere, in that vast green cathedral of dappled light and spreading canopies, there might possibly be something to eat. I was thinking cautiously about beetles when a voice behind me said, "You're not from around here."

I didn't have a knife, and the bow and arrows were on the saddle, which was lying on the ground ten feet away. I was wearing the hat, which covered my hair, and the coat covered the rest of me; I'd been too tired to take it off. The accent was quite like poor Giraut's. I speak Sashan fluently, but I knew I couldn't do the accent. "I'm lost," I said. "No, don't come close. I'm sick. Mountain fever."

"What's mountain fever?" the invisible man said nervously.

Oh, God, they don't have it in Hetsuan. Never mind. "Really bad," I said. "I got it at my last posting, up north." I was slurring and mumbling, the way you do when you're sick, hoping to mask the lack of accent. "You don't want to come too close, trust me."

"But you're sick, you need help. Look, our house is just down the road."

"No," I snapped. "Really. I wouldn't want you on my conscience. Look, if I make it through till nightfall, I'll probably be all right, and if not – well, so what?"

"You sure? You sound awful."

"It's all right," I said, sounding terribly brave and noble. "Look, the best thing you can do is make sure nobody comes this way till either I'm dead or well again. Say five days. Seven would be better. And if I don't make it, tell the district commissioner that Juifrez de Luzignac won't be joining his staff after all. Will you do that for me?"

"Sure. What's a district commissioner?"

Nuts. I covered by making horrible groaning and retching noises, followed by "Quick, get away from me", advice he must have taken, because I heard running noises. He was a lucky man. If he'd come any closer he'd have caught something fatal, though probably not mountain fever, so I'm glad he was sensible and stayed away.

I gave it an hour, which was as long as I could bring myself to stay put. Then I led the horse off the track into the trees, made a long loop and thrashed about in the undergrowth until I hit the track again. A competent tracker would be able to follow the trail, but ordinary folks would take a long time poking about in the bushes looking for where the poor stranger had crawled away to die. By then, of course, they'd have figured out that there's no such thing as a district commissioner (why not, for crying out loud? Every other society I've come across has them, so why not the Hetsuan?) and their hackles would be up, but by then, God willing, I'd be miles away.

God was willing. I crossed the river that night, leading the horse up to my neck in fast-moving water but never actually having to swim, and out the other side into more of those horrible cornfields. I knew I wouldn't be able to get across that lot in one night no matter how fast I rode, and I hadn't been able to see that far from my vantage point on the downs, so I had no plan and no ideas for when morning came. Dawn rose, finding me clueless and horribly exposed. I decided to keep going, and the hell with it.

The horse was making those noises but I daren't stop. I was flashing past people, individuals and groups, who stopped and stared at me as though I was a dragon breathing fire. I'd heard of top-grade cavalry horses and the special breeds they use for the Imperial mail that can keep that sort of pace up for four days and nights with only the bare minimum of stops. The horse did its best, and then some, and then it suddenly stopped, shook all over and dropped like a stone. I managed to scramble off just as it was collapsing, so I wasn't squashed under it. By the time I was on my feet again, the poor thing was dead as a brick.

I looked round. Two men in straw hats were staring at me. Here we go, I thought.

I knew I had to start talking quickly, before sheer terror jammed up my throat. "You've got to help me," I said. "It's really important."

The two men looked at me some more. "You're not from around—"

"It's an invasion," I said. "The Sashan have crossed the border. I just came from there. There's thousands of them, headed this way."

I realised that the hat had fallen off when I jumped off the horse. "They've got at least thirty thousand armoured lancers," I said. "They're killing and burning everything in their path. If I don't get to Midons and let them know, it'll all be over before we can do anything. You've got to help me. I need a horse."

Sheer terror is convincing, even when it's borrowed from one thing and lent to another. For that moment, I think I honestly believed in the Sashan invasion. I could see it in my mind's eye: houses burning, women screaming, massive dark shapes on huge horses riding down running children, it was horrible. "We got a horse," one of the men said. "Where did you say you were headed?"

Shit, I thought. I'd said Midons because it was the only place-name I knew, and my mind had gone blank so I daren't make one up. "That way," I said, waving as vaguely as I could. "We knew it was coming so we've been raising the army, but we didn't think it'd be so soon. Look, I really need that horse. Please?"

One of the men was kneeling beside the dead horse, getting at the bow and arrows. My heart froze, but he got them loose and held them out for me to take. I took them. "You got any food?" he said.

I shook my head. He took a cloth satchel from around his neck. "There's some bread and cheese," he said. "Sorry, that's all we got."

"Thank you," I said, not having to strain too hard for sincerity, and the other man reappeared, leading a horse. "What's your name?" I asked.

"Arnaut de Cadenet," he said. "But forget about the horse. It's the least we can do."

I was in the saddle in an instant, my hands grabbing for the reins. "Tell everyone to make for the woods," I said. "Lie up there as long as you can, don't come out for anything. They'll make straight for here to burn the standing corn, so you need to stay hidden. You got that? Don't leave the woods, no matter what. I'm sorry," I added, "I've got to go. Thank you."

"Just a minute." My heart stopped again. Arnaut stooped

for something – a stone? I knew all about well-aimed stones. But it was my hat. He handed it to me and I took it. "Thanks," I said, and then I was off.

The new horse wasn't nearly as good as the old one, but never mind. The other side of the grain belt was hills, heather and gorse and good visibility until the fog came down, and fog was even better, provided I didn't get lost. But I wasn't going to, because on the other side of the hills was a river that ran due north, so as soon as I hit it I'd know where I was. Up the hill, then down the hill till you reach a river. No, I was really glad to see the fog.

I'd spent a lot of the time since I met Arnaut and his friend in reliving my meeting with him, in horrible, slow detail, and I decided there was one thing I could do to improve my chances, so I did it. When I stopped for the night I took an arrow from the quiver, sharpened it by stropping it for an hour on a bit of flint, and used it to shave my head absolutely smooth, using spit as lubricant. A man with no hair can't have hair the wrong colour, and they must have bald people in Hetsuan. I kept stopping to whet the arrowhead some more as soon as I felt it pulling on the hair instead of slicing, so I got away with only a few minor cuts. I even shaved the eyebrows, just in case. That and the hat, I reckoned, would give me a sporting chance, though naturally there were a million other ways I could give myself away. And I washed the linen coat in a stream; it was pretty filthy by that point, and all the Hetsuan I'd seen looked clean and neat. I broke the sharpened arrow off about six inches below the head and tucked it into the cloth bag Arnaut had given me. It wasn't a knife but it could do many of the same things, and I feel like a snail without a shell unless I've got a knife on me.

The wet coat was still damp and soggy when I put it on again; so much for bright ideas. Luckily it started pouring with rain soon after I started off and I got drenched to the skin, so anyone seeing me wouldn't wonder why I was all wet.

Arnaut had lied to me. There wasn't bread and cheese in the bag. There was bread and cheese and an onion and two honey-cakes and a handful of black dried shrivelled things that looked like large dead flies but presumably weren't, since flies are God's creatures, too. Anyhow, I ate them and they were fine.

By the time I'd finished the last dead fly I reached the river, and I knew more or less where I was. It was too misty on the top to see far, but coming down I'd got an impression of more bloody farmland – small fields, lanes, grey smears that looked horribly like villages, more of what I'd just gone through by the skin of my teeth, only worse. The more you push your luck, the more likely you are to provoke it into pushing back. I really wanted to turn round and climb into the friendly mist, but I knew if I did that I'd lose precious time, and probably my nerve as well.

Instead, onwards. Naturally, the fog meant I couldn't see if anyone was tailing me, but if anyone was, he'd have a devil of a job picking up my trail again. I made a point of zigzagging about as I went down the hill, just to make his life a bit more interesting, if he existed.

I reached the edge of the moor, where it gave way to land that someone presumably owned and looked after. The fields were split up by a sort of hedge I'd never seen before. Someone had driven in two rows of blackthorn posts, about six feet apart, and woven about a million withies in between them, like you do when you're making sheep-hurdles. In the gap between the two lines of posts, he'd stuffed gorse branches, packed in really tight and stamped down – the same principle as a wattle-and-daub wall, except the filling was gorse rather than rubble. From which I gathered that there couldn't be many trees in the neighbourhood, but I knew that already. No big deal, except that these hedges were too solid to burst through and too high for the horse to jump, and they lined the tracks along which I was going to have to ride. I might as well be in a tunnel or a mineshaft for all the chance I'd have of darting artfully sideways if pursued.

The hell with it, I thought. I still had about six hours before nightfall, and there was nowhere safe I could crawl away and hide until then. Nothing for it but to blast through at top speed and keep going until I reached safe cover or the horse died. They haven't caught me yet, I reminded myself, and off we went.

The sky clouded over late afternoon and there was no moon to speak of that night, but the track I was on was pretty straight and mercifully free of ruts and potholes – we kept going in the pitch dark until I heard a loud splash and realised my legs were wet and the horse was leaping about trying to get rid of me. I'd ridden into a river I didn't even know was there; not the smartest thing I've ever done in my life, though not the stupidest, by a long chalk.

I calmed the horse down – it wasn't the fastest thing on four legs but it was pretty phlegmatic and forgiving, which was probably better than mere speed – and considered the position. It didn't seem to be a particularly deep river, at least not at that point. I guess it came up to my knees, so just below the horse's shoulder. I decided it might be helpful to ride upstream for a bit, in case anybody was following me – dark as a bag so he couldn't see me, and no tracks for him to follow in running water. The horse wasn't crazy about the idea but I used my casting vote.

An hour upstream and then the clouds rolled away and the moon came out, and I could just about see what I was doing. I saw a bridge over the river – if the clouds had stayed put I'd have ridden straight into it, bashed my head on it, fallen in the water and drowned – which suggested a track or road. The moonlight showed me how broad the actual river was; we'd been splashing along in the shallows, any further out and we'd have been swimming against a strong current. It's disturbing to realise you've just spent an hour or so a few feet away from certain death.

But no harm done; I rode up onto the bank and used the bridge to cross the river like a rational human being, and then we were off again, quick as you like. Dawn rose, and I saw a fair-size stand of pine trees ahead and to the right. Marvellous. I couldn't wait to get my head down and grab a few hours of blissful sleep, somewhere safe after all that danger.

I woke up and there was a ring of people standing round me, looking at me.

It's a feeling I've had on a number of occasions. First the chilling shock, which numbs you up and loosens all your muscles and tendons; you feel cold all over, I have no idea why, and it's like when someone's standing on your chest, pressing all the air out of you. Then, because you know it's all over and you don't stand a chance, almost a feeling of relief, because there's nothing you can do about it so you don't feel obliged to try. That doesn't make the chill or the empty lungs go away, but somehow you recognise that it's for the best, because the horrible burden of being you is about to be lifted off your shoulders. It's different when there's even the slightest possibility of getting away. That possibility is like someone's pressing a branding iron on your forehead and keeping it there; the pain of the possibility is so intense as to be unendurable and you've got to do something about it, even if it's just screaming and thrashing about. Total and absolute loss of hope, on the other hand, is quite different. It's actually not a bad feeling. I had the most appalling toothache once, so severe that I got Gombryas to rip the thing out with a pair of farriers' tongs. The toothache was really bad and the ripping out was no fun at all, and then there was just a sort of numb ache, which in comparison was practically enjoyable. A bit like that.

I could only count the ones I could see: fifteen or so, all men, between the ages of fifteen and sixty. There were more behind me, because their shadows were keeping the sun off me. I had a razor-sharp arrowhead in my satchel, which was about eight feet from my hand; no earthly use at all. Oh well, I thought.

It's well known in butchery circles that you really want the animal nice and calm before you kill it. If it's got itself worked up into a state, it taints the meat and gives it a funny taste. I took a deep breath, which called for a lot of effort, and let it go slowly.

"Are you him?" someone said.

I identified the speaker. He was probably the oldest man there, and the shortest, with a shiny head, a short white beard and those weird blue eyes I still hadn't got used to. It seemed like an odd question. I didn't know how to answer it, not that I could've spoken in the state I was in.

"The cook," the man said. "You're the cook, right?"

It occurred to me that the symptoms of numb terror might

easily be confused with not being a morning person. I had no idea what a cook was at that precise moment, but they didn't look like people who were going to stomp me to death for being one. I nodded.

They all relaxed a little. "Thought so," the man said. "They told us, look out for a guy with a shaved head. Just you're a day earlier than we were told."

I shrugged. Better too early than too late, I tried to suggest with shoulders that now wanted to tremble more than anything else in the world.

"You fit?" the man said. I nodded. Sooner or later I was going to have to speak, unless I could get away with being a mute cook. "Right, let's go. I expect you could use a wash and brush-up before we do the thing."

"Sure," I managed to say. "Thanks."

"No trouble." I gathered that I was expected to get up, so I did that. In doing so I saw that there were at least thirty of them all told. None of them was armed as far as I could see, but a slim young man with flowing copper hair had hold of the horse's bridle. I did the geometry in my head, and acknowledged the fact that I had the shakes too badly for anything athletic or demanding. The strangers didn't seem overtly hostile at the moment. Possibly a bad decision, but I chose to wait for a better opportunity. Why a cook, for crying out loud? Why were all these people waiting for a cook?

I remembered they were Hetsuan. I haven't got one of those lightning-quick pole-vaulting imaginations, but I managed quite well without.

We were walking along a track. I was out front, with the man who'd spoken to me. The rest of them were behind us, with someone leading my horse. "Come far?" the man asked.

"From Midons."

"Never heard of it."

"Quite some way from here."

The man nodded. "Darned good of you to come out like this," he said. "Our local guy broke his arm. Stood on a chair reaching a pot off a high shelf, for crying out loud." He rolled his eyes. Some people. "First time we've had anything like this around here since before I was born," he said. "Bad business."

"Really?"

He nodded. "Mother killed her own kid," he said. "How could anyone do something like that?"

I shook my head. "Beats me," I said.

"Me, too. Crazy. Just one day she ups and grabs it by the ankles and swings it against a wall. I know the family; they're good folks. Terrible thing. Terrible."

Ahead the track showed signs of turning into a street. I could see tiled roofs, smoke rising from a smoke hole. Nobody about. Something told me that was because of the solemn occasion. "So," I said, "what's the plan?"

I think I'd struck the wrong note, because he looked at me. "I guess that's up to you," he said. "Like I told you, we ain't never done anything like this before." A thought struck him. "Sorry," he said, "forgetting my manners. Fulcet de Blacatz."

It took me a moment to realise that was a name, presumably his. "Juifrez de Midons," I improvised wildly.

"Northerner?"

I nodded.

"Thought so," he said. "Never met one before. Sorry you had to come all that way."

"Not a problem."

We walked on a little way. "Mind if I ask you something?"

"Shoot."

"Why do cooks shave their heads?"

I nearly burst out laughing. "Hygiene," I said.

"Sorry?"

"Keeping clean," I said. "You don't realise it, but actually your hair is permanently filthy. Dirtiest part of you, actually." He raised his eyebrows. He wasn't as bald as me, but not far off it. "You need to keep clean when you're around food all day. Especially meat."

The word made him wince slightly. Not hard to understand why. I think he'd realised for the first time that he was in the presence of a monster; someone who did *that*, for a living. He tried very hard not to let it show. "Anyhow," I went on, "it's just a matter of convenience. Either you wash it four times a day or you shave it off and don't have to worry about it."

"Got you." He wished he hadn't raised the subject.

A single street, with a half-metalled track running between two rows of small, two-storey houses with pitched, red-tiled roofs. At the end of the street a tower; I remembered that these were nervous people with a vivid memory of persecution and hostility. You'd want there to be a tower you could run to if the bad people came. The rest of the time you'd use it for – what? Having a tower, a communal building that never got used for its intended purpose, would probably make you tend to be sociable. You'd go there for prayer meetings, most likely, and other sorts of get-togethers; you'd meet your neighbours and talk about things, and people who do that get into the habit of thinking about things, which probably explained why they had no lords, masters or district commissioners. You'd probably all gather there when something dreadful and unthinkable happened; and then you'd send for a cook.

I reminded myself that he didn't know the drill; presumably that meant I did. Probably better that way. "Is everybody meeting up at the tower?" I asked.

He nodded. "I ring the bell," he said. "I'm the sexton. Closest thing we got to a mayor in these parts." He hesitated; a question he had to ask but didn't want to. "What'll you need?"

"Oh, the usual."

That didn't help. "We ain't got much in the way of big pots and pans," he said.

"A spit?"

He shook his head. "Blacksmith could probably make you one, if you tell him what you need."

"Not to worry. But I will need a wooden box, about yay long and so wide. And plenty of salt."

"Salt we got." He smiled. "We got our own saltwater spring. Folks reckon our salt's the best in the south."

"Everybody says that."

"Maybe. But in our case it's true."

"Spices," I said. "I'll want anise, fennel, peppercorns, cinnamon, cloves. You got that?"

"Sure." Didn't even have to think about it. What the hell sort of place was this, anyway? "Anything else?"

I was racking my brains trying to remember the recipe for cured pork, Echmen-style. "Honey," I said, "the lighter the better. Sesame oil if you've got it, if not walnut oil will do at a pinch. Garlic, of course, and strong white wine—" I stopped; did these people use alcohol? Some people don't, and they get very funny about it. Then I remembered seeing vineyards on a hillside. "Black bean sauce," I said. "I don't suppose you've got any of that."

"Sure we got bean sauce. How much do you need?"

"A pint ought to do. That's about it. Oh, and of course I'll need three or four knives. A good strong one for chopping, a nice thin narrow one for boning—"

I was being distasteful again. "We can get you all that," he said quickly. "And walnut oil. We got loads of that."

"Sesame is better," I said. "But walnut will do. And I'll want a small copper saucepan, for clarifying the glaze."

Shut up, I was telling myself, you'll go too far in a minute. But now that I'd started it was difficult to stop; the cook would talk like that, and if I let go of him for a second I'd freeze solid and then I'd be the one they'd need anise and fennel for. Meanwhile I kept telling myself that I wasn't screwed yet, and a chance would come, or I'd think of something. All I had to do was keep calm, act natural, kill some woman I'd never met and cook her and then go on my way—

We'd reached the tower. There were two men standing on either side of a low door, looking very sad. They glanced at me and nodded politely. Not every day you meet a real live cook. "How's it going?" I said. They didn't answer, and I went inside.

It was dark in the tower. The only light came through arrowslit windows high up. A wooden staircase led to the gallery, built halfway up the wall, and more stairs connected the gallery to the belfry, right up at the top. In the middle of the floor was a table and a chair. The table was just a table, big enough to be useful in a farm kitchen. The chair was just a chair, and there was a woman sitting in it. She wasn't tied down or anything; no need, she was paralysed with fear and guilt and the knowledge that there was nowhere left to go. You see that look on a horse or a cow that's gone down and won't get up again. She'd reached a place she was never going to leave, but she wasn't going to be there very long.

There were five or six men and a couple of women with her, just standing about; one of the women was crying, and I guessed it was her mother. If the dead baby had a father he wasn't here; probably best not, because nobody wants a scene. Presumably there'd been a trial, or a hearing of some sort. She'd have walked to the chair and been told to sit down in it, and that was where voluntary movement ended for her. The moment she bent her knees and sat down, she'd made her last choice. You could argue that she'd made a choice when she grabbed the kid and smashed its head in. I wouldn't know about that. I'm not a woman at the end of my rope with a kid that won't stop crying. But I paused and looked at her, and remembered the occasions – note the plural – on which I'd sat and waited to be put to death; and here I still was, at least half a jump ahead of the anise, the fennel and the boning knife, and somehow it didn't seem right. Then again, I've never been entirely convinced that the correct response to crime is punishment. It's always struck me as a bit like putting out a fire with lamp oil. But you really don't want to pay any attention to anything I say.

"Right," said Fulcet de Blacatz, the sexton. "I guess we'd better make a start."

I nodded. "Any preference?" I said.

He looked like he wanted to throw up. "Happy to leave it to you," he said.

I bet. I walked forward, close enough to see the woman's face. She looked at me, but she wasn't really interested. I think she just wanted it to be over and done with. If I'd been her I'd have been doing the geometry in my head – angles, distances, speed and time to intercept, and is there anything handy I can use as a weapon? She wasn't. It made me feel ashamed.

She was somewhere between thirty and forty, leather-faced and thin – the cook would've asked for vinegar to add to the marinade. Her eyes were blue, just like the rest of those freaks. Would a woman who's just killed her own child want to go on living? Another question I didn't presume to know the answer to. "Just a minute," I said.

The sexton looked at me. "Yes?"

"Sorry, I should've asked earlier but it slipped my mind. When did this woman have her last period?"

He looked at me some more. "I don't know."

I raised my eyebrows; what do you mean, you don't know? He hesitated, then went up to her and whispered; she whispered back. He came back to me. "Six days ago. Why?"

Rolling my eyes would've been overdoing it. "For crying out loud," I said. "It's got to be within three days, or the meat's tainted. Don't you people know anything?"

I'd raised my voice so everyone could hear. "We didn't—" the sexton said. "We don't get this sort of thing around here, I told you."

"Yes, all right, fair enough." I was counting in my head. "Sorry," I said, "but I can't help you. I can't hang around here for three weeks."

"But—" Panic. He lowered his voice. "Nobody mentioned anything about that. I'm really sorry. We didn't know."

I took a deep breath. "This is very bad," I said. "How long has this woman been in custody?"

"Eight days. Does that—?"

"You do realise," I said, "you can't hold someone on a death sentence more than thirty days, it's the law."

"Is it?"

The ignorance of some people. "It's the stress," I told him.

"It releases toxins into the bloodstream. Poisons," I translated. "You eat meat that's full of toxins, you get sick. Really sick."

He looked horrified. "I didn't know that."

I forgave him. Ignorance isn't a sin. "Not your fault," I said. "But it's serious. People have died before now, eating tainted meat."

I could almost feel the weight crushing down on him, poor man. "Does that mean we got to let her go?"

"Don't ask me," I said, "I'm just a cook. But, yes, I imagine so. I've never actually come across a case like this before. I don't know, maybe things are different down here. But where I come from—"

He closed his eyes for a moment. "And you can't—?"

"Six days after a period? Absolutely not. It'd be murder, letting you eat meat tainted like that."

Why, he was asking the universe, did it have to be me? "Right," he said. "I'll tell them. Some folks are going to be pretty mad about this."

"You want me to talk to them?"

He was tempted, but I knew he'd refuse. He was a good man, to whom bad things were happening. "Thanks, but I'd better do it." He walked away and some of the men came forward to meet him. There was a quiet conversation, followed by a raising of voices.

It occurred to me that the real cook would be arriving tomorrow. I looked at the woman in the chair. I fancy she was somewhere else, a long way away, and I couldn't bring myself to believe I'd done her any substantial favours. Probably I'd made things worse, for her, for everybody. Except, I devoutly prayed, me. The sexton came back. "Nothing for it," he said. "We let her go. This is going to make a lot of people very sore."

I gave him my sad face. "The best thing you can do, if you ask me, is get her away from here straight away, as far as possible. I don't suppose folks round here will want to see her face again."

He nodded. We were thinking along the same lines, at least up to a point. "She's got cousins in Li Canz," he said. "That's a long way west. I can't see where they'd want her, but you never know."

"The sooner the better," I said. "And out of sight, out of mind."

"I reckon so. I told Raimbaut to get out his dog-cart and drive her over there. By tonight she'll be miles away, and maybe we can all settle down again. Folks have been crazy ever since it happened."

"Talking of which," I said. "I'm sorry to leave you in a fix like this, but I need to be getting home."

"Of course." There was a look in the sexton's eyes that told me he wouldn't be sorry to see me go. "Amarich's got your horse over at his place, I'll walk you there."

It wasn't far. When I got there, I found the horse beautifully groomed and munching oats in a nosebag. Amarich and his wife had filled a sack with bread and cheese for me, with a jar of wine in a plaited straw sling. "The least we could do," said his wife, "after all the trouble you've been to." She was a fat woman with a nice smile. She'd been crying quite recently, none of my business why.

I was on the horse. The sun told me which way was northwest. I'd even had the nerve to borrow a knife. I'd drop it in the next time I was passing, I said, which should be soon. Forget about it, Amarich assured me. Nice people.

"Oh, one last thing," I said. "Did you hear about the crazy man?"

They looked at each other. "What crazy man?"

"No idea if it's true or not," I said, "but they told me down by the river that there's a crazy man wandering around. He's not dangerous if you don't get him all upset, but he's making out he's a cook and they reckon he's dead set on killing some-one. They actually thought I was him," I added, pulling a face, "until they realised I'm not crazy. Sorry, I meant to tell you earlier but it slipped my mind."

One damn thing after another, their faces told me. "We'll look out for him," Amarich said. "Last thing we need round here is any more trouble."

Time to go. "So long," I said. "Thanks for everything. You've been very kind."

They shouted blessings after me as I cantered away. Nice people.

The horse was rested and fresh and full of sustaining oats, and we didn't hang about. We carried on until an hour or so after midnight, then risked a stop in a holly brake until the sun rose.

We'd been going uphill lately, and when I crawled out of the holly and looked round I could see that I was quite high up, with a good view behind me. I'd covered a lot of ground through the cultivated strip, and ahead of me were more hills, promising the prospect of moorland, where at least I could see what was going on, and there wouldn't be quite so many people. I gobbled some bread and cheese and tried to feel smug about the way I'd come through terrible danger, though it didn't seem to work very well. Then I saw something on the road below, a long way off but easily visible. Someone on a horse, riding fast, the way I'd just come.

Coincidence. No, probably not.

As I scrambled to my feet and fumbled the bit into the horse's mouth, I argued that if it was the villagers there'd be more than one of them; likewise any other plausible threat. If you set out to catch a malignant foreigner, you go mob-handed, surely. Maybe it was the real cook, on the run from a village of lunatics who wouldn't believe who he was. Possible. Unlikely.

I had another look just before I kicked the horse into a gallop. I'd been wrong. There were four of them. No, make that five.

Joy unbounded. But not to worry; the original plan still held good, or as good as it had ever been. I had a good head start. The moor is a good place to be prey, none of those damned gorse hedges. They hadn't caught me yet.

There's a science to not being caught on a moor, one which I'd never had an opportunity to study before. It's mostly to do with dead ground – that's dips and hollows that are practically invisible from a distance, unless you happen to know they're there. Heather and merino grass aren't exactly the best going for a horse race, but if you stick to the heather you don't leave an obvious trail; your pursuer has to dismount and poke about among the roots to find hoofprints. There are brooks, streams and tarns you can follow for a hundred yards or so, breaking the trail. There are granite outcrops you can duck behind and be invisible while you check up on the progress of the predators. Provided you keep thinking at about a hundred and twenty per cent capacity every second of every minute of every hour, you can do a pretty fair job of staying ahead of the pack on a moor. Mind you, it doesn't always work, as General Gorsevir found out at Suilden Moss, one of the very first battles I ever cleared up after. He was under the impression he'd kept well below the skyline and he was invisible, and now Gombryas has three of his toes.

Unlike its predecessor, the horse believed that slow and steady wins the race. I couldn't get it above a sort of lumbering canter over the heather, but it kept going hour after hour, right up to the moment when it put its hoof in a soft patch. I was thrown clear and hit the ground with my shoulder, and for a moment I thought I'd got away with it. But the horse couldn't get up; broken leg, forget it. The way I'd been carrying on, it was practically inevitable. My own stupid fault.

I didn't like leaving it there but I had nothing to kill it with – the bow was snapped clean in two, along with ten of the remaining eleven arrows – and I didn't dare hang about. A white horse on a brown moor is about as visible as you can get, and every second I stood there was a yard I could've run. I had absolutely no idea what I was going to do next.

I looked at the sky. A huge mass of cloud was about to blot out the sun. I looked for something I could take a bearing on, but you know what the moor's like, everything looks the same. If the cloud came any lower there'd be mist, which would hide me but wreck any hope I might have of navigating. The best I could think of was to start walking north-east and walk in as straight a line as possible, no matter what, until the sun came out again and I could adjust my heading. I had plenty of food left in the sack, but the fall had smashed the unopened wine jar. It all seemed pretty hopeless, and I was beginning to wonder if I could really be bothered any more. I decided that on balance I probably could, turned my back on the poor horse, and started walking. I didn't look round, for fear of what I might see. If the predators were still on my trail, they'd find and catch me, sure as eggs. Nothing I could do about that. Never mind, I told myself, they haven't caught you yet. Bloody stupid thing to say, even to myself.

It was one ridge after another, and each one the same – you reach the top and, below you, there's a dip and then the ground starts rising again. That meant that someone following me wouldn't be able to see me while I was in the dip, and a man on foot leaves practically no tracks in heather. I kept telling myself I'd be pretty hard to find, unless the predators got lucky, and it was far more likely that I'd die of starvation, thirst or exposure before they caught up with me. You have to keep reassuring yourself in situations like that, or you soon give up.

Then I reached the top of a ridge, just like all the others, and everything suddenly changed. Instead of the ground sloping gently downhill and then rising again, it fell away – well, not precisely like the side of a house but steeply enough to make it awkward to walk down unless you tacked from side to side; at the bottom of the slope, a long way away, I could see a river valley, with deep woods, probably holm oak, and on the other side a flattish plain yellow with gorse and white with wild cotton. You know what that means as well as I do.

I made it down to the river just as night fell. The river, as far as I could judge, ran north-west to south-east, so following it and using all that wonderful heaven-sent cover would take me seriously out of my way. The alternative was to strike out over the flat on the other side.

I thought long and hard about that. Wild cotton, also known as bog cotton, grows in sodden peat. I was telling you a moment ago about the Suilden Moss campaign, my first big score in the business. It was the start of my career and very nearly the end of it, because I thought it'd be a good idea to save time on the journey home by taking a shortcut across the Moss itself. A lot of bog-cotton grows on the Moss, and back then, being a westerner, I didn't understand its significance.

Fortunately, it was only a pack mule. One moment it was there, the next it had almost disappeared: just its head, sticking up out of the sticky black mess for about five seconds, and then it was gone. Needless to say we turned back, white and shitless with terror until we were back on the busy, unequivocally solid road. A life lesson for the cost of a twenty-kreuzer mule. You don't often get value for money like that.

You get no warning in wild cotton country. People say that if you know what you're looking for you can read the signs and stay safe; people say a lot of things and not all of them are true. On the other hand, only a lunatic would try and ride a horse across it, and if he tried there'd be one less lunatic and one less horse. As the sunlight faded, the white tufts of the cotton practically glowed red; going round it would mean a serious detour, no way of knowing how far because I couldn't make out the end of it from where I was standing. Well, then: a problem, but also an opportunity.

You'd have to be frothing-at-the-mouth crazy to walk across that sort of terrain in the dark, with no moon, so I did. Why not? Seeing where I was going wasn't going to help. Unless I could see the sun, daylight wasn't going to help me navigate. If I kept going nice and steady, I could get maybe sixteen miles into the bog by sunrise. Think of the implications of that. Anybody chasing me would have to give up, and news of why I needed to be chased couldn't reach where I was going until days after I'd left there. All I had to do in order to be safe and successful was to keep from putting my foot into a bog hole, invisible and imperceptible until it's absolutely too late; and if I did that at least it would be relatively quick. Not something I needed to think too deeply about. Just crack on and do it, before I lost my nerve.

It's not a journey I care to look back on, nevertheless. I took it slowly and carefully, feeling each step to see if it was firm before committing my weight; it sounds painfully slow but once you've got used to it, you can pick up a bit of speed. Once every half-hour or so I got it wrong, and there'd be the moment of sheer blind terror as my foot sank in and I struggled for balance, knowing that if I got it a quarter-inch wrong I'd be dead. The deepest I went in was crotch-level, six or seven times, and of course I lost both sandals fairly quickly. Heather is all right to walk on in bare feet if you have absolutely no choice in the matter, and you can feel more sensitively than if you were wearing anything. I think the only way I managed to keep myself going forward was knowing that it couldn't last much longer; a few more steps and then the bog would swallow me up and all my troubles would be over. I genuinely found that thought comforting, and so I kept going.

I stopped three times, when I reached the point where I couldn't bring myself to go a step further; all I could do was stay absolutely still until the panic gradually ebbed away. The fourth stop was just as the sun started to rise, though I couldn't see it, only a generalised pink glow. The sudden access of light nearly killed me; I started looking where I was going instead of feeling each step, and almost at once I was balls-deep with my right leg. I nearly ripped all the tendons in my left knee hauling myself out, and then as I staggered my left foot started to sink – it was a bad moment, and when I was safe again I resolved to stop where I was and pull what was left of myself together. That took longer than I thought, and by the time I was ready to go on it was broad daylight.

I looked back towards the river valley, but I couldn't see it, only a darker grey representing the moor above it. I gobbled some bread, which by that point tasted exclusively of mud, and I cupped my hands to draw off a quarter-inch of black surface water. In the Echmen liturgy they pray, *give us this day the food we need*; well, I had that, no more and no less. I don't think I'd ever appreciated what that prayer really means before then.

Eight more stops the next day, and each time I stopped I fell asleep; the eighth time I woke up and it was pitch dark, which panicked me until I remembered that walking by night was actually safer. Then more of the same, and more; I woke up after a stop and it was daylight again, and an actual visible sun just above the horizon showed me exactly where due east was, and straight in front of me a beautiful, beautiful mountain. Not long after that I slipped into a bog-hole with both feet and very nearly died, which only goes to show that you can't trust hope as far as you can spit.

And more of the same, which I won't bore you with, until the ground started to rise and dry out, until it was hard enough to make my poor feet hurt like blazes. I had the mountain to take my bearings from, and just enough stale crust and cheese rind left to get me to the horizon.

When I got there it was mostly merino grass, which is tough and sharp-edged and cuts bare feet to ribbons. I took off my hat, cut it in half and repurposed it as two very inefficient socks. Gradually as I walked that day it struck me that if I was going to die it wouldn't be any time in the next half-hour. I found the thought mildly depressing.

I said I wasn't going to bore you, so we'll skip that day's walking, and the next. I have to confess, walking isn't my favourite thing. Any walk, even a stroll along a beach on a warm summer day with your true love at your side, can only be rationalised as a foul-up in the transport arrangements. Trudging uphill through merino grass with blood seeping through your improvised footwear has nothing to recommend it whatsoever, and don't you let me catch you doing it, or I'll be seriously annoyed. At least the sun was out of the clouds most of the time, so I had a handy compass to set my course by. Sooner or later, if I stuck to the right line, I'd see three big, round hills sticking out of a flat plain with a river snaking round them. Forty miles beyond those hills would be Midons. Piece of cake.

It rained in the night; no cover, no hat, I huddled on the ground and got wet. The sun came out shortly after dawn, but there wasn't enough warmth in it to dry me out properly. A third day of walking; I had to sit down and rest every hour or so. It didn't seem to matter much. There was nobody and nothing about. Sheep can't eat merino grass; nothing can. No sign of the three round hills, which I ought to be staring straight at. I couldn't even see crows in the air, and where there's life there's crows, to eat it when it dies. This is no country for crows, I remember solemnly telling myself, over and over again; not for crows, and not for me. No wars here, no eyes to peck out or rings to pull off dead fingers, no predators, therefore no scavengers, not even any prey, except me and nobody seemed interested in eating me. Probably by that point I wouldn't have tasted very nice anyway. Halfway through the morning I stopped for a rest and tried to remember what I was doing there in the first place: running, hiding, keeping one step ahead of the pack? Yes, naturally, that's what I do, but I had a vague idea there was something else as well. The name Apoina floated into my head, and after a bit I remembered who she was, and burst out laughing. I must be out of my tiny mind, I thought, then realised, sobering thought, that by this point I probably was.

Screw it, I decided. It didn't really matter what had motivated me to get into this mess: love, good intentions, idealism, all that bag of tricks. The only relevant thing was that I had reduced myself to prey in its purest form; a creature that lives by grazing as it runs, its existence shaped and governed by the need not to be caught, killed and eaten, defined by its predators; life in its most basic manifestation. The only reason I had a life was so as to lose it, as belatedly and as reluctantly as possible, after the maximum of futile effort. They haven't got me yet, emblazoned on my brow in letters of fiery gold.

You and me both, brothers and sisters. The only thing is, you don't realise it.

9

I woke up. A man was standing over me.

I remember when I was a little kid, and I went for a walk with my father. As noted above, walking doesn't agree with me; never did. We walked for a long time. Are we there yet? I asked. No. When will we get there? Soon. We walked on for an eternity, and I asked, Is it soon yet?

Define *yet* . . . I could feel those fiery letters dispersing on my forehead. The man was big and strong and he had a sword in an ivory scabbard stuck through his belt. He'd caught me. Well, fair enough.

"I say," he said. "You're in a real mess."

I looked at him again. I was feeling particularly stupid at that moment, but even so I could recognise a number of things that made no sense. The first one was the ivory scabbard. The second was the man's dark skin, curly shoulder-length black hair, brown eyes and long, plaited beard. The third was his purple coat embroidered with gold thread. This man, I realised, wasn't Hetsuan.

He was talking Sashan, but not with that ghastly singsong accent; it was perfect upper-class diction, clear as rainwater and sharp as a razor. Not only wasn't he Hetsuan, he was definitely and positively something else. "You're Sashan," I thought aloud, and he grinned.

He was leaning forward with his hands resting on his knees. "Bit of a moot point, actually," he said, then he frowned. "You're not from around here, are you?"

By which he meant I wasn't Hetsuan; that cracked me up, and I laughed. For some reason, laughing hurt. "I'm not from around here," I said. "Neither are you."

He was looking worried. "You shouldn't really be here, you know," he said. "It's against the law."

"Is that right?"

He nodded. "Properly speaking I ought to turn you in to the authorities, but if I did that—" He gazed at me. I was causing him trouble, not that he blamed me, but, nevertheless, I'd put him in an awkward spot and he didn't like it. "The thing is," he said, "I'm a guest in this country. Here on sufferance, to be absolutely—" He stopped to think. I could see thinking was a skill he'd attained by long and diligent training, rather than something that came naturally. "Oh, buggery," he said. "Come on. Can you stand up?"

It turned out that I could, though not at the first or second attempt. Apparently there was something wrong with my feet. "What the devil happened to you?" the nice man asked.

I shrugged. "Walking," I said.

I was a conundrum, and no mistake. "It's all right," he said, "I'm not going to turn you in. We'd better go back to my place and think what we're going to do with you."

Behind him – I hadn't seen it because he was in the way and

he wasn't exactly small – was a chariot. I kid you not, a chariot. Of course nobody uses them any more, except in Sashan, for very special occasions. But a chariot was what it was; not a trap or a fly or a chaise or a buggy. Four magnificent milk-white horses were harnessed to a coachbuilder's dream of lightweight rigidity sitting on top of two insubstantial wheels you could've built a city on. "That's a chariot," I said.

He roared with laughter. "Yes," he said, "it is. Built it myself, as it happens, just to pass the time. Silly, really. My only indulgence."

This from a man in a purple robe embroidered with gold thread. "Hop in," he said, but I was about a mile and a half past hopping, and he had to help me. "Who the devil are you, by the way?" he said, grasping the reins as the horses surged into wind-swift, silk-smooth motion. "My name's Vistam."

"Pleased to meet you," I said, gripping the handrail like grim death.

"Not my real name," he went on, as the moor flashed past. "Well, it is but it isn't, if you follow me; it's complicated. Who did you say you were?"

"Florian," I said. "My real name," I added. "But nobody calls me that."

He laughed. I was clearly a bundle of fun, one way or another. "The thing is," he said – we bounced over a large stone, but the chariot's suspension was flawless – "the only foreigners supposed to be in Hetsuan are me and the missus and the kid. They give us a certain degree of leeway, but one doesn't like to take the piss, if you follow me. What happened to your hair?"

"Shaved it off."

That puzzled him, so he did a bit more thinking. "Smart,"

he said. "They can't see it's the wrong colour if you haven't got any. Did you know that in Hetsuan men with shaved heads are always government officials?"

"Yes," I said. "No. I thought they didn't have a government."

"Not as such, no." I had to shout to make myself heard over the rumble of the wheels, but his was the sort of voice that didn't need raising for anything short of an earthquake. "Closest thing they've got is the cooks. You know about the cooks?"

"A bit."

"Well, you look like one of them." He thought some more. He was quite good at it once he got going. "I see," he said. "You did it on purpose, to look like a cook. That way you can go about freely without looking out of place. Clever devil, aren't you?" Then he thought some more and stopped the chariot. Being still was absolutely bliss. He pushed me out of the chariot and drew his sword. "Look here," he said. "Are you here to kill me?"

What a question to ask. "No," I said, "absolutely not."

He considered me as though I was a simultaneous equation; I could be solved, but was it worth the effort? "Well," he said after a while, "if you are, you're in no fit state to be dangerous just yet. Get back in and keep your hands where I can see them."

Only too delighted to oblige; both of them clamped to the handrail, the knuckles showing white. Vistam, I thought. I haven't heard that name before, but then again, I wouldn't have, would I?

A short digression. The Sashan, who in my opinion are probably the most marvellous people on earth except for the

Echmen, wrap names up in a vast cocoon of mystique. Every Sashan male has three names; A son of B from C is the first one, and anybody's allowed to know that. Then there's his name-in-religion, which in theory is known only to himself, his priest and the Eternal Flame – my name-in-religion, incidentally, is Sayathiya, and how I come to be entitled to one is a long and tedious story. In practice, that's what your family calls you and you share it with close friends. That's who you think of yourself as being, if that makes any sense; it's what your wife calls you in bed, and if you had a dream and an angel appeared to you, that's the name he'd use. Then there's a third name, which is a deadly secret between you and your father; not even your mother knows what it is. Unless, of course, you happen to be the king of the Sashan, the Great King, King of Kings – in which case, that's what everyone calls you and it's chiselled up in inscriptions and spelled out on the fronts of coins, and I imagine the effect must be living your entire life stark naked in public, but presumably they get used to it.

Anyhow, that's the men. Women are A daughter of B (male) from C, and A is usually the name of a flower or a synonym for Pretty. In Sashan society, women are supposed to be meek, decorative and silent.

Note, supposed to be. That's why I like the Sashan so much. For the Sashan there are two realities, both equally valid and equally real: the way things are, and the way things are supposed to be. They believe in both simultaneously with equally absolute faith, even when they contradict each other, which is ninety-six per cent of the time. Thus, for example, women should be seen and not heard, and in practice they run the government, most of the great landed estates and well over half of the major business organisations. The Great King is by definition seven feet tall and broad as an ox, with forearms like the trunks of thorn trees – you know this is true, because there's pictures and sculptures of him on the money and every street corner – and he's never lost a battle. In Sashan it never rains in summer and the sky is always blue.

I like the Sashan. I've seen Sashan cheerfully dying in agony who know they're perfectly fit, because the priest has been and splashed them with holy water, and the pain is obviously just an illusion so they ignore it. Nobody can ignore an illusion like a Sashan. They are, of course, the Master Race, and because they know this is true they don't feel obliged to go about proving it all the time, just as they don't need to prove the existence of the moon just because there happen to be clouds. The Sashan keep the rest of humanity the way you and I keep pets. They're kind to them, they indulge them, they spoil them – probably because if they didn't there might be a war, which of course they'd win, but there might be an illusion of defeat. This means the Sashan are generous hosts and humane masters, when it's absolutely convenient; they have complex and inviolable laws of hospitality, and if a Sashan saves your life in the desert, he's lumbered with you until further notice. Whether this applies on the moor as well as the desert is a grey area, since there were no moors in Sashan territory when the rules were formulated. Vistam, however, struck me as the sort of man who'd be inclined to give me the benefit of the doubt. Besides, I had a sneaking suspicion of who he was, and if I was right, I was laughing.

"You're him," I said. "Aren't you?"

He smiled. "Yes," he said. "How did you know?"

"Lucky guess."

"Buggery." He didn't do anything, but the horses picked up speed. They'd know to do that, because the Great King is master of all living things, human and animal.

Except that Vistam wasn't the Great King. At least he was, but he wasn't; very Sashan. About forty years ago, the Great King died – he was immortal, but he died – leaving a three-month-old baby as his rightful heir. This posed a problem, since the Great King is seven feet tall and as strong as a bear, which is difficult when you're only three months old. The finest minds in the empire gave the problem a great deal of thought and realised that the baby wasn't the Great King after all; that was just an illusion. The Great King was really the late Great King's nephew, who happened to be seven feet tall and strong as a bear, or close enough as made no odds, and the baby was just a figment of the imagination. Since he was imaginary it wouldn't matter if he died, but on the other hand there was no need to do anything drastic, since he didn't actually exist; he and his mother were packed off to a castle in Cisbataan, which by coincidence housed a Guards regiment, and the dubious alternative reality faded away like ripples in water after the fall of a dead sparrow.

But although the new Great King won all his battles and stamped the enemy flat until the earth knew them no more, he also lost a major campaign against the Echmen, one which I'd have given both ears to have had the rights to, and failed to put down a rebellion in the unimportant north-western provinces, where so much of the wheat comes from, and certain deluded people with long memories wondered if these particular illusions might somehow be connected with the illusory hiccup with the succession. If the Great King wasn't really the Great King, undoubtedly heaven would mark its displeasure with significant events, such as military reverses, and although nothing of the sort had actually happened, it bore thinking about, which they did. There were even a few minor scuffles between the Army of the East and the Army of the West, after which the baby (who was now twenty-seven) left the castle in Cisbataan in a laundry basket and was never seen or heard of again. He didn't die, because if he had his head would've been displayed on a pike in the palace forecourt; it was, of course, but a great many people who ought to know better suffered an illusion that it wasn't the baby's head and didn't even look like him. It goes without saying that all the resources of the empire were deployed to find him, even though he'd never existed; the fact that he was never found proved beyond doubt that he'd never been anything but an illusion. Then the genuine Great King gave the Echmen a hammering they'd never forget, proving that Heaven was satisfied and everything was fine, and the point became moot.

Now then; given the efficiency and power of the Sashan covert intelligence division, which really is the best in the world – if they looked for a certain person and couldn't find him, where could he possibly be? It would have to be somewhere nobody could go; eighty feet down inside an active volcano, or the bottom of the deepest trench in the ocean, or Hetsuan.

The illusory Great King's name had been Balas, but of course nobody but his father and every single human being in the world would've called him that. He'd have had another name, A son of B from C. Vistam, maybe? Apparently, yes.

"You came here to escape," I said. "To be safe."

"Too bloody right." We were slowing down, from unthinkably fast to merely terrifying. Ahead I could see a wall. Behind it, dim on the horizon, three rounded hills. "My cousin, God bless him, would have my liver for a pincushion if I ever stuck my nose over the border. Here I'm all right, because our lot are scared stiff of the savages. Who aren't so bad, actually, provided you have absolutely nothing to do with them."

The wall was in fact a compound, like an army fort. Belay that; the place *was* a fort, built on the time-honoured Sashan pattern, if it ain't broke don't fix it for the past thousand years.

There are hundreds, maybe thousands of the things all along the frontiers of the empire, as near identical as such things can be. You've got your gatehouse, with a heavy-duty double gate, the tower above serving as the main accommodation block; a yard enclosed by the wall, which is sixteen feet high, crenellated and backed by a wooden catwalk on solid brackets; the back wall is a casemate with rooms for storage and barracks for the twenty or so soldiers of the garrison. The yard itself, just over half an acre, is supposed to be a parade ground, therefore is a parade ground, this being a Sashan installation; it's also a meticulously tended walled garden where the soldiers grow cabbages, onions, leeks, carrots, peas, beans, lentils and vines trained up the north-facing wall, the south and east walls being reserved for espaliered apples, cherries and pears. There's stabling for eighteen horses along the west wall, ensuring a strong cavalry presence for defence in depth and plenty of manure for the strawberries.

"You live here?" I said, a singularly pointless question.

"Yup," he said. "The savages built it for me, part of the deal. They allowed me a staff of twenty, all Hetsuan, obviously. Down in the dip on the other side I've got seventy acres, piss-poor soil but we're gradually making something of it. And that's my lot, I'm afraid. It's not much, but it'll do me."

Seventy acres and your own castle: not much, if you're the rightful King of Kings. And if that not-much will do you, you're a wiser man than any Great King who ever sat on the Rainbow Throne. "You've got twenty Hetsuan working for you? Really?"

He nodded. "It was all a bit tense to start with," he said, "what with me being an abomination in the sight of heaven and all that, but we've sort of got used to each other and now we get along famously. Splendid chaps, the lot of 'em. Can't do enough for you." The chariot rolled to a halt in the shadow of the gatehouse. The gate was shut. "How they'll react when they see you I just don't know," he said. "No visitors is something of a condition of the deal. Of course, they'll see you aren't one of them in two shakes."

Comforting. "In that case," I said, "maybe I shouldn't come in. I don't want to make trouble for you."

That laugh again. "Bullshit," he said. "You're my guest. I found you starving in the desert, so I'm stuck with you. What did you say your name was?"

"Florian."

"Florian. Like that chap on Sirupat a while back."

"Yes."

"Heard about that. One of my revered cousin's less idiotic decisions." He advanced to the gate and booted it with a colossal left foot, making the massive timbers shudder. "I'm allowed letters," he said. "One in, one out, every month. Benhart, you idiot, what took you so long?" he added, as a tall, dignified looking Hetsuan in a white robe opened the gate. "Put the cart away and see to the horses, there's a good chap."

The Hetsuan looked at me. He saw the shaved head and the filthy, tattered coat. "Who's he?"

"Guest."

It wasn't that long a silence, objectively speaking, but it was plenty long enough for me. "Right," Benhart said. "I'll see to the cart."

Inside the gate, a garden. Things to eat on the west side, flowers and stuff on the east. If there's a more beautiful thing in the world, I haven't seen it and I'd have trouble imagining it. Dead centre was a fountain, spouting and chattering. The Echmen have this concept they call Paradise, which is where you're supposed to go when you die if you've been very good. They envisage it as a beautiful garden. I'd be able to tell the next Echmen I met that they'd been right about that all along.

"What you need," Vistam was saying, striding through Paradise as though it wasn't there, "is some grub and a change of clothes. I think we can run to that. Betriz! Eloiz! Visitor," he said, as two women in long white dresses appeared from a doorway. "Brioche and honeycakes and cranberry juice in the arbour, quick as you like." The women stared at me, then went away. "And a bath," he added firmly. "Sorry to mention it, but you stink to high heaven."

I said he was probably right. He pointed to a bench next to a stone table under an arch of trellis, messy with trailing honeysuckle. I sat down, a shabby monster in heaven with scraps of cloth glued to his feet by clotted blood. "Got to ask," he said. "What's a foreigner like you doing in the middle of Hetsuan?"

"I'm trying to reach a place called Midons," I said.

"Well, you're in luck, it's just over the hill there." He nodded his head vaguely north-east. "What's in Midons?"

"My wife."

"Ah."

"And my daughter," I said, "who I've never seen."

He looked at me, thinking, little white mice scrambling round inside ponderous wheels. "You married a Hetsuan."

"No," I said.

"Interesting. Excuse me if I'm being rude, but what's your wife's name?"

"Apoina."

I have good reflexes, honed by a lifetime of bad experiences. Usually I see it coming. Maybe I was too tired and run down, or maybe Paradise had got to me. I didn't see it coming. He was on his feet and his fist was slamming into my face before I realised what was happening.

The back of my head went bump on the granite paving slabs and my head swam. He was standing over me, blurred, bright sunshine blazing on the blade of his sword, the very tip of which was pricking my throat like a bramble. "What did you say your name was?"

"Florian." Saying the word moved my throat against the sword point, dangerously.

"Sure about that?"

Something in my face or eyes or body language told him I wasn't a threat just then; he reduced the pressure on the sword-point just a little. "I also go by Saevus," I said. "Saevus Corax."

I think he'd already figured that for himself. "Fucking God almighty," he said. And then he bellowed a name. "Get up," he said. "But if you try anything, guest or no fucking guest I'll cut you in half."

I sat on the bench beside the stone table, in Paradise. "She's here," is all I could say.

"Yes," he said. "My wife, you arsehole."

I realised I wasn't doing the geometry. It's automatic with me, I can't help it. When I'm in trouble and there's guards or soldiers or hitmen or whatever, instinctively and without thinking I do the geometry. It runs something like: I move there, he moves to intercept, is there time for me to get to there before he gets to there, what if I take a long circling step to the right, in which case by the time he's there, I'll be there – all in a fraction of a second. I can see it as if there were fiery lines hovering in the air; it's second nature, just like breathing. But this time, I simply couldn't be bothered. All beside the point. I heard myself say something like, I can explain. The look on his face told me no, I couldn't.

A door opened and there she was. My wife, in Paradise.

She looked at me and screamed. "It's all right," Vistam said quickly, "I've got him. He can't hurt you."

"Kill him," she said. "For God's sake, Vistam, kill him. You don't know what he's like."

"He's a guest," Vistam said. "Look, it's fine, really. Go back inside and lock the doors. It'll be fine."

Dear, sweet, clever Praeclara. I hadn't realised she hated me so much. The thought of all that malice sobered me up like nothing else could have. "She thinks I want to hurt her," I said. "I don't. Really."

He looked at me. The Great King can read men's minds like a book, and from his eyes no secret can be hidden. "That's not what I heard," he said.

"I take it you've met my mother-in-law."

That gave him pause for thought. "Poisonous woman," he said. "Can't say I liked her very much. But that's neither here nor there."

"No," I said, "I don't suppose it is. Praeclara told you I want to kill Apoina. It's not true. I love her."

Not the most tactful thing to say, maybe, but I think he

believed me. The Great King trusts his own judgement, because he's the wisest man in the world. "Maybe you do," he said. "Which would explain why you went to so much trouble to get here. Jealousy. She dumps you; you kill her."

"No," I said. "Praeclara was telling lies. All lies."

He was considering me as a proposition, something that could be solved. I hoped he was right. But, I thought, this is the Great King, the wisest man in the world, in the Sashan sense. It was all up to him, and he knew it. But the Great King makes decisions like that a thousand times every day. "Oh, for crying out loud," he said, and he sat down and laid the sword across his knees. "You don't want to murder my wife."

"No."

He nodded. "Can't see why anybody would want to; she's a doll. Mind you, I'm biased." Small grin. "Well," he said, "I'm sorry, but you've had a wasted journey. That Praeclara," he added. "A real piece of work. Never liked the woman."

"Me neither."

"Well, there you go." His eyes were upon me, and I felt the power of twenty-six generations of Sashan kings. "Sorry," he said, "but that's how it goes. She may have cared for you once – my wife, I mean – but that was then and this is now. We're happy together. We both have everything we want. And – well, I believe you, but I don't think she ever would. Dearest mother-in-law's stitched you up good and proper, and there's nothing you can do about it, unless you'd consider cutting her throat. But I won't encourage you to do that, because after all, she's Poina's mother and she's fond of the old viper, God only knows how but she is, and if ever she found out, I'd be in shit up to my earlobes. Sorry," he repeated, "but that's that."

Over the years I've got used to thinking I'm smart. It's hard to accept just how stupid I can be. "Can I ask you something?"

"Sure. Fire away."

"How did you two—?"

He laughed. "Dearest mother-in-law," he said. "She brokered the deal with the Hetsuan, so I could come here. I don't know to this day how she managed it."

I told him. It made him angry, I could see. "Like I said, a real piece of work. Anyway, me marrying Poina was a condition: marry her and take her with you; it's the only place on earth she'll ever be safe. Which I was only too pleased to do, once I'd met her. Like I said, she's a doll." He paused. "You know that, of course."

"Yes."

"Fair enough. We hit it off right from the start. And Eudocia—" He stopped. "That's your daughter," he said.

"Eudocia," I repeated. "Nice name."

He nodded. "Great kid," he said. "I couldn't love her more if she was my own." He stopped again. "Sorry," he said, yet again, "but things have moved on. Even if she were to believe you—"

Imagine you're lying flat on your back on a table while surgeons cut out your internal organs, and on the ceiling there's a mirror, so you can see the whole thing, the view from above, as though you were simultaneously you and God. A bit like that. "I get the picture," I said.

"Good lad." Praise from the Great King is praise indeed. "I'll get Poina out here again in a bit and you can hear it from her if you like. I mean, like I said, I'm biased. But I know she'll say the same as me. To be honest with you, I wouldn't have lasted a day out here without her. She's—"

"A doll, yes. You told me." He let me have that one, which was generous of him, in the circumstances. "You're right," I said. "I've been wasting my time."

"You have rather. All that bloody woman's fault, I'm sorry for you, really." He paused, as another thought began seeping through his mind, like water through limestone. "Hang on," he said. "Who told you she was here?"

"Praeclara."

His eyebrows rose. "Did she, by God? That's interesting."

It was my turn. He'd figure it out eventually, of course, being the wisest man in the world, but it was only polite to save him the effort. "Quite clever, really," I said. "I'm guessing here, of course, but I don't suppose I'm all that wide of the mark. The situation in Sashan has changed and now they want you dead. I imagine they're offering money, or something else Praeclara wants. So she fixes things so she can tell me that Apoina is here, knowing that I'll go through hell to get to her, and that I'm smart enough and dangerous enough to get halfway across Hetsuan without being killed and eaten. Under other circumstances I'd take that as a compliment, but I don't think I will, somehow. I get here, I find she's married to you, so I kill you. That's how she reads me," I added. "And of course it has the added benefit of torturing me more than anything else possibly could. Good plan."

"A real piece of work."

"Quite." I shook my head. It didn't help one bit. "She was wrong, of course, so the plan was fundamentally flawed. Her prejudices clouded her judgement. She thought I'd kill you, thinking that if you were dead I'd get Apoina back. But I'm not that stupid. That's where she misjudged me."

He nodded. "Figuring," he said, "that you'd kill me and then Poina would hate you even more. I could see why she'd want to believe it of you. From her point of view, it's pretty well perfect. It just needed you to be how she wants you to be, and it'd work."

"Wishful thinking," I said. "Clouds the judgement, even for the best of us. I really thought, if only I could see her again—" I shrugged. "Wishful thinking."

"Yes," he said. "Really, someone ought to shred that woman into little bits with a cheese grater. But not me, I'm afraid, because Poina would never forgive me. You can, though. After all, you've got nothing to lose."

Maybe the one quality the Great King lacks is tact. "I can't be bothered," I said. "Besides, I don't kill people, not unless I absolutely have to."

"Good lad. Anyhow, being Praeclara's the worst punishment I can think of. Changing the subject somewhat, have you given any thought about how you're going to get home?"

"No," I said. "Somehow I didn't anticipate that happening. Not that I've thought about it. I've had other things on my mind."

He took a deep breath. "If you want," he said, "you can see them. Poina and Eudocia, I mean. I think that's only fair, if that's what you want. They won't want to see you, but I'll try and explain."

I took a moment to look round at the garden. There's that bit in Saloninus's elegies:

Thou, beside me singing in the wilderness,
O, Wilderness were Paradise enow!

"Thanks," I said. "But what would be the point?"
"No point at all," he said. "Sorry."

I took a deep breath and let it go. Where does dead breath go to, I wonder? "She's got a Sashan sort of mind," I said. "Praeclara, I mean. She can believe in me as I ought to be, in her version of the world."

"A crazed, vengeful killer. Yes, I can see what you mean."

"Her preconception becomes reality. Quite Sashan," I said. "No offence intended."

"None taken. Of course she is Sashan. On her mother's side."

"Really? I didn't know that." I looked at him. A nice man. The thought made me laugh. "You're right," I said, "I'm in a real fix."

"You are," he said. "Did you have much trouble getting here?"

"A bit."

He nodded. "Going back the way you came probably isn't an option," he said. "It's fine stirring up a hornets' nest if you're just passing through, but going back the same way would probably end in tears."

"And a garnish of onion rings."

He looked startled, then diagnosed it as a joke and smiled. "Quite," he said. "On the other hand, if you try going north, you'll have a hell of a way to go before you get anywhere. And the south is pretty thinly populated. North of here you'll run into the towns and big cities. I don't think you'd last five minutes."

"Probably not. And, of course," I added, to save him the trouble, "I can't stay here."

"Not really, no. Sorry."

"That's fine," I said. "But to be honest with you, I don't really give a damn."

He frowned, the Great King's sympathy. "You must have loved her a lot."

"Yes. After all, what's not to love? She's a doll."

He took that one, too. "Even so," he said, "life goes on."

"Though not necessarily for very long. How about due west?"

He thought about due west. "Don't know an awful lot about it, to be honest with you. It'd be a hell of a drag from here to the coast. Actually, east would be better. Also a hell of a drag, but eventually you'd reach the Antecyrene border rather than just the sea. Unless you're a really good swimmer, I don't suppose the sea would be a lot of use to you."

"I hate Antecyrene," I said. "It's so hot."

"Really? Never been there myself. That's what I'd do if I was in your shoes."

"What do you know about it, in that direction?"

"Not a lot." He scowled in thought. "There's about eighty miles of rather scruffy farmland," he said, "then a couple of big towns you'd have to detour around, then a lot of sort of steppe country and then you're into the desert. Lots of that, and then you're in Antecyrene. It doesn't sound very hopeful, but I guess it's better than the alternatives."

Not that it mattered. "I don't suppose I could see my daughter," I said. "Just for a moment. Through a doorway or a window."

He shook his head. "You decided it'd be better if you didn't, and you were quite right," he said. "Besides, if she found out she'd be livid. I don't think she'd ever forgive me. You're the devil, you see. Ever since she was born, she's been told that. The fact that I've let you out of here alive is going to be a very big issue for a very long time. Sorry."

I could have pleaded. I could have gone down on my bended knee, grabbed a stone and plugged him right between the eyes. But that would have been – rude? That's the word that popped into my mind, and it made me giggle. He frowned. "Joke?"

"Ignore me," I said. "I'm a bit overwrought, to tell you the truth. All right, then, tell me something about her. Anything."

He thought long and hard. "She's a great kid," he said. "Really."

She's a great kid, said the Great King. I wanted to hit him for that, just as one time I was in a crowd of people in the market square at Semivartis and some clown in a high tower started flinging sixpences from a balcony. Later I found out that that was why the crowd had gathered. But I didn't know; and suddenly there were people barging into me and shoving me and crushing me, and then I was on the ground and someone trod on my head. I could've killed that man in the tower for being so viciously generous. He had all the sixpences in the world and the people down below didn't have any, and they swarmed like goldfish being fed in a pond, and someone trod on my head, just as Vistam was doing, though he didn't realise it. He thought he was being generous. I looked like I could use sixpence, so he tossed me a coin from his heaped sackful of moments and hours and days and years he'd get to spend with my wife and my daughter. She's a great kid, he said, and the pressure crushing my earlobe against my skull shifted as he lifted his heel and put his weight on his instep.

"Thanks for that," I said.

"No trouble at all." He looked at me some more, maybe hoping I'd metamorphose into the Dragon King of the West, the way flies do when princesses rescue them from drowning in a bird bath. Something like that would be just another day at the office for the Great King, who makes miracles real and the real miraculous, but maybe he was having an off day. "You'd better go," he said. "I'm going to have a lot of explaining to do as it is." He clapped his hands, a noise like thunder. Two Hetsuan in white gowns appeared instantly. "Saddle the strawberry roan," he said. "Put up two big saddlebags of travelling biscuits and a couple of cheeses and a skin of last year's sweet red. Very good year for the sweet red, last year," he assured me. "You'll like it. Oh, and a couple of blankets, two of the linen coats from the stable, two pair of sandals, couple of hats – anything else?" he asked me.

A coin falling from a great height and skipping off the stones as it landed. Even a coin can kill, if it falls far enough. "I'll be fine," I said. "Thank you."

"Oh, and a bow and two dozen bodkins and a sword. Do you prefer a Twelve or a Fifteen? We've got both."

"A Fifteen," I said.

"And a jar of pickled walnuts," he added. "Cook does the most delicious pickled walnuts ever," he added reverently. "Now then, money won't do you any good because they don't use the stuff, but this might come in handy. Besides, it's sort of the usual drill, if you get me."

He took a ring off his finger. It was Sashan, a signet ring. They very rarely come up in the West, so putting a value on it would be largely speculation: say a hundred thousand staurata, or half a million. But you wouldn't sell it. They'd have to cut your finger off to get it. The Great King's seal – well, one of them. He'd have spares, probably a sackful. Even so. The usual drill; at parting, the Great King gives his guest a gift of fabulous, unimaginable value. This probably happens several times each day, every day of the year, but the Great King can afford it. That's how you know he's the Great King.

"Won't cut any ice with the Hetsuan," he said. "Still, you never know, you might get through." He thought for a moment. "Do me a favour?"

"Anything."

"If you do get out and if anybody ever asks, tell them I'm dead. Really dead." He smiled. "It's been a pleasure meeting you, really it has, but on the whole I don't much care for visitors."

He hadn't mentioned it, but someone had tucked a map into the left-side saddlebag. It was only a sketch; a few scratches and dots on a wooden tile coated in beeswax, a few words in Sashan wedge-letters – mountains, river, sea, that sort of thing. Luckily I remembered that Sashan maps have east at the top, or I could've got myself in a right old pickle.

Not that it mattered. He'd said go east, so I went east. I started out at sunset, having memorised as much of the landscape as I could see from the top of the fort's west wall. The horse was the sort I could never afford, and when we pick them up running loose on a battlefield I don't let anyone ride them in case they go lame. He'd chosen a strawberry roan because they're common as muck in Hetsuan, though anywhere else they go for silly money.

I'm guessing that Vistam had a word with his sister, the Moon, because she came out from behind the clouds and did a grand job of letting me see where I was going, that night and the following night and the night after that. I was glad I'd gone west, like he told me. If I'd gone east, no doubt it would've been as dark as a bag and the horse would've put its hoof in a rabbit hole. We have free will, you see; we can do as we're told and everything will be fine, or we can do what we want and make a complete mess of our lives, but the choice is up to us. But he'd said go east, so I was going east. I may be stupid, but I'm not an idiot.

At daybreak on the fifth day I found a nice dense thicket of willows beside a small lake, made a nest for myself among the tall reeds and went to sleep. I woke up, and there were people standing all round me. They were Hetsuan, with spears and bows. One of them had a shaved head.

10

"On your feet," he said.

I did the geometry. It wouldn't come out. Distance to the nearest weapon, too far. Triangulation of antagonists, not favourable. I did as I was told.

One of them led the strawberry roan out from where I'd skilfully concealed it. "Up," said the cook. I got into the saddle. The geometry was still wrong; in fact, it was worse. The Hetsuan were watching me with intense, educated attention. They knew all about this sort of thing. They had horses, too, and they mounted quickly and smoothly, allowing me no opportunities. I got the impression that the cook wasn't just any cook. I bet he could do you a pot roast to die for.

"What happens now?" I asked.

"Shut your face," the cook snapped back, which was me told. There were no reins on the strawberry roan, just a leading rein which the cook took charge of personally.

It's a terrible thing when, after a lifetime of doubt, you finally achieve true faith, only to find you've been had for a fool. For a while back there, I actually believed in Vistam. I'd crossed the wilderness and met Him, vicegerent of the Eternal Flame, brother of the Sun and Moon; he hadn't felt able to let me see my daughter and he was screwing my wife, but he'd given me a really fine horse and a magic ring and arranged all that useful moonlight – but no, apparently not. Maybe even he could only operate in a strictly limited geographical area, say a fifty-mile radius of home. Now I was making my last journey, no idea how long, no idea where I was headed. I felt disappointed, but I knew that none of it mattered. The geometry was all over the place and, besides, could I be bothered any more? Not really. The convention is that once you've made the journey and had the beatific vision, you spend the rest of your life in contentment and inner peace. Clearly the rest of my life was going to be relatively short, but how I spent it was up to me. Contentment, inner peace: why the hell not? As I think I may have mentioned earlier, the calmer and more relaxed the animal, the better it tastes. And I was a guest in these people's country. I wouldn't want to leave a bad taste in their mouths, it'd be rude.

As usual, missing the point. The function of prey is to be caught; as prey you keep score, know how well you're doing, by the length of time during which you can honestly say, they haven't got me yet. Meanwhile the salmon struggles gamely upstream until he gets where he needs to go. Once he's got there – fine. I'd struggled against the current as far as Vistam's castle, under the mistaken impression that I was seeking my mate. I got there and found that my mate was much better off without me, which when you think of it amounts to pretty much the same thing. My mate was in Paradise, for crying out loud; surely that was enough, and no further action required on my part. Now let the salmon depart in peace, and you'd have to be downright churlish to deny the otters a decent meal.

We had a long ride, uneventful and boring. I tried asking: where are we going, why is it taking so long, are we there yet, is it soon yet? Shut your face. The more I asked, the angrier the cook got with me, so I gave up. When we passed through villages, people hurried inside and shut the doors. I got given a fair ration of bread and water each day, and I got to see a lot of the scenery of Hetsuan, which you can have, and welcome to it. I felt like a man falling off a very, very tall tower. It's relaxing, wallowing lazily in a cushion of air, and quite boring after a while, and then the journey comes to an end and all your troubles are over—

It was about three hours after sunrise. I stood up in my stirrups and looked straight ahead. I recognised that low, featureless rise ahead of me. About a mile away, though of course I couldn't see it from there, was a ditch. The other side of the ditch was Sashan territory.

I did the geometry and it was hopeless. They were riding in star formation, with me in the epicentre; I hadn't noticed them shift position, which shows how demoralised I'd got. Well, I said to myself, here we are and this is it. Presumably it has to be here, because this is where I murdered Giraut de Borneil and stole his excellent horse. Fair enough. Just one more ditch to cross, so to speak, and I'm in the place where I truly belong.

We carried on. They were watching me the way guard dogs do, when they've come bounding up, howling bloody murder, and they surround you, and then they stop dead and stand there, doing that special low growl that loosens your bladder.

We were getting closer and closer to the border, close enough that I could see the ditch; close enough to see a bunch of people on the other side. Hang on, I thought.

Closer still, and I could make out the faces of the people on the other side. There was Eudo, and there, in a red cloak and pretty as a picture, was Stauracia. They were all on horses, and behind them was a farm wagon, and more people I couldn't quite make out, on horses, clustered round it in what looked very much like that classic star formation.

The cook stopped his horse on the very edge of the ditch. "Hey, you," he called out.

Stauracia and Eudo rode up to their edge. They didn't say anything. Someone behind me told me to get down off the horse, so I did. The cook turned and beckoned, and I saw bows being drawn.

"That him?" the cook said.

"That's him," Eudo said.

The cook took his foot out of its stirrup and booted me in the face. I toppled over and fell in the ditch. I lay there, wondering for a moment which side I was supposed to clamber out on. "Come on, for fuck's sake," Stauracia yelled at me. I scrambled a bit, and I was on Sashan soil, with a dozen Hetsuan arrows pointed precisely at me.

Eudo turned and waved to the men beside the wagon. The wagon rumbled forward until it reached the ditch, the tailgate dropped down and a dozen or so people got out: four women, the rest kids. The women climbed awkwardly into the ditch and held up their arms to help the children; five or so Hetsuan dismounted to help them up the other side. The archers unbent their bows, keeping the arrows nocked on the string.

The cook looked at me. "Arsehole," he said. Then he gave a

signal with his hand, and the Hetsuan turned and rode away, in star formation around the women and the kids.

Something crashed into me. It was Eudo, giving me an enormous hug. Oh, I thought.

"We didn't expect gratitude," Stauracia said. "Still, there's no need to be a total shit about it."

"You must have been out of your tiny minds," I yelled at her. "You could've started a war."

I was seriously angry. I'm still not entirely sure why. "So what?" Stauracia said, tightening her horse's girth. "War is good for business. I'd have thought you of all people—"

"It was all we could think of," Eudo said. "I mean, you didn't exactly make it easy for us, suddenly going off like that."

"All *I* could think of, you mean," Stauracia interrupted. "This idiot here was all for sneaking across the border at night and hoping for the best. Fortunately, one of us has a brain."

Was I angry because I was still alive, and they'd saved me? That wasn't supposed to happen. I was a lamb going serenely to the slaughter. "You know about these people, for crying out loud," I growled at her. "Kidnapping innocent women and children—"

She put her foot in the stirrup and mounted the horse. Nearly everything she does is graceful, a pleasure to watch. "You prick," she said. "I should've let them eat you."

Eudo was already mounted. They'd provided me with a big chestnut mare, cavalry surplus. Compared to the horses in Hetsuan, it was a big slab of dog meat. When I was on it, I felt like I was a hundred miles off the ground. "We need to get away from here as quickly as possible," I said. "If they come across the border, I want to be very hard to find."

It was, of course, Stauracia's idea. When she realised what I'd done, she had hysterics (according to Eudo and Gombryas) and had to be restrained from charging off after me. Ten minutes later, she'd come up with the plan: hire some local muscle, cross the border at night, snatch as many civilians as they could round up and still have enough time to get back across the ditch by daybreak, and then send one of them home with a message.

The message was: our friend, who's a lunatic and not responsible for his actions, is trespassing in your territory. If you bring him back to us unharmed, we won't kill the hostages.

"I've met these people," I nagged at her, as we raced across the moor. "You really don't want to play games with them. This is just the sort of thing that confirms what they think about us already."

"Actually," Eudo put in, "when you look at their record of actually going to war, they don't, usually. For a start there's all those checks and balances. When you think that over the last fifteen hundred years they've only—"

"Shut up," I said, because he was probably right. I'd met the Hetsuan. They were vicious savage bloodthirsty monsters, in the Sashan sense. We think they're ravenous predators. They think the same about us. We're both right.

By the time we stopped for the night I'd calmed down a bit, and the feeling of disappointment and loss was wearing off. "So," Stauracia said, raising the topic for the first time, "how did you get on? Did you get there?"

"Midons?" I said. "No. I think I may have seen it in the distance."

"So you didn't find her after all?"

"I found her," I said. "Saw her, for about fifteen seconds."

"That's not very long," Eudo said. "Was there a problem?"

Bless him. "You could say that," I said. "She thought I'd come to murder her."

"But you explained."

"No," I said. "Can we talk about something else?"

"You didn't explain."

"I explained to her husband," I said.

Stauracia looked at me. I couldn't see her face very well, because it was dark and she was leaning back from the light of the campfire. "And?" she said.

"He's a nice guy," I said. "I liked him."

"And then you cut his throat."

I sighed. "No," I said. "That would've been pointless. He explained that Apoina and Eudocia – that's my daughter – were absolutely convinced that I was hell-bent on killing them both. More to the point, they're both about a million times happier than they ever could be with me in their lives. So—"

"So you gave up."

"It seemed the sensible thing to do," I said.

Long silence. Then Eudo said, "I think you were quite right. No offence, but you're not exactly premium husband-and-father material, and if they're happy, why spoil everything? And if you killed the husband, I don't suppose that would have endeared you to her particularly."

Stauracia and I stared at him for a moment. "My thoughts exactly," I said. "So, yes, I gave up."

"Fair enough," Stauracia said. "Only I wouldn't have thought you'd have done that. I assumed—"

"So did Praeclara." And I explained to them what Praeclara had assumed. It left them silent and thoughtful for a moment or so. Then Stauracia said, "Smart woman. We really ought to kill her for that."

"For being smart?"

"I wish I'd thought of it," she said. "It's – what's the word I'm looking for? Economical."

Eudo was gazing at me. "You really met the rightful king of Sashan?"

I nodded. "Nice man," I said. "I liked him."

"So that's why you didn't kill him?"

"No."

Which wasn't strictly true. Or it wasn't the whole truth. "Anyway," Eudo said, "that's a wonderful thing, meeting a real live king like that."

Eudo is like the toothache. For a long time, you tell yourself it's not so bad and you can bear it. Then you reach the point where you no longer can. "I think I'll go to sleep now," I said. "It's been a funny old day."

But I couldn't sleep, needless to say, and after a couple of hours lying on my back looking at a bunch of disappointing stars I got up and went for a walk about. I found Eudo still sitting by the fire, reading a book.

"So it was her idea," I said.

"Oh, yes. We all tried to talk her out of it, but she was dead set."

"I can imagine," I said.

He closed the book and laid it down. "Do you think the Hetsuan—?"

I shook my head. "Probably not," I said. "Luckily, nobody actually got hurt, and I managed to get away without doing anything particularly bad while I was over there. And they've only got two choices: all-out war or pretend it didn't happen. If it'd been Antecyrene or Tyrsenia, they might well go to war. But I don't see them committing themselves to wiping

K. J. Parker

the Sashan Empire off the face of the earth if they can possibly help it."

He thought about it for a moment. "That's all right, then."

"Yes, probably it is. What's that you're reading?"

"Oh, just something I picked up somewhere. It's pretty boring, actually."

He handed it to me to look at. I glanced at the title, written on the spine in typical librarians' abbreviations. *Concerning Textiles*. "Where did you say you got this?"

"Can't remember. Actually, yes I can. I picked it up at that castle place. It was just lying about, so I thought—"

I wasn't listening. I was leaning as close to the fire as I could get without my eyebrows getting burned off, so I could read the librarian's precis on the title page; *a book concerning the manufacture, use and decoration of textiles, with some irrelevant digressions about different types of loom used in remote countries, notes about dyestuffs and an inaccurate account of the life cycle of the silkworm. The first edition; later copies were amended and much spurious and unsubstantiated material omitted.*

"What's the matter?" Eudo asked. "Are you all right?"

I ignored him. Dyestuffs; first edition; much spurious and unsubstantiated material omitted. "Just lying about," I said.

"Yup. It was in that room in the tower. I fancied something to read."

"You lunatic," I said. "Do you know what you've done?"

He gave me a blank look. "It's just a rather dull book about flax," he said. "Isn't it?"

I considered him, the way Vistam had considered me: an equation, difficult but capable of being solved   actually, I wasn't at all sure about that. "You maniac," I said. "All right, wake everybody up. We're moving."

"But it's the middle of the—"

"Now."

I thought about it carefully, and decided that Stauracia probably needed to know, or that I owed her something for something. She was sleeping peacefully, like an angel curled up in a blanket. I prodded her shoulder with my toe and she was awake instantly. "What?"

"The book," I said.

She didn't need to be told which book. "What about it?"

I showed it to her. "Know what this is?"

"It's a book. So what?"

"It's *the* book."

She can go from fast asleep to wide awake in a heartbeat, like a cat. "The one Praeclara wants."

"Yes."

"How do you—?" She didn't bother finishing that. She trusted me.

"Eudo had it all the time," I said.

Her eyes went round. "The fucking shit."

I shook my head. "I don't think he realised," I said. "I think he just wanted something to read."

"The *arsehole*." So much, in her view, for reading books. "You're sure?"

"Pretty sure. I'll have to look through it to confirm, but it all makes sense now." I paused for a moment. "It'll be worth a lot of money," I said.

We both knew what I meant by that. We didn't have to use it as a lure to trap Praeclara. We could sell it and be stupidly rich, and all our troubles would be over. "Fuck it," she said.

"Sure?"

She grinned. "You know what?" she said. "I've spent my

life on the trail of the big score, ever since I can remember, and it's always been so close I can practically smell it. So, fuck it. There'll be another one along in a minute. There always is."

I looked at her. I couldn't see her, because it was still dark, but I could see her clear as day in the Sashan sense. I imagine it was the magic of the Great King's signet ring, or something like that. "No," I said. "I mean a *great deal* of money. *Enough* money. Even for you and me."

She was only human. She hesitated. Maybe a whole second. "Fuck it," she repeated. "And there's no such thing as enough, believe me."

The long ride to Beloisa was no fun. We were all terrified, every step of the way. We took longer than we should have because we went the long way round any settlement bigger than a village. We had every right to be scared. We were exposed in open country, moving painfully slowly; anyone could have found us and scooped us up, and that would have been that.

When we got there it was even worse. Out in the open, we could see them coming. Beloisa is one of the biggest cities on our side of the Friendly Sea. Spotting an enemy there is like looking out for one particular mackerel in a shoal.

I found Gombryas in the Nine Pillars of Understanding, where the booze is toxic but reasonably priced. He was meeting a small-time dealer who claimed to have a kneecap of Carnufex the Irrigator. It turned out to be a fake, as Carnufex relics almost invariably are, so he was understandably annoyed. "Where the hell did you get to?" he demanded. "We've been stuck in this shithole for a week."

I gave him a condensed version. He stared at me. "You're crazy," he said. "You're fucking lunatics, the lot of you."

"Yes," I said. "How did it go?"

"You really kidnapped a load of—"

"Yes. How did it go?"

He pulled a sad face. "All right," he said. "Lousy hot weather and everything crawling with flies, but we cleared two thousand net. Polycrates got blood poisoning from a rusty arrow but the doc pulled him through."

You can't have everything. "You've sold the stuff."

"I just told you, didn't I? Did you really—?"

"So we're ready to move out."

"Yes."

We moved out. There were a lot of complaints. Polycrates made the valid point that he and the rest of them had just carried out a relatively successful operation with absolutely no help, guidance or input from me, so what did they actually need me for? He also raised the issue of where we were going, and when I told him, back to the castle, he asked why. Shut your face, I suggested, and there the matter rested, but I could see he wasn't happy, and neither were most of the others. We went, all the same. Mostly, I think, through force of habit; and if I were to step down as leader of the gang, who'd replace me? Better the arsehole you know, seemed to be the general verdict, even if he does keep leading us into mortal peril and we never seem to make any money.

On the way we stopped over in Eisi Celeuthoe, where I got into a bidding war with the Company of Vultures for a small police action just over the Blemyan border into Doria. I only did it to draw attention to myself, and let everyone know that I was back and very much still in business. The Vultures made sure of that, telling everyone who'd listen about pissy little cowboy operators who gave the industry a bad name by over-bidding and driving up prices generally.

"You realise," Stauracia said, "that you've just told the entire trade where you are and where you're going to be in eight weeks' time. I thought we were keeping a low profile."

"Really?" I said. "What made you think that?"

"But—" She gave me that look, the one that deals with my exaggerated opinion of my own intelligence, and various related issues. I'm so used to it that I've got callouses on my face, from where she glares at me. "You want Praeclara to know where you are."

"Now that we're back in the West, yes," I said. "I figure it might save us a long journey."

It did. We were two days from Beloisa, camped in a wood on top of a hill, at the foot of which the Southern Main snaked along the bottom of the Calama Downs. It was an ideal defensive position, where you'd feel safe from any trouble. Accordingly, I posted three cordons of sentries, and told everybody to sleep with strung bows and an arrow nocked on the bowstring.

It was a clear night, so I figured she'd make her move about four hours after midnight, when the dark would be starting to thin out. She'd come for me there anticipating that I wouldn't bother to be careful in such a strong position. She underestimates me, which is the only advantage I have in dealing with her.

My orders were to let her through the first two cordons; the third cordon greeted her with shouts and yells, picked up straight away by the two cordons that were now right behind her. They made enough noise to give her the impression she was surrounded by superior forces, which she was, in the Sashan sense. She'd have made a fight of it, knowing that my followers were sincerely chickenshit when it came to violence, but her people weren't prepared to get into a fight with sharp weapons on her say-so and gave up immediately. Carrhasio dragged her in by her hair, pushed her to the ground and stood with his foot on her neck until I told him to pull himself together, which he did with a bad grace. She got up and glowered at me in the red light of dawn.

"I'm not talking to you," I said.

"Arsehole," she said.

From my pocket I produced the book. I opened it so she could see the librarian's inscription on the front page, and held it in front of her face. "Is this it?" I said.

"Yes."

I snapped it shut and stuffed it in my pocket. "Fool you twice, shame on you," I said. "I think I'll keep it. I earned it, after all."

She looked straight at me. "Why do you say that?"

"I did what you wanted," I said. "I killed Vistam. That's what you sent me to do, isn't it?"

I could almost hear her heart ringing inside her like a bell, but her face didn't change. "Say that again. You killed Vistam."

"Yes." I let that sink in. "Pity, really. He was a good man. She loved him, you know. Of course, that's why I killed him."

A moment ago she'd had her nose in the leaf mould, and Carrhasio's boot on her spine. Now she had to fight to keep the joy out of her voice. "I told you the truth," she said. "I didn't lie to you. I told you where to find her, and there she was."

"You arranged for me to assassinate the rightful Great King," I said, "to suit your maniac agenda. So what? We're just two deeply unpleasant people who were able to do each other a favour. But I get to keep the book. It's worth a great deal of money."

She had to ask. "How the hell did you get out of Hetsuan?"

"My friends rescued me."

Not what she'd expected to hear. "What, that lot?"

"Loyal and resourceful," I said. "And brave as tigers. You didn't anticipate that, I don't suppose."

She was thinking. I knew the name, Vistam; how would I have found it out unless I'd actually been there? Therefore I was telling the truth. "Apoina," she said.

"Oh, exactly as you'd set it up," I said. "She now hates me worse than ever. Eudocia, too, they both think I'm the devil incarnate. I had nothing to lose on that score, so I killed him and came home. As far as I'm concerned the whole thing was a total washout. Still, it's nice to go to new places and meet new people. Which reminds me," I added. "Got something for you."

"Go on, then."

"Just a moment." I nodded to Eudo, who came forward with a razor, a basin of water and a bar of soap. "Oldest trick in the book," I said, as Eudo started shaving my head. "Luckily they don't seem to have read Rodebart's *Chronicles* in Hetsuan."

Eudo took his time, because I didn't want to get even the slightest cut or nick on my scalp. "There," I said, leaning forward so she could see."

She read what Vistam's valet had tattooed on my scalp; fortuitous that the Hetsuan have a long tradition of body decoration. Like I said, the oldest trick in the book; shave the messenger's head, tattoo the message, let the hair grow back. Not only is the message highly unlikely to be found by anyone intercepting the messenger, but the messenger himself can't see what's been written. "She begged me," I said. "She went down on her knees. I reckoned it was the least I could do, since I'd just murdered her husband."

Actually, I knew exactly what it said, because Vistam and I had composed it between us. I knew roughly what I wanted it to say, and he tweaked it so it sounded just like Apoina, including the secret codeword she only used when writing to her mother, so Praeclara would know the message was genuine. Credit where it's due: it was Vistam's idea, though he would've been content to forge Apoina's handwriting on a piece of paper. But I'd come up with the tattoo thing, which I remembered from reading the *Chronicles*; partly because I didn't trust his ability as a forger, partly because if I was captured (as indeed I was) they'd search me and find it. And they did search me, but they didn't find it. I imagine they're now under the mistaken impression that foreign savages tattoo weird talismans on their scalps, along with all the other bizarre things we do to ourselves.

I can't remember word for word what we came up with, but the gist was: Saevus has murdered my husband; I'm all alone here and I'm terrified; please come immediately – followed by a detailed account of the secret passwords, safe houses et cetera she'd need to cross Hetsuan unmolested. It's fortunate I have rather a large head, or the valet would never have been able to fit it all on.

Anyway, Praeclara read it, turning paler and paler every second. "Well?" I said, when she'd finished. "Will you go?"

She sublimated her fear into hatred for me, a useful knack. "You bastard," she said.

"I didn't do anything," I said. "It was all your idea. And now your daughter's stuck in the middle of Hetsuan, and only you can save her. Your own silly fault, if you ask me."

"How do I know it's safe?"

"You don't," I said. "It's what Vistam set up, just in case

something like this happened, but whether or not it'll work I have absolutely no idea. You might get there, or you might not. Your choice."

The fear made her look ten years older. "How do I know—?"

"Oh, come on," I said. "I'm smart, but even I'd have difficulty tattooing my own head, in a language I don't even know. And if you think I had it done after I got back, use your brain. My hair doesn't grow that fast."

She thought about it, very carefully. She was thinking that while she was there she could surreptitiously acquire Vistam's head, as proof, always assuming nobody had thoughtlessly cremated him. But the Hetsuan wouldn't like that, so the head was probably still around somewhere . . . "The book," she said. "I need the book."

"What for?"

"For when I get back," she said. "For the next stage, now that Vistam's dead."

I sighed. "You really take the cake, don't you? Tell you what. You go and rescue Apoina and bring her back, and then we'll talk about it."

"No," she said. "I want the book now, or I'm not going."

(And that's how I won my bet with Stauracia; most expensive bet I've ever won, but I'm not complaining.)

"The hell with what you want," I said. "I'm sick to death of you and your constant manipulating. If you want the book you can buy it, cash money."

"How much?"

"Since you're family, half a million. I could probably get double that from the Knights, or the Poor Sisters."

"I haven't got half a million."

"It sucks to be poor," I said. "How much have you got?"

She breathed at me through her nose. "Two hundred thousand," she said. "In the Merchant Venturers' in Auxentia City."

"Just a moment," I said, "while I confer with my associates."

I staged a little huddle, in whispers. "What's she talking about, two hundred thousand?" Gombryas said. "Shut up," I replied. "And keep your voice down or you'll ruin everything."

Huddle over. "I'll need a sealed bill of exchange," I said. "You've got your seal with you, naturally."

She called me a rude name. I pointed out that I could seal the bill just as easily with the seal still on her severed finger. She took it off and threw it at me: a nice touch, I thought. "Thank you," I said. "Here's your book."

I put it down on the ground with my foot resting on it. She got down on her hands and knees and teased it out from under my toecap, expecting to get the other boot in her teeth. I disappointed her, which gave me much more satisfaction.

Needless to say, there was no account in her name with the Merchant Venturers'. Gombryas and Polycrates were upset about that; they'd believed her, and insisted on traipsing back to the coast and taking a boat to Auxentia City. They rejoined us at Xedes, the nearest port to where we were going in Blemya, and gave me a hard time about going all that way for nothing.

But, as I explained to Stauracia and Eudo the next day, it was only fair that Praeclara should've lied to me, since I'd lied to her about Vistam's carefully planned escape route and network of safe houses, which was of course a figment of Vistam's and my imagination. For what it's worth, I have no positive proof that Praeclara got caught and eaten by the Hetsuan. Nobody's heard anything about her since that night, but it's quite in keeping with her way of doing things to disappear for long periods of time. For all I know she may still be alive and well and brimming over with malice same as ever.

Stauracia said I was stupid to give her the book, maybe because she was sore about losing her bet; she couldn't believe that Praeclara would have the nerve to make the book a condition of saving her own daughter's life, and told me she had ten staurata that thought the same way. She was lying: she didn't have ten staurata. I told her she could owe it to me. She still does. But (she went on) I was still stupid. I should've killed Praeclara when I had the chance, instead of making up that idiotic rigmarole with the faked message and the shaved head, the scars of which would stay with me the rest of my life. She was right, of course; she generally is. But when Vistam suggested it, I knew immediately that it was the right thing to do. It would mean, he said, that the only decent, human thing Praeclara ever did in her entire life would result in a horrific, terrifying death; a solemn lesson, to those of us in the know, about how vital it is for the leopard not to change its spots.

"You're still a moron," Stauracia said. "That book was worth half a million, and now it'll end up chucked under a hedge somewhere in Hetsuan and be no good to anybody. That's just a pointless waste."

"It's not quite as bad as that," I said. "I may have been able to salvage something from the wreck. We'll see."

She sat gazing into the campfire for a while. "You really hate her, don't you?"

"Yes."

"That's not like you. You don't usually hate people."

"She has that effect on me."

"Because of your wife."

I nodded. "That's what love does," I said. "I've always

reckoned the positive emotions cause more harm than anything else in this life. It's like altruism and idealism. Altruism and idealism have caused more wars and more deaths—"

"Don't start all that again," she said, reasonably enough. "And you don't know the first thing about love. All you're interested in is saving your own skin."

I looked at her. "If it wasn't for love, I'd never have needed to," I said. "Two people in my life I've really loved, my brother and my wife. Things don't tend to go well with people I love, or with me because of them. I'd be rather more comfortable with a pet scorpion. At least they only sting you if you tease them." I thought about that for a moment. "Part of me wants Praeclara to make it after all. I couldn't have killed her in cold blood. This way, at least she's got a chance. A properly small one, but a chance all the same."

She gave me an odd look. "You're pathetic," she said, and left me to my brooding.

The trivial little police action in Doria had started by the time we got there, but we had no trouble finding it; just follow the trail of burned-out villages and crucified insurgents. "This is a complete waste of time and money," Polycrates said, as we rattled along an arrow-straight military road through sand and thorn-scrub. "The savages aren't going to fight a pitched battle with the Blemyan military. Nobody's that stupid. They'll just play hit and run a few times while the soldiers round up their women and their cattle, and then the Blemyans will go home and that'll be that. How much did you say you paid for the rights to this piece of shit?"

I wasn't really listening to him. I was more interested in the crows. They're not especially common in Blemya, where the main scavengers are kites, which miaow like cats when they're circling and whistle when they're scared. We'd been whistled at for most of the morning, as we put up dozens of kites from every gibbet and cross we passed, and when I heard crows screaming in the distance it almost made me homesick.

The crows were circling around a small lake or large pond – there's a technical term in Blemyan – and I decided to take a look. Always follow the crows; they know what they're doing.

Easy to figure out what had happened. Two regiments of Blemyan regular heavy infantry and a squadron of lancers had stopped at the lake for the night. They knew the lake was there, it was on the maps, and their route had been carefully planned to make sure they never ran short of water. They hadn't seen hide nor hair of the bad guys for three days, and if they were being followed, they'd have seen a dust cloud. So there was nothing at all to worry about. They reached the lake just before sunset, pitched their tents, filled their water bottles, posted their sentries and went to sleep.

The rebels, of course, had got there first. I'm guessing they'd been there for five or six days, knowing that the enemy would have to stop there to get water; they'd dug shallow trenches on the edge of the belt of greenery surrounding the lake and roofed them over with thorn branches. If the sentries heard them coming, it didn't matter. It would all have been over in five minutes or so. They managed to take most of the Blemyans alive; presumably the poor fools thought they were being given a chance to surrender, but I guess that by that stage in the relationship the rebels were good and mad at them. They nailed the officers to tree trunks by their hands and feet, beheaded the rank-and-file, stacked the heads in a neat pyramid and slung the bodies into the lake. Nobody would be drinking that water for a good long time, which meant a further punitive expedition was out of the question. I guess the rebels belonged to the small subsection of humanity who think more clearly when they're angry. It's not a bad character trait to have, if you ask me.

If we'd got there a day later, the whole lake would've been stinking and we'd have been in serious trouble. As it was, there were a couple of smaller subsidiary pools that hadn't got polluted yet, and we were able to fill up our water jars for the trip home. Once we'd got that done, we were able to turn our attention to business.

The only thing the rebels had taken were the horses; everything else was where it had been when the rebels burst in and started rounding people up. A thousand tents, nearly three thousand sets of bedding, mess kits, boots, uniforms – too hot to sleep if you're wearing anything, so everything was laid out neat and soldierly, armour sand-polished, boots paired and gleaming, belts and straps freshly whitened with pipeclay, unissued arrows bundled in three-dozens in sealed cloth bags, cooking pots and kettles cleaned out and burnished, ready for tomorrow's breakfast; the rebels had even left the food, barrels of pork and apples, twenty-gallon jars of olives and pickled cabbage, sacks and sacks of oats for the horses, all neatly stacked ready for us to load onto the carts, as though we'd been expected. We dug a pit for the heads and the desiccated officers, and that was all we had to do. "I really like these people," Olybrius said. "Let's hope they invade the empire. They're so clean and tidy."

We left the crows shrieking at us, without even sun-dried officers to eat, and rumbled back the way we'd come. We cleared twenty-six thousand eight hundred staurata when we got to Boc Bohec, net of shipping, harbour dues and local taxes; it was one of our best jobs ever, and far and away the easiest.

"What's she getting a share for?" Dodilas wanted to know, when we did the split after I'd cashed the bills we'd been given. "She's not even a member."

"She did her share of the graft," I said.

"What, helped lift a few barrels onto a cart?" Carrhasio wasn't impressed. "The hell with that. If she's not a member she's not entitled. What's she doing, anyway, still hanging around? I don't remember anyone being asked if she could tag along."

"Fine." Stauracia got up. "Fuck the lot of you, then." She looked at me and I had a fair idea what she expected me to say, but I didn't say it. I vaguely remembered a conversation we'd had, about her staying with us as far as Boc Bohec; presumably it had slipped her mind. "She gets a full share," I said. "She can have mine. I'd be a pile of turds in Hetsuan right now if it hadn't been for her."

"That's your business," Polycrates said. "But if she's joining us, we need to vote on it, and I wouldn't trust her as far as I can piss."

I'm not what you'd call a gesture person. I don't wave my hands about, yell or stamp my little foot, and I try not to do things simply because they feel right at the time. But nobody's perfect. "No problem," I said. "She goes. Me, too. I've had it with you people. From now on you can look after yourselves, and the best of luck to you."

There was a stunned silence as everyone wondered: does he mean it? They should have known me better than that. I stood up and walked away, out of the gate of the livery yard where we were staying, down an alley that led into Cornmarket, across the square and into the Kindly Light. Technically I was still barred from the Light for antisocial behaviour, but that was five years ago and it had burned down twice since then. I spent two of my five remaining thalers on a jug of beer and a rather indifferent sea bass with spinach and almonds, and considered what I'd just done. All in all, I couldn't find much wrong with it.

I'd finished the sea bass and I was picking my teeth with one of the big bones when Eudo came in, looked round and saw me. "What was all that about?" he asked.

I shrugged. "It's about time I moved on," I said.

"We're your friends."

"Exactly," I said. "I'm doing them a favour. They don't need me, and I keep getting them in trouble."

He sighed. I poured him some of the beer, which was all right but nothing special. "This is about Stauracia, isn't it?" he said.

"No, not really."

"You're not running away from us. You're running away from her."

I yawned. "I'm not sure I've got the energy left to run anywhere any more," I said, "to or from anyone or anywhere or in any particular direction. The hell with running. Drink your beer."

"You can't just take off like that."

"Oh, I think I probably can."

"Really? Got any money?"

I showed him my three thalers.

"That's not going to last very long."

"True," I said. "But when that's gone I'll just have to get some more." I stood up. "I suppose I ought to go and find Stauracia," I said. "She'll be wanting someone to shout at."

He looked up at me. From above, I could see where his hair was starting to get thin. He'd be bald as an egg in five years, at that rate. "You really don't get it, do you?"

"You what?"

"You think you're really smart and you know about people, but really you haven't got a clue. I'm sorry for you."

Nobody's been sorry for me since I was twelve. I sat down again. "Sorry," I said, "I don't follow."

"She rescued you, for crying out loud," he said, leaning forward into my face further than was strictly necessary. "She cares about you. She—"

"Oh, come on," I said. "It's not like that with her and me." I stood up again. "I know her. All she's ever been interested in is the big score, which is why she's such a mess. The sad part of it is, one of these days she'll make it, and what will the robin do then, poor thing? Till then, though, she's as single-minded as an arrow. Get a grip on yourself and don't read so much poetry."

He looked at me. "You're an idiot, Saevus. Sorry, but you are."

I looked for her but I couldn't find her, and then it was dark and I decided I didn't want to wander around Boc Bohec when I couldn't see people's faces. So I went back to the Light. Eudo had gone, leaving a message at the bar that he'd be back in the morning. One thaler for a bed for the night, which is robbery, even in Boc.

Someone had been round nailing up proclamations on all the inn doors, which was a scandalous waste of expensive paper. I helped myself to one – something about a rise in municipal property tax – and borrowed the landlady's pen and ink from her cubbyhole in the cellar. Then I retired to the overpriced ten square feet of hayloft floor and wrote something down before

I forgot it. While the ink was drying (like a fool I'd forgotten to steal any blotting sand) I looked around and found the ideal place, a little space between two rafters, just the right size for wedging a government proclamation, folded four times. I daubed a bit of spiderweb over it to help it be inconspicuous.

Eudo was there bright and early. I found him talking to Gombryas, who jumped up as soon as he saw me. "You're coming back, right?" he said.

"No," I said.

"Fuck that. You're coming back. Otherwise it'll be that clown Polycrates. He'll get us all killed inside a month."

"Then don't elect him," I said. "Tell you what, you can be leader. Or Olybrius. Not Carrhasio, obviously, or Dodilas, and definitely not Polycrates, but it's not exactly difficult work, or else I couldn't have done it all these years. You'll get on splendidly, trust me."

We argued for a bit and Gombryas went away in a huff. I hoped I'd see him again someday, but I was glad he'd stalked off calling me an arsehole. Anything more tender than that would've upset me. "You mean it, don't you?" Eudo said. "You're leaving them."

"Yes," I said. "Before I bring down something really nasty on them. They're my friends. I don't want anything bad to happen to them."

He nodded. "I think you're probably right," he said. "By the way, I'm sorry. Last night. I was out of line."

"Were you? I can't remember. I wouldn't worry about it."

"Did you find her?"

I shook my head. "She'll turn up," I said. "She always does, when you need her least."

He didn't think that was funny. "I got to thinking about it," he said. "It's the same as with Gombryas and Carrhasio and the lads. Anybody you really care for—"

"Is better off without me, yes. I learned that in Hetsuan. No, I tell a lie, I've known it for years, Hetsuan just reminded me, very forcefully. So I think I'll just go a long way away and make a great deal of money. So long, Eudo. Thanks for rescuing me, even if you did try and start a major war."

He frowned. "Any idea where you'll go?"

"Echmen," I said. "Not straight away, of course, but it's where I plan to end up eventually. They have more money in Echmen than any other country on earth."

He grinned. It was forced grin, strained for, like bad constipation. "Here," he said, and on the table he placed four staurata, one on top of another in a neat column. Neatest man I ever met in my life. "Pay me back when you're stupid rich."

"Of course I will," I said, and left him.

11

To get to Echmen eventually, the best way is west. Echmen is, of course, due east, but I was in no hurry.

West, therefore, as far as Brotoe, a thaler and two bits on the carrier's coach and wine with my dinner at some godforsaken fleabag along the way. At Brotoe the money changes, florins for thalers and angels for staurata. The exchange rate happened to be in my favour, for the first time ever.

From Brotoe – you can get practically anywhere from Brotoe, which was handy, since that was where I was headed. I spent one of Eudo's staurata on a boat trip to Scona. I hate travelling by ship. On Scona I went to see a man I hadn't spoken to in years. He was surprised to see me, but he calmed down after a while, at which point I told him what I'd got to sell. He suddenly went very quiet, and when his wife came in he yelled at her to go away. I told him I was going the rounds asking for offers, and how much was he prepared to pay? He said, you can't put a price on something like that. Try, I told him.

He lent me ten angels, and I took a boat and a mail coach

to Choris, where I went to see another man I used to know. He suggested a sum of money. I told him I was just shopping around, but I'd let him know; meanwhile, if anybody asked after me, I'd died of the fever in Blemya. He nodded. It's nice when you can trust people.

My next port of call was En Chersi, where I knew a man I hadn't seen for a long time. On the way I stopped off in Traco, just in time for the first of the new season strawberries. I went to the inn for a bed for the night. The landlord and I go way back. "There was someone in here looking for you," he said.

"Is that right?"

He grinned. "Not like that," he said. "It was some woman. Tasty."

My hair was just starting to grow back, but most nights when I closed my eyes I was back in Hetsuan. "That's not a nice expression," I said.

"A doll," he said. "If it was me, I'd let her catch me."

I described Stauracia. He nodded. "How long ago?" I said.

"Three days. Nice clothes and a ten-angel horse. I asked her if she was thinking of someone else."

"If she comes back," I said, "tell her I'm in En Chersi."

A doll, I thought. A coarse expression. Maybe, maybe not; none of my business. I caught the stagecoach to Psaulis, just in case she was still there, but she'd left two days earlier. There wasn't a stage from Psaulis to En until the day after tomorrow.

The hell with it. There's only one inn in Psaulis. I got something to eat, but it didn't agree with me. No matter; I'd come to the right place for all that.

The Imperishable Hope in Psaulis is just another coaching inn, but its owners are endearingly optimistic. They argue that all sorts of grand and impressive people use the road from Choris to En Chersi – diplomats, provincial governors, high officials, famous actors – and although they invariably stay at the Flawless Diamond in Reuza, nine miles up the road, maybe this wouldn't always be the case; accordingly they built a detached block of superior accommodation on the downwind side of the stable yard (nobody's stayed there yet, but you never know) and the only running-water shithouse east of the Cardauli. It's a square brick building straddling the brook that runs down the hill to join the mill leat; you sit on a plank with a hole in it (diligently sanded smooth, so no splinters) and admire the view across the valley with the castle ruins in the distance. On a pleasant evening there's no sweeter spot in the Duchy; just as well, since I was doomed to spend some time there. I settled in with my trousers round my ankles and a dual-purpose copy of Macrinus's *Sonnets*, and I was thinking beautiful thoughts about money when someone crept up behind me and hit me on the head.

I opened my eyes and there was Eudo. I recognised the back of his head. He was driving the cart I was lying in. I couldn't move my hands or feet, because of the ropes.

"Eudo?" I said.

"Quiet," he replied.

"Eudo, what's happening?"

He sighed. "Sorry," he said. "Now please shut up. We've got a long way to go. I'll stuff your mouth with wool if I have to, but I'd rather not."

At that point the dizziness caught up with me, and I was too preoccupied with not throwing up to bother about much else. I was lying on my chest and lifting my head made the dizziness much worse; you really don't want to vomit when you're face down and immobile.

"Are you all right back there?" Eudo said.

"No," I said. "I think I've got concussion. My head's swimming and I want to puke. For God's sake stop the cart."

"Sorry," Eudo said, "I don't believe you. I mean it about the wool."

I had a feeling he did, and the last thing I needed in my condition was a stuffed-full mouth. "At least turn me over on my back," I said.

"No can do. Sorry."

Attention to detail is the mark of a clear, sharp mind, though it's also irritating when carried to excess. It's one of Eudo's strong suits; for example, he'd tied my hands behind my back, but the knots were at the front, digging into my stomach; furthermore, he'd chained my right ankle to a heavy-duty staple driven into the floor of the cart, to keep me from wriggling anywhere. I remembered telling him stories of various brilliant escapes from custody and confinement I'd made over the years while we were sitting beside various campfires; clearly he'd been listening. "Why are you doing this?" I asked.

"Money," he replied. "And I'm sorry, I really mean it. And the next time you say anything, I'll stuff your mouth."

It was a long day. The jolting of the cart kept me from drifting away into sleep, which would have been the end of me, and the dizziness and the nausea gradually wore off, by which time I was dying of cramp, though my upset stomach appeared to have sorted itself out, which was really just as well. I had a big splinter stuck in my nose and another in my left cheek just below the eye. Not that it signified. Money, Eudo had said. I knew what that meant.

He stopped the cart around noon to water the horses at a stream. "How are you doing?" he asked.

"How much?" I said.

"Seventy thousand staurata, actually," he said.

I was disappointed. A year or so back, in the aftermath of the business on Sirupat, my brother-in-law the Archduke lost most of his money. This meant, among other things, that the bounty he'd placed on my head fell dramatically; at one point it had soared to half a million. How the mighty have fallen. "I'll give you double that if you'll let me go," I said.

"I don't think so," he said.

"Straight up," I said. "You know that book you were reading, the one you took from the turret room in the castle?"

"What about it?"

"It's a very rare book," I said.

"Actually, it isn't," Eudo said. "I looked into it. It's the standard work on textile manufacture. Every library in the West—"

"It was the first edition," I said.

He thought about that for a moment. "Big deal."

"Yes," I said, "it is. There were sixteen copies. When they brought out the next edition, the copyists left out a paragraph on the fifth page of the fourth book. I gather it was just an oversight. But that paragraph was Saloninus's formula for synthetic blue paint."

He turned round and stared at me. As well he might.

In case you live in a cave on a mountaintop and eat snails and drink rainwater collected in a bucket, maybe I ought to explain. Blue paint has always been the rarest, most expensive luxury item in the world – worth double its weight in truffles or murex shells or pink diamonds and much harder to get hold of, because the only way to make it is to grind up a block of lapis lazuli. Precisely because it's so rare and so very hard to come by, blue is the must-have colour for any artist with claims to be taken seriously and any patron who doesn't want to be written off as a hopeless cheapskate. That's why the Holy Mother's gown is invariably blue, in every fresco and triptych in every temple and monastery in the West. The only source of lapis is a single mine in Gapenthe, and the revenue it produces funds the staggering defence budget of the small but strategically vital kingdom of Chastel, a long, narrow mountain strip wedged in between the Sashan Empire, Aelia and Antecyrene. As long as the demand for lapis holds up, Chastel can use its fabulous wealth to hire mercenaries and keep the peace of the world; hence the saying that all that stands between civilisation and Armageddon is the thickness of the Holy Mother's robe.

But people will always want blue paint, so not to worry. Not, that is, until Saloninus invented synthetic blue. The legend has it that he was trying to discover the philosophers' stone and turn base metal into gold; when he accidentally stumbled on the secret of synthetic blue he forgot all about making synthetic gold, since blue paint was far more valuable. Making and selling the paint would've brought him in a comfortable income for life; not making and selling it proved to be the once and future big score he'd been searching for all his life.

It was a fundamental term of his contract with the kings of Chastel that the formula would die with him, and he was smart enough to realise that, if he abided by it, the formula would die with him just as soon as the king's men found out where he was hiding. So he wrote it down, and let the Chastellans know that if any harm came to him, the formula was in a safe place and would be made available to every alchemist within a month's ride of the Friendly Sea. He was lying, naturally; there was only one copy of the formula, scribbled in the margin of one of his countless notebooks, buried deep in the jumble of papers on his study floor – he was notoriously the untidiest man who ever lived. When he died, most of his papers were bought by a local scrivener, who scoured the ink off the parchments and sold them as blank stationery. But the notebook with the formula came into the hands of the monks of the Steel Briar, two thousand miles away in fire-worshipping Echmen, and fifty years later one of them set out to write a book about textile production. During the course of his research he came across the notebook in the monastery library, and copied out the formula as a curiosity. The story of the priceless formula hadn't percolated as far as the Steel Briar, and in Echmen the colour blue is considered unlucky, so blue paint isn't used much. Accordingly, nobody had any idea that Saloninus's recipe was worth anything.

In due course the monk's book was translated into Robur – the Echmen original was lost when the Hus sacked the Steel Briar and burned it to the ground. The translation ended up at the Silver Rose monastery on Ogyge; nobody bothered to read it, because it was just some commercial how-to book, but over the course of a decade they made sixteen copies to give away as prestige gifts to generous patrons, most of them illiterate, before technical advances in flax-retting made the original book obsolete and the abbot commissioned a new, revised edition. At some point after that, Sashan intelligence discovered that the formula had been in the first edition and turned the entire known world upside down looking for a copy. They couldn't find one, but they were able to account for all sixteen, lost in fires or ground down for parchment. Saloninus's formula, they declared, had been lost for ever, and probably just as well. What they hadn't accounted for was the original, from which the sixteen copies were made, and that was what Praeclara had traced to the Silver Rose, where my old friend the abbot used to let me store my stock-in-trade in one of the disused charcoal cellars—

"You're kidding," Eudo said.

"No," I said. "And you know I'm not making it up, because you saw how desperate Praeclara was to get hold of it. She didn't want it for money; she wanted to start a war."

"And you gave it to her."

"Yes," I said. "And now it's rotting in the long grass beside some road in Hetsuan, along with her shoes and her scalp and the other bits they can't eat. And good riddance, if you ask me. Except," I added, "I memorised the formula."

He gave me a long, thoughtful look. Money, war, the future of civilisation west of the Friendly Sea; a lot of factors to cram into one equation. "I believe you," he said. "That's just the sort of thing you'd do."

"More money than you could possibly imagine," I said. "All I'd have to do is write the formula on a wax tablet and send it to the kings of Chastel. You can bet your life they've got a copy of it, very carefully preserved. Stupid money, for as long as we both live."

But that wasn't telling him anything he hadn't already thought of himself. "The trouble with that is," he said eventually, "I know you. You're smart and resourceful, and you're very good at getting away. And I don't need silly money. Seventy thousand's more than I could spend in a lifetime, and

I wouldn't have to lie awake every night of my life wondering when you're going to come and slit my throat."

"I wouldn't do that," I said. "No point. There'd be so much money it wouldn't matter. I'm not a killer, Eudo."

He considered that, too. "Sorry," he said, "but I think you are. Praeclara thought so, and she had excellent judgement."

"She was wrong. I didn't kill Vistam."

"I've only got your word for that," he said. "I think you'd kill me because I was your friend and I betrayed you. That's what I'd do, in your shoes. Perfectly right and proper that you should," he added. "I'm not proud of myself, believe me. You were a good friend to me."

"Eudo—"

"Sorry," he said, "but it's not worth the risk. Your brother-in-law's offering seventy thousand alive, fifty for just your head. I'd kill you right now, only I don't want to get that close to you. You're a very dangerous man, Saevus. In fact, you scare the life out of me." He stood up and pulled a canteen from under his seat. "I'm going to give you a drink of water," he said, "but no food. If I give you anything to eat you'll pretend to choke, and then when I try and unblock you, you'll bite my throat out, like you did in Lentousis."

"That wasn't me," I said. "That was somebody else."

He shrugged. "Makes no odds, I'm still not going to risk it. If you starve to death before we get there it'll cost me twenty thousand, but at least I'll still be alive. For what it's worth, I think you're probably the most dangerous man in the world. That's probably a compliment," he added, with a grin. "Sorry, but that's how it is."

At least we were talking. "You've been planning this all along," I said.

"Of course," he replied. "And don't pretend you haven't been suspicious. You're smart. You didn't trust me back in Sosis, when I said I'd infiltrate the cartulary for you. You got that woman to do it instead. You've had your eye on me all along. I realise that."

"That's just me," I said. "It's the life I've led. And you've just proved me right, incidentally. There really isn't anyone I can trust."

"No," he said, not without sympathy, "there isn't. Hell of a way to live your life if you ask me, every man's hand against you, no real friends. Except her, of course, but you're too stupid to realise that."

I didn't want to talk about Stauracia. "I thought you were different," I said.

"No, you didn't," he said. "You couldn't be bothered to figure me out, that's all. In your shoes I'd have cut my throat a long time back. I don't know, maybe you aren't a killer after all. Did saving you from the Hetsuan put you off the track? I was livid with you for going off like that. I didn't think you'd do it, to be honest."

"I thought you liked me," I said.

"Oh, I do." Said with genuine sincerity. "Like I told you, I'm not proud of myself. I do like you, as it happens. Makes no odds in the long run. When I was a kid we had a calf one year; it had a crumpled horn, cutest thing you ever saw. I loved that calf, but when it was eighteen months old we slaughtered it, and very good eating it was, too. You've got to be sensible about these things."

"Listen," I said, pleading. "I understand. You're only doing what I'd do. It's all right. But it's not sensible. It's a waste. All that money—"

"I told you, I'm not interested. A bird in the hand, and all that. You're only saying this because you've figured out how to jump me and kill me and get free. Sorry, but I'm not going to fall for it. I learned a lot from you. Don't play around with dangerous people, especially when they're smarter than you are."

"If my sister and my brother-in-law get their hands on me—"

He sighed. "I know," he said. "Or I can guess. That's why it's an extra twenty thousand if you're alive. If I wasn't so scared of you I'd kill you now and spare you all that, and the hell with the money." He laughed. "It's your own fault for being so valuable. Nobody's ever going to pay seventy thousand for me." He got up, sat in the seat and picked up the reins. "I've changed my mind about giving you a drink," he said. "Too risky."

"Please," I said. "I'm so dry I can hardly breathe."

"Sorry," he said, and the cart started moving again.

By late afternoon I was so thirsty I could hardly swallow. I started begging. He ignored me. Please, I said, over and over again.

"I know what you're doing," he said. "You want me to come back there and gag you, and then you'll make the move you've been planning. I've been trying to figure it out, but I can't see it. Still, like I said, you're much smarter than me. Sorry, but no dice."

"Please," I said, or at least I tried to; it came out as a croak, but I guess he got the message. He stopped the cart and got to his feet.

"The hell with it," he said. "I'm going to stuff your mouth, before you break my heart. By the sound of it you're too weak to be dangerous, and you're driving me mad."

He felt in his pocket and found a wad of sheep's wool and

came and kneeled down beside me. He hesitated. I tried to say "Please", but no sound came out. He sighed, and put his fingers in my mouth, and I bit down hard.

The wetness of his blood was delightful. He tried to pull back, but I held on like a dog; the more he pulled, the more I tore his flesh and the more it hurt. He tried to use his other hand to prise my jaws open, at which point the geometry slotted into place. I kicked with my feet, which gave me just enough distance to reach his throat with my teeth.

On reflection I bit much harder than I needed to. Blood spurted in my eyes, all down my face; he was jerking madly, so I bit harder, and then he jerked again and got free, but only because he'd left a large part of his throat in my mouth. I could feel him thrashing about for a bit, and then he stopped moving.

I had to spit out my mouthful, even though I was starving hungry; my throat was too dry, and the blood was too salty to do me any good.

A farmer on his way home from a fair found me the next morning. When he'd finished throwing up he cut me loose and gave me a drink of cider from his jug. I explained that the dead man had kidnapped me and was going to murder me, which was more or less true. He was horrified; we had to report it to the magistrate, he said. So I hit him with his jug when he wasn't looking and stole his horse. He got two perfectly good horses and a cart in exchange, so I didn't feel too bad about it.

The last of my strength ran out about a mile shy of Soutalis, which is so close to En Chersi it's practically a suburb. I pulled off the road into a holly brake, made sure the horse was secure and went to sleep. When I woke up I managed to crawl to the ditch, which had a little muddy water in the bottom. I drank some of it and washed the blood off my face. Fairly soon the farmer and the magistrate's men would be along, making trouble. A provincial magistrate's jurisdiction wouldn't apply in En Chersi, so I pressed on and got inside the walls well before noon. I know people in En Chersi. They weren't pleased to see me, but nobody ever is.

Stauracia isn't hard to find. Just ask around: Have you seen a beautiful woman on her own acting like she owns the place?

"Is that dried blood?" was the first thing she asked me.

"Yes," I said.

"Yours?"

"No."

"Ah." She frowned at me. Needless to say she looked well-groomed, elegant and sophisticated, and here I was, ragged and blood-soaked and scary looking, not the sort of man you'd expect someone like her to associate with. If the landlord of the inn saw us together, he might get to wondering whether he should've made her pay for her room in advance after all.

"You were looking for me," I said.

"Was I? Oh yes. I was concerned about you, stomping off in a huff like that. Then I decided you could look after yourself." She paused and looked at me again. "Presumably I was right."

"More or less."

"That's all right, then. What happened to you, by the way?"

I answered straight away, no hesitation. "I had a run-in with a bounty hunter," I said. "Apparently these days I'm only worth seventy thousand, which came as a bit of a blow, but never mind. I have broad shoulders. I can take it."

"Hence the someone-else's blood."

I nodded. "And there may be legal complications," I said, "so I won't be stopping here long. But that doesn't matter, because I'd already made up my mind. I'm going to Echmen. One of the eastern provinces, I fancy, on the other side of the Heavenly Mountains."

"They're a myth," she pointed out.

"Really? Oh well, never mind. There's bound to be some really big mountains in a country that size. They'll do just as well."

She considered me for a moment. "You came looking for me to tell me that."

"You were looking for me."

"So I was. Echmen," she said. "Can you speak the language?"

"No," I said. "But that's a plus, as far as I'm concerned. I seem to get into trouble when I talk to people."

Silence. Usually we have no trouble making conversation. "What about money?" she said.

"What about it?"

"I can't give you any, if that's what you're after," she said. "I'm broke. Spent my last few staurata on these clothes and a nice horse."

"I'm fine," I said. "While we're on the subject, by the way, have you got a bit of paper and something to write with?"

"No."

Awkward. I looked around, but all I could see was the food she'd been eating when I interrupted her. There was a thick slice of dense, waxy Suromaner cheese. "Give me a hairpin," I said.

"Why?"

"Please?"

With the pin, I picked out the formula, in Sashan cunei-
form, on the slice of cheese. "What's that supposed to be?"
she asked.

"Read it."

She read it. She's the only woman I know who can read
Sashan. Her face went completely blank. "Is that—?"

"Yes," I said. "It's what Praeclara was after. It was in one of
the books."

"But we went through them—"

"Eudo stole it before we looked," I said. "I stole it back.
Then I gave it to Praeclara."

"Oh, for crying out loud."

"Anyway," I told her, "the only written record of the formula
anywhere in the world is now that piece of cheese. I suggest
you don't eat it."

She put it down very carefully. "For once I think you're
right," she said. "Why?"

"Why what?"

"Why give it to me, you moron?"

I decided I'd earned the right to smile. "Because it's what
you've always wanted," I said. "The jackpot, the motherlode,
the one and only big score. You have it. I don't want it. I'm
going to Echmen, where I'll be safe."

She looked at me. She has beautiful eyes. "What's the catch?"

"Figure it out for yourself," I said. "Besides, what do you
care? More money than even you could ever possibly want,
and you don't have to steal it or kill anyone. Just write out the
first two lines and send them to the Chastellan ambassador in
Beal Regard. After that you'll probably have to change your
name and live in a castle, but not to worry. With that sort of
money you can afford to buy a dozen, one for each month of

the year. Probably not a bad idea to have several, so you can keep moving around."

"What's the catch?" she repeated.

"Does there have to be one?"

I stood up. At this point, if there was any justice in the world or a god up in the sky, a raven would have swooped down, skewered the cheese on its beak and flown away. "Of course, you still know the formula," she said.

"True," I said. "Tattooed on the inside of my head. It's a shame you can't forget things deliberately. That's a talent I really wish I had."

There didn't seem to be anything else that needed saying, so I walked away.

I didn't go to Echmen after all. I got as far as New Perimadeia, but then I got arrested and thrown in jail – some nonsense about a valuable icon going missing from a temple. I kept telling them I hadn't got it, which was perfectly true; I'd sold it three days earlier. It's twelve years in the slate quarries for stealing from temples in that particular jurisdiction, so I made a fuss and yelled and screamed and kicked the door until they fetched a minor official from the Sashan embassy.

"Know what this is?" I asked him.

He looked at the ring on my finger. "Yes," he said. "Where did you—?"

"Get me the ambassador."

They got me the ambassador. The ambassador got me out of jail, the district magistrate apologised profusely for any inconvenience, and I was back outside in the sunshine. "May I ask where you got that?" said the ambassador.

"No," I said. "I need a thousand staurata."

He didn't have that much on him, reasonably enough, so he had to send someone to get it. When I'd got the money he asked me, "Is he still alive?"

"No."

"Are you sure?"

"Yes," I said. "I killed him." Which was true, in the Sashan sense.

He nodded. "Is there anything else I can—?"

"No," I said. "That'll be all."

A thousand staurata. In return, I'd killed a man I genuinely liked, which is all he ever asked of me; we were quits.

I bought myself a straw hat and sat under a chestnut tree in the town square with a plate of honeycakes and a small flask of dry white wine, and thought about Echmen. A very long way away; too far for anyone to travel for a miserly seventy thousand staurata. That, unfortunately, wasn't true.

So instead I thought about predators and prey, and that special in-between category to which I aspired to belong, scavengers. We don't kill, we just clear up what the killers leave behind – a chance to eat meat without having to do any actual violence. True, by the time we get to eat it, the meat is generally tainted and rotten; it's an acquired taste, let's say, but sun-dried or slightly gamey, it's not so bad.

The question was, would I be better off on my own or in company with, say, five hundred others loosely bound to me by bonds of enlightened self-interest? It occurred to me that most scavengers keep from being prey by operating in flocks, or packs. Birds of a black feather flock together; you can see how that came about. One day a solitary crow saw a dead fox and swooped down to feed. A dozen other solitary crows, cruising the empty air, saw him swoop and rushed down to get their share. The arrangement worked; four hundred and ninety-nine crows feed while one crow keeps watch, and then another crow takes over sentry duty while the sentinel has his turn at the bones and gristle. From what I've seen, crows don't like each other much, but if you want genuine entertainment, go and watch a mob of crows seeing off a buzzard.

Friendship had left me with a bad taste in my mouth: salty, with strong undertones of iron. Love had nearly got me eaten, except that at the last moment two of my fellow crows had seen off the buzzards, and then one of the crows turned out to be a hawk in disguise – thoughts like that kept trying to drag me where I didn't want to go, like the draught when you pull the bung out of a basin of water. I was only ever in love once and look where it got me.

That's a fine line to end a paragraph on, but as it drains away it draws me towards the gurgling hole. Because I was in love, I got to meet the Great King, brother of the Sun and Moon, who made it possible for me to deal appropriately with Praeclara and gave me a magic ring. That wasn't what I went for, but it was what I got – like the man who climbed the highest mountain in the world looking for dragons' eggs, met God and went home without any dragons' eggs. By the same token, Stauracia saved me from the shaven-headed cooks and in return got the one true big score, what she'd been searching for all her life. The rule seems to be that you get your heart's desire when it's not the thing you actually want most.

Love and friendship, I decided, were strictly for predators: lions and lionesses, eagles and their mates nesting in the turrets of castles. Instead, consider the lark. When she sees the predator's shadow hurtling towards her across the ground, she leaves her nest and her nestlings and soars into the air, shrieking as loud as she can, to lure the bad things away. Greater love, then, hath no man than this, that he gets the hell out of it at the first sign of trouble.

I looked at my hand. I had a magic ring. With something like that, I could make a real nuisance of myself. Or I could go back to working for a living – consider the myth of Danderic, or Oneager the Unbeaten, or all those other heroes who were rescued in infancy from their wicked uncles, whisked away to far-distant lands and brought up by kindly strangers, all so that they could one day return, slay the usurper and set the fatherland free. Everyone thinks it's wonderful when Oneager slaughters a thousand palace guards with the jawbone of an ox. I haven't killed anything like a thousand palace guards, but the ones I have killed lie on my stomach, like rich food late at night. Personally I think it would have been much better for all concerned if Oneager had stayed in Permia and got a job.

Consider the predator. Four times out of five, he fails and the prey gets away. Consider the prey: he always gets away, except for one time. It must be incredibly frustrating being a lion or a hawk, whereas the deer and the sparrow have a hundred per cent win ratio until their dying day.

To hell with all wildlife. I finished my wine, threw the last honeycake to the birds and went down to the Market Square to buy a horse.

"Oh, for God's sake," Polycrates said.

"Sorry," I said. "I'm back."

They weren't pleased to see me. No one ever is. But since I'd been away things hadn't been going so well. The Asvogel boys had outbid them for every job worth having, and all they'd been able to find in their price bracket was a miserable little rebellion in north-west Aelia. Without Eudo or myself to keep the peace, they were at each other's throats; Polycrates and Papinian against Gombryas and Olybrius and Dodilas, with everybody else changing sides so fast it'd make your head spin, and Carrhasio loudly threatening to cut Polycrates's ears off and make him eat them every time he saw him. Better the arsehole you know, I told them; nothing unites disputing factions like a common loathing of the boss. They saw sense, especially when I mentioned that I had five hundred staurata which I was prepared to plough back into the business. Two months of Polycrates's and Gombryas's joint leadership had reduced company funds to twenty staurata and a handful of coppers. We went to north-west Aelia, where it snowed and we made a loss. On the way back I pointed to a small, low hill I'd read about in a book. That's reputedly the tomb of Prince Oneager, I told them.

Bullshit, they said. Oneager's just a myth.

Humour me, I insisted; so we dug down into the mound, broke through a stone dome and found ourselves in a burial chamber. They lowered me down on a rope – nobody else fancied going in there, for some reason – and I lit my lamp and looked around. The lamplight reflected back the colour of honey.

We could probably have made five times as much if we'd sold the stuff from the tomb as works of art, but there are times when you just want to take the immediate money and run, so we chopped it up into bits, built a simple clay furnace and melted it down into ingots; a whisker over seventeen thousand staurata, which is a lot of money. "We should've done like you told us," Gombryas said mournfully when we delivered the gold bars to the Imperial Mint at Thugatra. "Seventeen grand is all right, but we could've been rich."

I thought of Eudo, who could've been rich but who was satisfied with the prospect of seventy thousand; and Stauracia, who ought by now to be the richest woman in the world. "Shut your face," I told him.

The story continues in ...

Saevus Corax Gets Away With Murder

Keep reading for a sneak peek!

extras

orbit

meet the author

K. J. PARKER is a pseudonym for Tom Holt. He was born in London in 1961. At Oxford he studied bar billiards, ancient Greek agriculture and the care and feeding of small, temperamental Japanese motorcycle engines. These interests led him, perhaps inevitably, to qualify as a solicitor and immigrate to Somerset, where he specialised in death and taxes for seven years before going straight in 1995. He lives in Chard, Somerset, with his wife and daughter.

Find out more about K. J. Parker and other Orbit authors by registering for the free monthly newsletter at orbitbooks.net.

if you enjoyed
SAEVUS CORAX CAPTURES THE CASTLE

look out for

SAEVUS CORAX GETS AWAY WITH MURDER

The Corax Trilogy: Book Three

by

K. J. Parker

From one of the most original voices in fantasy comes a heartwarming tale of peace, love, and battlefield salvage.

If you're going to get ahead in the battlefield-salvage business, you have to regard death as a means to an end. In other words, when the blood flows, so will the cash. Unfortunately, even though war is on the way, Saevus Corax has had enough.

extras

There are two things he has to do before he can enjoy his retirement: get away with one last score, and get away with murder. For someone who, ironically, tends to make a mess wherever he goes, leaving his affairs in order is going to be Saevus Corax's biggest challenge yet.

1

Isn't it nice, I remember thinking as I tried to yank an arrow out of a dead soldier's eye, when things unexpectedly turn out just right? And then the arrow came away in my hand, but the eyeball was firmly stuck on the arrowhead. I glared at it. A standard hunting broadhead, with barbs, which was why it had dragged the eye out of its socket. I could cut it away with a knife, but could I really be bothered, for an arrow worth five trachy?

Everything about this job (apart from the flies, the mosquitos, the swamp and the quite appalling smell) had been roses all the way. For a start, Count Theudebert had paid *me*, rather than the other way around. In my business – I clear up after battles – you have to pay the providers, meaning the two opposing armies, for the privilege of burying their dead, in return for what you can strip off the bodies. Since we're a relatively small concern and the big boys (mostly the Asvogel brothers) outbid us for pretty well every job worth having, we tend to get contracts with wafer-thin margins, and our profits are generally more a state of mind rather than anything you can write down on a balance sheet, let alone spend. But the Count had written to me offering me a flat-rate fee for clearing up the mess he intended to make in the Leerwald forest, plus anything I found that I might possibly want to keep. That sort of deal doesn't come along every day, believe me.

I could see where the Count was coming from. Five thousand or so of his tenants, living in a clearing in the vast expanse of the Leerwald, had decided not to pay their rent and had killed the men he'd sent to help them reconsider their decision; accordingly, he had no choice but to march in there, slaughter everything that moved and find or buy new tenants to replace the dead. The tenants didn't own anything worth having, so no reputable battlefield clearance contractor would want the job on the usual terms. Either the Count would have to do his own clean-up, or he'd have to hire someone.

He wasn't exactly offering a fortune, but times were hard and we needed the work. Also, as my good friend and junior partner Gombryas pointed out, chances were that the Count's archers would probably do a fair amount of the slaughtering, which would mean arrows... Nothing but the best for Theudebert of Draha, so they'd be bound to be using good quality hard-steel bodkins on ash shafts with goose fletchings – again, not exactly a fortune but worth picking up, and if what people were saying was true, about a big war brewing in the east, the price of high-class once-used arrows could only go up. Also, he added, according to the Count's letter there'd be dead civilians as well, and even peasant women tend to have some jewellery, even if it's just whittled bone on a bit of string. And shoes, he added cheerfully, everybody wears shoes. At a gulden six per barrelful, it all adds up...

Gombryas had been right about one thing. There were plenty of arrows. But they turned out to be practically worthless, which was wonderful—

"Over here," Gombryas yelled. "I found him!"

I chucked the arrow with the eyeball on it and shoved my

way through the briars to where Gombryas was standing, at the foot of a large beech tree. Its canopy overshadowed an area of about twenty square yards, forming a welcome clearing. Nailed to the trunk of the tree was a man's body. He'd been ripped open, his ribcage prised apart and his guts wound out round a stick. Piled at his feet were his clothes and armour: gorgeous clothes and luxury armour. Nothing but the best for Theudebert of Draha.

"Charming," I said.

Gombryas grinned at me. "I guess they didn't like him much," he said. "Can't say I blame them."

He had a pair of clippers in his hand, the sort you use for shearing sheep or pruning vines. I could see he was torn with indecision. Gombryas collects relics of dead military heroes; relics as in body parts. His collection is the ruling passion of his life. Mostly he buys them for ridiculous sums of money from dealers and other collectors, and he's not a rich man, so he finances his collection by harvesting and selling bits and pieces whenever we comes across a dead hero in the usual course of our business. Theudebert was definitely in the highly-sought-after category. Hence the agonising decision: which bits to sell and which bits to keep for himself?

The point being, Theudebert had lost. He'd led his army into the Leerwald, knowing that his tenants were forbidden to own weapons and therefore expecting, reasonably enough, not to have to do any actual fighting, just killing. What he'd overlooked was the tendency of forests to contain trees, which any fool with a few basic hand tools can turn into a functional bow in the course of an afternoon... Tracing the sequence of events by means of the position of the bodies, I figured out that Theudebert was only about half a mile from the first of the villages when he walked into the first ambush. About a third of his men were shot down in what could only have been a matter of a minute or so. Understandably he decided to turn back, figuring that the tenants had made their point. He was wrong about that. There were further ambushes, about a dozen of them, strung out over about five miles of forest trail. Finally, Theudebert had turned off the road and tried to get away through the dense thickets of briars, holly and withies which had grown up where his late father had cleared a broad swath of the forest for charcoal-burning. The beech tree was, I assumed, the place where the tenants had finally caught up with him and his few surviving guards.

"Will you look at the quality of this stuff?" Olybrius said, waving a bloodstained shirt under my nose. "That's best imported linen."

"It's got a hole in it," I said.

Olybrius gave me a look. "Funny man," he said. "And you should see the boots. Double-seamed, and hardly a mark on them."

I should've been as delighted as he was, but somehow I wasn't. I wasn't unhappy, either. We'd lucked into a substantial windfall, at a time when we badly needed one, and for once the work wouldn't be particularly arduous (except for the flies, the mosquitos, the swamp and the truly horrible smell) – and, God only knows, my heart wasn't inclined to bleed for Count Theudebert, even though he was a sort of relation of mine, second cousin three times removed or something like that. Quite the opposite; when you've spent your life either imposing authority or having it imposed upon you, the sight of a head of state nailed to a tree with his guts dangling out can't fail to restore your faith in the basic rightness of things. Just occasionally, you can reassure yourself, the bullies get what's coming to them, so everything's fine.

I decided that whatever was bothering me couldn't be terribly important, and got on with the work I was supposed to be doing. Since I'm nominally the boss of the outfit, it's more or less inevitable that I get the lousiest job, which in our line of business is collecting up the bodies, once they've been stripped of armour and clothing and thoroughly gone over for small items of value, and disposing of them. Usually we burn them, but in a dense forest packed with underbrush it struck me that that mightn't be a very good idea. That meant digging a series of large holes, a chore that my colleagues and I detest.

Especially in a forest. It's the nature of things that forests grow on thin, stony soil; if there was good soil under there, you can bet someone would've been along to cut down the trees and plough it up a thousand years ago. Typically there's about a foot of leaf mould, really hard to dig into because of the network of holly, ground elder and bramble roots. Under that you find about ten inches of crumbly black soil, along with a lot of stones. Then you're down into clay, if you're lucky, or your actual rock if you aren't. On this occasion Fortune smiled on us and we found clay, thick and grey and sort of oily, which we laboriously chopped out with pickaxes. Two feet down into the clay, of course, we struck the water table, which turned our carefully dug graves into miniature wells in no time flat. Still, we were only burying dead soldiers, so who cares? Let them get wet.

Gombryas and Olybrius had finished stripping the bodies and loading the proceeds onto carts long before we got our pits done, so they and their crews gathered round to give us moral support while we dug. I was up to my waist in filthy water, I remember, with Gombryas perched on the edge of the grave explaining to me the finer points of relic collecting. For instance: singletons – organs of which there are only one, such as the nose, the heart and the penis – are obviously more

334

valuable than multiples (fingers, toes, ears, testicles), but complete sets of fingers, toes, ears &c are more valuable still. But you can make a real killing if a rich collector has got nine of so-and-so's fingers and you've got the missing one, which he needs to make up the set. Accordingly, after much deliberation, Gombryas had decided to keep Count Theudebert's heart and liver (preserved in honey) and one finger; the rest of the internals and extremities would probably be alluring enough as swapsies to net him either the complete left hand of Carnufex the Irrigator – with most of the skin still on, he told me breathlessly, which is practically unheard of for a Warring States-era relic – or the left ear of Prince Phraates; he already had the right ear, but the First Social War wasn't really his period, so the plan was to swap both ears for the pelvis of Calojan the Great, which he knew for a fact was likely to come up at some point in the next year or so, because the man who owned it had a nasty disease and wasn't expected to live...

"Gombryas," I interrupted. "How much is your collection worth?"

He stopped and looked at me. "No idea," he said.

"At a rough guess."

He thought for a while, during which time he didn't speak, which was nice. "Fifty thousand," he said eventually. "Well, maybe closer to sixty. Depends on what the market's doing at the time. Why?"

I was mildly stunned. "Fifty thousand staurata," I said. "And you're still here, doing this shit."

He was shocked, and offended. "I'd never sell my collection," he said. "It's taken me a lifetime—"

"Seriously," I said. "All those bits of desiccated soldiers are worth more to you than a life of security and ease. Fifty thousand—"

"Keep your voice down," he hissed at me.

"Sorry," I said. I straightened my back and rested for a moment, leaning on the handle of my shovel. "But for crying out loud, Gombryas, that's serious money. You could buy two ships and still have enough left for a vineyard."

"It's not about money." This from a man who regularly went through the ashes of our cremation pyres with a rake, to retrieve arrowheads left inside the bodies. "It's about, I don't know, heritage—"

"Talking of which," I said. "You've got no family. When you die, who gets all the stuff?"

He shrugged. "I don't know, do I? None of my business when I'm dead."

"Maybe," I suggested, "your fellow collectors will cut you up and share you out. Wouldn't that be nice?"

He scowled at me. "Funny man," he said.

I gave him a warm smile and started digging. Quite by accident, I made a big splash in the muddy water with the blade of my shovel, and Gombryas' legs got drenched. He called me something or other and went away.

Six feet deep is the industry standard, but I decided I'd exercise my professional discretion and make do with four. I called a halt, we scrambled up out of the graves and started tipping the bodies. They rolled off the tailgates of the carts and went splash into the water, displacing most of it in accordance with Saloninus' Third Law, and then we filled in, making an eighteen-inch allowance for settlement. Not that it mattered a damn in the middle of a forest, and we'd been paid in advance by a man who was now exceptionally dead, but there's a right way and a wrong way of doing things, and I hate it when Chusro Asvogel goes around making snide remarks about the quality of our work.

if you enjoyed

SAEVUS CORAX CAPTURES THE CASTLE

look out for

NOTORIOUS SORCERER

The Burnished City: Book One

by

Davinia Evans

A dazzling fantasy debut bursting with wild magic, chaotic sword-fighting street gangs, brazen flirting, malevolent harpies, and one defiant alchemist.

Welcome to Bezim, where sword-slinging bravi race through the night, and where rich and idle alchemists make magic out of mixing and measuring the four planes of reality.

Siyon Velo, Dockside brat turned petty alchemist, scrapes a living hopping between the planes to harvest ingredients for the city's alchemists. But when Siyon accidentally commits an act of impossible magic, he's catapulted into the limelight—which is a bad place to be when the planes start lurching out of alignment, threatening to send the city into the sea.

It will take a miracle to save Bezim. Good thing Siyon has pulled off the impossible before. Now he has to master it.

Chapter 1

Siyon couldn't get the damn square to line up, and the hangover definitely wasn't helping.

He squinted at the ash lines on the floor. The tiles tessellated in a not-quite-repeating pattern of swirls and spirals that could probably cause headaches all by itself. It was left over from before this place was taken over as the Little Bracken bravi safe house, when it had been a... temple? Church? Whatever. They called it the Chapel now, so probably one of those. Siyon didn't know much about all that religious stuff. He'd been born and bred here in Bezim, where they preferred the certainty of alchemy instead.

The building was nice; tidy brickwork, tall pitched roof, narrow windows of coloured glass. From the pale hair and impressive beards on the figures, Siyon thought the stories probably drew from the cults and myths of the North, not the remnants of the Lyraec Empire he was more familiar with.

The Chapel was quiet right now, with the morning sun

338

cutting through the dust motes dancing around the lofty beams. The bravi were denizens of the night—the feet that rattled fleet as a passing rain shower over your roof tiles, the midnight laughter that promised mayhem and crossed blades and adventure. Last night they'd been all of that, the stuff of the dreams of children and poets, and now they were sleeping it off. So the tall, vaulted space—which might otherwise be cluttered with the scrape of a sharpening sabre, the clatter and call of training duels, the bicker and bellow of arguments over style—was all at Siyon's disposal.

He still couldn't get his delving portal square.

Siyon's tea had gone cold on a pushed-aside pew. He lifted the tin-banded glass, high and higher, until the light through the stained-glass windows both made him wince and turned the remaining liquid a fiery golden orange. A colour burning with righteousness. An *Empyreal* sort of colour.

Siyon *reached* through that connection and snapped his fingers.

And then nearly dropped the suddenly scalding glass.

Allegedly Kolah Negedi—the long-dead father of alchemical practice—had strong views about casual use of the Art. Something about the essence of another plane not being a dog to fetch your slippers. Poetic, but frankly, the great Kolah Negedi didn't seem all that applicable to the life of Siyon Velo. Let the fancy azatani alchemists, with their mahogany workbenches and expensive bespoke glass beakers, debate his wisdom. All Siyon did was fetch and carry for them. And that's all he'd ever do, unless he could scrape together enough hard cash to pay for lessons. Today's work would barely add to his stash, but one day, maybe...

In the meantime, at least he could have hot tea.

Siyon blew gently across the surface of the liquid, took a

careful sip, and sighed as the blissful heat smoothed out the jagged edges of his hangover.

"Sorry," someone said. "I can come back later if you're enjoying your alone time."

Not just any someone; that was the tight, pointed accent that went with leafy avenues and elegant townhouses and lace gloves. That was an azatani voice. Siyon cracked one eye open, and looked sidelong toward the doorway.

The young woman wouldn't have come up to his chin, but she stood straight and tall, barely a trace of a girl's uncertainty in the way her weight shifted from one foot to the other. She was clad head to toe in bravi leathers—sturdy trousers, tight vest, bracers laced up to her elbows. They creaked with newness, and the sabre at her hip gleamed with oil and polish. The tricorn balanced atop her tied-back ebony curls had an orange cockade pinned on with a Little Bracken badge.

They'd probably run the tiles together, two fish in the great flickering school of the Little Bracken, but Siyon never paid too much attention to the azatani recruits. They joined, they had their youthful adventures, they left to take up their serious adult responsibilities. None of his business.

But here she was, getting in his business. "What are you doing here, za?" he demanded, though he had a bad feeling he knew the answer.

"I was sent by the Diviner Prince to…" Her words petered out, uncertainty conquering the assurance she was born into. "Er. Assist you? Hold something?"

Siyon snorted. "I need an anchor, not a little bird. Go back and tell Daruj—"

"No," she interrupted, her chin coming up in a belligerent jut. "I can do it. I'm bravi. Same as you."

Siyon sauntered out into the aisle, where she could in turn

get a good look at him. At the fraying of his shirtsleeves and the scuffs on his boots, at the battered hilt of his own sabre, at the lean length of his limbs and the freckles and even the glint of red in his brown hair that said *foreign blood*. That confirmed he was a mongrel brat.

She could probably trace her family back a few hundred years to the end of the Lyraec Empire. They'd probably helped overthrow the Last Duke and claim the city for *the people*. People like them, anyway. They'd renamed the city *Bezim*—in Old Lyraec, that meant *ours*.

"Yeah," he drawled, stretching the Dockside twang. "We're peas in a fucking pod. How old are you, anyway?"

"How old are *you*?" she demanded right back. There was a flush of colour in her warm brown cheeks, but she wasn't backing down. Was it even bravery when you hadn't heard the word *no* more than a dozen times in your life?

"Twenty-three," Siyon said. "Or near enough. And I've been on my own since I was fourteen, delving the planes since seventeen. That six years of crossing the divide between this plane and the others tells me I'm not trusting you"—he jabbed a finger at her, in her new leathers with her boots that probably got that shine from the hands of a servant—"to hold the only thing tying me back to the Mundane. No offense, princess."

She hesitated in the doorway, but then her chin came up again. "Fuck you," she stated primly. "I can do it. And I'm all you've got, anyway. Daruj went down to the square; Awl Quarter have called public challenge." There was a twist to her mouth. It stung, to be sent to do this, rather than being included in the party to bare blades against another bravi tribe, even in a small morning skirmish.

Siyon knew what that felt like. He drained his tea and set the glass down on the pew next to him. "You're well out of it. It'll be dead boring. Lots of posturing, barely three blades getting to kiss daylight. No audience in the morning, see? So no pressing need to fight."

She really did look like a doll playing dress-up, but she hadn't fled. And if Daruj was off playing *Diviner Prince* (Siyon never found his friend's bladename less ridiculous, whatever its proud history), then she probably was the best Siyon was likely to get until later this afternoon. Which would be cutting it fine to make his deliveries.

He sighed. "What's your name again?"

She grinned, sudden and bright and blindingly pretty. She was going to carve her way through society when she set aside the blade to take up a ball gown. "Zagiri Savani. And I'm eighteen. If it matters."

Siyon shrugged. "Not to me. Come on."

His ash square still looked a little skewed at one corner, but he wasn't redoing it again. "How much did Daruj tell you about what's involved?"

Zagiri stayed well back from the lines of ash, so at least she was sensible. "You're going to raid one of the other planes. For alchemical ingredients."

Basically right, but she'd need more than basics. "I tear a hole between the planes," Siyon elaborated. "Which is what the square is for. Keeps the breach contained. There's no risk—not to you, not to the city." The inquisitors might feel differently, but they weren't here, and what did they know anyway? "That also cuts me off from the Mundane, so to get back, I need a tether."

She nodded. "Which I hold."

"Which you hold." Siyon watched her for a moment. Clearly a little nervous, but she had a strong grip on herself. That irritating azatani arrogance might be good for something after all.

He unhooked his sabre from his belt and set it down on a pew, picked up a coil of rope instead. It was rough stuff, thick hemp and tarred ends, liberated from docks duty. As mundane—as *Mundane*—as rope could get, heavy with work and sweat and dirty, fishy business. "One end ties around me," Siyon said, looping it around his waist, under his shirt and the weight of his cross-slung satchel. "And you hold the other. You hold it no matter what you see, or what you hear, or how much it jerks around. You hold on to this."

She wrinkled her delicate little nose as she set a hand just above the thick knot tied in the end. She'd probably never put her pampered hands on anything this coarse in her life. "What happens if I don't?" Not a challenge, more curiosity.

Siyon smiled, tight and brittle. "I get stuck in there. Since I'm delving Empyreal today, that means I'm trapped in unforgiving heat with the angels on my back until either I can find a way out or you"— he prodded at her shoulder—"scarper off and find someone to summon me back. I recommend Auntie Geryss, you can find her through the tea shop near the fountain in the fruit market. If, y'know, you fuck up completely."

Zagiri swallowed hard, wrapped the rope around her fist, and braced her heels against the tiled floor. At least she was taking this seriously. "All right."

"Don't worry." Siyon grinned, the thrill of what he was about to do starting to tug at him as surely as a tether. It never got old. "I'll be right here. Well. Right here, and on the other side of reality at the same time."

She didn't look reassured.

Siyon stepped into the ashen square and vanished into heat haze.

Follow us:

f **/orbitbooksUS**

🐦 **/orbitbooks**

▶ **/orbitbooks**

Join our mailing list
to receive alerts on our
latest releases and deals.

orbitbooks.net

Enter our monthly
giveaway for the chance
to win some epic prizes.

orbitloot.com